The Love Book

Nina Solomon

KAYLIE JONES BOOKS

ALSO AVAILABLE FROM KAYLIE JONES BOOKS

UNMENTIONABLES BY LAURIE LOEWENSTEIN
SING IN THE MORNING, CRY AT NIGHT BY BARBARA J. TAYLOR
STARVE THE VULTURE BY JASON CARNEY
FOAMERS BY JUSTIN KASSAB
WE ARE ALL CREW BY BILL LANDAUER
LITTLE BEASTS BY MATTHEW MCGEVNA (forthcoming)

Published by Akashic Books
©2015 Nina Solomon

ISBN-13: 978-1-61775-317-6
Library of Congress Control Number: 2014907316

Kaylie Jones Books
www.kayliejonesbooks.com

Akashic Books
Twitter: @AkashicBooks
Facebook: AkashicBooks
E-mail: info@akashicbooks.com
Website: www.akashicbooks.com

For my parents,
still holding hands after sixty-three years

Acknowledgments

I owe a debt of gratitude to all the people who have contributed to the writing of this book, providing inspiration, information, guidance, and encouragement along the way. To Kaylie Jones, my mentor and friend, who had a dream and allowed me to be part of it. None of this would have been possible without her. To Johnny Temple, publisher extraordinaire, who guided this book to completion with a steady hand and clear vision. To Ibrahim Ahmad, Johanna Ingalls, Aaron Petrovich, Susannah Lawrence, the brilliant crew at Akashic, who made this process feel easy. To Elizabeth Crane, my first reader, spell-checker, cheering section, and best friend in the world. To Barbara Taylor, one of my guinea pigs, for sharing her experiences, critiquing my drafts, and showing me what it means to have an open heart. To Theasa Touhy, for teaching me to say yes and always keeping the pink champagne flowing; "swim away" was the best advice anyone has ever given me. To Laurie Loewenstein, for reading draft after draft and being an abundant source of insight and inspiration. To Deirdre Sinnott, Liz Dalton, Suzanna Filip—three members of the best little writing group ever! To Maggie Crawford, who read an early incarnation and gave me invaluable editorial input and direction. To Albert LaFarge for giving the book a final sweep. To my agent Irene Skolnick for always having my back. To M.M. Cooper, my toughest reader and the inspiration for this book, who cooks the best saffron risotto in the world, and always insists I reach higher.

A special acknowledgment to Katherine Woodward Thomas, for helping countless people, including me, find "The One."

And finally, to Nathaniel Reicher, my awesome son. I couldn't have written this without you, and I wrote it for you.

*If my book is any good it will gently tickle
many a feminine wound. One or two will smile
when they recognize themselves.*
—Gustave Flaubert

C HAPTER ONE
THE FOUR FURIES

IT WAS DOOMED FROM THE START. One after another, the cycling singles who had oh so bravely embarked on the Tour de Flaubert bike trip through the cow dung–laden back roads of Normandy had wilted faster than rose petals in a hopeful lover's hand. Chugging over hill and dale on khaki one-speeds probably left over from D-day was no picnic, especially at the mercy of red-faced farmers in their royal *bleus de travail*, pickled in calvados, careening down the middle of the road. The coup de grâce was simple arithmetic: nine frisky women divided by one gay man does not equal romance.

The flytrap excuse for a tour began in the quaint port of Honfleur and ended in "Yonville" at the fictional home of Emma Bovary, that femme fatale par excellence and her hapless *cocu* of a husband, Charles. The attrition had occurred with neither fanfare nor regret. First to go was a self-described former beauty queen who, after failing to seduce the almost always AWOL tour guide, found solace in the arms of a pudgy but well-heeled bon vivant in Deauville. The next was called home allegedly to tend to her corgi, whose spastic colon was wreaking havoc at the kennel. Then there were the annoying Canadian sisters who, unhappy with the accommodations, called their travel agent, obtained a full refund, and repositioned themselves on a first-class trip down the Nile at the height of terrorist season. A nondescript woman (*Qui? Qui?*) disappeared at some point, but had she left, had they lost her, had she even been there in the first place? Orlando, a bear of a man with a penchant for too-tight bike shorts, had fallen head over heels with the patron of a "clothing-optional" B & B and moved into his cozy manse near the cliffs at Etretat. The last to go was a mousy Englishwoman who finally lifted her nose out of her overly thumbed copy of *Madame Bovary* and realized she was surrounded by a gaggle of high-pitched cluckers, lovelorn sad sacks with excess luggage no amount of pedaling or therapy could burn off. There was no love lost when she bid them a quick adieu and warbled away in an Austin-Healey to meet her sister back home in the Lake District.

By the time they arrived at Emma Bovary's home, a petit bourgeois affair with severe shutters and a pitched shingled roof, only three little Lonely Hearts remained, all Americans—or four, if they counted Madame Bovary herself, that cloaked figure who seemed to shadow them in her Hirondelle.

There was Emily, a single mother and divorcée from Manhattan, the Upper *West* Side to be precise, the "shtetl" of overly opinionated upper-middle-class artsy Jewish intellectuals, not to be confused with the "snooty" and provincial Upper *East* Side. (Like Flaubert, she had a love-hate relationship with the hamlet she called home.) Her dark Mediterranean looks made her feel self-conscious around blond, blue-eyed Midwesterners. She checked her phone for messages umpteen times a day. She hadn't received a single SMS from her ex-husband, Charles, since she'd gotten there. Was he really so small that he couldn't send her a simple *Zach is fine,* or an *All good here*? A *Zach misses you* would have been way too much to hope for. At this point she'd even have settled for a *Zach mugged a third grader and skinned his knee.* She tried to focus on the notes she was jotting down in her Moleskine: *Soldier on, girl, work will set you free.*

Then there was Maxine, a twentyish personal trainer who ran five miles every morning before they set out each day, and kept her blond hair buzzed danger short on one side and butch on the other. Her only care seemed to be her determination to prevent her body fat from exceeding 12 percent. Whatever Max felt about the tour or France or life or love, and the world, she kept it to herself. The others agreed she must have wound up with them by mistake, though none of them knew for sure. In fact, the trip had fallen in her lap. One of her clients had won it in a silent auction for the benefit of an anthroposophist commune in the Hudson River Valley, and given it to Max.

And last but not least, Cathy, a perky special ed teacher who came prepared for everything short of Armageddon . . . endless rolls of aloe-scented toilet paper, Band-Aids, EpiPens, hand sanitizer, iodine pills for purifying water, pills for constipation, pills for Giardia, pills for you name it, and probably some gold coins, escape maps, and a forged ID. What really set her apart was her different pair of floral stirrup pants for every day of the week.

In the early days of the Tour de Flaubert, before the weak were weeded out, as they rode up chalky hills and coasted through the cool air of the gold-speckled beech forests, the cathedral-tall canopy of branches shading them from the sun, they'd seen occasional flashes of a fiery redhead. She was elegant in her tweed skirt, zipping along on a blue lady's bicycle and slaloming between the *bouses* (the ubiquitous piles of dried cow dung) that decorated Picardy. No one knew quite what to make of her, though the best guess was that she was either Countess Aurelia of *The Madwoman of Chaillot* or an Avon Lady.

One day, during a downpour so torrential it seemed as if the rain might dissolve their bodies into the Normandy soil, Emily, Cathy, and Max found themselves stranded from the rest of the group. Soaked to the bone and famished, they made inquiries at an auberge but the innkeeper spoke no English and merely shrugged off their *excusez-moi*s and *s'il vous plaît*s and sent them pedaling back out into the deluge. They could barely wheel their bikes through the soggy salad of a road without slipping and falling every few minutes.

Shipwrecked and downcast, they stumbled upon an old chalk grotto and took refuge from the storm. Cathy set up an LED lantern, rummaged through her backpack for her official Girl Scout compass in a green Bakelite case to determine their coordinates. But what good was a compass without a map? (The supposedly waterproof Michelin Guide had long ago disintegrated in the rain.) She spritzed them with hand sanitizer and told them what to do in case they encountered any cave-dwelling snakes.

Despite Cathy's admonitions, Max convinced them to venture further into the cave. Neither Cathy nor Emily had any desire to be left alone in the dark. With only the flickering lantern to guide them, they discovered a gothic archway carved into the chalk, and countless crumbling sculptures depicting heroines of the ages, from Joan of Arc to the female cyborg in *Ghost in the Shell*. The walls were covered in graffiti, a lot of it in neon reflective paint. The mud-splattered ground was littered with little green beer bottles. Further in, a big pink blob revealed itself to the light. It turned out to be an army tank, repainted in pink camouflage, the gothic crosses replaced with hot-pink hearts. Behind the tank was a circular crab apple press, jury-rigged to the tank's engine. There was also a tarnished copper alembic, which they would later discover was an illegal still.

Stacked up on the far wall were hundreds, if not thousands of dusty bottles of apple cider. Max popped the first cork by holding the bottleneck between her thighs. Several others exploded spontaneously. The cider was light, dry, and refreshing, and before long the women, excluding Max, who did not drink, were feeling very festive, especially Cathy, who said they didn't sell this kind of cider at the Tice's Corner farm stand. They were even inspired to play a drinking game, a hybrid of Truth or

Dare and Fuzzy Duck, which prompted some deep truths about human nature and personal revelations, only to be forgotten in the morning.

Emily jotted down some notes: *Allecto, the angry one; Megaera, the jealous one; Tisiphone, the avenger of murder. The three Furies.* She'd helped her son Zach study for a test on Greek mythology last year. The reference had seemed fitting at the time; they were in a sort of underworld, although she couldn't quite pin down who was who, or make heads or tails of her handwriting when she tried to decipher it later.

This wasn't the first time they had been separated from the group. Their tour guide, with his gold signet Cracker Jack ring and endless and inextinguishable font of Madame Bovaria didn't consider small details, like whether everyone on the tour was accounted for, to be on his *cahier des charges*.

They had sung quite a way down from "Ninty-nine problems and you're hearing them all" when they first became aware of stamping feet and then shouting. The footsteps were coming closer. They shushed each other, extinguished the lantern. Without so much as a *bonjour*, two imperious Frenchmen in long white aprons marched them up several flights of stairs, finally emerging into the quaint old kitchen of an auberge where pots simmered and pans sizzled. The gendarmes were about to be called in to decide the fate of the three cider pilferers, when the mysterious redhead of the blue bike appeared from the *salle à manger*.

"*Excusez-moi*," she said with her Midwestern accent, "I'm Beatrice, allow me." Napkin still in hand, she quieted down the hosts making assurances that the cost of the applejack would be reimbursed; and, despite the lack of passports and *cartes d'identité*, clean rooms, hot baths, and a Norman feast were quickly arranged. The only thing she did not provide was a squad of French lovers, although Max had no trouble conjuring one later on her own.

The aubergiste couldn't have become friendlier. "*Trouvez-*

moi une table pour ces mal baisées d'américaines," he ordered the garçon, who seated them at a cramped table near the kitchen. The *soupe à l'oignon gratinée,* so thick it was easier to eat with a fork than a spoon, was washed down with a *trou normand* (a spoonful of homemade apple sherbet floating in calvados), a *blanquette de veau,* another *trou normand,* followed by the *plateau de fromages,* another *trou normand,* then, palates sufficiently cleansed, a molten *tarte Tatin . . .*

"Calories never tasted so good," declared Max, very likely calculating how many miles she'd have to run to get back to ground zero.

Their savior, Beatrice, had replaced her usual biking tartan with a linen dress the color of buttercups and a strand of amber beads. Luckily, Cathy had several days' worth of one-size-fits-all outfits in her emergency backpack. She had changed into her favorite fuchsia stirrup pants, the ones she usually wore on Saturdays, and an oversized white T-shirt. Emily was in Cathy's cornflower-blue Monday pair, and Max was barely dressed, in a sports bra and men's boxers with the waistband rolled down, exposing her hipbones. No sunflower Sunday stirrup pants for her.

Dinner cleared away, Beatrice ordered *café calva*s, in what turned out to be the first of many nightcaps.

"So, enjoying the calvados?" she asked the women. "You've certainly earned it. I've seen you pedaling along each and every byway."

"Yes, I think we've crossed paths a few times," Emily said.

"Calvados?" Cathy asked. "I thought it was apple cider."

Beatrice laughed. "It doesn't mean *save our souls* for nothing. There's magic in those apples. Do you want to know how calvados got its name?" Emily's pen was poised to take notes. Beatrice patted her hand. "Don't think you're going to find this on Wikipedia."

Calvados, Beatrice told them, was named for the Spanish

sailors who washed up on the shore after their ship the *San Sal-vados* sank on the rocks off Arromanches. The only thing they had to eat was an exotic variety of bittersweet Iberian apples. *Marineros* and apple seeds took root and spawned the famous crab apple orchards that are the pride of Normandy and the source of the world's finest ciders and apple brandy.

Beatrice took a sip of her drink. "Et voilà!"

After the first dessert course was cleared, the conversation, as it had been wont to do on the Tour de Flaubert, turned to men, to the delight of everyone except Emily who was too absorbed in her thoughts and writing them down to pay complete attention to the overall soap opera.

Her mind was elsewhere, cycling, actually "recycling," a thought that made her smile, through quaint towns with timber-framed houses and down quiet country lanes. On the Tour de Flaubert everything was Madame Bovary. Even the street signs. They stopped for a nibble at Bar Bovary and bought trinkets at Le Grenier Bovary. In the automaton museum, five hundred remote-controlled mannequins reenacted scenes from *Madame Bovary*: Emma and Charles dancing on their wedding day; Emma in a cab with Léon, impulsively ripping off her chemise; Charles sawing off Hippolyte's leg; Emma fainting in the kitchen when she receives the basket of apricots from Rodolphe with a Dear Jane letter tucked inside.

Their tour guide had delighted in frightening them with ghost stories at every opportunity. At Mortemer Abbey, he recounted the legend of the White Lady and her feline goblin companion that "knows naught of no." Cathy didn't get a wink of sleep that night and was dressed and ready to go at the crack of dawn.

They visited the grave of Delphine Delamare, Flaubert's model for Emma Bovary, and rode up a hilltop where Emma and Rodolphe had ridden on horseback. After a while it became hard to discern truth from fiction—for instance, which, if either, of the two stuffed parrots was the actual one that had sat on

Flaubert's writing table? The only place reality was not in question was in Flaubert's library, now housed in the town hall. Surrounded by his books—Cervantes, Shakespeare, Voltaire—still in the original bookcases, everything was black and white.

"Ah, *l'amour l'amour, toujours l'amour*," Beatrice sighed. "My days of love are over. Now I take French lessons."

"What about Albert?" Cathy asked. "You just said he was the love of your life."

Beatrice had brought her level of inebriation to cruising altitude and hadn't even remembered mentioning Albert. "I guess you could say that, but he was also a heck of a lot of trouble. French isn't all that much easier, but at least it doesn't get cancer and die or leave its socks on the floor. Or have a wife."

She summoned the garçon and her glass was swiftly replenished. Emily had diluted her drink with water and was pretending to take tiny sips of the now milky opalescent liquid. Max asked for another Perrier. Cathy was still working on her herbal tea. Was Beatrice the only one drinking? She'd always considered it a badge of honor that she could drink most of her male colleagues under the table.

"Wait, Albert was married?" Cathy asked.

"Naturally. It was the perfect arrangement," Beatrice said. "We had a grand adventure."

"No regrets?" Emily asked, finally emerging from her fog.

Beatrice gave a throaty laugh. "Non. Rien de rien. Je ne regrette rien."

Emily refused to drop it. "How did you deal with the guilt?"

Beatrice pushed her glasses onto her forehead. "Guilt? That's quaint. Are you suggesting that I infringed the law?"

"No, but there's always collateral damage."

Beatrice lost a bit of her color, and took a moment to look at the bibelots adorning the bare and hand-hewn rafters. "Oh, I get it now," she said. "You cheated and left your husband, thinking the grass is always greener."

"My husband was the one who left," Emily clarified.

"Okay, whatever you say, *Emma*."

Emily avoided the other woman's gaze, her eyes filling with tears. The others exchanged glances. Max gently maneuvered Emily's snifter to the other side of the table.

"Cry if it makes you feel better," Beatrice said. "But when you're finished, do something about it. Toughen up, babe. People today have such thin skins. They make much too much out of anything. You think wallowing in so-called guilt and self-pity will make things right? What a waste of time—unless you're a glutton for punishment. Albert and I didn't hurt anyone. So what if he was married. So what if he had a few girlfriends on the side. Good for him. Stick your nose in your own business."

Cathy gasped. "He had other women besides you? Not counting his wife, I mean?"

"De temps en temps, oui!"

"And you tolerated that?"

Beatrice laughed. "Why would I begrudge him his liberties, when I was taking mine?" The reaction didn't surprise her. Her espousal of free love, in the Victoria Woodhull sense, had never been met with acceptance, though for the life of her she couldn't imagine why anyone would want the government interfering in her personal life.

"Weren't you afraid that one day he wouldn't come back?" Cathy asked.

"And be with a man who felt obligated to me? That's the beauty of being free that you don't understand, that obviously terrifies you."

Cathy seized upon the opportunity for a teachable moment. "On Super Soul Sunday I heard you have to *be* the perfect partner to *attract* the perfect partner. If you ever want to find your soul mate—"

"Let's get something straight," Beatrice interrupted. "I don't want a man hither, thither, or yon, thank you very much. If you're waiting for Mr. Perfect, you're going to be waiting for a very long time."

"I'll wait as long as it takes," Cathy said. "My soul mate and I are destined to find each other."

"Don't wait, take those dogs for a walk."

Max shook her head and laughed, muttering something under her breath. They all looked at her. "It's nothing," she explained. "I was just thinking how interesting it is to spend time with all of you in this place where I never—ever—expected to find myself."

"What do you mean?" Cathy asked. "You're here to find your one and only, your soul mate, aren't you?"

Max rolled her eyes. "Read a lot of Harlequins?"

Beatrice liked straight shooters, and though Max was probably right—hope *was* a killer—for some reason she felt protective of Cathy.

"What are you doing on a singles bike trip then? Chasing butterflies?" Beatrice asked.

"That's what I'm going to ask the bitch who traded this freak show of a trip to me," Max said. "No offense intended."

Cathy looked at Emily. "*You* want to find your soul mate, don't you?"

Emily shook her head. "Sorry. For me, this is actually an . . . assignment. I'm writing an article for a travel magazine." A half-truth. In fact, she was planning to write a freelance article and see if she could sell it to a friend who wasn't answering her calls. But given the chance, she would have welcomed a brief foreign entanglement before returning to her real life.

"None of you wants to find your soul mate?" Cathy pressed.

The garçon brought over a plate of champagne truffles, which were consumed in silence. Emily thought, Did they all really want soul mates, and if they did, would they even know what one looked like? Was there even such a thing? A soul mate? *Pfffft!* How many times had they been disappointed in love before? What would make them take a chance on something so fickle again?

Beatrice finished her digestif, every drop of which she'd savored as though it was her last. When she lifted her glass, Cathy peered at her expectantly. The Knights of the Round Table may all be assembled, their "quest" yet to be determined, but Beatrice had no intention of raising a metaphorical sword to make a pledge of allegiance to love and soul mates; she just wanted a refill.

After an effusion of *mercis* to the *aubergiste*, who was slightly less effusive, the four women retired to their rooms, much to the relief of the *aubergiste*, who was waiting for them to turn out the lights so he could sneak into Max's chamber.

Upstairs, Cathy scanned the bookshelves lining the low crooked hallway in search of a cure for insomnia. She decided upon a slender book with a red leather cover, gold leaf, and onion-skin pages, chosen solely and precisely for the title embossed on its spine: *The Love Book*.

The next morning, not five minutes after they'd said their *au revoirs*, the tires of their bicycles sinking deeply into the squishy *bouses* that the rain had democratically spread across the road (even *cow dung* sounded better in French), Beatrice swerved to avoid a tractor zigzagging down the road and fell, twisting her ankle and bruising her hip. The handlebars of her Cooper were mangled, and her now mud-cum-manure-covered belongings were strewn everywhere, most notably an old French novel. That's how they discovered that Beatrice was on her own *Madame Bovary* pilgrimage.

"Through with love?" queried Emily, as she wiped the mud from the cover.

Max did triage, both on Beatrice and the Cooper, and Cathy quoted a Buddhist master, "No mud, no lotus," and no one was the wiser for it. The tour guide finally reappeared and Beatrice was conveyed by van to the nearest doctor.

After much grumbling about preferring to be a free agent, Beatrice agreed to unofficially join their Tour de Flaubert. Everyone had pegged her as least likely to keep up with the twenty-plus kilometers of cycling per day. Not overtly athletic, the sixty-nine-year-old former DA from Albany looked like a middle-aged beauty who'd been left in cold storage for perhaps a decade or two, with little ill effect. She turned men's heads of any age with her infectious laugh, shoulder-length auburn hair, nouveau cool purple sunglasses, manicured fingernails, and the perpetual twinkle in her emerald eyes. No amateur she, Beatrice had planned her trip as methodically as a woman chooses a man and plants her crosshairs on his heart. She ordered a brand-new Cooper shipped to France, with a wicker basket, gears, a bell, and a Brooks seat. A Cooper was the only thing a sensible woman would put between her legs, she liked to explain.

Even with her injuries, she turned out to be real Tour de France material, rarely breaking a sweat, never complaining, though she could not quite understand how the French could claim to be more civilized, without ice cubes or air-conditioning.

One might suppose that these four intrepid women, despite their age differences and disparate backgrounds, would become fast friends, bonding over their shared passion for *Madame Bovary* and their mutual, if not acknowledged, fear of love. But while they binged liberally on carbs and male-bashing sessions; commiserated over cheating partners or lack thereof; complained about inclement weather and French bathrooms; lost their way in the largest hedge maze in the area; and spent many a sleepless night in ramshackle farmhouses, with creaky beds covered in plastic and currents of tiny flies swarming around a bare bulb— in truth, they could barely tolerate each other. Between Beatrice's increasingly self-assured and preachy pronouncements, Emily's moodiness, Max's overcompetitiveness, and Cathy's

voodoo soul mate–conjuring rituals, the sooner this trip was
over the better.

C HAPTER TWO
THE INVITATION

THE INVITATION APPEARED in Emily's in-box early one September morning, two weeks after she'd returned from the bike tour, in a swirling pink font with tiny pulsing hearts: Soul Mate Soirée!

Had it been scratch-and-sniff like the key lime pie T-shirt Zach had brought home last summer from a trip to Disney World with his father (the air gun had been confiscated at airport security), it would have been strawberry shortcake. She almost deleted it, thinking it was yet another chain letter promising all sorts of blessings that would rain down on her if she forwarded it to seven friends—money, fame, love—which she invariably did, not because she was afraid of suffering the karmic consequences, but because she didn't want to disappoint the person who'd sent it, even at the cost of annoying the friends she sent it to. But curiosity got the best of her and she opened it.

The proposed soirée was at Cathy's home in Bayonne, New Jersey—probably, Emily imagined, in some kind of life-sized Polly Pocket Dream House. She hoped she could use Zach as an excuse, then looked at the date. It was Charles's weekend. She'd never been a good liar, except when it came to Nick, the married man she dated toward the end of her own failing marriage.

After the second postscript, Cathy had written: *BYOB*. For Cathy, who was basically a teetotaler, this seemed a bit odd. She couldn't possibly have meant *bike*, could she? Emily had roomed with a girl like Cathy freshman year, who wore frosted lip gloss, wielded a curling iron, and used double-sided tape to affix posters of orange kittens in baskets to the dorm room's cinder-block walls. All year the girl had tried to get Emily out of her dark "urban" clothes and into one of her flouncy Laura Ashley dresses, finally succeeding for an Easter brunch in Philadelphia with her sorority pledges. Emily looked like a Jewish Laura Ingalls Wilder.

Her hand floated over the delete button. How easy to send the email to spam and pretend it had never arrived. She looked at the names of the other recipients. What must Max be thinking? Or Beatrice? Would any of them make the trip to New Jersey for this?

The following day *The Love Book* arrived from out of nowhere. Emily stuck it on the windowsill with the other two copies that had already "manifested" through no effort or desire on her part. The first was the multicolored Post-it–festooned copy Cathy had swiped from the auberge and accidentally left at Charles de Gaulle. The second was from Emily's mother, who thought her daughter needed a little help in the love department. She'd even inscribed it: *Time to find you another fella!* Joyce's concern about her daughter's love life was purely financial in nature. Spousal support ended in January. Like Charles, she had little faith in Emily's ability to be self-supporting. And now, this third copy of *The Love Book* of mysterious provenance with no identifiable markings other than the words *Return to Sender* stamped in red. She was tempted to look online for an antidote for unbidden self-help books. The last thing she needed was a soul mate. And definitely not another copy of *The Love Book*.

Emily made a pot of tea and sat by the window. It was Zach's first day of school after summer break. She'd let him sleep a little longer. Her view, a patchwork of rooftops and water towers, had always seemed so exotic. She should have been working on a post for a friend's blog, but she was thinking

about the muddy ride from Lyons-la-Forêt to Ry, a soggy but
not unpleasant two hours. It had given Emily a chance to think.
Max had raced ahead with the tour guide, Beatrice was keeping
Cathy company in the rear, walking their bikes up even the most
gradual inclines, and Emily was lost in thought as she mean-
dered along the quiet country road, her rain slicker flapping in
the wind, trying not to worry about Zach, who was hiking with
his father and Charles's fiancée, Clarissa, in Yellowstone and, in
Emily's opinion, precariously out of cell phone range. Not that
Zach needed to call his mother; he was a well-adjusted, independent ten-year-old. It was her issue and she knew it. Of the
two of them, she often felt like the child, and, for the two weeks
she was in Normandy, one whose pacifier had been yanked unceremoniously out of her mouth.

Her friends were concerned that she was isolating. Since di-
vorcing Charles, she hadn't made any attempts to meet someone, let alone gone out on a single date. Even Zach had tried
hooking her up, first with his phys ed instructor, then a divorced
dad from the stables where he rode, and last spring, when a
sanitation worker whistled at her, Zach observed, "Maybe he
wants to marry you?"

The divorce hadn't been a complete surprise. Emily had
known before they'd married that she was wrong for Charles,
but he had been so certain. Of everything. And his certainty had
made her feel safe, providing her with guidelines, parameters,
and consistency. He wanted a wife and four children in a house
in the suburbs with dinner on the table when he pulled into the
driveway.

She'd failed miserably on all accounts. She hated cooking
anything other than brownies, and miscarried with a vengeance,
as if her uterus was triple-coated with Teflon. The mere idea of
the suburbs gave her anxiety, and every morning she'd wake up
like Martin Sheen in *Apocalypse Now*, freaking out in his hotel
room in Saigon, waiting for a mission.

In sum, she was a pretty useless housewife. She understood perfectly Charles's disappointment. He thought he was getting Madame Homais, the pharmacist's dutiful wife, but wound up with Emma Bovary instead.

When they were newlyweds, a bowl of M&Ms or cheese and crackers had sufficed for dinner; and at least in those first years, Emily had more than made up for the lack of food with an overabundance of passion. She was a freelance writer and had a tendency to lose track of time when she was in her office, a tiny alcove off the kitchen overlooking the courtyard. If there was food in the fridge, it was often spoiled or inedible, which infuriated Charles who hated to waste anything. That all changed when she discovered she was miraculously pregnant.

For the next nine months *What to Expect When You're Expecting* became her Bible. She'd morphed into a food Nazi, eating only organic, unprocessed food with no caffeine, no preservatives, no artificial colors or flavors, practically no *anything*, to Charles's complete and utter and maddening dismay.

Then Zach was born, and it was happily back to M&Ms, though now she dispensed with the bowl.

By the time Charles came home from work, usually past midnight, Zach finally and safely asleep in his crib, Emily was in no mood to get up and prepare anything, let alone talk to Charles about his latest case, or welcome his sexual advances. She'd pretend to be asleep, listening for the whir of his electric toothbrush, the sign that she was off the hook; he never made love after brushing his teeth. He began referring to the mound of pillows she erected between them to protect her lower back when she was pregnant as Hadrian's Wall, a line of defense that persisted even after she gave birth. The few times Charles did manage to surmount the wall, she'd say she was too tired to put in her diaphragm.

When Zach was in preschool, she'd started going to the gym and discovered that she could still catch the eye of the occasional man. Or two. Charles spent more and more time at work, until over breakfast one day he said, "Emily"—and she said, "I know, Charles, but how will we tell Zach?" The next week Charles moved into the Harvard Club, then a small furnished studio. Six months later he was living with Clarissa.

Now that it was all finally over with, the sound of the guns no longer reverberating and the smoke cleared from the battle-field, she was sincerely glad Charles had found someone new. She wanted him to be happy, and Zach seemed to like Clarissa, except for that one time he locked her out of the apartment and disabled the doorbell when she went out with the garbage.

Emily and Clarissa even went to lunch at Fred's, on the ninth floor of Barney's, at Clarissa's suggestion. Emily waited and waited for Clarissa to say whatever she felt she had to say, but *die neue suburban Hausfrau* just picked at her chopped salad for an hour, scanning the room, more interested in seeing and being seen than engaging Emily. It was all a little too post-modern for Emily and something she hoped to never do again.

Emily's friends were wrong; she hadn't been manless for the last four years, only for the past two, except for several unfor-tunate instances of phone sex with her college boyfriend, but it had been decidedly one-sided, so in her mind it didn't really count. There had been some "overlap" between her marriage to Charles and her relationship with Nick, for which she would probably never forgive herself. The *if only*s still kept her awake at night.

Nick had been one of her first interviews after she began freelancing again. They'd met at one of those interchangeable "authentic" brasseries in the theater district. As he spoke about his work in landmark preservation, the intensity of his gaze had ignited something in her like a leftover cassoulet brought back to life. Somehow, the lines of discretion had been blurred by denial or depression or something, she wasn't even quite sure. None of her friends would have suspected or believed her capable of having an affair. Utterly "uncharacteristic," they would have said—that is, if they'd found out. She'd never imagined she was capable of it either.

She came to enjoy these interludes. No talking, no having to dress up or make dinner or do her hair. Just passion. An hour later, she'd walk Nick to the door and drift off to sleep as if it had never happened. A close call several years ago prompted Emily to put an end to the affair, an end that turned out to be one of many. Zach had been asleep for hours. It was one of those occasions when Nick would arrive unannounced already half-undressed when she opened the door and carry her to the bedroom for a quick romp. But on that night, they'd accidentally fallen asleep. Nick bolted awake at 5 a.m. and was sitting on the foot of the bed, hurriedly putting on his shoes, when Zach came in, rubbed his eyes, and, still half-asleep, said, "Daddy?"

Emily put her arm around him and walked him to his room. "Go back to bed, sweetie," she said softly.

In the morning, when Zach asked why Daddy had been there, she told him that it had only been a dream, the first time she'd ever lied to him, another thing she'd never forgive herself for.

Emily had been meaning to mail *The Love Book* back to Cathy, but kept forgetting. The fact that Cathy had left something at the airport wasn't surprising; she'd been in a complete daze from the time-release tranquilizers she'd taken to counteract her fear of flying, not having anticipated a three-hour delay. Despite gulping down a double espresso, every time Emily glanced up from her magazine, Cathy had slipped a little bit further down in her chair. But *The Love Book*? Since finding it at the auberge on that postdiluvian night, Cathy had never let it out of her sight, lugging it in her backpack along with her other emergency supplies. The red leather book was so often in her hands that her fingertips were stained red as though she'd eaten pistachios laced with red dye. By the time Emily noticed the forsaken book, Cathy had already boarded her plane back to Newark.

All of their flights had been "eventful," everyone's except Beatrice's—she'd flown Swissair. Her flight had not only taken off right on schedule, but she was bumped up to first class and wound up sitting next to one of her college roommates from Holyoke whom she hadn't seen in over thirty years.

Max's plane had mechanical problems and spent eight hours idling on the tarmac; Cathy was waylaid in Atlanta, after missing her connecting flight; and Emily's bags were lost. If Emily bought into the belief that *The Love Book* was, as Cathy professed it to be, the Rosetta Stone of the Law of Attraction, and that like attracts like whether you like it or not, it might appear that the universe was just mirroring back what each of them had been expecting. But she didn't. Lost baggage was nothing more than an inconvenience.

Emily realized she'd been absently flipping through the copy of *The Love Book* her mother had sent her. A quote by Marianne Williamson, one of many, dotting the margins like a Rorschach test, caught her eye: *It is our light, not our darkness, that most frightens us.*

Already she found her mind wandering.

Like clockwork, at precisely seven fifteen, the telephone rang. She let it ring several times. It was Charles calling to say he'd be swinging by in a taxi to pick Zach up at five thirty that afternoon and could she have him waiting downstairs. Charles took Zach Wednesday nights and alternate weekends. Wednesday was the hardest night of the week especially when it was also Charles's weekend, as this one was. The distance between Friday and Sunday seemed interminable, a no-man's-land. How many episodes of *What Not to Wear* or baths could she take? Nick had known her particular susceptibility to loneliness and used to call hoping this time she'd succumb and invite him over. He hadn't called since before she left for Normandy. She didn't know if she felt relieved or rejected.

"Can I talk to Zach?" Charles asked.

"He's not up yet."

"But he has to be at school in an hour."

"I'm about to wake him. Do you want him to call you?"

"Just tell him I'm picking him up at five thirty."

"Yes, Charles. Like always."

"When I say five thirty, I don't mean five thirty-seven, okay?"

"Charles—"

"Because Clarissa thinks—"

"I know what Clarissa thinks." She'd heard it enough times. If Zach was five minutes late because he forgot to pack his math homework or had a stomachache, it was her fault; she was being manipulative. She could hear Charles take a deep breath and exhale through clenched teeth, like steam from a sputtering kettle.

"Do me a favor, just have him ready. That's what I pay you for."

"You didn't actually just say that, did you?"

"Emily, don't start. It would be nice if you could accommodate us once in a while. Clarissa and I babysat while you were off riding a bicycle in Normandy—"

"Babysat?"

"You know what I mean. So, do we understand each other?"

"Don't worry, Charles, Zach will be downstairs at five thirty."

"Alone, okay?"

"Yes, alone."

In the space of a thirty-second phone call, the usual low-grade self-doubt that hovered in her consciousness had multiplied like the fruit flies that circled the overripe bananas on the kitchen counter, too far gone even for banana bread.

Zach was on the bottom bunk of his loft. He'd kicked off the blanket. He was wearing Spider-Man pajamas and a Knicks jersey, just as he'd done every night for the last five years, since the first game Charles had taken him to at Madison Square Garden.

His Beanie Babies collection, handed down from an older cousin, was lined up on the top bunk. He'd dressed the squirrel like a road hog, with a leather jacket and bandanna, and put him on Batman's motorcycle. The cow was wearing a tutu. In a place of honor on Zach's red beanbag chair was the talking Yoda Charles had bought him when Zach was four and expressed a desire for a three-foot-tall My Size Barbie, which Charles had thought was wrong on so many levels. Emily saw it differently; he was an only child and just wanted a playmate. One night when Zach was in bed, Emily heard him whispering to Yoda, "Will Daddy come back?" But even with her ear pressed to the door and holding her breath, she couldn't hear the answer.

For years, Charles had been urging her to donate Zach's baby toys and clothes. She'd kept his first shoes, the red fleece onesie he wore when he learned to crawl, his snowsuit, the quacking beagle pull toy he used to take for walks in the park. He might want to give it to his children someday. So what if she was a little bit overly nostalgic. Weren't most parents? It didn't take up that much space in the closet.

A few months after they separated, Charles stopped by without calling (he still used his key, which enraged her, but not so much that she bothered to change the locks) to collect the rest of his things, like the red Craftsman toolbox filled with brand-new, top-of-the-line tools Emily had given him for their fifth anniversary.

When Zach discovered the toolbox missing, he said, "How am I going to fix things?"

Emily took him in her arms and tried to keep from crying. "It's not your job, Zach. It's not your job."

But there were times she wondered too.

After school that afternoon, Zach was racing down Broadway on his Razor scooter with Emily trailing behind, reminding him to stop at the lights. She'd been at the computer all day and even though she was technically outside, she was still at her desk in her state-of-the-art ergonomic chair—the one Charles had given her on their last Valentine's Day together. Her friend the editor had liked the piece about the Tour de Flaubert bicycle trip but not quite enough to publish it. With a little work, he told her, maybe. They'd discuss it over lunch tomorrow, already the second lunch they'd rescheduled. She had an idea and stopped to jot down some notes when, in the window of Barnes & Noble, she saw a giant poster for a reading by the author of *The Love Book* and took it as a sign. She'd write a Valentine's Day article about soul mates. She might be able to sell it to a major women's magazine, not just one of the free periodicals printed on recycled paper and dispensed on street corners. She was still scribbling as she stepped off the curb without looking, and bumped into a man on a BMW motorcycle.

"Hey! Watch where you're going!" she shouted, grabbing Zach protectively. She'd lived her whole life in Manhattan—in the same zip code, actually—but only since Zach was born had she developed the ability, the chutzpah, to yell at strangers. Charles thought it unbecoming.

The man on the motorcycle apologized. When she didn't let up, he told her to take a chill pill.

"A chill pill? You nearly run over my son and you want me to take a chill pill? You should have your license revoked."

"It was my light," he said. "You were jaywalking."

"The pedestrian always has the right of way."

"But I wasn't even moving."

Emily noticed Zach had put his hood over his head and taken refuge under an awning.

"Zach, are you all right? Did this maniac hurt you?"

"Maniac? You're the one flying off the handle, lady!" the guy shouted.

Zach tugged on her jacket. "Come on, Mom, let's go. I'm going to be late for Dad."

His voice quavered. He'd pulled the strings on his hood so tight that only his eyes were visible. He looked like an anteater. She put her arm around him, scowling one last time at the motorcycle guy before walking off.

"That man was an asshole," she said. "I'm giving you permission to say that word, but only if the situation calls for it. And you have to say it like you mean it. We'll practice later. You still can't use colorful language like that at school or around your father," she added.

Zach stopped and glanced behind him. "That was Kenneth, my math teacher."

"Are you sure?" Emily asked. "Maybe he just looked like him."

"It was Kenneth."

Emily had met Kenneth last week, but the biker outfit was a far cry from the chinos and conservative blazer he'd worn to Open School Night. The only thing that seemed to cheer up Zach was her suggestion that they stop at Alice's Tea Cup for a chocolate chip banana scone and peppermint tea.

The bells tinkled as they entered and walked down the stairs. Stevie and Justin were behind the counter. Zach was smitten with Stevie, a twenty-four-year-old waitress with sapphire-blue eyes and short dark hair. Alice's was a magical place where little children dressed up in tulle skirts and angel wings and were sprinkled with fairy dust when they entered, and grown women sat at antique sewing tables having tea and scones and remembering what it was like when everything was pretend.

Justin scooped up his teacup poodle, Apricot, and led them to a table. Apricot was wearing a miniature camo doggie hoodie and could have been mistaken for one of Zach's Beanie Babies. A few minutes playing with Apricot and Zach seemed to have forgotten the run-in with his math teacher. Emily was glad Alice's ignored the "no dogs allowed" policy enforced in most New York City restaurants.

On the way out, Stevie was talking on the phone, giggling and blushing. Young love, Emily thought, but she could barely remember.

When they were almost home, Emily saw Charles standing out front, arms crossed. He beckoned to Zach, who sped ahead. Charles walked out into the street and hailed a cab. She barely had time to kiss Zach goodbye before Charles slammed the taxi door. But she'd be getting a call soon—she was still holding his backpack.

She was at her desk, staring out the window, when the phone rang. It was Clarissa. Emily didn't even have a chance to say hello.

"I know how difficult it is for you to have Zach ready when Charles comes to pick him up, especially since you're so, so busy. But some of us have real jobs."

Emily had just read a poem by Rumi in Cathy's copy of *The Love Book*, which she'd opened at random. *If I love myself I love you. If I love you I love myself.* She'd never really understood this notion. It seemed like a tautology. A chicken-and-egg situation. In any case, she took a breath and tried to remain poised and receptive.

"I'm sorry, Clarissa, but we were only five minutes late. Charles should have called. We were just around the corner."

"No, you should have had him ready. Emily, you're not pretty enough or thin enough to be a prima donna, so stop acting like one. And nobody likes you."

"You can't talk to me like that," Emily said. "Put Charles on," but the line was dead.

Rumi had obviously never met Clarissa.

Emily closed the book. Her fingertips were stained magenta, a hint of which remained for days, leaving traces like rose petals on everything she touched. Across the courtyard, a fat naked man was staring at her from his window. She pulled down the shade and prayed that Nick would not call tonight.

C HAPTER THREE
PLAYING WITH FIRE

ENGINE COMPANY SIX of the Bayonne Fire Department breaking down her door at 3 a.m. was not how Cathy had envisioned her soul mate arriving. If she had, she would have changed out of her flannel nightshirt and pink Uggs into something a little more *je ne sais quoi*. But with her house burning down, she had no time to ponder the specifics. The firefighters, their faces streaked with black, sledge-hammered their way inside. Glass splintered across the carpet. She ran from room to room gathering what valuables she could and trying to wrangle her cat, but every time she was within striking distance the cat would dart away and whatever possessions she'd collected slipped from her grasp. The firemen told her to leave the premises but she paid them no heed. She'd go to the ends of Hades to save Mrs. Beasley.

The last thing she'd done before going to bed were the bonus exercises for Day Seven in *The Love Book:* Cutting Toxic Ties. She'd followed the directions to the letter, compiled a comprehensive list of all the chi-sucking people and situations in her life, and done the meditation on letting go, but rather than burn the list as instructed in order to sever the energetic cords, she'd flushed it. She'd never been one to take unnecessary risks and was especially careful with fire, ever since putting a flaming pot holder into the utility drawer last Thanksgiving. A septic issue she might have expected, but not a fire!

She'd been kneeling in front of her soul mate altar, a low marble bench positioned in the feng shui relationship sector of her house beneath a painting of lovebirds, doing her affirmations. *I was born to be loved. I deserve to be cherished. My soul mate adores me.* She'd spent hours agonizing over her Toxic Ties list. Whenever she turned out the light, another chi sucker would spring to mind. By the time she finished, the list was three pages long. The only thing she'd forgotten to do was blow out the candles.

Mrs. Beasley shot out from under the dining room table as the bulbs in the crystal chandelier exploded like fireworks. In closets and cabinets, dusty keepsakes, heirlooms, hand-me-downs, all the treasured relics Cathy had been charged with preserving after her mother died, were devoured by flames. The emulsion on her grandparents' wedding photo melted off the paper, the image changing from positive to negative until wisping into nothing.

Then she felt herself scooped up into a firefighter's sturdy embrace.

"You're coming with me," he said.

Cathy shouted, "Mrs. Beasley!" at the top of her lungs, but he ignored her, charging through the smoke and carrying her a safe distance from the house, before dropping her on the grass. He disappeared into the smoke and returned a few minutes later with Mrs. Beasley howling, but unharmed, in her cat carrier.

A million droplets of water sprayed into the sky. Tiny bits of ash fluttered like parched petals. Even from where she was standing, the heat from the fire was like a blast from a hot oven. The whole pajama-clad neighborhood had assembled around her house. Lawrence Weiner was leaning against the pumper truck talking to the fire chief, using words like *deflagration* and *pyrolysis*. He had a PX Series helmet with TrakLite and was wearing his volunteer fireman windbreaker over the standard uniform he'd worn all through high school: parachute pants, a patterned sweater vest, and those stupid tasseled loafers. When she looked carefully, she saw that today they didn't even match: one was black, the other brown. He was already in the process of narrating his timely rescue, bragging about how he'd been the first responder on the scene. Of course he was! He lived next door! All he had to do was slip on his mismatched loafers. When he swaggered away, Cathy met eyes with one of the firefighters who muttered, "Gear queer."

Luckily, she'd managed, despite all the chaos and commotion, to grab her purse, car keys, and, at the last minute, *The Love Book*. This was the third copy she'd bought since forgetting hers at Charles de Gaulle. The first replacement, she'd doused with coffee in the teachers' lounge. The second, she'd accidentally returned to the library with a stack of Harlequins, never to be found again, although one might have detected a rosier glow in the librarian's visage. And this, the third in the succession of replacements, had only just barely escaped annihilation by incineration.

Until Emily emailed to tell her *The Love Book* was safe and sound, Cathy had believed it irretrievably lost. For all she knew it was the only copy in the Western Hemisphere, maybe even the world. The book seemed to have been typed on a Smith Corona, though Cathy wouldn't have been surprised if it had appeared spontaneously out of the ether. The information contained between the red leather binding was priceless, so priceless she had been willing to risk copyright infringement—when she returned to the States she'd planned to make several photocopies to distribute to all her single cousins. The secret to finding true and lasting love needed to be shared. And then *poof*! Just as quickly as this magical book had come into her life, it vanished.

The other day, she was browsing in the Human Growth and Potential section at her local bookstore, though her heart wasn't really in it, when suddenly there it was, *The Love Book*, if not in the flesh, then at least in black and white. Somehow it had

miraculously "jumped" into her bag. Cathy didn't even bother
to speculate. There are no answers to certain questions. *Ours
is not to reason why*, her favorite and most misused Tennyson
quote. She'd gone back to pay for it, but the irony of a book on
the law of attraction finding *her* was not lost on Cathy. Now she
could lose as many copies as she wanted, the only consequence
a spike in Amazon ratings.

Every self-help book on relationships she'd ever read (and
there were few that she hadn't) recommended putting oneself in
a target-rich environment. So, like a Navy SEAL, she self-deployed
on carefully planned search-and-destroy missions, more search,
less destroy, in free-fire zones, recklessly diving into sports bars
and happy hours, comic book and Star Trek conventions; she
worked out at the YMCA during peak times near the basketball
court; and she shopped at Trader Joe's, the mecca of convenience food for suburban bachelors. But she hadn't met a single
man, at least not one with any "potential." Still, she tried to
remain open. As her mother used to say: *Mr. Right doesn't have
to be Mr. Perfect*. But Mr. Right was definitely not going to be
wearing parachute pants and a fireproof, environmentally controlled, shock-resistant, overpriced plastic helmet, PX Series or
not.

As plumes of smoke and copper flames poured out of her
second-floor window, she thought that if she couldn't find a
man here, in this mother lode of men, an entire squadron of
sexy firefighters delivered by the universe right to her door-
step, a fundraiser calendar come to life, maybe she was beyond
self-help.

The sun came up and finally the fire was contained. The
crowd dwindled to just a few stragglers. Lawrence hovered
nearby like a stubborn patch of pigweed.

She was hugging *The Love Book* when the fireman who'd
so unceremoniously deposited her on the lawn walked toward
her. His suit was covered in mud and his hair was matted down

with sweat from his helmet. At the time, Cathy hadn't noticed how clear and bright his eyes were, the kind of eyes that cut through fog. He was carrying the pretty pink glass thing she'd found in the attic when she'd first moved in, embalmed in cobwebs. It was shaped like a hollow glass pomegranate and filled with some sort of liquid. She'd dusted it off and hung it by its metal bracket in the kitchen.

The next thing she noticed were the firefighter's sturdy boots. They were the boots of a man who could be counted on. A man's man. No tasseled loafers for him.

"There's quite a lot of smoke and water damage," the firefighter said. "But consider yourself lucky. If the fire had spread to the kitchen, this grenade extinguisher would have exploded from the heat. People think they're kitsch. But they're highly toxic kitsch. Tough luck if you're standing there when it blows up in your face."

Cathy hadn't known what a grenade extinguisher was until she went on a tour of FDR's house with her sister's family. The tour guide, a perky female ranger, had explained that because of FDR's lifelong fear of fire after witnessing his aunt's death by conflagration, he had grenade extinguishers, glass bulbs filled with a chemical fire retardant, attached to every doorframe.

"I like it," she said. "It's pretty."

The fireman was staring at her. "Funny how pretty things can come in lethal packages," he said.

She blushed. The fireman wiped his brow. This law-of-attraction stuff really seemed to be working. And it was only day seven! She hadn't expected anything, not even a nibble, until at least week eight.

His name was Sean O'Dardy. A black Irishman. Dark hair and blue eyes. The Dylan McDermott of New Jersey. He was getting some guff from his fellow firefighters for flirting on the job.

"Whenever you're ready, Romeo," the fire chief called.

Sean put on his helmet. "Our revels now are ended," he said.

"Did you say *our revels*?" Cathy asked. All the Shakespeare she'd studied hadn't been for naught. "As in *this insubstantial pageant faded*? What you're calling a revel was just my life that burned down."

A grin spread across Sean's face. Prospero stood there dazed in his fire boots, wavering on the shore. Wasn't being rendered speechless a sign of falling in love? He wrote his number on the back of a Starbucks napkin. If she wasn't busy, there was a regional production of *Hamlet* next Friday. And then it hit her: as surely as fire finds the fuse, her soul mate had found her.

She'd been waiting to be swept away in a torrent of love her entire life, with "great thunderclaps and bolts of lightning," like in *Madame Bovary*. Maybe not into an abyss; she'd prefer a town house in Mahwah, but close enough.

Her indignation faded away. Why play hard to get with The One? A fireman bard! What were the odds? And so thoughtful! He even offered to dispose of the grenade extinguisher for her. She said yes with no further ado.

After the fire trucks wailed away, she made short work of loading the few scraps and trinkets she'd salvaged into her trunk. She was almost finished packing up when Lawrence Weiner sidled up beside her.

"I hope you have insurance," he said. "It's going to take weeks to repair all this damage. If you want, you can bivouac at my place. I have an emergency air mattress in the garage."

Cathy had no idea what bivouac meant, but there was no way she'd ever do it with Lawrence. "Thanks for your concern," she responded, bending over to pick up the cat carrier.

"I couldn't help noticing," he said. "And now that I'm finally getting a good look, that's a very furry pussy you have there, isn't it? My Maine coon is as hairy as a Greek sailor."

Cathy straightened up, smoothing down her nightshirt.

"My special ed students have more tact," she snapped. "Even on Ice Cream Fridays!"

Lawrence stuck his finger in the little hole on the side of the cat carrier and wiggled it. Mrs. Beasley hissed.

Cathy slammed her car door and sped off. She knew she'd left someone off her Toxic Ties list!

She pulled into the gravel driveway of the house she'd grown up in and retrieved the key from under the mat, brushing aside some stray pine needles. A fake poinsettia with a red velvet bow was sitting on the dining room table. She heard her father's labored breathing coming from the den. He looked up when he saw her, turned off *The Price Is Right,* and removed his oxygen tubing. He smiled, stretching his arms wide. His little girl was home.

C HAPTER FOUR
SUDS AND BUDS

MAX PUT ON HER GARDENING CROCS and stepped through the sliding screen door to her garden, a twelve-by-fifteen-foot paradise. The backyard actually had more square footage than her apartment, even counting the closets. The usual background sounds—strains of salsa music, a passing siren, honking cars—were not quite drowned out by the constant hum of the building's air-conditioning system. A few tomatoes were still hanging on the vine. The basil was growing like a weed.

When she'd first moved in, the "garden" was an unruly rectangle of concrete and stinkweeds, with the promise of peaches, azaleas, and roses climbing the worn wooden fence and now the last of this season's late bloomers. The outdoor space was one of two reasons she'd taken the ground-floor studio in East Harlem with fifteen-foot-high ceilings and a wall of windows, but barely enough room for a pullout couch. The other was that the building, a block from the river, was thirty-five stories high. She was a "tower runner." Every morning at dawn, she religiously did one hundred flights of stairs, two at a time with a weighted backpack.

The Empire State Building race was in January and this year she wasn't going to settle for runner-up. As Grandpa Calvin always said, *Qui audet adipiscitur.* Who dares, wins, a motto from his days in the British Army.

She'd spent summers with her grandfather, Caleb "Calvin" Forsythe, a physics professor at MIT and devout atheist, while her parents did their yearly grand tour of Europe. Two months every summer were spent barefoot and in cutoffs. He taught her to garden, drive a tractor, shear alpacas, and even to box. When she was fourteen, her parents, fed up with her rebellious nature—smoking, drinking, cutting school—took her out of private school and sent her to live with Calvin full time. They considered it a punishment. The captain in the Royal Army would put her through her paces—but for Max it was the first taste of freedom she'd ever had. Calvin let her buzz her hair, tend his beehive, and didn't get angry when she accidentally let the chickens out. He was also the first one to call her Max. He liked to say she was the best grandson a man could ever want. And so much like her grandmother, Evelyn, though Max had never known her. She died of cancer when Max was only six months old.

Calvin and Evelyn had met at Allied Forces headquarters in London during basic training. She was an officer in the United States Women's Army Corps, in the first battalion sent to the European Theater of Operations. They were both in the Eighth Air Force, Calvin a fighter pilot and Evelyn assigned to an aerial reconnaissance mapping team. A fourth-generation New Englander and one of seven girls, she'd joined WACs because she wasn't interested in staying home and doing those "humble homey tasks"; she wanted to serve her country. Getting married had never been on her radar. But it was love at first sight, at least for Calvin. He'd never met another woman who could do more pushups than he could. His family was brokenhearted when, after the war, he abandoned his country to marry a Yankee. But he followed his heart and never looked back.

Max turned off the garden hose, then collected the cigarette butts and joint filters that the new tenants on the second floor regularly tossed off their balcony into her yard. Last week she taped a note to their door. *Please don't litter in the garden!* But today she wouldn't be so polite.

* * *

Later that afternoon, when Max returned from a sixty-mile bike ride up the Palisades, she found an unmarked package wrapped in newspaper in front of her door. A very "successful" drug dealer lived next door and he frequently received deliveries and questionable visitors late into the night. Max had never dared peer over the high fence that separated their adjacent gardens, but she knew it was no Versailles.

The drug dealer's door opened; he was wearing a white tank top and overalls, the straps down around his waist. Max appreciated his well-defined physique. The rich dark color of his skin made his body look even more ripped. He pushed his Prada sunglasses onto his forehead. His pet ferret was in its usual spot around his neck.

"Shorty, you're looking fine today," he said.

She gave him her shut-you-down glare. She was in no mood to fend off yet another proposition from the drug dealer.

"This must be for you," she said, handing him the package.

"No, Shorty, not mine. I opened it by mistake. I should have known with all the glitter and shit."

Max lifted the edge of the newspaper. Pink confetti hearts fluttered to the floor. Another copy of *The Love Book*. The first had come by FedEx and Max had refused to sign for it. Cathy was nothing if not persistent.

"Fuck!" she said.

"Can't now, Shorty," the drug dealer said. "I might have time if you want to link up later."

"My name's not Shorty and not in this lifetime, Simon."

"Why the attitude, mon? Did I do something?"

"Would you tell your 'friends' I'd appreciate if they not ring my buzzer in the middle of the night?"

"Hush, I told you last week I'd take care of it."

"And if I find the service door open one more time I'm calling the landlord."

"Why you blaming me?"

"It doesn't take a brain surgeon."

"You're in luck, then. Here I am. Your own personal neuro-surgeon."

"Interesting euphemism."

He laughed. The ferret was getting restless. Simon cradled it under one arm, rubbing its underside. "Truce?"

"I guess," she said. "For now."

She read the first and last line of *The Love Book* before tossing it in the recycling bin. *Everyone you meet is a mirror.* The sort of trite crap found on the back of bags of Famous Amos cookies.

She showered, put on her last clean pair of board shorts, stuffed her gym clothes and regular clothes—not that there was much difference between them—into her grandfather's army duffel bag, slipped on her "street" Crocs, and headed to the all-night laundromat. A conspicuous trail of glitter led to the drug dealer's door, and surprisingly, but also somehow not, *The Love Book* had been removed from the trash bin.

Before leaving the building, she slammed the service door so hard it rattled. No point being subtle.

At Suds and Buds, after dumping her clothes in a washing machine, she grabbed a seltzer from the glass refrigerator case, found a stool by the window, and opened the well-worn copy of *The Sorrows of Young Werther* she'd found at the Strand. Squeeze was playing on the stereo, an album that conjured a time fixed in her memory like Calvin's chloroformed beetles.

Her father had been livid when she announced she was dropping out of the premed program at Harvard. Moving to New York? After all the strings he'd pulled to get her in? Maxine Latham Forsythe, valedictorian, daughter of the chairwoman of the local Junior League, a fitness instructor? But she'd made up her mind. She'd rather be groped by muscleheads than limp-dick, lard-assed professors with mint-masked sardine breath and all the power.

She would have stayed with Calvin forever, but her parents had enrolled her in summer school before sending her to Deerfield Academy for her senior year. A month after she left, on June 6, 2004, the sixtieth anniversary of D-day, Calvin killed himself. After the funeral, Max drank, snorted, or screwed whatever or whoever was in front of her, trying to dull the pain and quiet her mind and the incessant thought: if only she hadn't left him. The pain was still right under the surface. It began with pressure behind her eyes, then flickers of light, a knife in the base of her skull. Drinking had masked it, sex had numbed it, exercise had given her the feeling she could get beyond it. But it was only an illusion.

Now that you have gone, there's no other . . .

A group of rowdy guys crowded around the beer cooler. Like many people at the laundromat, they were more into the free Buds than suds. Max wondered how many of these guys would eventually end up in AA. She'd been clean and sober for almost two years. She'd tried to do it on her own, to cut down, only drink on the weekends, after five, muscling through the days like her workouts, but eventually she couldn't remember entire evenings or how she'd wound up in some stranger's bed, again. Giving up drinking had felt like a betrayal of her grandfather's memory. It had been Calvin who had taught her to hold her liquor when she was fourteen, shown her how to mix and throw back one martini after another as they sat watching the sunset from the porch.

"That's my boy," Calvin had said proudly the first time she didn't puke.

The Golden Hour, he'd called it. The only time of day he ever spoke about being in the trenches.

She'd read only a few pages when she sensed someone behind her.

"*Mi hermosa*," Hector said, kissing the back of her neck. Just the sound of his voice aroused her.

She and Hector had met five years ago at a dingy gym on Nineteenth Street when she'd first moved to New York. He was a gorgeous Adonis of a man as serious about weightlifting as she was. It didn't take long before they became training and—though his sexuality was somewhere on the Kinsey continuum—sex buddies. He gave her a lead on an apartment in his building—a tiny walk-up in the East Village with a bathtub in the kitchen—helped her move in, and built her floor-to-ceiling bookshelves. She had few possessions, mostly disposable, except for her books and whatever she'd managed to salvage after Calvin shot himself with his army revolver: his maroon beret, an ivory chess set, a glass-covered box containing his rare beetle collection, and a fisherman's sweater that she'd worn so often it had unraveled at the neck. After a few months, like every other guy she'd ever slept with, Hector started getting serious. She'd thought he'd been a safe choice, and it was a shame, because he rocked in bed, but he said she was the first woman who'd ever satisfied him. She told him they were done and moved uptown. It was self-preservation. Calvin would have been proud; he'd taught her well.

Hector straddled a metal chair. He smelled irresistible, a mixture of salt, sand, and sun, and if she knew what was good for her she'd get away from him as quickly as possible. She checked the time on the machine. The wash cycle seemed to be taking forever. She considered lugging home her wet clothes and hanging them in the backyard.

"Hiding from me again?" Hector asked.

"I was in Normandy."

"Oh, right. Pam."

Pam was her rich client with the Central Park South duplex who'd just had shoulder surgery and couldn't go on the Tour de Flaubert. One of the perks of being a personal trainer was that she was the recipient of her clients' hand-me-downs and castoffs, like never-worn outfits from Bergdorf's, all-inclusive vacations, and the occasional man.

The only reason she'd accepted the bike trip gift had been to honor Calvin's memory. While the rest of the group went to *Madame Bovary* sites, Max would take off, visiting military cemeteries, D-day museums and battlefields, paying her respects to the lost soldiers including her grandfather, who had made it home though part of him had never returned.

"I knew I'd find you here," Hector said, leaning on the back of the chair.

"How?"

He smiled. "We're *almas gemelas*."

"There is no more *we*. We're done."

"We'll never be done."

Suddenly, there was a commotion. Someone rushed over with a bucket and mop. Water and suds covered the retro linoleum floor.

"Shit," she said.

Hector laughed. "Didn't anyone ever teach you all things in moderation?"

She transferred her clothes to an available washer and deposited six more quarters. When she sat down, she felt the throbbing begin behind her eyes. She'd already done her hundred flights. *Suck it up, Max*, Calvin used to say.

Hector got up and sat behind her, his thighs wrapped around hers. He always seemed to know. "Close your eyes," he said, pressing his thumbs into the knot at the base of her neck.

Memories of it still keep calling and calling, but forget it all I know I will . . .

"*Mi cariño*," he whispered. Of course the word for beloved in Spanish would be gender neutral.

The next morning, Max was on her final flight of stairs, making good time, but she knew she could do better. When she reached the top landing, she rested for a few seconds, hands on hips. A rusty bicycle was leaning against the fire door. She disabled the alarm, pushed the door open, and stepped out onto the roof, breathing in the misty morning air. The steeple of the Methodist church just three blocks away was barely discernible. She could still feel Hector's hands on her skin like a sunburn. At least he'd had the decency to leave before dawn. It was Sunday, after all.

C HAPTER FIVE
BLACK AND WHITE

THE BLINKING CURSOR HADN'T BUDGED in over an hour. For Emily, it was starting to feel like an admonition, just like the stack of bills in her peripheral vision. Her friend the editor still wasn't satisfied with her second stab at the Tour de Flaubert article. He actually said it had no point of view, no personality. Not surprisingly, she hadn't written a word all day.

She shut down her computer, packed her gym bag, and, hoping an intenSati class would boost her spirits, set off for the gym. But today, as she performed lunges and leg lifts, and chanted the group affirmations—*Every day, in every way, I'm better, I'm better, I'm better! Yeah!*—she didn't feel any more empowered afterward than she had before. If anything she felt *worse, worse, worse, yeah!* Clarissa was right. No one liked her, and Emily least of all. She was at the water fountain when one of the trainers complimented her on her rear delts. She thanked him, though she didn't know exactly what or where her rear delts were. Christophe was a twenty-nine-year-old bodybuilder from Israel, basically a sweet overgrown kid who gave her training tips and occasionally took her for lunch at the burrito place around the corner. But today he was looking at her less like a big sister and more like his next meal.

"Give me your number," he said. "Maybe we can hang out sometime."

Like she needed another son. Zach and Charles were enough.

When she came out of the locker room, a man with dark shoulder-length wavy hair and a scruffy beard was doing squats on the Smith machine. He'd angled the bench in such a way that it was blocking the exit. Like most regulars, he had his never-ever-changing routine. First, he'd preen in front of the mirror; his daily adulations complete, he'd regretfully tear himself away for an hour of heavy lifting; thirty minutes on the recumbent bike with the newspaper; hit the mats for his own version of a Bulgarian stretching routine; then shower and change out of his singlet and back into his ubiquitous three-piece suit. She didn't know what to make of him. In Manhattan, he could just as easily be a CEO of a Fortune 500 company or underemployed. She'd been to enough church sales to know that princes and beggars could be standing side by side, scouring the week's inventory. More likely the latter, as she'd once overheard him haggling with the sales manager about an increase in his membership dues.

When she squeezed past him, he stared right through her without blinking as if she weren't even there.

The days were getting shorter. The sky was now the same slate gray as the sidewalks and it had turned chilly. Emily left the gym and walked down Broadway, past familiar stores like the Town Shop—a lingerie store that had been there for over a century, with its iconic pink sign—and various chain and box stores that seemed to have popped up overnight. With fewer and fewer exceptions, the whole neighborhood was beginning to look like a strip mall. The restaurants and bookstores that used to line this stretch of the Upper West Side when she was growing up were now as much memories as the places her grandparents used to wax nostalgic about: Gitlitz, Bloom's Bakery, the Automat on Seventy-second Street, Schwartz Candy where women in white aprons and hats made homemade chocolates, nonpareils, and fudge. She was thinking how much she wished things didn't have to change—she wanted there to be some continuity for

Zach—when she realized she was standing in front of Barnes &
Noble again, right where she and Zach's math teacher had their
run-in. Poor Zach. He said Kenneth had been picking on him
all week. She dreaded going back to an empty apartment and
the blank computer screen. Her editor was right: her article had
no point of view.

Her cell phone rang. As she was searching for it in her gym
bag, an older couple passed by, arm in arm, laughing. They were
probably in their early seventies, a little older than Beatrice.
They stopped to look at the display of books. On the phone,
Zach was telling her about the paintball party he'd gone to that
morning. She probably wouldn't have noticed the couple except
that they were so colorfully and exquisitely and deliberately
dressed, like a nineteenth-century painting. Though she couldn't
hear them speak, she knew they were definitely not American.

The woman was tall and thin, with aristocratically stooped
shoulders. She wore a knotted green turban, a lavender blouse
with a huge collar under a fitted brocade jacket with a peplum,
a long silk skirt with splashes of green and red and peacock
blue, and blue suede ankle-strap shoes. Her fine gray hair had a
hint of purple. She wore no makeup except for magenta lipstick
and a dusting of powder on her translucent skin. Her companion was her complement, in pink trousers, a blue blazer, and
an orange bow tie, with a shock of wavy white hair and a full
beard.

Standing next to this Technicolor couple, Emily felt as
though she and the rest of the city were in black and white. It
wasn't just the couple's artfully put together attire, or the way
the woman smiled as the man pulled her close—the way Emily imagined they must have done hundreds of times—it was
their vibrancy, their joyful spirit that eclipsed everything around
them. Emily had been staring at their reflection so intently that
she hadn't noticed that her own reflection was superimposed on
the poster of *The Love Book* in the window.

Perhaps it was something about the sight of this perfectly in-sync couple, but whatever it was, she knew exactly what she needed to do to make her article work. It wasn't a sudden epiphany. The solution just came to her as if it had been there all along. After she and Zach hung up, she turned back to the couple, but they were gone. The streets were once again dull and colorless, just shades of gray, and she felt a sense of loss, though for what, she didn't know.

Beatrice was at the Victory Café on North Pearl Street with Bob and Mary, two former colleagues who kept her up-to-date with the internecine goings-on at the DA's office, and who also enjoyed a good single malt. Beatrice had retired last May with full benefits. She loved her job but it had begun to take its toll. She'd worked with victim advocates for thirty years and had prosecuted enough First Street Goonies, Second Avenue Goonies, Crips, Bloods, and SBOs for several lifetimes.

Bob and Mary were making fun of her for bringing her own bike to Normandy and being, as the tour guide had referred to her, such a *poule de luxe,* which at the time she thought meant *deluxe chicken,* but later discovered was another name for a high-class prostitute. She wasn't sure whether to be flattered or offended. She believed in the rights of sex workers, but knew Bob and Mary weren't quite so enlightened.

It was true; she hadn't been the easiest of traveling companions—one thing Beatrice had never been called was easy. She'd tried to be a good sport, but after an entire day biking around Rouen and environs, when they arrived by van at the place they were supposed to stay for their last night of the tour, she'd pretty much lost it. She was tired and looking forward to a nice lunch, relaxing by the pool, and turning in early. So when she saw the tumbledown brick cottage with a trellis of bare branches on an overgrown patch of land, she knew it would have neither room service *nor* a heated swimming pool.

"What exactly do you mean, *self-catering*?" she'd inquired of the tour guide. "We have to cook?"

Because of a "small" miscommunication when the cottage, an old Norman farmhouse, had been rented, there was no cook or housekeeper as advertised, only two small bedrooms, a *god-awful* outhouse, and a "scenic" view of the largest hedge maze in the area, to which Beatrice said, "Oh great, we can get lost in some old bushes!"

Bob and Mary were sitting on the opposite side of the booth. For some reason they weren't finding her story about saving Emily, Max, and Cathy at the auberge during the deluge as amusing as she'd thought they would.

"You should have seen the look on their faces when the aubergiste threatened to call the gendarmes," Beatrice said. "They were shivering like sopping little mutts. It was *très amusant*!" She finished her scotch. "I guess you had to be there. Well, what are you waiting for? Isn't anyone going to order another round?"

Bob took a deep breath. "Beatrice, Mary and I—"

"Oh, please, not again. Save your breath. We've been over this before. What do I always tell you?"

"Bea—"

"Come on, Bob, you should have this part down by now."

"You were the best DA in Albany, probably the state. No one's disputing that. We just think it's time for you to consider cutting down."

"Have you forgotten that I rarely lost a case and could argue circles around the other prosecutors? Still could. Loosen up, Buster Brown. You're being a real downer. Are you going to drop this, or should I just get the check now?"

"We're your friends, Bea," Bob said. "We care about you."

"If you really cared about me, you wouldn't try to change me."

"Beatrice Callahan, you're a stubborn old—"

"Old?"

"You know what I mean."

"Yes, I think I do."

"I'm sorry, that came out wrong."

"Words matter," she said.

"We're just worried about you. You know it's been a good ten years since Albert—"

"If I were you I'd stop right there," Beatrice said.

Bob was about to continue, but Mary touched him lightly on the arm and he sat back. He always gave up too easily in court *and* in bed; surprising, since she'd trained him.

"Okay, Bea, if you're sure."

She laughed. "You know I always am," she said, hoping it sounded convincing.

They had their usual cheesecake and Irish coffee, but the conversation from then on was stiff.

"*Zut alors!* Where did the time go? You kids should be heading home. It's a school night," Beatrice said, though it wasn't even nine.

Bob helped her on with her coat and offered to drive her home, but Beatrice told him the night air would do her good. She turned her cheek when he tried to kiss her. She wasn't about to get in his car after he'd accused her of being a lush.

It was a half-mile walk down Sheridan Avenue to Lark Street in Center Square, where she lived on the first and parlor floors of a nineteenth-century row house. She'd lived in the landmarked Albany neighborhood since getting her first job out of law school. But tonight she was distracted and got a little disoriented, eventually finding herself in an area she didn't recognize. The streets were deserted. The further she went, the more unfamiliar the area became. She thought of the hedge maze at that ramshackle farmhouse and getting lost in the thicket of branches past nightfall. Beatrice had stayed with Cathy, who'd grown more anxious the deeper into the maze they went. Beatrice had thought the maze would be a snap, child's play, like the corn mazes she and her cousins used to run through on Halloween when they were children. The first one out got a hayride.

But the hedges on either side of them on that last night in Normandy were ten feet high and impenetrable. Every route, every path, brought them to another dead end, but she'd never let on that she didn't know the way. She was the brave one. The one everyone leaned on. The one who never admitted she was hurt, or lonely, or afraid, or had had too much to drink.

In the distance, she heard a series of pops. Gangbangers. Why hadn't she taken Bob's offer to drive her home?

Emily held out until 9 p.m. before giving in to her craving for black-and-white cookies. The deli guy recognized her voice and all he asked was, "How many?" She ordered two fewer than she really wanted, along with a quart of soy milk, as though that could make it seem like she was a health-minded person. The subterfuge to hide her cookie habit was getting expensive. She didn't need any more soy milk; she didn't even like soy milk. Charles would have a fit if he knew she was planning on pouring it down the drain.

Her friend the editor had been very enthusiastic when she'd called and told him the new angle for her article, a soul mate experiment. She'd be the guinea pig and "do" *The Love Book*, apply the soul mate–seeking techniques in her own life, record every encounter with anyone of the male species, and then report on her findings, e.g., after eleven weeks, did she find The One? How much more personal could it get?

The buzzer rang and Kalman, the doorman, escorted the delivery guy upstairs. Emily handed him a fifty but he didn't have change.

"I think I can break it," Kalman said. He reached into his wallet and pulled out some bills along with a business card. "Did I tell you I work at a martial arts school?"

Last week Dominic, the other part-time doorman, had given her a coupon for salsa lessons at the dance studio where he taught. They must think she was the loneliest tenant in the building.

When she called to say goodnight to Zach, Clarissa answered his cell phone.

"Can I talk to Zach, please?"

"Zach's busy."

"Tell him to call me before he goes to bed."

"You already spoke to him twice today. Give the kid a break, Emily. I studied social work. He doesn't need to talk to you every five minutes."

"He's my son," she said, but Clarissa had already hung up.

A little after midnight, she was reading the introduction to *The Love Book* when her phone beeped. It was Christophe. With more cookies. She closed the book. Tonight was off the record.

Getting lost in a neighborhood she'd lived in for over forty years had sobered Beatrice up, but not enough that, without taking off her coat, she didn't immediately pour herself a snifter of brandy when she got home. She'd been an insomniac for ages, probably since Albert had died ten years ago, though things were getting a little blurry these days. She reread the email she'd gotten from Cathy that morning. Poor kid, she thought. A blue chat box suddenly appeared on the side of her computer screen accompanied by what sounded like air bubbles.

It was Emily: *Did you get Cathy's invite?*

This instant-messaging stuff wasn't Beatrice's thing. She'd rather pick up the phone. They were both up, after all.

Yes, got the book too.

I was hoping we could beg off.

Beatrice was surprised by Emily's insensitivity. Well, she supposed on the Upper West Side it wasn't fashionable to extend yourself to those in need, unless it came with a tax deduction.

It wouldn't be nice, Emily. After everything Cathy's been through, first with her father in the hospital and now the fire.

Fire???

Beatrice had passed on the news to the other women on the bike trip right after she'd heard. Hadn't she? She checked her sent mail. Oops! Well, she'd certainly meant to.

Cathy's house burned down yesterday morning.

To the ground?

Well, maybe not to the ground, but enough for her to have to move in with her old man.

There was silence. A long silence. The cursor blinked in waiting. A very pregnant pause. Had Emily fallen asleep? Some people can't deal with the ups and downs of life. They hide their heads in the sand instead of facing reality. Emily needed a wake-up call. There was no reason for her to punish herself forever. So she fudged her way out of her marriage. That wasn't an actionable offense. Not that Beatrice would wish unhappiness on anyone, but if anyone could use a real tragedy to put things in perspective, it was Emily.

Finally a ping. Emily was alive!

That's awful. Gotta run! I'm getting another call.

Hmmph. Isn't that rich!

The next morning, Emily was in the kitchen making two cups of coffee in the French press when the front door opened and Zach walked in. He was wearing his blue-and-white soccer uniform.

"Zach!" she said surprised. "What are you doing here?" She glanced at the closed bedroom door then gave him a hug.

He wriggled out of her arms and went to the closet. "I need my cleats. Dad's waiting."

She'd forgotten all about Zach's Sunday-morning soccer league. "I'm sorry, I should have packed them."

"They're not here."

"They should be in there somewhere," she told him. "Let me help."

"Zach, are you coming?" Charles called out, opening the door and surveying the apartment, to his obvious dismay. "Nice housekeeping."

"Here they are," she said. When she closed the closet door, Christophe's gym jacket fell off its hanger.

"You have to be kidding," Charles said. "Clarissa was right: you have a revolving-door policy."

"Charles, please, not in front of Zach."

"Come on, Zach, we're going to be late for your game."

"What time will you be dropping him off?" she asked.

"We'll see."

"Next time it would be nice if you called to tell me you're coming over."

"Next time don't forget his cleats."

She gave Zach a quick kiss. "Have a good game, sweetie. I'm making chicken strips for dinner."

"I had chicken yesterday," he said, sounding a little bit like Charles.

"I love you."

"Bye, Mom."

"Bye . . . I love you."

She watched from the window as Zach and Charles crossed the street and headed toward the park. She'd forgotten to give him a juice box. The next weekend Zach was with Charles, she'd ignore any calls from Christophe . . . or from anyone, for that matter.

C

CHAPTER SIX
INCREDIBLE OEDIPAL

BEATRICE WAS ON THE PETER PAN BUS wearing a floppy blue hat with polka dots, a short black knit dress, and sandals, on her way to the Black River Wildlife Preserve. Libby, her roommate from Holyoke, had arranged for them to have horseback riding lessons. She'd specifically told Beatrice to wear boots with a heel, but sandals were Beatrice's footwear of choice all year long—she hated to be constrained—and if the horse knew what was good for it, they'd be just fine.

Beatrice was not a horse person, by any stretch. But next month she and Libby were going to Montana to celebrate mutual friend Rob Roy's seventieth birthday. At a dude ranch of all places! And Libby thought they should at least know how to get on a horse. Luckily, Beatrice had planned ahead and brought provisions for a picnic lunch: duck confit, crusty bread, and a half bottle of Merlot, so all would not be lost. No creamed corn and American cheese sandwiches from the concession stand for her.

She reached into her straw tote bag for the latest Stephanie Plum novel. She had a friend in publishing who kept her well supplied with advance copies. She'd been chomping at the bit to read this latest installment of the Jersey girl turned super sleuth, but instead of the juicy mystery novel, she'd mistakenly packed *The Love Book*, which fell out of her hands when she touched it, like a hot potato.

A man in the seat across from her, a not unfriendly looking man, dressed all in khaki and wearing a large-brimmed mesh hat as if about to embark on a safari, leaned over, picked up the book, glanced at the title, and handed it to her. He smiled, obviously wanting to engage her, but Beatrice ignored him, opening the book and pretending to read. Unfortunately, the book opened right to the chapter entitled "Clitorally Speaking." She quickly flipped to a more innocuous section on forgiveness called "Pardonnez-Moi." A moment later, Safari Man leaned across the aisle and tapped her on the shoulder.

"*Pardonnez-moi,*" he said.

Beatrice scowled at him; she hated being scrutinized. She covered the book with her tote bag.

"Say, you look awfully familiar," he said. "And I pride myself on never forgetting a face."

She peered over her half-glasses and examined his features. "People are always mistaking me for someone," she said. "But I really don't think we've ever met." She continued the pretense of reading, but sneaked a look and the man was still staring at her. She would have changed seats, but the bus was completely full.

"I've got it!" he said, hitting his forehead. "San Miguel. I used to go there with my late wife."

"Sorry, never been."

"Captiva Island?"

She shook her head.

"Long Boat Key Club?"

"Still not ringing any bells. Now, if you'll excuse me."

Safari Man sat back. Beatrice had only a few moments of peace before he began pestering her again. "This is driving me crazy, I'm positive we've met. I'm Malcolm McBride."

"Holy mackerel!" she said. "I dated your brother in college."

"I told you I never forget a face!"

"You're Freddy's little brother. The one who played hockey."

"One and the same," he said. "And you're Beatrice Callahan. As lovely as ever."

"What a small world. How is Freddy?"

As Malcolm gave her the details of Freddy's life—the kids,
the wife, the seven grandchildren, the house in Bedford—along
with his private number in case she wanted to get in touch with
him, Beatrice slipped back into a time she'd all but forgotten, or
at least had tried to forget, almost fifty years ago.

She and Libby had bummed a ride from a girl at Holyoke
up to Hanover for Winter Carnival. They thought the girl was
"square," but she did possess a functioning automotive vehicle and a valid driver's license, so they ditched her as soon as
they reached the green. Those were the days when Dartmouth
was really the College on the Hill and the Seven Sisters its loyal
sperm bank. She and Libby had found a bench downstairs at the
DOC House on Occom Pond and laced up their skates. Beatrice
had borrowed her mother's white fur skating jacket, which she
wore over a blue dirndl skirt. She'd done her hair in a neat page-
boy, a hairdo that would be her signature look for decades to
come. Some dork, who she later discovered was Freddy's younger
brother—Safari Man—brought them two mugs of hot cocoa
laced with something and then stood there looking every bit the
imbecile who'd swallowed his tongue. Hormones, they'll be the
death of us all. Party weekends with the Wah-Hoo-Wahs always
involved pretty heavy drinking. Not a place for debuting debu-
tantes if they knew better. Freddy pushed Malcolm aside and
pulled her onto the ice without even asking her name, and a bit
later, after they were just tight enough, they skated down to the
darkened end, where his frat brothers had sawed through six
inches of ice. There they stripped to their birthday suits, took a
few fortifying shots, and did The Dip. The rest was history. They
dated for three years. At the end of his senior year he proposed,
but Freddy's mother said Beatrice would never fit into Highland
Park society, no matter how smartly she was dressed, so the

engagement was put on "hold." When Freddy didn't stand up to his mother, Beatrice took a job as a clerk to a district court judge in Albany. The next fall she enrolled in law school. She'd spent years resenting Freddy's snooty mother, but in a way she owed her entire career to her. If she had a drink she'd raise her glass. Here's to you, Mama Evil.

"Where are you headed?" Malcolm asked.

"Black River. You?"

"Cape May for the fall hawk migration. Hoping to see some osprey too."

"That explains the outfit." Beatrice flipped open her phone, which had begun to vibrate.

Malcolm adjusted the collar on his safari jacket. "Are you a birder?" he asked.

"Oh my heavens, no!"

"We're not a bad sort," Malcolm said. "You just have to get used to us."

"I didn't—I mean, I wasn't talking about you. It's my friend Libby. She's been in a terrible accident."

Cathy's deviled eggs were always a big hit at parties and church dinners, and were also, along with her spaghetti casserole, a Thanksgiving favorite, so she made an extra dozen for the Soul Mate Soirée. All three women had accepted the invitation. She decorated the eggs with pimento hearts then arranged them on a pink daisy platter, which she hid on the bottom shelf in the refrigerator where she hoped her father wouldn't find them. She knew there would be a few missing in the morning, despite his doctor's strict orders.

She tested the flameless tea lights (she wasn't taking any chances on burning down her father's house too), and plugged in a rose-patchouli air freshener, which she bought only after extensive research and was satisfied her fear that they were a fire hazard had been proven unfounded. She surveyed the room.

Everything was perfect for tomorrow's party. Now, if only the ladies could keep on schedule, soul mate–wise. She did the calculations: if they met every two weeks, skipping New Year's Eve, of course, the final Soul Mate Soirée would be the day before Valentine's Day, when, providing everything went as planned, all of them, even Max, would be with their soul mates. Talk about divine timing! Cathy had already bought a set of pink satin sheets and a blue terry cloth robe as visual representations of her beloved's imminent arrival. With a little luck she could have the robe monogrammed with a certain fireman's initials before long.

Satisfied, she went to get dressed for her date with Sean. She'd done several days of "prepaving," putting forth her intention for a wonderful night, down to the smallest detail, from imagining the kiss on the porch to doing a "sensualization" of the two of them watching their first child sleeping in a wicker bassinet. She'd be an inspiration. Nothing was more powerful than being a living, breathing example of love fulfilled.

Her father was standing by the window when she came downstairs. "You look like your mother more and more every day."

Even though he was smiling, Cathy could detect a mournful quality in his voice. "You're having quite a crowd for your ladies' lunch tomorrow, I see."

"Just a few women I met on the bike trip."

"Your mother, God rest her soul, used to send me on an errand when she had her bridge club. Don't worry, I'll make myself scarce. I'll go to the lodge."

"No, I'd like you to meet them," she said.

It was true; she'd been wanting her father to find a female companion, and now that the soirée had been relocated to his house, there might just be an opportunity. He and Beatrice would be perfect for each other. Yet another manifestation of synchronicity thanks to the fire!

"Dinner's in the oven," she said. "I made your favorite, stuffed shells."

"You're spoiling me. I'll never let you go at this rate."

She gave her father a kiss. "I won't be late. I have my phone if you need me."

"Just have fun, Princess," he said, suppressing a cough. His breath smelled like cherry lozenges.

Suddenly, her feet felt nailed to the carpet. "I can cancel if you want."

"I wouldn't hear of it. Now go. You don't want to keep Mr. Wunderbar waiting."

On her way to the fire station, she recited her love mantra: *Men are attracted to me like bees to honey. I am a magnet for love. I was born to be loved, treasured, and adored. And so it is!*

She'd left early. She was not a good navigator, and lo and behold, even with the GPS her father had won at the church raffle, she found herself driving around in circles and only getting more and more lost.

The third time she passed the same general store, she unplugged the GPS and went in to ask for directions. The store smelled like cinnamon. Jars of penny candy lined the shelves behind the counter.

"Welcome to Bixby's. Can I help you, ma'am?" the clerk asked.

She wasn't used to being called ma'am, especially not by someone around her own age. It made her feel ancient although she was only thirty-two. Her father and his friends still treated her like she was that sweet ten-year-old who worked the register at her father's secondhand bookstore on school holidays.

"Can you tell me how to get to the fire station?" she asked.

"It's about a mile up. Go straight until you hit Union Street, then make a right and it will be on the next corner across from the post office. If you pass a KFC you've gone too far."

She was already completely turned around, but she didn't

want him to think she was the cliché clueless female driver, even though that was exactly what she was.

"Thanks," she said. "Left at the second stop sign?"

"Maybe I should draw you a map. I'd take you there myself if I wasn't the only one here. My brother works at that firehouse."

She looked at the guy's name tag. "Sean O'Dardy?"

"Yes, indeed."

"I have a date with him tonight," she said.

He lit up. "Are you that cat lady whose house burned down last week?"

Cathy nodded.

"He said you were cute, but he didn't do you justice."

She was trying to process the *cat lady* comment. She didn't think of Mrs. Beasley as just a cat. More of a spiritual companion. A few months after her mother died, Cathy had gone to the mall and there was Mrs. Beasley in a Bideawee adoption trailer outside the pet store. She purred when Cathy put her hand through the cage to pet her. From that moment, she knew they were meant for each other. That was sixteen years ago.

"Sean hasn't stopped talking about you. Can you believe what a killing he made on that grenade extinguisher?"

"A killing?" she asked, wondering what he'd blown up.

"Yeah, somebody paid twenty-five hundred dollars for it."

"He sold it?"

"On eBay."

"How could he do that?"

"Easy. He sells lots of things on eBay. There was a bidding war. Isn't that jim-dandy?"

"Yeah, you could say that again," Cathy said, turning to leave.

"Hey, don't you want the map?"

"No, that's okay, I don't need it anymore."

Beatrice was waiting until Libby fell asleep in her hospital room at Saint Claire's before she went in search of the cafeteria for a cup of dross. What she really needed was a drink. The half bottle of Merlot hadn't even made a dent. It wasn't easy to see Libby in a full body brace, but she'd tried to put on a brave front. The prognosis was two weeks of bed rest, then months of physical therapy, and still no guarantee that she'd regain full mobility. But she was alive and as feisty as ever and that's all that mattered. She laughed when Beatrice read her Cathy's chipper daily inspirational message: *What you give out, the universe gives back to you. If you want love, you have to give love. If you want health, you have to feel health.* By this logic Libby had caused her own accident, and in that case Beatrice was in for a doozie. In the last half hour, though, Libby had started to get maudlin, which Beatrice attributed to the drugs.

"It's true, Bea. We're all alone. And it serves us right for being so darn independent. There's no one to take care of us when we need them."

"Look, Libby, I'm here, and if you want some practical advice, you should try not to fall off a horse, let alone get on one again. Once you're up and around you'll realize how fortunate you are to be unencumbered. No ingrate children to ask you to cosign car loans or insufferable dinners with in-laws. You've got nieces and nephews, but even they can be tiresome. How many school productions of *Guys and Dolls* can one person go to? You should thank your lucky stars. You have a career, an extended family of good friends and colleagues. A husband? What for? So he could criticize the way you cook, or iron his shirts? Be careful what you wish for. I sure don't want to be anyone's nursemaid, or burden for that matter."

Finally, Libby closed her eyes and Beatrice slipped out. Prepared for a tasteless cup of tepid coffee, a Starbucks kiosk just meters away from her looked like a mirage.

"You don't happen to have a bottle of Baileys back there, do you?" she asked the young man at the counter.

"The closest we have is hazelnut liqueur. But there's no alcohol in it. I can whip you up a mocha cookie crumble if you like. It's insane."

Her usual inclination would have been to say something snarky. But he was looking at her with such an earnest expression—as if giving her what she wanted was actually important to him, that the only thing that mattered was that the one thousand–calorie dessert masquerading as coffee please her—she just couldn't do it. He was only a kid, probably nineteen at the most.

"Never mind. I'll take a tall coffee. Black. No sugar."

As she sipped her coffee, Libby's words were still rocking around in her head, and no matter how much internal shooing she did, they refused to budge. *We're born alone, we die alone.* That was what Albert always said. *All else is vanity and vexation.* And he'd done just that, died alone in a Four Seasons after a three-course dinner. Beatrice hadn't gone to the funeral, not out of respect for the grieving widow, who knew all about her, turning a blind eye every time Albert "missed" the last train from Rensselaer Station, but because she thought funerals were morbid.

Had it really been ten years?

She threw her empty cup in the trash and then, like a case study in point-of-purchase marketing, impulsively grabbed from the display a CD of Elizabethan madrigals and a bag of peppermint malted milk balls. She pulled some bills out of her wallet, but the kid behind the counter waved her off.

"It's on me. You remind me of my grandmother. She loved malted milk balls. Hope whoever you're visiting feels better."

The kid gave her a high-beam smile she couldn't help returning. It was probably just some mirror neurons on the fritz— *monkey see, monkey do*—but it warmed her from the inside out, better than a good shot of whiskey. He could be her grandson and for some reason she didn't find the thought all that objectionable.

In the elevator she looked at the back of the CD. Coincidentally, the very first track was a song that Freddy and the Aires, the Dartmouth a cappella group, used to sing at Christmastime: "Lirum, Lirum." She couldn't believe she still remembered the first line: *You that wont to my pipe's sound.* As soon as she stepped off the elevator she dialed Freddy's private number.

"Freddy . . . it's Beatrice."

"Beatrice, well now, it has been a day or so."

Cathy's father had left the yellow bug light on. She felt like a teenager breaking curfew, something she'd never done, as she sneaked around back and sat on the swinging bench, careful not to let the hinges squeak. She was planning to stay out there until eleven, the time she would have gotten home had she gone on the date with Sean. The last thing she wanted was to cause her father any needless worry that yet another man had disappointed his daughter.

The porch wrapped around the side of the house like an embrace. Her mother used to complain about the no-see-ums getting in, so her father had replaced the screens with a finer mesh. Now the porch was impervious not only to all manner of flying things, but to summer breezes too, and Cathy was convinced it was harder to smell the honeysuckle.

Her father had always been overprotective, but he'd become even more so after her fiancé left her at the altar five years ago. If he had his druthers, he would keep her behind glass like one of his rare books in a climate-controlled environment away from natural light, not in a lending library where she was prey to the plight of dirty fingers, tattered pages, and a broken spine. But there were other perils even more insidious than an infestation of mites or silverfish—those dreaded mildew spores, or books being consumed by acid page by page until eventually disintegrating to dust, for which there was no defense. So, for a father and true book lover, there was little reason to be sanguine. Either option was fraught with potential disaster.

For a moment, as she sat on the swinging bench, it seemed like the porch was swinging and she was stationary, a feeling that persisted as she entered the house and tiptoed past the den where her father was dozing in his recliner. An infomercial was playing about a spray-on product for bald spots. She deleted Sean's three voice mail messages without listening to them then went upstairs. So much for Mr. Wonderful.

CHAPTER SEVEN
TUNNEL VISION

MAX HAD BEEN A TOMBOY HER ENTIRE LIFE. Still, she knew how to put herself together when the occasion required. Like tonight. In order to make some extra money, she'd been hostessing at Philomel, a chichi restaurant on East Fifty-seventh Street. Tight and short, the owner had suggested, and a pair of killer heels; the tips would be worth it. The heels were where Max drew the line. She wouldn't compromise her feet for the sake of a few dollars more in tips from some drunken, hot-to-trot businessman, so she wore her biker boots over a pair of fishnets. But judging from the tips she'd been collecting, it turned out the tough-girl look was pretty popular with slimeballs too.

The subway was surprisingly empty for a Friday evening. Two little girls in matching white cardigans and Mary Janes were playing with a gyroscope. Their mother, laden with pink Conway bags, seemed totally oblivious to the degenerate exposing himself three seats down. What was it about New York City that attracted these creeps? Ever since she'd gotten back from Normandy, they seemed to be coming out of the woodwork. Did the unseasonably warm weather cause miscreants to multiply faster than mealworms in a science experiment? The woman finally noticed the flasher and pulled her young daughters to the far end of the car. When the train pulled into the station, Max glared at the man until he zipped his fly. If she ever had a daughter, she'd teach her to kick ass, just like Calvin had taught her.

Philomel was packed with well-dressed couples. It wasn't difficult for Max to tell which women had been recently dumped by rich husbands for younger versions of themselves; she could pick them out a mile away. They comprised half her clientele. The ones with frozen faces wearing tight-fitting tops to show off their hard, fake boobs and well-toned tanned arms, who laughed at every word uttered by their young male companions, often trainers or aspiring actors in recovery. Max had no sympathy. It was their own fault that they hadn't seen it coming. No one would ever get the chance to dump her. She was always ready with a preemptive strike. And then there were the ones who acted as if they had no part in their husbands' leaving. The "victims." But Max knew better. If a husband left it was either because he'd found someone else or his wife had cheated on him.

Friday nights, Antoine, the French chef/owner, performed his cabaret act, crooning while women in low-cut tops swooned around the piano. The first time he'd tried to seduce Max, she just laughed in his face. But her rebuffs only egged him on, so she had changed tactics, giving him exactly what he thought he wanted against the tiled bathroom wall until he begged for mercy. Worked like a charm. Always did.

Her cell phone pinged. It was a reminder about the Soul Mate Soirée tomorrow (why had she agreed to go?) and another of Cathy's daily inspirational messages: *Prepare for your Soul Mate! A twenty-minute salt bath will cleanse the body of psychic intruders!*

She felt like texting Cathy back and telling her there was no tub in her studio apartment, only a stall shower, and she wasn't about to buy a kiddie pool at the dollar store for the backyard.

Antoine must have put something in the water because she hadn't even been working ten minutes before she got her first proposition. A gentleman well into his nineties with a red silk pocket square folded as intricately as an amaryllis and carrying an ivory cane offered her ten thousand dollars to travel abroad with him for six months. Before she could answer, he nodded off.

Around ten, one of the waiters brought her a club soda with lime and whispered in her ear, "You have an admirer."

At the end of the bar was a ginger-haired man with red glasses who reminded her of an older version of a chubby child star who used to do commercials for bologna.

"Him?"

"No," he said, leaning close and pointing to the lounge area. "Him. I hear he's some hotshot entrepreneur. And loaded!"

Across the room was a man with perfect hair. A young Robert Redford type. But he was way too tan and his starched white shirt was open one button too many. He raised his glass. Max turned away.

"He asked me to put a bottle of Clos du Mesnil on ice," the waiter said.

"Tell him I'm not interested."

"Tell him yourself, he's coming this way."

"I've been watching you," the man said, adjusting his cuffs so that his gold Rolex glinted in the light.

"And?"

"I've decided that today is your lucky day."

"Wow, that's amazing. You're absolutely right," Max said. "Because you're going to leave now."

The man smiled with his perfect teeth. "I could make all your dreams come true."

"Fuck off," she said.

"*You're* rejecting *me*?"

"Damn straight, asshole."

"It wouldn't have worked out anyway," he said, slapping a hundred-dollar bill on the bar. "I don't date women who curse."

Max laughed. "Oh well, then suck my dick." She walked away.

Antoine finished his set, told Max to bring a round of Crème de Violette to a table of particularly adoring female fans, flirted with them for a bit, then made the requisite rounds, gracing the ladies with his super-suave French charm.

By the window, a group of naval officers sat in a booth, celebrating with a bottle of Stoli and caviar. Only one man at the table was not in dress uniform. He was wearing a bomber jacket and chinos. He and Max locked eyes. There was something familiar about him; he reminded her of a photograph of Calvin she'd found stuffed in his army trunk, wearing his khaki battle dress uniform. She sipped her club soda and tried not to look at him.

Max sensed him approaching without turning around. The hairs on the back of her neck stood up and then, like an endorphin rush, she felt a cold euphoric tingling, from her temples to the top of her head. It was a sensation she'd only experienced on rare occasions, when she witnessed something truly breathtaking like a star-filled sky, or a beautiful piece of music, or the sound of her grandfather singing "Waltzing Matilda" in the kitchen.

The guy leaned close. He smelled like licorice. She thought of the round yellow tin of Cachou pastilles her grandfather always carried in his jacket pocket. "A wise man once told me never to fly JAFO. I have a feeling you don't either."

Of all the pickup lines she'd ever gotten, this was the strangest. The only person she'd ever heard use that expression was Calvin. *Promise me something,* he'd said to her on her seventeenth birthday, a few months before he killed himself. *I don't care what you do in life so long as you promise never to fly JAFO.*

What does that mean, Calvin?

You'll have to figure that out on your own.

Now she looked this guy straight in the eye and said, "I'm not a fucking anything, but I'm definitely not Just A Fucking Observer."

The man smiled and put out his hand. "Garrett."

"Max, but I can tell you right now you're wasting your time."

"I never waste anything," he said. "Especially not time. Your grandfather taught me that time's our most precious gift."

"You knew my grandfather?"

"I studied with him at MIT. He's the one who convinced me to join the navy and become an engineer. Calvin was my professor and mentor, but I thought of him more like my spiritual father. I even visited him at the farm, met you once or twice. You look a little different than you did when you were a fifteen-year-old smoker with a shaved head downing martinis."

"How'd you know who I was?"

"I didn't at first. Your hair's a little longer than it used to be, at least on this side," he said, lightly touching her behind her earlobe. "But you have his eyes and you're wearing his beret."

Max touched the maroon Airborne beret on her head, straightened the winged medal pinned to the front. On the back was a rainbow peace sign and a *Make Love, Not War* patch. He wore it every day, backward. She could still see his sparkling cool blue eyes, the way they lit up when he looked at her, crinkled when he smiled.

Garrett opened his jacket. The same patch was sewn into the frayed lining. "I hope you don't mind my asking . . . but how long have you been sober?"

"Two years," Max answered. "How could you tell?"

"Your eyes. They're as clear as an arctic lake. And nearly as deep."

On the subway platform on her way home, she received a text: *The left seat is all yours. Pick you up tomorrow at seven.* And just like that her weekend plans changed. She knew she didn't have to bother calling Cathy to cancel. If anyone would understand, she would.

C HAPTER EIGHT
LOVE GURU

EMILY HADN'T EXPECTED Barnes & Noble to be so crowded. A smattering of people, perhaps, not standing room only, to hear the author of *The Love Book*. Apparently soul mates were a hot commodity, very much in demand.

She spotted a seat and began homing in on it when an unshaven guy in a three-piece suit brushed past. It was the self-obsessed guy from the gym. Finally, he acknowledged her presence in the aisle. She expected him to do the gentlemanly thing, but he just gave her a nod and draped his jacket over the back of the chair. The label was showing. H. Huntsman & Sons, the Savile Row purveyors to the likes of Sir Winston Churchill and the Duke of Windsor. It didn't take long for Emily to figure out why he was there. What better way to put the law of attraction to good use? He was the only man in a room full of single women. The narcissist!

Her feet were already getting sore in her new shoes, an emergency purchase when the heel of her clog broke in half on the way over. It had been slim pickings on the sale rack at Harry's, at least in her size. She'd settled on a pair of slip-on weatherproof shoes when a pair of red suede Mary Janes with four-inch stacked heels one size down caught her eye. Rarely did Emily feel inspired by a pair of shoes, but they made her look ten pounds thinner, and, though snug and completely impractical in a walking city, she left the dog-walking shoes on the rack and gave in to the impulse. But after fifteen minutes, it was clear that not only were they not walking shoes, they weren't even standing shoes.

Finally, there was an announcement: the Love Guru was a no-show. Her publicist, a woman in a white pantsuit with a meringue of white hair who clearly hadn't seen any action since the early nineties, would read in her stead.

People got up to leave, but Emily leaned against a bookshelf and opened her notebook. She was on assignment: Love Guru or no Love Guru, she had a deadline.

Lady Meringue stepped up to the podium, put on a pair of sparkly red glasses, and began reading: *"Are you blocking the flow of love? Are you 'off duty'? Switch your Heart-Light to 'I'm available!'"*

Emily jotted notes, but was flummoxed by the alleged correlation between soul mates and taxicabs. If there was such a thing as a Heart-Light, hers was on such a low-wattage dimmer that the risk of her being flagged down anytime soon was next to nil. It was true that the timing of her relationship with Nick hadn't been ideal, but neither had it impeded her in any way. She'd been in transition. He was the one who was unavailable.

They hadn't seen each other in months. The last time had been accidental, at a gala opening of the Alexander McQueen exhibit *Savage Beauty* at the Met. The place had been packed, so crowded that she found herself at various times unable to move, but the dresses in the exhibit were so excruciatingly beautiful, severe, haunting, almost sadomasochistic, that she barely noticed. As she took notes for an article she was writing for an online fashion blog, she'd imagined what it would feel like to wear McQueen's creations. Like the silk gown that undulated in waves, or the dress appliquéd with real flowers, or the costume of black ostrich feathers with taxidermy hawks holding up the straps, or the one made of iridescent oyster shells. The crowd had eventually begun to thin, migrating to the champagne reception. Emily had lingered in front of a holographic box in which a three-dimensional image of a model twirled in a fluttering white dress. Then, there in the hall of mirrors, she'd seen Nick with his hand on a woman's lower back. His wife? Another mistress? On either side of the hall, mannequins spun in mirrored cubicles. She had tried to block out her own image, but she was entwined with reflections of Nick and the woman in multiples too numerous to count.

The white pantsuit lady droned on and on . . . "*You are the creator of your own experience.*" Yada yada, blah blah . . . "*You create your own reality.*" Yada yada yawn.

Emily closed her notebook. If she could create her own reality, she wouldn't be here listening to a lady who looked like a piece of plastic pie. It was after nine. She needed to call Zach before he went to bed. And that's when she saw Clarissa, cocooned in a white fur vest, lining up with dozens of eager soul mate seekers, waiting to have their books signed. Her emerald engagement ring flashed brighter than a traffic light as she rummaged in her purse that probably cost more than Charles and Emily's first couch.

Trouble in paradise?

She was in no mood for an encounter with Clarissa, especially when she was in slum mode, in one of Zach's T-shirts and ripped jeans, so she made a beeline for the escalator. And just her luck. Right behind her was Pretty Boy Who Can't Shave from the gym.

"I'm thinking about getting a restraining order," he said. "There's a fine line between stalking and manifesting."

Manifesting? What the heck was he trying to say?

She turned, annoyed, but her annoyance was short-lived, short-circuited by his smiling blue eyes. She was surprised that his voice had so much resonance. He was a little shorter than average, but in her new heels she towered over him. Maybe he was an out-of-work actor, a go-to guy for voice-overs.

"I got the nights mixed up," he continued. "I thought I was here for a talk about Vietcong opium fields."

Three obviously single women, freshly armed with *Love Books,* rode behind them on the escalator.

Lowering his voice, he asked, "You're not . . . one of *them*?"

"No," Emily said, stepping aside to let the women pass. "I'm just writing an article. For a magazine," she added.

"Ah, you're a writer."

"I do some freelance."

"That makes two of us," he said.

She braced herself, accustomed to people trying to use her as a contact, sending her unreadable manuscripts, asking if she knew any agents who handled post-apocalyptic, zombie-inspired bodice rippers. These encounters never ended well.

"Really?" she said, glancing at her phone.

"Yes, there's a potentially toxic concentration of struggling artists in this postal code. We're worse than kudzu."

She buttoned her coat. Another day, another struggling artist. What a tired cliché. "Guess I'll see you at the gym."

"Or here, next week," he said, pointing to a life-sized poster in the window emblazoned with his photograph.

"You're Duncan Lebow?"

"At least according to my driver's license," he said, after pretending to look over his shoulder.

"I'm so embarrassed." Emily realized she was slouching the way she used to in junior high when all the boys were five inches shorter than she was.

"Don't be. This is New York. Everyone's someone."

"I loved the excerpt of your novel in *Esquire*," she now gushed.

"I appreciate that. What did you respond to most?"

"I liked it all, but particularly the line about revelation being more perilous than revolution. That really stuck with me. I wish I could write with that much muscularity."

"That's one of my favorite lines too," he said. "I was riffing on Nabokov."

The revolving doors spun, letting in the fresh cold night air and disgorging the last of the Upper West Side schlumps with their anointed *Love Books*. Behind them, like an aurora borealis floating down the escalator, was the lovely older couple she'd seen the other day. How had she missed them upstairs?

Duncan zipped his Barbour. "If I didn't have a 6 a.m. flight to Oslo for Nobel week we could continue this conversation. I love to help fellow novelists."

"I'm not a novelist," Emily said. "I write fluff pieces for women's magazines."

He smiled as though he knew some secret. "Call me, I'm in the White Pages."

In the middle of the crosswalk, something made Emily stop and turn. Duncan was still standing in the same spot. Horns blared, the light blinked red. He waved, and motioned for her to hurry up and not get hit by the horde of oncoming taxis.

When she had safely reached the other side he set off in the opposite direction. She may have misjudged him. But *Call me, I'm in the White Pages?* Who says that? Then she quickly dismissed the thought.

On the way home she stopped at the deli for cookies and unfortunately ran into her neighbor Mrs. Weisenbaum. Adele was notoriously nosy. Probably not even four foot ten, always dressed in animal print and metallic kitten heels, with a Virginia Slim in her mouth, she made it her business to know everybody else's.

"I never see you with a man," she said. "Dating anyone?"

"Not right now. If it happens, it happens."

"My daughter used to say the same thing when she was your age. Now she's way past her prime. You should try Internet dating. You have to cast a wide net to catch a live one. They have sites for over-forties."

"Three black-and-whites," Emily said to the deli guy. "Thanks, Adele, but I'm not quite there yet."

"You should watch your sweets. Metabolism starts to

change when you hit perimenopause. I see the boxes from Mag-
nolia in the recycling bin."

"They're for Zach."

Adele squinted her eyes. "And I only pretend to smoke."

The deli guy was looking at Emily strangely. Was everybody
judging her? She'd only ordered three cookies.

"You're that actress," he said.

"Excuse me?"

"You're that actress in that show."

"I'm not an actress," Emily said.

"You look just like that lady on *Weeds*. You know who I
mean?"

"Yes, my nephew says I look like her too," she said. "But
trust me, I'm not."

The deli guy persisted, handing her the bag of cookies. "You
are her, aren't you?" he said.

Emily shook her head. "Sorry, I'm just a writer."

"I get it," he said, winking, as he finished ringing up her
purchase. "I won't tell anyone."

Adele gave an impatient sigh. "Who's he talking about?"

"Mary-Louise Parker," Emily answered as she turned to
leave the store. "She's an actress."

"I know who she is. You don't look anything like her. Three
packs of Virginia Slims. With matches, this time."

Emily was in the elevator when she heard Mrs. Weisenbaum's raspy voice and heels echoing in the marble lobby. She
automatically put her hand out to hold the door.

"I didn't get my *Women's Wear Daily*," Adele complained
to the doorman. "Can't you people keep track of the mail?"

"Sorry, Mrs. Weisenbaum," the doorman said, "I only work
nights."

"This is the second time this month. Believe me, this
doesn't happen at the Schwab House. And another thing . . ."
Adele said, as Emily quietly pressed *Door Close*.

Upstairs, five Brooks Brothers shirts, arms stuffed with pink tissue paper and pinned back like straightjackets, were hanging from the door. Clarissa had been bemoaning the fact that Emily still hadn't gotten around to changing her name now that the divorce was "finally" final. When and if Clarissa became "Mrs. Charles Andrews," she wanted to make darn sure there wasn't another Mrs. Charles Andrews in the same zip code. Emily's rationale was that it was her professional name, not that her byline had been on more than a handful of articles. Also, she thought it would make Zach feel like she was denying half of who he was. When Clarissa found out that not only the dry cleaner but also the Georgetown alumni association, Charles's dentist, and the county clerk still thought he lived with Emily, the white fur would fly.

In her study, Emily took a bite of her first cookie, the chocolate side first, so she could savor the vanilla. She turned on her computer to do some preliminary research on May Soon Nu, the author of *The Love Book*. The photo on the back cover was small and out of focus. The author was an attractive woman, probably in her early forties, with long dark hair parted down the middle, wearing a flowy white top and crocheted headband, a Joan Baez type. With the Internet, gathering information on her would be a snap. Even Salinger wouldn't have been able to avoid the scrutiny of search engines. Oddly, though, the only thing that came up was Cheat-o-Matic, a Scrabble word builder, which Emily was loath to admit she had used once or twice. May Soon Nu was an anagram of Anonymous. She checked to make sure she had the spelling right, and tried various searches for the Love Guru. There were dozens of *Love Book* groups around the country, but not a single mention of the author. The ISBN number came from the acquiring publisher and while Emily was able to track down the original source of the book to a small press in Idaho, the author had a clause of anonymity. When she scanned the photo into Google images, it turned out it was of an Indian actress who'd died decades ago. Emily's meeting with her friend the editor was on Monday. She couldn't very well tell him the author was untraceable.

Mrs. Weisenbaum's television was blaring through the wall. Last week it was a Truman Capote biopic at one in the morning. Tonight it was *Jeopardy!* She tried to tune out the sound of Alex Trebek's voice and concentrate, when she realized that Adele's intrusive question might just be the answer.

In love, as in research, it was best to cast a wide net. She began by updating her LinkedIn and Facebook accounts, joined Instagram, Tumblr, Hubpages, Wordpress, Google+, Pinterest, Vine, even something called CafeMom. Her new Twitter handle was @LookingforLoveBook. Excited to get started, she dropped her first 140-character lure into the worldwide web. Within minutes she had ten followers and one share.

An email from Cathy appeared. Pink, of course, with pulsing hearts and exclamation points after every line:

Reminder about the new venue for Soul Mate Soirée tomorrow! Bring your soul mate wish list! Games! Prizes! Love Potions! More!

It sounded like a child's birthday party. Emily wondered if there would be cotton candy and a petting zoo. Instead of writing up her notes from the reading, she found herself Googling Duncan Lebow. She downloaded his latest book and immediately began reading. His prose resonated with her on a deep level, her heart beating in anticipation of each new page. His words touched places in her that even she didn't know could be accessed. She felt connected to him, as if he was speaking to her personally. He was so unlike Charles and his staid and controlled demeanor. His words exploded in all directions into vibrant colors, igniting her imagination, opening her up.

By the time she looked up from her computer it was after

midnight. She'd finished all three cookies, with no recollection of having eaten them, and had forgotten to call Zach.

The next morning, she couldn't believe she was doing it, but she actually looked up Duncan's address in the White Pages. She never would have supposed that an author as famous as he would have a listed number. But there it was and he lived only ten blocks away. His number was one of the old New York exchanges, the kind that used to begin with names like ENdicott, PEnnsylvania, PLaza, TRafalgar, or BUtterfield, and that conjured for Emily silk peignoirs and soigné apartments straight out of a Noel Coward movie. It was the equivalent of urban carbon dating. Whoever lived there hadn't moved or changed the number for at least half a century. She left a message, something she wouldn't have done if he hadn't been on his way to Norway. Then she grabbed her purse and *The Love Book*, almost forgetting Charles's shirts, and headed out for the Soul Mate Soirée.

"Perfect timing," Charles said, taking the dry cleaning from her when she stepped off the elevator.

Zach was showing Kalman how he could "walk the dog" with his new light-up yo-yo. Clarissa was in the car, wearing a huge pair of sunglasses. Emily was tempted to tell Charles that she'd seen Clarissa at Barnes & Noble the night before, but then would have to admit she'd been there too. He'd always said she was a good writer and was wasting her time writing fluff pieces.

Charles gave her that stony stare he'd perfected these last few years and that she could even detect over the phone.

"Didn't I tell you to give the dry cleaner's a change of address?"

"That's not in my job description."

"Are you trying to screw things up for me? Because you're doing a very good job."

"Charles, please," she said, looking at Zach, who gave no indication that he'd been listening. But Emily knew better. He heard everything.

"And try to limit yourself to one call a day," he said.

"You're telling me I can't call my son?"

"Clarissa finds it intrusive."

"Tell Clarissa not to answer his cell phone if it bothers her so much."

Charles smirked when he noticed the subtitle of *The Love Book*. "*Eleven Weeks to Finding Your Soul Mate?* A cellmate's more like it. I have a book for you. *Eleven Weeks to Stop Being a Bitch*."

"It's for an article. Maybe you should get a copy for Clarissa."

Charles shook his head. "Still can't take a joke, I see."

Emily rolled up her windows as she entered the Lincoln Tunnel. Ordinarily, she would have avoided the tunnel altogether, but the bridge was closed for repairs. As much as she loved Manhattan, living on an island had its drawbacks. She was not a fan of tunnels. Or subways. Or elevators. The grotto in Normandy had made her break out in hives. Venturing underground was something she did only when absolutely necessary. To Charles, the subway, even in the sweltering summer heat, was freedom. In any city around the world, he could glance at the metro map, determine the most direct route to his desired destination, however remote or off the beaten path, and arrive within minutes. Emily, however, would rather walk six miles to jury duty than risk getting stuck between stations.

She was still thinking about Duncan when the vehicle ahead of her stopped short and she had to slam on the brakes. Cars began honking. There was the sound of a distant approaching siren. Lights flashed in her rearview mirror. She rested her head on the steering wheel. No coffee, radio, or cell phone reception. Her only diversions were *The Love Book* or an old Rafi tape. She chose *The Love Book*, the lesser of two evils. When a Rafi song got into her head, it was impossible to get it out. She read a quote in the margin: *The light at the end of the tunnel is not an illusion. The tunnel is.* Maybe Rafi would have been the safer choice.

By the time she emerged from the tunnel, the sky was a wash of magenta and midnight blue. A motorcycle and a New Jersey Transit bus had collided, blocking both lanes. She took out her cell phone to apologize to Cathy for missing the party, and noticed that she had a missed call.

"*With the jets firing behind me, I must be quick. Your message was like a breath of fresh air. I return from Oslo on the fifteenth. Until then, here's my email . . .*"

A message from Duncan and the George Washington Bridge had reopened to traffic. Maybe there was something to this law of attraction stuff, after all.

Cathy waited until nearly five o'clock, when she was sure that no one was going to show up, before turning off the flameless candles and wiping the white board clean. She'd spent hours highlighting the salient details of the chapter and summing up this week's lessons with a PowerPoint presentation. She'd even concocted love potions and made soul mate goodie bags. The distraction and intention to offer guidance and support to her unlucky-in-love friends had helped keep her spirits buoyed after the fiasco with Sean last night. But Max hadn't even bothered to call. And while Emily and Beatrice both had good excuses, particularly Beatrice who was taking care of a friend who had fallen off a horse, she was still disappointed. Her father was due back from the lodge soon. Under normal circumstances, she would have packed up the deviled eggs and taken them to her aunt's house or to the soup kitchen—waste not, want not—but she couldn't muster the energy. She said a quick prayer asking for forgiveness, as one by one she shoved the eggs down the garbage disposal, ran the water, then flipped the on switch.

C HAPTER NINE
DRESS CODE

BEATRICE WAS AT THE BAR at the "21" Club waiting for Freddy. They'd arranged to meet for lunch. *Très civilisé.* If you're going to do it, do it right, she always said. She'd left Libby in the capable hands of Ursula, another college friend of theirs, who'd offered to pitch in from time to time until Libby was up and about. Beatrice was wearing a deep green jacquard shift and matching jacket. Freddy had always liked her in green. Funny, the things one remembered. She'd come in early for a little primping at Elizabeth Arden. In the mirror behind the bar, her hair shone as brilliantly as burnished copper. Coiffed and dressed and ensconced in old New York, she was beginning to feel like her old million-dollar self. One week of hanging around the hospital had taken its toll. It felt good to be out in the world.

Yes, Freddy was right: it had been a day or so. But it felt like yesterday.

She watched as the young male bartender assembled a Manhattan. Into a Yarai cut mixing glass, he poured bourbon, sweet vermouth, dry vermouth, and a splash of bitters. He gave it a quick stir with a slender silver mixing spoon until it formed a liquid tornado, then poured the perfect concoction into a sparkling cocktail glass.

Beatrice appreciated his attention to detail. There was nothing she liked more than for things to be done *comme il faut.*

"I always thought a Manhattan was supposed to be shaken

to fox-trot time," she said, playfully. She was quoting *The Thin Man*. She realized a moment too late that the flick was probably made before the bartender's grandparents were born.

"I'm a purist," the young man said. "I believe that a Manhattan, like a beautiful woman, deserves to be treated with care, though I do on occasion like to jitterbug my martinis."

She was enjoying trifling with the young man. He seemed flattered. The interesting ones often were. There was something to be said for sticking with younger men. The ones who still had some imagination.

"If you shake it," he said, "the ice bruises the bourbon, and adulterates the taste."

"But what would Bond say?" Beatrice teased.

He smiled. "James Bond? The womanizer with the drinking problem?"

She was about to offer a rejoinder, when there was a small kerfuffle at the door. A tall brunette walked in wearing blue jeans under a plum-colored velvet tunic with a pair of killer five-inch strappy gold heels. The diminutive maître d' looked aghast and took the woman aside. Beatrice found the whole thing terribly amusing. How could anyone not know about the dress code at "21"? Then she reprimanded herself for being so bourgeois. Hadn't Glen Campbell been asked to leave when he'd come in wearing a pair of dungarees? But the tall woman wasn't going anywhere. She disappeared into the powder room, emerging only moments later, before the brouhaha had even abated, in just the hip-skimming tunic, bared legs and gold heels, her jeans stuffed into her huge Birkin bag. The maître d' apologized profusely as he led her to her table, but she laughed it off. According to the bartender, she was one of the women from the *Housewives* reality series, possibly even a countess. Pretending to be impressed, Beatrice said, "They ought to require aristocrats to learn a thing or two about dress codes before they're allowed to roam freely."

She sipped her drink and swiveled in the bar stool, and there was Freddy walking with the maître d' toward her like Moses emerging from the Sinai. She felt a shiver up the back of her neck. He looked exactly as he had at graduation in 1962. Well, all things considered he seemed in pretty great shape for a seventy-year-old man. He was wearing a blue blazer with gold *D* buttons, gray flannels, and a Tartan tie. His thick dark hair was now a lustrous shock of silver. But she would have known him anywhere.

Emily dressed in her most conservative outfit for her meeting with the school headmaster, a charcoal-gray suit and pumps she'd last worn when she and Charles went to the mediator, the first of two, both of whom Charles eventually "fired." She looked like a paralegal.

Charles had found her less-than-conventional fashion choices charming, even alluring, when they were first dating—fancy skirts with old T-shirts and jet beads—but it wasn't long before he began to criticize the way she dressed. Especially when he was up for partner. *You came to my office wearing that?* Suddenly, her quirky outfits didn't quite cut it when all the other women were in tasteful black cocktail dresses and Mikimoto pearls. He'd tried to steer her toward a more conservative style and at first she'd welcomed his input. It reminded her of her maternal grandmother who called her a ragamuffin with her macramé vests and magenta bell-bottoms with torn knees. Whenever she visited, they'd go to Bergdorf's where Emily would be transformed into a little Renoir girl with a rabbit muff and princess coat. After lunch in the Tea Room they'd sit on one of the boudoir chairs and freshen up in the pink art deco bathroom. But it never stuck. She'd be back in her torn jeans and work shirt before dinnertime. Charles must have thought he was getting the put-together Emily, not the woman with a tendency to get so lost in writing she'd forget to dress or make dinner.

Zach's school was no less conformist. Emily felt like an im-
poster at school functions when she put on the "uniform" worn
by the other mothers: black twill or khaki pants, leather for evening, sweater set, flats, and diamond studs. Then there were the
overdressed mothers from the Upper East Side whose children
hadn't been accepted at one of the single-sex, Ivy League–feeder
prep schools, who dropped their children off in their black
SUVs and shopped at Barneys.

The only other time Emily had been called in to see the
headmaster was when Zach was in first grade, right after she
and Charles separated. The huge bearlike school psychologist
was on hand each morning until November to wrench a crying
Zach out of her arms. It took all of her resources not to run
back in and make sure he was all right. Of course, Charles never
had any problem when he dropped Zach off at school. In fact,
he didn't even get out of the taxi, letting the boy go up in the
elevator with the other kids. *He's not a baby*, he told her. But
when she asked if he could drop Zach off more often, it wasn't
possible because of *a little thing called work*.

At that first conference, Charles had sat smug and self-
satisfied in his pinstriped suit as though about to win a case.
The school psychologist told her that Zach's separation anxiety
stemmed from his concern about her well-being and that she
should let him know that it wasn't his job to take care of her.
Again, all her fault. That's what Charles had said when they
went for marriage counseling. He'd leaned forward, elbows on
his knees, and, as if renegotiating a deal, told the therapist to
"fix" her.

The door to the office opened and in walked the headmaster
and the school psychologist, followed by Zach's math teacher,
Kenneth, wearing his usual khakis. Zach was still complaining
that Kenneth had been picking on him in class since that day
she'd chewed him out on Broadway.

After the usual pleasantries, the headmaster put his hand

on her shoulder. "Emily, we've given the matter a lot of thought and decided that a three-day suspension and probation until Christmas break is fair."

"Probation? I don't understand. Zach's an excellent student."

"This is not about academics," he said.

"Then what is it about?" she asked.

"Sexual harassment," the headmaster answered.

"You can't be serious. What are you accusing him of?"

"Snapping a girl's bra," he said.

"A bra? They're ten years old. Girls in fifth grade don't wear bras." She looked at the school psychologist for support. "You know Zach. He's a good kid. Boys pull pranks like this all the time, don't they?"

The psychologist shook his head. "No, Emily, they don't. Not at this school. It shows a real lack of respect for women. And it's not an isolated incident."

"Zach's a good kid," she said. Her voice quavered. She took a deep breath. She was not going to cry. "I'm sure he didn't mean to do it."

"We're concerned that if we don't deal with it now, the underlying issue will only get worse. It's most likely a cry for help."

She felt tears pressing behind her eyes. Charles would take care of this. With all of his faults, he was a very protective father. He'd probably threaten to file suit.

"If it's all right with you, Emily, we'd like to bring Zach in. He's waiting in the hall."

She stared at the spines of books that lined the shelves. *The Launching Years. Letting Go. The Fiske Guide to College. Cracking the SAT.* When the door opened, she half-expected to see the little five-year-old boy with the head of curls, but instead, in walked a preteen wearing a backward Knicks cap. When had he grown up? He slumped into the chair, mumbled a hello, and fidgeted with the strap of his backpack.

"You know why you're here, don't you?" the headmaster began.

Zach nodded.

"We've been discussing a suitable consequence for your actions. You'll be on probation until Christmas break. Do you understand?"

He nodded again.

"Zach, tell them you didn't do this," Emily said.

He was silent.

"Zach?" she whispered, but he wouldn't look at her. "You didn't, did you?"

For a brief moment, the boy had the expression on his face she'd seen so many times before, on the playground when he fell down the slide; when Charles's cell rang during one of Zach's baseball games and he missed seeing his son's home run; the morning they took him to the wisteria arbor in Central Park and told him they were separating.

Finally, he nodded.

"But why?" she asked.

He shrugged. "I don't know. For fun."

Freddy asked to be seated in the Bar Room in one of the red-leather banquettes. The hexagonal space was as precious as the inside of an antique music box, with the famous collection of antique toys and sports memorabilia hanging from the ceiling. Elegant waiters in white tuxedo jackets did figure eights around the tables as if on skates. They ordered oysters and littlenecks, lump crabmeat and fois gras for starters, and two bottles of champagne. Beatrice pointed out the pantless "countess" and they laughed and talked about everything and anything, except Freddy's wife at home. Freddy had two sons, both of whom were legacies at Dartmouth, and now his eldest grandson, his namesake, was applying early decision. She shook her head. Was it college or a cult?

When the waiter cleared their plates, Freddy smiled and looked into her eyes. He reached for her hand across the table. "Your eyes, Beatrice. I can get lost in them. You're even more enchanting. How did I ever let you get away?"

"Your mother, remember? Boy, was she ever a piece of work!"

Freddy laughed. "You never did beat around the bush, Beatrice. I miss that."

She pulled her hand away. "Let's skip this part, Freddy. No need to get maudlin. What's done is done. How about we just pick up where we left off? No fuss, no muss. No strings. I don't believe in all that nonsense anyway. You're lucky you didn't marry me. I would have made a pretty mediocre wife."

"But you would have been *my* mediocre wife, and that's all that matters. We should be celebrating our forty-fifth wedding anniversary."

"God, that sounds awful! Like Gloria Steinem said: I can't mate in captivity. Madame Bovary, *c'est moi!*"

"If that's my only choice," Freddy said, clasping her hand in his. "Then I'll be Rodolphe to your Emma."

"I'll be *your* Rodolphe is more like it," she said.

A gray-haired couple at the adjacent table pretended to be surveying the menu but could barely conceal their shock. The man looked like a research librarian and the woman was dressed in a blue cardigan with a severe bob, probably a nun who had just leapt over the wall. Of course two old fogies would find it shocking, but Beatrice didn't care. Life was short. Look at the contessa. She had her pants off even before she sat down for dinner. In the old days they waited at least a few dates. Besides, what did she have to feel guilty for? She and Freddy had preceded his relationship with Muriel, so she could plead the case that she was just reclaiming what was hers. But that judgmental look from Freddy too! She hated hypocrisy. He'd probably had numerous affairs. A man in his position and with his looks was bound to stray now and then; that was fine. She didn't want him to leave his wife and have to deal with the fallout of divorce, the resentful adult children, financial burdens, regret. What a bore! He'd mope around for months like a lost puppy and probably want to move in with her. Men his age couldn't be alone. But they still had plenty of life in them, with the right woman to prime the carb, inspire them, and that's what she intended to do.

He kissed her hand. "I see you haven't changed."

"And not planning to. Take me or leave me," she said.

"If that's the only choice, then I take you, Beatrice, to be my ever and always."

Ever and always, Freddy. That's how he had signed his letters.

It was nearly four o'clock; Beatrice couldn't leave Ursula hanging. Freddy looked bereft when she said she had to catch the bus back to New Jersey.

He placed fifty cents in the basket for the coat check girl and helped Beatrice on with her coat.

"I have to see you again," he said.

"Isn't that what ever and always usually entails?" Beatrice teased.

"How about two weeks from Thursday? The Plaza Hotel? I'll arrange everything."

For some reason Beatrice hesitated. She glanced over at the bartender who was shaking two cocktail tumblers like maracas. But this was no foxtrot flirtation and there was no bar between them as a buffer. This felt like more of a plunge than that frigid dip in Occom Pond fifty years ago.

"Well?" Freddy said again. "Meet you in the Oak Room?"

"I'll be there with bells on," she replied.

As he embraced her, Beatrice caught her reflection in the mahogany mirror above the bar. Burnished, polished, but soon to tarnish.

In the cab to Port Authority, Beatrice slumped against the backseat. The Plaza on Thursday? What on earth was she thinking?

Emily couldn't even look at Kenneth as she and Zach walked out of the headmaster's office. They took a taxi straight to Charles's office. She'd packed his clothes and snacks for the Jitney and had no intention of being late. She wouldn't give Charles the ammunition or Clarissa the satisfaction.

Charles didn't react at all the way she thought he would when she told him about the meeting. All he said was, "If he worked at this firm, he'd be fired."

An hour later, she was walking home from Whole Foods when her cell phone rang. It was Charles. "Guess where we are?" he asked.

"On the Jitney?"

"No, Brooks Brothers. We missed the Jitney, thanks to you. I don't know why I trusted you. You were supposed to pack Zach's bag."

"I did."

"We're going to the Hamptons, not a surfer convention. Billabong? American Eagle? Why do you do this to me?"

"Charles, he's ten. That's what kids wear."

"I told you he needed a blazer. Maybe you should spend less time with your loser boyfriends and pay more attention to your son. Now we're going to be stuck in traffic for hours."

"Can I talk to Zach?"

"He'll call you Sunday. Oh, and I'm deducting this from next month's child support."

She felt entirely frozen, incapable of an appropriate response. His cruelty had only increased since their separation and while she knew she should not accept such insults from him, she didn't know how to make Charles stop.

A few months after Charles left, Zach had come in to her

room, all dressed except for his tie, his first real (not clip-on) tie. She told him that someone at the bar mitzvah would put it on for him. But he refused to leave without it. She looked up Windsor knots in *How to Do Just About Anything*, a book she would come to rely on when she needed to fix the toilet or repair a leaky faucet.

Now she pictured Zach in his Brooks Brothers outfit, a blue blazer, khaki pants, and red-checked oxford shirt—a miniature replica of Charles. It still made her sad that the doorman had been the one to teach Zach how to tie a tie and not his father. She'd always blamed Charles, but it was her fault. Maybe she was unfixable.

CHAPTER TEN
IN THE ZONE

EMILY WAS AT HER DESK rereading an email Duncan had sent her while he was in Oslo. For the past two weeks or so, she and Duncan had corresponded several times a day. The sound of her phone pinging caused in her a Pavlovian response. Her heart would pound and she'd feel blood rush to her cheeks. His emails struck a nerve in her. Composing her responses was a painstaking process. Every word had to be right. She'd press send, then wait. An hour felt like agony. Had he forgotten her? Then *ping!* And all was right in the world. She'd never felt so alive, so present, so inspired. Duncan said they were *atomes crochus,* which she cut-and-pasted into Google Translate and very much liked the sound of. One particularly arresting email was written entirely in French. A tiny part of her wondered at first if it had actually been intended for her, but she shooed the thought away. It was too racy for Google and even for Babble-fish. What little she could understand caused her to be tongue-tied for hours. Anyway, it was two weeks of sheer pleasure that she never wanted to end. According to *The Love Book* a woman doesn't fall into love, she falls into obsession, although to Emily it was a semantic distinction. Whatever the technical term for what she was feeling—love, obsession, or a mixture of both—she didn't care. It was intoxicating. Even rereading his emails momentarily stopped her heart.

*I am willing you the spirit of John Donne today. He will
sit on your shoulder and be your muse, and if you lose
concentration he is authorized to enter your heart!*

It was the last day of Zach's three-day suspension and
Charles didn't think he should be allowed any "privileges," including spending the night at his apartment. He'd sprung this
on Emily at five thirty, on the dot, just as she was about to send
Zach downstairs. Having Charles stay with Zach this evening at
her place would never have been Emily's first choice, but there
was no time to make other arrangements. Duncan had returned
from abroad last night and invited her to a literary salon. He
said he'd "collect" her at seven. She liked the idea of being collected. No one had ever said that to her before. So many of the
things he said to her, whether in email or during their five-hour
phone conversations, had rendered her speechless. Even a recipe
for homemade mayonnaise recited by Duncan could slay her.
Commercial mayonnaise, he told her, was poison.

Emily went to say goodbye to Zach. Charles and Zach were
in the middle of a highly competitive Nerf basketball match.
Charles was up by nineteen points. Zach had just stepped on
his father's foot trying to block a shot. Charles was at the foul
line. He was wearing one of Zach's old Knicks jerseys and a pair
of tight white athletic shorts. He looked like one of the Village
People. Emily had chosen her outfit carefully, a black knit dress
and knee-high boots, an outfit Clarissa might wear.

"Interesting choice of outfit," Charles said from the foul line.

She took a deep breath and practiced being Zen, imagining herself covered in bubble wrap. She wasn't going to let him
throw a poison dart at her but neither was she going to play
doormat. He seemed disappointed when she didn't react.

"It's Rosh Hashanah not Halloween," he said, preparing
for his second shot. "When did you become a member of the
Einsatzgruppen?"

"You should talk, Charles," she countered, almost tempted to do the arm motions for the song "YMCA." "Make sure Zach does his writing journal. His teacher says he hasn't been keeping up with it."

"Jawohl, Herr Kommandant!"

"*Jawohl*, Mom!" Zach echoed, giving Charles a high five.

"See you later, Zach, sweetie. Love you."

"Air ball!" Zach shouted, jumping to get the rebound.

"Love you," she said again.

"I heard you. Bye."

She stood at the front door, listening to the reassuring sounds of a father and son playing in the other room. It was as if time had collapsed, four years hovering in midair like the blades of a revolving propeller, an optical illusion. A feeling surfaced, which she tried to push away. And though it was an undeniably fractured image of hearth and home, it was comforting all the same. Someone was waiting for her.

Duncan kissed her hand when she stepped off the elevator. "I have a present for you," he said, presenting her with a hard copy of his book. "It's a first edition. I inscribed it."

> *With tenderhearted feelings to a*
> *fellow writer and friend.*
> —*Duncan Lebow*

A *fellow writer*. She liked the sound of it. But after their two-week correspondence, she felt like much more than a friend. The book did not fit in her handbag and therefore she would have to carry it around all night in the crook of her arm.

The salon was on Central Park South at the home of a man who was on the board of directors at the National Endowment for the Arts. The living room was all windows and glass. Emily sat next to Duncan on a white leather couch. He was wearing a form-fitting ribbed turtleneck and black jeans. She wasn't certain, but his hair seemed to have a slightly coppery tinge. It was probably just the lighting. When Emily was a girl, her father's gray hair had turned yellow from the fluorescent lights in the kitchen. Every once in a while Duncan would press his thigh against hers, which made it hard to concentrate on the discussion of art and gender politics. Afterward, he clasped her hand and they made the rounds as if choreographed. Duncan mingled among the guests, all of whom he knew on a first-name basis, tossing bon mots more effortlessly than finger rolls.

"Liam! How the hell are you?" he said, slapping a man with a thin goatee on the back. "I hear you've been nominated for the National Book Award. *Chapeau!*"

Swish!

Emily admired how he worked the room. He was the "big man" on his home court, in the "bubble," navigating his way through conversations with film critics, award-winning novelists, philanthropists, editors, as proficient as a top athlete in the zone. He had the Midas touch, never once losing possession of the ball. He made easy layups, assists, showed off with a few no-look bounce passes, *Dime!* established his pivot foot, dribbled past defenders, hit every three-pointer and free throw, and then scored with a huge slam dunk. "Why of course, I'd be honored to give the keynote. Here's my publicist's number." *Bang!*

The evening was so unlike the dreary real estate dinners where Emily had often felt like an accessory for Charles, a pair of cuff links, a mouchoir or pocket square, where the only topics of discussion were apartment renovations or summer vacation homes. It was easy—all she had to do was smile and not say anything controversial—but deadening. Whenever attention was turned to her, it was always the same. *You're a writer. How interesting! Have you ever been published?*

This was something altogether different. Duncan was in his element, drawing people out, making introductions, congratulating them on successes, empathizing over lackluster reviews. It was a level of networking she'd never witnessed, all accomplished without the least hint of the flagrant self-promotion that it could be construed as. He was the Merv Griffin of the intelligentsia and took pleasure, maybe a little pride, in "making things happen" for other people. He even introduced her to a features editor at the *Atlantic* who gave her his card and told her to send her portfolio and clips. She felt like she was in the HOV lane, on the fast track to her heart's desire, even though she was the only passenger in the car.

While they were on line at the buffet, Emily explained that she had to be home early because Charles was watching Zach.

"You seem to have a very amicable relationship with your ex," Duncan said.

"I wouldn't say that, exactly. He can be a little, well, very controlling. He's a lawyer."

"I'm not a controlling man," he said, and picked every single poppy seed off a whole wheat bagel before spooning tuna fish onto it. She wondered if he knew it was probably made with gobs of mayo.

"I believe in self-empowerment," he said.

A tall woman entered, a yoga bag over her shoulder, drawing all eyes, including Duncan's, to her. She shook her blond mane of a ponytail. She was wearing a miniskirt and a fitted red leather jacket. In her arms was a basket of exotic fruit, a traditional Rosh Hashanah gift. Emily assumed it was for the host and hostess, but the woman handed the basket to Duncan.

"*Shana Tova*," she said, kissing his cheek. "For a *very* sweet New Year."

"Lara, late as always," he replied. "This is Emily. Lara is my research assistant. Her husband is a colleague of mine. How is Cyrus?"

Lara gave him a Cheshire cat smile then wiped some tuna

from the side of his mouth. Emily had noticed the tuna fish and a poppy seed or two between his teeth, but would never have presumed to even mention it. She watched his reaction, but ever gracious, Duncan laughed it off.

Around ten, when Emily told Duncan she had to leave, he said, "I'll walk you home."

She smiled. "That would be nice."

"It's on the way," he said.

Lara touched Duncan's arm. "I was hoping we could discuss that project . . ."

"Ah, yes, I'll call you later," he said.

Lara didn't say goodbye to Emily and neither did Emily feel the need to mention to Duncan that he had forgotten the basket of fruit at the party.

As they neared Lincoln Center, a four-piece band was playing and people were dancing by the reflecting pool. Duncan took her in his arms and, whispering the lyrics to the Burt Bacharach song in her ear, waltzed her around the plaza. The sky was a deep blue. There was a sliver of a moon. A new moon. The burden of the past seemed to lift. Emily felt hopeful. New York had never looked so beautiful.

Upstairs, she hung her coat in the closet. Charles walked into the front hall, his face crosshatched with the pattern of Zach's comforter. His expression was more impenetrable than a piece of carbon hardened under pressure deep in the earth. She knew he was waiting for her to thank him for staying with Zach, but she couldn't utter the words.

"Parents' night is next Wednesday," she said.

"I know, Emily. He's my son too."

"Zach wants to ride twice a week now," she said.

"If you want to pay for it, fine."

"Child support is supposed to cover afterschool activities."

"Did you get my name off the proprietary lease?"

"The board will never approve me without a guarantor. I don't make enough money."

"Get a job," he said.

"I'm working."

"I know you're a good writer, Emily, but an article here and there isn't going to pay the rent. I guess you're going to have to bite the bullet and sell this place."

She held the door open. "Goodnight, Charles."

He stood in the doorway shaking his head. She knew what he was thinking even without him saying it. She'd been having entire conversations with him in her head for the past four years. *Fucking little bitch.* It was hard to defend herself against voices that were all her own.

CHAPTER ELEVEN
THE BLUE LOTUS

ALTERNATIVE MEDICINE had never been Cathy's thing, but Dr. Oz said acupuncture could cure vertigo, and she'd been feeling dizzy for the last two weeks, ever since the fiasco with Sean. Her health insurance paid for ten wellness visits, including Reiki and Rolfing, provided they were at participating facilities. Luckily, she found one that looked good and was in her plan, so she made an appointment for Friday after school. But the real reason she'd agreed to being stuck with needles was that according to *The Love Book*, opening up meridians (whatever they were) could speed up her soul mate's arrival. So it was all for a worthy cause.

The Blue Lotus Center for Acupuncture and Healing Arts was in a generic strip mall between a Cold Stone Creamery and a Subway sandwich shop. Once inside, though, bonsai plants, fountains, and Oriental figurines created a tranquillity rarely found on Route 9. A snow-white cat slinked through the maze of objects. Jasmine blossoms were scattered on every surface, like tiny snow angels. It was hard to believe New Jersey was just beyond the double glass doors.

In the reception area, she sent a group email with the new date for the rescheduled Soul Mate Soirée. Her school district closed on both Jewish and Muslim holidays and next Friday was Yom Kippur. She knew Emily was Jewish, but four hours before sundown seemed a safe bet. It was that or put it off until

Eid al-Adha, the Muslim Festival of Sacrifice in November, but
that would throw their whole schedule out of whack. Somehow
a soul mate arriving on the Ides of March did not have quite the
same appeal as Valentine's Day.

Emily texted back immediately: *Why don't we meet at Alice's? It's a cute teashop with a private back room.*

Sounds perfect.

Good luck with the acupuncture.

Thanks, I'll need it.

She made a mental note to ask her brother-in-law to program Alice's into her GPS.

The only positive outcome of the incident with Sean was
that he'd shown her that her "compass" was off-kilter. She never
would have attracted a man of such low moral fiber if her Love
Vibration had been clear of interference. Men like Sean were
"tests," their sole purpose to help a woman refine her intention
and bring into high relief any remaining blocks to love. And
Sean was one big hulking block. Sure, she was getting more
male attention than usual, like the man wearing a Hawaiian
shirt and patterned balloon pants at TGI Friday's who asked
if she was taking applications for husbands or the guy she'd
gone to first grade with who sent her a message on Facebook
telling her they were destined to be together. These were all
very good signs—she was "magnetized"—she just needed to
do some fine-tuning.

The white cat nuzzled her legs, meowing insistently like
Mrs. Beasley did when she wanted to take her somewhere.
Cathy closed *The Love Book* and followed the cat through the
Oriental garden into an open studio. Stenciled on the bamboo
floor was a large geometric pattern, a maze, only without the
sides. It reminded Cathy of Stations of the Cross, a game she
used to play in Sunday school. The object was to maneuver a
silver ball through a series of concentric circles with a tiny magnet on the end of a string. Always, right before getting to the

center, the Resurrection of Jesus, the silver ball would roll back
to where it started.

She imagined she was looking at the hedge maze in Normandy from an aerial view, and it didn't seem nearly as inscru-
table from this perspective as it had in real life.

Despite initial reservations, Cathy had gone along with Beatrice's plan to explore the maze their last night in Normandy.
Max and Emily had set off in different directions—first one out
got the single room. She'd decided to stay with Beatrice, who
forged confidently ahead. The ten-foot-high hedge on either side
of them was as dense as a brick wall. Even though it was getting dark, she felt like she was in good hands, but after an hour
of coming to dead end after dead end, she began to panic and
stopped in the middle, refusing to continue.

"We'll never get out," she said.

"Where's your sense of adventure?" Beatrice asked. "We
just have to keep going. We'll make it out eventually, even if we
have to be airlifted by French Special Forces."

"I don't want to keep going. It's dark and we're getting
more and more lost."

"You can't just stay here."

"Yes, I can."

She knew she was being unreasonable, but she wanted to
know the right way to go, not make any more wrong turns.

"If only we had a map."

Beatrice took her hand. "What fun would that be? Don't
worry, I'm not going to leave you."

I'm not going to leave you. The magic words.

In the center of the maze the cat rolled onto its back. "Mrs.
Beasley would like you," Cathy said, kneeling to stroke it behind its ears. Talk about being magnetized! This cat knew how
to get what it wanted. The receptionist called her name. When
she stood up, the room began to spin, then pixilate, until finally fading to black. The next thing she knew she was on a

padded table in a small cubicle surrounded by a white curtain.

A woman in a bright fuchsia sundress was taking her pulse. She was short, a little pudgy, with a mop of curly dark hair and frosted lip gloss, the spitting image of Cathy's dental hygienist cousin. Her name was Joy Baumgarten, the acupuncturist.

"Good, your color's coming back," she said. "We've never lost anyone in the labyrinth before," she said, laughing.

"The what?" Cathy asked.

"The meditation labyrinth. The thing you were doing before you went down. I do it every day. It reminds me that there is mystery in design and simplicity in intuition."

Cathy took a sip of water. "Oh, I was just following the cat."

"How long have you been feeling dizzy?" the acupuncturist asked.

"About two weeks," Cathy said.

"Anything going on lately?"

"Where should I begin?"

About to launch into the story about her disastrous date with Sean, she remembered in the nick of time that it was advisable to "turn away" from unwanted things, not give them attention, which, for the law of attraction, was the equivalent of saying "Yes!" to what you don't want. But it was hard not to think about Sean's sparkling blue eyes. And that smile!

"Just a little stressed, that's all," she said.

Joy asked a slew of questions about her diet and sleep habits. "You really should try to eat more vegetables," she said.

"They make me gag."

"I'll give you the recipe for kale chips. You'll be a convert. Cute sandals."

"Bloomingdale's. Short Hills Mall," Cathy said. "They're having a blowout sale. I got them in three colors."

Joy placed a rolled-up towel under Cathy's knees.

Cathy suddenly felt her tongue go dry. Her heart was pounding in her ears. "I've never had acupuncture before. I don't like needles."

"You'll barely feel a thing," Joy said, smiling to reveal lipstick on her teeth. "See?"

"That's it?"

Joy nodded. "These three points will help nourish yin and anchor the liver yang," she said, covering Cathy with a soft blanket. "Empty your mind. I'll be back in twenty minutes."

Cathy closed her eyes, but emptying her mind was easier said than done. If nature abhorred a vacuum, her head was an air popper filled with confetti. She decided to block out her thoughts with some mantras from *The Love Book* she'd committed to memory:

> *I am open, available, and receptive. I am responsible for my relationship success. I take care of me first. I love to receive, especially from cute available straight guys with good jobs! I enjoy giving back in appreciation, but never go Dutch!*

Cathy had added the part about sexual orientation. She figured that the more specific she was, the better. The never going Dutch was from her father.

She had gone through the mantras so many times she'd lost count when Joy returned to remove the needles.

"How do you feel?"

Cathy opened her eyes. "Relaxed. Kind of floaty."

"Dizzy?"

"Actually, no. The room's not spinning anymore."

"If you'd like I can do a quick tune-up to raise your vibration and clear any blockages."

"Sure! That sounds great," Cathy said.

In her present state of receptivity, she would probably have said yes to just about anything, even cruciferous vegetables or, perish the thought, an advance from Lawrence, Jerk of the World. *Cancel! Cancel!* Note to self: never make dating decisions post-acupuncture.

Joy opened a velvet-lined box containing tuning forks of various sizes, and struck the largest one on a round disc. Holding it about twelve inches above Cathy's feet, she spiraled it up and down Cathy's body until the sound faded. She shook it off as though it was wet, put it down, and picked up the next one.

"I'm opening up your meridians," Joy explained, spiraling the tuning fork a few inches above Cathy's pelvis, "so all of your organs are in harmony."

This time Cathy flinched. She felt a tingling sensation in her lower abdomen, like an electric shock.

Joy abruptly set down the tuning fork. "I don't mean to be rude, but when was the last time you had sex?"

"It's been a little while, I guess," Cathy said quietly. More than awhile. She hadn't been with a man since her fiancé jilted her.

"Nothing to worry about," Joy said. "We all have dry spells. Maybe this isn't your season of love. Ask the receptionist for one of my *Feminine Power* meditation CDs on your way out. It has a link to my website. I'll see you in two weeks."

But Cathy was barely listening. She walked, or rather floated, back through the jasmine-scented Oriental garden and out the double glass doors to the parking lot. With all the endorphins circulating in her system, it didn't even register that she'd forgotten to take *The Love Book*.

It was raining and she stepped into a puddle getting into her car. Her new turquoise sandals looked like endangered exotic birds after an oil spill. She was definitely back in New Jersey.

Cathy and Veronica hadn't had a girls' night since Veronica's third child, Cathy's goddaughter, was born almost a year ago. Pat's Tavern wouldn't have been Cathy's first choice. It was a neighborhood hangout and invariably they'd run into someone they went to school with. But Veronica knew the owner and got half-price drinks. Luckily, Cathy always kept a few pairs of emergency shoes in the backseat so she didn't have to drive all the way to her father's. The black "Kalinda" boots would go well with her plaid skirt, giving it more edge than her now sludge-covered sandals. She'd had the skirt tailored, but instead of it being just at the knee, it was several inches above. One of her students said she looked like a Tyrolean dancer.

As she pulled into the parking lot, Cathy got a text from Beatrice, punctuated with smiley faces wearing sunglasses. Beatrice was pretty "with it" for a woman her age—actually, for anyone. Her father wouldn't know how to send email, let alone an emoticon.

Guess where I'm going next Thursday! To the Plaza! With Freddy! I'm turning into you with all your soul mate hooey! And using too many exclamation points!

Cathy responded only with a thumbs-up. What she needed to say required more thought than a dashed-off text. Did Beatrice really want to get involved with another married man?

Her cell phone pinged again. She looked at the caller ID and pressed decline. It was her ex-fiancé, Rob, the third time he'd called since she'd begun doing *The Love Book*. For now it was an annoying nuisance she was willing to suffer in order to call in her soul mate. She listened to his message. He said he needed closure. Apparently, throwing his things in the street hadn't been closure enough.

Pat's wasn't too crowded, just the regulars, solo drinkers slumped at the bar watching the game, a symbolic empty seat between them, which a social scientist might have interpreted as both a hopeful and self-protective gesture. As intimate as they might appear to be, sharing drinks and their life stories, they were alone, and would still be alone even when every seat was taken. "Nondrinker" was on the very top of her soul mate list, in bold and underlined in neon pink.

Veronica was late as always and harried. Even before having children, she'd arrive like a squall, a bundle of scarves and bags and windswept hair and a dramatic story that drew everyone in. Cathy missed her. Baby showers and Gymboree parties with the kids were no substitute. All the girls they'd gone to high school with were married, even Debbie Finster, with the unibrow and size eleven feet.

They ordered fried mozzarella sticks and "Virgin" Virgin Marys. It was their joke, since both of them had waited to lose their virginity until they were engaged. The difference was that Veronica was still having sex.

Cathy debriefed Veronica on her latest dating disasters. The pilfering firefighter, the guy with man boobs who'd tried to pick her up at the gym, and the cute guy she'd flirted with on Professional Development Day who she later found out had Asperger's. She knew she was "sexertaining"—using her misadventures with men to define herself—something *The Love Book* advised against, but it was all in fun, and besides, her friends loved it. She was about to tell Veronica about Rob calling, when in walked Lawrence with his friend Josh. Lawrence was wearing a bulky light-blue sweater vest. It had either shrunk in the wash or he'd put on some weight since she last saw him. And brown slacks. Slacks!

Veronica leaned over to Cathy. "What happened to Lawrence Weiner?"

"I know, isn't he such a—"

"What a hunk!" Veronica made her swooning face.

Before Cathy could stop her, Veronica started waving like the cheerleader she used to be. Lawrence's face lit up when he saw them. The next thing Cathy knew, he and Josh were coming over with a tray of drinks.

"Ladies, I'll need to see some ID first," Lawrence said.

Veronica giggled. "You always were such a card!"

Lawrence set down the tray and slipped into the booth next

to Cathy. Three shots and a glass of ginger ale. Was it possible that he remembered Cathy rarely drank? If so, he had one thing—and one thing only—going for him: a very good memory.

Veronica reached for a shot, which Cathy intercepted. "You're driving."

"Since when did you become the fun police?" Veronica asked. "Look how little it is."

One glass remained on the tray. Lawrence placed it in front of Cathy.

"Cathy's a virgin all the way," Veronica said. Somehow their joke didn't seem so funny anymore.

"I don't drink much either," Lawrence said. "I'm Josh's designated driver so he can get as sloshed as he likes."

Veronica and Josh knocked their drinks on the table and tossed them back.

"It would be a shame to let this one go to waste," Josh said, pouring half into Veronica's glass.

Cathy gave her a look.

"Stop being such a worrywart," Veronica said. "Isn't it so cool that we're all here together and none of us have changed one bit? Cathy even has the same haircut! I can't wait for the reunion. Fifteen years! But it won't be nearly as much fun without Cathy."

"Why aren't you going?" Josh asked. "You didn't gain that much weight since high school."

"Thanks, Josh. That does wonders for my self-esteem."

"Tell them why, Cathy," Veronica prodded.

"There's nothing to tell. I have other plans, that's all."

"You do not have any plans. It's because of Debbie Finster."

"What about Debbie Finster?" Lawrence asked.

"She's married," Veronica said, laughing, reminding Cathy why she didn't like it when her friend drank.

"I hear Finster's hot now," Josh said.

"Unibrow? Seriously?"

He nodded. "Doug Houser ran into her in Asbury Park."

"That makes it even worse," Veronica said.

"Who cares? As long as you're happy," Lawrence said.

"Lawrence," Josh said, "you really should think seriously about taking up drinking. You need to loosen up. How about another round? We can toast Debbie Finster."

As soon as Lawrence and Josh left the table, Cathy tried to move to the other side of the booth, but Veronica pushed her down.

"What do you have against Lawrence? He's being perfectly pleasant. What did the guy ever do to you?"

"Homeroom? Seventh grade?" Cathy said.

Seventh grade. The year every girl had to have her hair cut like the girls on *Friends*, only Cathy's turned out more mullet than Rachel. Everyone tried to be nice. *You don't look so bad. It'll grow out. Maybe you could use a flat iron.* But the last straw was Lawrence Weiner cracking everyone up in homeroom: *Why is Bon Jovi sitting in Cathy's seat?*

"That was eons ago," Veronica said. "That's what boys are like at that age."

"You don't outgrow being a jerk."

"Cathy, it was seventh grade."

"Look who's talking, Miss Congeniality."

"I'm just having fun reminiscing with some old friends. When I go home I have another life."

"I have a life too," Cathy said. "I teach, I'm social . . ."

"And where are you living?"

"You know very well why I'm staying with my father."

"I told you that you're welcome to stay with us."

Cathy's phone buzzed.

Veronica raised an eyebrow. "I rest my case."

After their second round, Veronica and Josh went to check out the jukebox. Each minute alone with Lawrence was more agonizing than the last. He said something, but with the jukebox blasting "We Are the Champions" and Veronica and Josh singing along at the top of their voices, Cathy could barely hear a word.

"What did you say?" she asked.

He repeated it but she still couldn't make it out.

"What?" she said louder.

He leaned toward her and cupped his hand to her ear. "Nice boots," he said, this time with a huge grin. The same grin he had that day in homeroom.

Cathy's cheeks grew warm. "Did you just say you liked my boobs?"

"I sure did. They're awesome. They look very aerodynamic. I wish they made them in my size, but I don't think I could pull them off."

Veronica and Josh slid back into the booth with another round of drinks. "What'd we miss?" Veronica asked.

Cathy scrambled over Lawrence and out of the booth. Hands on her hips, she said, "Lawrence Weiner, you were an insensitive oaf in high school, and now you're just an older and more insensitive oaf. *With* love handles!"

The shot glass was in front of her on the table. Her first thought was to throw it in Lawrence's face. Her second, to chug it. And though she hadn't had a drink since she'd mistook calvados for apple cider, she went with her second inclination and downed it.

"Now, if you'll excuse me. I'm going home."

Slightly on the wobbly side, she made a show of stomping away, but with all the sawdust, she might as well have been wearing bedroom slippers.

Pat's had filled up. Most of the empty chairs at the bar were now occupied. The barflies didn't look like lonely, miserable drunks anymore; they looked happy and like they were having a good time. Since when had she become the fun police? Had she always been a Debbie Downer like Beatrice called her? Yes, her mother sometimes drank to excess, sometimes passed out in the living room with her coat on, but she'd also made every day a holiday. International No School Junk Food Day, when she and her sister got to stay in their nighties all day and have cherry cheesecake and soda for breakfast. Make Christmas cookies in October just because. Stay up late watching *When Harry Met Sally* instead of doing homework. Ride the merry-go-round at Seaside Heights until the amusement park closed.

The jukebox was playing Dancing Queen, her all-time favorite Abba song. She and Veronica had been in the high school production of *Mamma Mia!*

Veronica caught up with her. "Cathy, Lawrence wasn't—"

"I don't want to talk about it." Cathy threw her bag on a chair and pulled Veronica onto the dance floor. She'd forgotten how much she liked to dance, and her boots provided surprisingly good support, despite the four-inch heels. Josh joined them. Lawrence, glum-faced, leaned against a pole and watched.

One song turned into two, then three. "I haven't had so much fun in years!" Cathy said to Veronica, who gave her a high five and a hip bump. "I love you guys! I love Pat's! Aren't we the best?"

The next song was Pink Floyd. People migrated off the dance floor. Only a couple of flannel-wearing Dead Heads and Veronica and Josh remained. Cathy went to the bar for a glass of water. The bartender was cute. Clean-shaven, and wearing a work shirt and striped red-and-blue tie. Neat, but not too conservative.

He smiled. His teeth were perfect. "What can I get you?" he asked.

Were those his real teeth? Cathy wondered. Or veneers? In any case, they were sparkling white and probably tasted like mint. Instead of asking for water, she tilted her head and said, "Guess."

"You look like you'd be an appletini kind of girl."

"How'd you know?"

"'Cause it's sweet. Just like you."

Into a frosted tin shaker, the bartender poured several different liqueurs, one even named "pucker," which seemed fitting, gave it a good shake, placed a napkin on the bar, then poured the caterpillar-green drink right to the tippy top of a chilled cocktail glass. Cathy had never actually had an appletini before, but it looked like candy. How strong could it be?

"I can't carry it," Cathy said. "It'll spill."

"That's the point. I want you to stay here with me," he said with a wink.

She turned so Lawrence was out of her line of sight then took a sip. "Yummy, but I don't know if I can finish it. I had acupuncture today." Somehow the non sequitur had made perfect sense when she'd formed it in her head.

"I had acupuncture to quit smoking," the cutie-pie bartender said.

"I hear you need to sleep with staples in your ears for that."

Cathy was about to ask him if he had ever been "tuned," when Veronica rushed over and pulled her to her feet. "Josh just put on the Pointer Sisters!" she exclaimed, her mouth forming the OMG-I'm-so-excited-I'm-about-to-scream shape.

Cathy put down her drink. "I have to dance to this song," she said. "Save my seat."

"You got it," the bartender replied, smiling. He even had dimples!

Veronica and Cathy had danced to this album so many times in Veronica's parents' basement and they still had the choreography down pat. Somewhere in the middle of "Jump," Cathy started to feel a little woozy, but this was their big finish. Veronica took her hands and they spun around. The next thing she knew, she was flat on the floor, spitting sawdust out of her mouth.

The bartender vaulted over the bar and helped her to her

feet. Embarrassed, but fine, she limped off the dance floor—and that's when she realized she'd lost the heel of her new boot.

"Ah, shoot!"

"Have no fear," Lawrence said, immediately beginning a search-and-rescue operation. "Where you stumble, there lies your treasure."

Cathy was furious. Not only didn't she need his help, she also resented his willful misuse of one of her favorite Joseph Campbell quotes.

"Lawrence, please. I don't need you to put on your head-lamp or night vision goggles or whatever other gear you have and come to my rescue. I'm perfectly capable of managing just fine on my . . ." Her voice trailed off as she ran to the bathroom, making it there just before she thew up.

She splashed water on her face and looked in the mirror. She looked slightly peaked. Nothing a little blush couldn't fix.

The bartender's name was Richie. He told Cathy a little about himself as he drove her home in his Jeep. He was attending business school part time, planning to go into his brother-in-law's business, something to do with cars. The world had finally stopped spinning. Her father was visiting her sister for the weekend and wouldn't be home until Sunday. The bartender could be her *trou normand*. A minty palate cleanser before the next course of true soul love.

Richie parked the car in front of the house and cut the en-gine. He helped her to the door. She was walking more Captain Hook, less Kalinda, than she would have liked.

"I'll have one of the guys drop your car off in the morning."

Holding onto the railing and balancing on one foot, Cathy pecked him on his clean-shaven cheek. He smelled like lemons. Was he waiting for a signal that he could kiss her? She closed her eyes and lifted her chin, anticipating the feel of his lips on hers. But nothing. When she opened her eyes he was walking down the steps.

"See you around," he said, clicking his car lights on.

Maybe Joy was right; it wasn't her Season of Love.

First thing the next morning, Cathy drove to the Blue Lotus Center. *The Love Book* was on the bench right where she'd left it. Before leaving, she took a little detour to walk the meditation labyrinth, hoping to understand what Joy had meant when she said there was mystery in design and simplicity in intuition. She walked slowly, still dizzy and hungover, but with each step she felt a little clearer, more sure-footed. When she reached the center, she found the white cat curled up with a black cat, like yin and yang. Not wanting to disturb them, she turned around and went back the way she'd come. And then she realized that the end of the labyrinth and the beginning were the same.

When she returned home, there was a small box on the front porch and a note from Lawrence: *Sorry for being such a heel.* She didn't have to open it to know what was inside.

CHAPTER TWELVE
UNSOLICITED MATERIAL

EMILY SAT IN THE COMMUNITY GARDEN on West Eight-ninth, a secret oasis tucked between crumbling brownstones, going through a stack of manuscripts. It was the first week of October, but it felt like summer. Amazingly, there were still some fragrant blooms on the rosebushes; some that hadn't even yet opened.

Since the salon, she and Duncan had met for lunch several times (a business expense), and he'd even offered her a job as an assistant to the literary editor (an unpaid but "influential position") at a "prominent" left-wing periodical where he was a contributing editor. They hadn't gone beyond a platonic peck on the cheek, but for Emily it was the most exciting relationship she'd ever had. Duncan was cerebral; his mind was her aphrodisiac. For all she knew he was asexual. She was relieved actually that they hadn't progressed to the next level. Flings had a tendency to throw her life off balance. With Duncan, the lines seemed clear. No sexual power plays, no bouts of insecurity. He treated her like an equal, albeit an unpaid one. He even said she might have a novel in her.

For the past few weeks she'd been Tweeting and Tumblring and had even started a daily blog about her experiences "doing" *The Love Book*. Remarkably, she already had three hundred followers and almost as many subscribers. She'd hoped to have something concrete to tell her friend the editor when they had coffee later that day, but so far no luck.

Finally, Duncan arrived, wearing a dark suit and a pair of weird sunglasses that looked like flying goggles. He grinned and gave a world-weary sigh, as though relieved to be back on terra firma. He sat on the wrought-iron bench and slathered his face with sunblock until his skin was Marcel Marceau white, then fastidiously positioned himself toward the sun. As an afterthought, he offered some to Emily, but she was wearing SPF 15 makeup.

"That's not enough," he said. "I want to be looking at a beautiful woman in twenty years."

That was all it took. She closed her eyes while he applied lotion on her face the way she used to do for Zach when he was little. His hands were softer than her massage therapist's, a luxury she couldn't really afford since her divorce.

He thumbed through her rejection pile. "You have no idea how much this helps. I can't afford to waste my time wading through slush. Can't these people read? No unsolicited material." He picked up a story, glanced at the author, and looked at her. "This, is in the rejection pile?"

"Yes, it's very . . . derivative," she said.

"Pierre Aboulay derivative?"

Duncan's goggles were black holes. She couldn't even see her own reflection. She thought of a line from *The Love Book*: *Everyone you meet is a mirror.* She felt ungrounded, like she didn't exist.

"Who is Aboulay?" she asked. "Should I know him?"

"He's only the world's greatest French author of the twentieth century. Perhaps of all time!"

She braced herself. "Have you read it?"

He removed his goggles and laughed. "That was priceless. Aboulay's a hack. He's been hounding me for years to publish his drivel." He reached into his messenger bag and took out a chocolate chip cookie. "It's spelt. Want a bite?"

"No, thanks," she said, looking at her watch. "I have an appointment. I should be going." She didn't like being laughed at.

"You can't leave yet. I have another stack of submissions. They're upstairs. It'll only take a minute. I promise."

Max waited for Pam to catch her breath. The reservoir was crowded with wannabe Type A's jostling each other as though they owned the jogging path, while the real movers and shakers had already been at work since dawn. They were trying for a ten-minute mile, but it wasn't looking too promising. The pace was torturously slow and Max was doing everything she could think of to avoid going crazy: walking lunges, chassés, high knees, running backward, but it felt like she was stuck in molasses and still Pam lagged behind.

As always, Pam was wearing a full face of makeup. It was only ten minutes in and already she was dripping with sweat. With any luck she'd be too winded to talk about her latest quandary: whether to get Fraxel laser on her lower abdomen or a tummy tuck. She'd begun to get some upper body definition, but nothing would help that muffin top or those stubbornly jiggly potato thighs, only accentuated by a streaky spray tan. Max found cellulite repulsive. Anything that moved of its own accord when it wasn't supposed to, she could do without. It was one of the reasons she was glad she wasn't well endowed. No elephant breasts flapping around when she was tower running.

They rounded the south side of the reservoir where it crossed the bridle path. Pam stopped for a drink of water at the gatehouse. This side of the path always conjured haunted memories for Max. A glimpse of the Twin Towers used to be visible through the trees. Today, without the endorphins to numb her out, to "lidocaine" her until she felt nothing, her thoughts turned dark. To suicide. The first recorded suicide in the reservoir was in 1884. An unidentified man in evening dress jumped into the water, a gun in his pocket. Not long after, a woman who called herself Titania walked quietly to the edge, leaving only a note and her lace gloves floating on the surface. Romanticized versions of an act that often defies explanation. Several suicides had occurred each month until a ten-foot fence was erected as a deterrent. After Calvin shot himself, Max had only brief respites from thinking about the horror, but they were fleeting, the reason she'd spent so much of her late teens and early twenties wasted. And a fence, no matter how high, wouldn't have prevented him from putting a loaded gun to his temple.

Garrett understood this. He'd felt the same sense of loss, the bottomless grief, guilt, anger, a blinding torrent of emotions. Calvin had been like a father to him. She didn't have to explain herself when, now that she was sober, instead of anesthetizing herself with booze, she had to push herself to her absolute physical limit and then beyond, otherwise it was more than one person could stand to bear alone.

This past weekend, Garrett had borrowed a friend's Cessna and they'd flown up to Falmouth, Massachusetts. Garrett was participating in a conference at Woods Hole Oceanographic Institution on the role of oceans in climate change. Grandpa Calvin had an old Cessna Caravan and used to take Max to local air shows. He'd promised he'd make it sea worthy and teach her to fly, but when he died, the Cessna, along with most of his other treasures, was sold for scrap. Her grandfather had been Garrett's mentor, so she knew he was no slouch, but she hadn't realized he was an expert in the field. Next summer, he was leading an expedition in western Greenland to study glacier and ice-sheet melting. His eyes sparkled like Calvin's as he discussed a promising study of bioavailable iron concentrations released by Greenland's melting glaciers, which could potentially slow global warming and improve marine life and air quality.

At the end of the first day of the conference, they rented mountain bikes and did the 3.2-mile, single-track loop in Beebe Woods five times. This was hard core, not the "conversationals" she'd endured in Normandy. Garrett was as skilled on two wheels as he was in the air, navigating the rocky passes and terrain as if he knew every inch of the dirt trail. He never once looked back to see if she was keeping up. He was in his own zone and so was she. The ride down the ridge was fast and treacherous, with steep drops on both sides.

She was thirsty, her quads and hamstrings ached, and her hands were numb from the vibration, yet there was no time to think about anything but the next turn, the road ahead.

Back at the house where they were staying, Max soaked in the huge whirlpool tub and gazed through the skylight until the October sky exploded with stars. When she pulled the plug, a trail of sparkling blue bath salts disappeared down the drain. She didn't believe in rituals like salt baths to banish psychic intruders—Calvin had taught her to only put her trust in empirical evidence—but there was no denying that she felt cleansed, released, free, and ready to start fresh.

Max had never planned further ahead in any relationship than the next morning when she'd make her exit, but Sunday, as they ate lobster rolls and littleneck clams on the deck of the *Captain Kidd,* watching the old drawbridge go up to let the tall sailboats in and out of the harbor, she could see herself sitting next to him at the foot of Leverett Glacier next summer, not with fear, but hope for new beginnings.

Pam was bent over, trying to catch her breath. "That was the best workout I've ever had," she said, adjusting her sports bra.

"Next time we're going to try to break the twelve-minute mile," Max said. "There are grandmas who walk faster around their kitchens than you run."

"You're such a bitch! So, are you coming tonight? I want you to meet my new client and you still haven't told me squat about this pilot guy."

"I told you I'd let you know."

After workouts, they always went to Le Pain Quotidien,

where Pam would consume more calories in one sitting than the average woman ate in a day. As they walked down Eighty-fifth Street, Max caught a glimpse of Emily walking into the courtyard of a building with a man Max recognized from the gym. Emily wore an embroidered hippie coat and clogs, and Count von Stunning was in a suit and dark glasses. They looked so mismatched. Max called to her but she didn't turn around. Either Emily was snubbing her or was so entranced by her companion that nothing and no one else existed. Max had fallen hard for Garrett, but there was no way she'd ever let anyone pull her under water again.

Emily followed Duncan through the arched entrance of the fortress-like building. The Belnord's rent strikes and landlord problems were legendary, but so were the stratospheric ceilings, ornate working fireplaces, and rooms of vast proportions. She'd always wanted to see what the landmarked apartments looked like. Her vision didn't even come close. Duncan had one of the last rent-controlled apartments in the building, a three-bedroom inherited from his great-aunt Bernice. It looked like he had also inherited the old lady's dilapidated antique furniture. It was a cluttered mess, but one Emily could easily get lost in.

He told her to explore to her heart's content. She wandered down crooked corridors with floor-to-ceiling bookshelves. One shelf was a shrine entirely devoted to Duncan's books. She touched their spines. Maybe one day . . . but a voice in her head mocked her. Silly girl, dream on.

At the end of the hall was an octagonal drawing room. Seashells and green apothecary bottles were lined up on the windowsills; antique canes and peacock feathers seemed to be growing out of the umbrella stand. The only anachronisms were a huge flat-screen television and modular black leather couch, probably the only furniture Duncan had ever purchased himself. Framed photographs, mostly of Duncan (one with Bill

Clinton), were three-deep on the mantelpiece. Stacks of books, newspapers, and dust of every variety covered the surfaces. A brand-new pink feather duster idled on the windowsill.

She heard file cabinets opening and slamming. Duncan's fingers pelted the keyboard like a hailstorm.

"I'll just be a second," he called from the other room. "I have to give Tarantino a quick call."

He'd changed out of his suit into jeans and a T-shirt and was pacing around wearing a headset like an air traffic controller.

Emily settled into the window seat and gazed at the alabaster fountain in the central garden, pretending to ignore his pretentious prattle. Was this a show, or was he for real?

Then he was typing again. And back on the phone, this time in French. Had he forgotten her? Finally, just as she'd decided to leave, he appeared behind her, swaying to music apparently only he could hear.

He spun her around slowly. Each time she made a full rotation, her gaze landed on a basket of exotic fruit on the coffee table, until the basket became just a blur of color when he finally kissed her.

He led her to the leather couch. "You're going to be late to your appointment," he said.

"I'm already late," she said.

"*Tant pis*, this appointment is more urgent."

Emily tried to relax, staring at the ceiling as he unzipped her jeans.

Two weeks. That was how long she and Charles had waited before sleeping together. But he'd already told her he loved her and met her parents. Two months later they were engaged.

Why now, of all moments, was she thinking of Charles?

As much as she'd enjoyed the feeling of being lost in Duncan's apartment, was she ready to lose herself again, and to this man? Since ending her affair with Nick, she was only just now finding her way out and back up to the surface.

He sensed her tensing up. "I've got you," he said.

She didn't know why, but the words made her feel safe. She melted into the couch as he pushed her knees apart. With Charles, this sort of thing had usually been relegated to national holidays, vacations, and birthdays, and only occasionally successful. Duncan, though, was a demonstrably accomplished linguist.

She'd always thought security and passion were mutually exclusive. Maybe there were two types of men: the ones she felt safe with, and the ones with whom she could cut loose.

Her inhibitions were dissolving. She was floating above the couch, watching herself. She thought of "Prufrock": *Like a patient etherized upon a table.*

More ether, please.

So, Duncan was literary, cerebral, complex, and more than a little bit egotistical, but he was certainly not asexual.

A few hours later when Emily gathered her things, the sky was a deep midnight blue. Her hair was still wet from the shower they'd taken in the clawfoot tub, the showerhead so strong it felt like needles. She'd welcomed his presence behind her, for an "encore." She'd heard him unwrapping something, probably putting on a condom. But when he turned her around, she saw that his hair was tucked into a pink-striped shower cap from the Beverly Hills Hotel, and he hadn't thought to offer her one.

Duncan said he'd drop her off in a cab on his way to a "working" dinner with his assistant Lara. In the elevator, he handed her a Rite Aid sack of manuscripts and a Penguin tote bag filled with advance reading copies of not-yet-published books.

"In case you can't get to sleep tonight, these work better than sleeping pills," he chuckled.

As they crossed the landscaped courtyard, passing ombré-leaved pear trees and formal flowerbeds, she felt protected, shielded from the chaos of the city. She imagined the literary parties, intimate dinners, and late-night discussions with luminaries that they could host. They'd be one of those couples. Before exiting the carriageway, she counted five stories up to Duncan's window. The Juliette balcony would be the perfect spot for a flower box.

"What are you doing for *yontif*?" he asked, as the cab pulled up in front of her building.

"It depends."

"If you're free Friday afternoon we could continue our quest for the elusive triple mitzvah."

She was glad she hadn't donated the book her mother-in-law had given her on setting up a Jewish household, so she could look up the definition. But she guessed the meaning and hoped they'd find it. It was only Wednesday. Zach was with Charles. She wished they could begin their search tonight.

"To be continued, then," he said, kissing her goodbye, "during the Days of Awe."

Upstairs, Emily found a crumpled note in the bottom of the Rite Aid bag: *To the sweetest fruit of all.* Signed *Lara.*

Working dinner? My ass.

Whenever Max socialized with clients outside the gym, she wound up feeling "less than," like a pair of canary-yellow patent-leather Louboutins bought on impulse for a black tie something-or-other, worn only once and, after collecting dust for several seasons, boxed up and sent to Housing Works or another worthy cause. It came with the territory. She'd dressed for the part, in laser-cut leather shorts, a backless halter, and combat boots to show them she could kick ass. But she felt like an impostor. She'd never had a problem separating herself from the situation. Why tonight? Had she really changed that much since meeting Garrett?

Pam and her entourage were at the Cabanas, an uber-cool

bar on the roof of the Maritime Hotel, a white-brick building with porthole windows that in one incarnation had been a
shelter for runaway teens. The way she was feeling, the setting
seemed uncannily appropriate.

Pam was sitting on a blue-and-white-striped bench at a low
teak table. Paper lanterns and amber-colored heat lamps hung
from the rafters. She waved, whispering something to a pudgy
British guy with a pink button-down and side-swept blond hair
sitting next to her.

As Max drew near, she heard the pudgy guy say, "Seriously?"

Pam nodded. "It's true; ask her."

"You went to Harvard?" the man asked Max when she sat
down.

She'd been down this road before. A fitness trainer who
went to Harvard didn't compute with this set, engendering
question after question as they tried to discover the fissure in
her character, how in the world she ended up training spoiled,
out-of-shape trust-fund babies like him.

She shot a look at Pam. "Yes. Amazing, but true."

"What house?"

"Cabot."

"Premed?" he asked. She nodded. "What year?"

"Class of 2005, but—"

"Perhaps you knew my brother Eric. He was also premed,
captain of the squash team?"

"You're British?" she asked.

"Yes, I grew up in Hampstead."

"London," Max said, feigning interest. "So you must know
Tony Blair."

The guy colored, blathered a bit, then said, "Right," in that
polite British way, before turning to his neighbor to discuss the
Republican primary.

She hadn't just known the pudgy guy's brother; she'd slept
with him and subsequently half of his Club brothers. It sur-

prised her that she remembered him at all, considering she'd
been in a bottomless tequila blackout after Calvin died.

The waiter brought a $1,000 bottle of Russo-Baltique to
the table and seven chilled crystal glasses. Max could practically
feel the cool burn of the first swig of vodka.

"Please don't tell people I went to Harvard," she said to
Pam.

"What's the big deal?" Nothing was ever a big deal to Pam,
as long as the story was entertaining and made her look good.

"Because my life is none of their fucking business, that's why."

But Pam wasn't even listening. She was waving to Count
von Stunning. Everyone at the gym had a nickname. He got his
because he dressed like Nureyev in *The Nutcracker* and couldn't
take his eyes off himself. A lightweight. Max could bench him
without breaking a sweat.

He kissed Pam and gave a tentative smile when he saw Max,
trying to place her. "I don't think we've met," he said.

"You know Max, Duncan," Pam said. "She's my trainer."

He looked at her blankly then opened his eyes wide. "Oh, of
course! I've never seen you dressed!"

The rest of their group broke into uproarious laughter, especially the pudgy guy who seemed to think it was the funniest
thing he'd ever heard.

"Sit with us," Pam entreated. "I heard your book's been
optioned."

"Sorry, I can't. I'm meeting someone." He kissed Pam's
cheek. Then to Max: "If you can squeeze me in, I'd love a private training session sometime." Count von Stunning held out
his card, but Max refused to take it.

"That'll cost extra," the pudgy guy said. He was drunk, but
not drunk enough for her to let the comment slip by. While the
rest of the group was discussing their upcoming winter holidays
to St. Barthes or Vail, Max slid closer to him until their thighs
touched.

"Do you work out?" she asked.

"I play tennis twice a week at the Paris Club. With the pro. I also play a little golf," he added, sucking in his stomach.

"You have good genetics," she said. "If you gave me six months, I could get you in the best shape of your life."

"I was actually thinking of getting a trainer. To build up my endurance."

"Plus other things," she said, casually placing her hand on his crotch. His cheeks flushed redder than a teenager caught with his father's *Playboy* magazine.

"What other things?" he asked, trying to act as if nothing untoward was occurring under the table. She slowly uncrossed her legs and slid her ankle along his calf.

"That for every ten pounds a guy loses, he gains an inch."

The table suddenly grew silent.

"No guarantee, but we can only hope," she said, spilling a glass of water on his lap as she rose to leave.

Pam caught up with her at the elevators. "What kind of stunt was that?"

"That guy's a shithead," Max answered.

"You're the shithead. That guy *was* my client, past tense, thanks to you."

"And you used to be mine," Max said. "Good luck with your muffin top."

If she'd learned one lesson from her grandfather, it was to get them before they got you. Self-love is self-protection.

CHAPTER THIRTEEN
THE MAD HATTERS

WHEN CATHY HADN'T SHOWN UP BY 4 P.M. for the Soul Mate Soirée at Alice's Tea Cup, even Max expressed concern, though that hadn't stopped any of them from ordering and nearly polishing off the Mad Hatter, a three-tiered, aptly named extravaganza. The waiter had recommended the Jabberwocky, an unlimited affair, but Beatrice, already on her third scone and second cup of coffee, thought it excessive. To her, tea was just a waste of hot water, or so she'd tell anyone who inquired. The real reason was that it reminded her of stuffy afternoons in Freddy's mother's chintz-upholstered drawing room.

Emily took a sip of her chamomile tea, hoping to calm her monkey mind. Duncan had been so remote when she'd spoken to him that morning.

"This is a very emotional time of year for me," he had said when she inquired if something was wrong. "I'm feeling very fragile."

"Is there anything I can do?" she'd asked.

"No, there's nothing anyone can do. I'll be better in January."

She chalked it up to Yom Kippur, this solemn fast day in the Jewish calendar. Emily never fasted or went to synagogue. She wouldn't consider herself observant—she was raised celebrating Christmas and Easter—unless making jelly donuts for Hanukkah and chocolate chip hamantaschen for Purim counted. Charles was always in a very black mood if he skipped a meal.

She used to give him the benefit of the doubt with regard to his moodiness, until the darkness began consuming entire weekends, despite how consistently she monitored his blood sugar levels. Duncan could be prediabetic for all she knew, but then she remembered Yom Kippur didn't technically start until sundown.

The private party room in the back was decorated with balloons and crepe paper for a little girl's fifth birthday party. The theme was *Fancy Nancy*. A gaggle of little girls dressed to the nines with pink boas and tiaras drank tea with their pinkies out, Fancy Nancy style. Even Justin's teacup poodle, Apricot, was wearing a rhinestone collar and sparkly fairy wings.

The change in the other women since Normandy was remarkable. Beatrice looked twenty years younger. Her skin was luminous, her eyes glowing. And Max was no longer the lean adolescent jock Emily had met there; she looked softer. She was even wearing a dress, a silk python-printed shirtdress with gold buttons, and motorcycle boots. She said she had to leave early; Friday nights she worked as a hostess.

Beatrice drained her cup. "Between you and me," she said, "all this love stuff isn't really my thing. I'm just here because Cathy's a sweet kid. The only thing I want to conjure is another scone." Though she scoffed, she had indeed read the first chapter of *The Love Book*, and the one after that. She'd boarded the bus from New Jersey and settled into her seat for a little escapist reading when she discovered that once again she'd mistaken *The Love Book* for her Stephanie Plum novel. Surrounded by glum-faced commuters, she'd passed the time by reading and then doing a silly quiz at the end of the chapter. She'd used a pen just like she did the *Times* crossword puzzle. She never put down an answer unless she was certain, and she always was.

Question One: In a movie, when the bride makes a run for it at the altar, your first thought is . . .

Smart cookie to have the taxi driver keep his meter running!

Question Two: If a man sent you loving emails three times a day, your first response would be . . .

Spam lists were invented for a reason!

Question Three: The last person you lived with . . .

She'd hesitated. An image of Albert, looking forlorn, his bags packed at the door, came to mind. She chose C, the only answer that came remotely close: *Moved out because they were cramping your style.*

Question Four: A man you're dating is transferred to another country. You . . .

Wish them luck. What else?

She completed the quiz, all twenty-five questions, and reviewed her responses. She'd felt satisfied. She was a strong independent woman who'd have made Betty Friedan proud. She tallied her score and turned the page.

If you scored 25 or above, you are a commitmentphobe. Seek professional help immediately.

"Hogwash!" she'd muttered. She was alone by choice. Several passengers had glanced up from their newspapers. It wasn't that she was averse to the idea of having a man take her to dinner occasionally. Once you got them home and unwrapped, even Albert, they were all the same: basically useless.

Beatrice thought about something Albert used to say before he was diagnosed with cancer: *I'll sleep when I'm dead.* What she would give to have one more night with him, just to tell him she was sorry for bailing on him when he needed her most.

Justin arrived with a scone and ramekin of clotted cream, but suddenly Beatrice couldn't eat another bite.

Emily glanced at her watch. "Traffic can't be that bad. I'm going to give Cathy a call."

She went to the front of the shop for better reception. Stevie was at the counter, her head resting on her hand. Last time Emily had been there, Stevie had been bubbling over about a new guy she'd met at her acting class—unlike today, when she looked like she'd rather be in bed under the covers. Emily knew how that felt; she'd spent the first three months after Charles left in a pair of flannel pajamas and a ratty cardigan.

"What's wrong with Stevie?" she asked Justin.

"Her boyfriend broke up with her. She's taking it pretty hard. It must be going around. My boyfriend dumped me too. From now on it's just me and Apricot."

The call to Cathy went directly to voice mail. When Emily returned to the table, Beatrice's tote bag began to chirp, an electronic orchestra of crickets.

"Cathy!" Beatrice said, answering her phone. "Where in God's name are you? We were getting worried . . . What's that you said? . . . The wrong Alice's?"

"She must have gone to the East Side Alice's," Emily said.

Beatrice shushed her. "I can't hear."

"Tell her we're at the Alice's on Columbus Avenue."

"Stockbridge? How the heck did you wind up in Massachusetts?" Beatrice listened, a look of disbelief on her face. She covered the phone. "Her GPS went kerflooey. Apparently her brother-in-law programmed it for the wrong Alice's. The Arlo Guthrie Alice's in the Berkshires."

Max rolled her eyes. "A four-year-old in a pink Barbie car could drive from New Jersey to Manhattan without a GPS."

Beatrice put Cathy on speakerphone on the top tier of the tea tray so she could give them detailed instructions for the release ceremony. Cathy had devised the exercise herself. It borrowed from several traditions and this one was fitting for the Day of Atonement. They were supposed to throw bread in the water to symbolize cutting emotional ties with past lovers. Beatrice didn't know from cutting toxic ties, but she didn't want to be a spoilsport, so she told Cathy they'd throw in a couple of slices for her.

The first step was to write a letter of forgiveness to someone with whom there was still unfinished business. Emily handed out mini legal pads, envelopes, and pens.

Beatrice pushed her pad away. There was no one she needed to write to; Albert was dead. And if she had anything to say to Freddy, she'd say it to his face.

Max wrote one line, tore off the top sheet, and crumpled it up.

Emily's letter to Charles had started out fine—clear and detached—but then took a strange turn. *Charles, I'm so sorry. I didn't deserve you. Please forgive me.* She slipped it into the envelope, then between the pages of Cathy's *Love Book*.

After paying the bill, they went to a dingy supermarket across the street to buy bread. The sound system was tuned to a call-in radio show about relationships. Beatrice was saying something, but Emily didn't seem to hear a word as though she were a million light years away. The relationship expert was giving advice to a caller. *Listen, you may never get over him. You might be alone forever, for all I know . . .*

Beatrice was quickly losing patience. Earth to Emily! What had gotten into the woman? She'd seemed fine a few minutes ago. "I'm going to grow mold if we don't get a move on," she said, tossing a loaf of marked-down bread into the basket. "The ducks won't care if it's white or wheat."

When they emerged from the store, it was as if the heavens had opened up. The release ceremony would have to wait for better weather.

Max headed off to her hostessing job and Beatrice agreed to wait out the storm at Emily's. Emily made hot chocolate and they watched *The Women* on TCM in the den. Emily had brought in the bag of marshmallows. She took the ratio of hot chocolate to marshmallows very seriously. She thought they'd only watch until the rain let up, but two hours later they were still watching. Near the end of the film, Norma Shearer, dressed in a silk peignoir, reads a passage from Kahlil Gibran's book

The Prophet. Emily had seen the movie at least three times but had absolutely no recollection of the scene. *Love gives naught but itself and takes naught but from itself.*

In the next scene, Norma Shearer runs off to be reunited with her estranged husband, uttering that famous line, "*Dignity is a price a woman in love can't afford,*" which Beatrice found amusing.

"What a bunch of simps. I say, skip the bromide. Give me some straight gin. Not one man in the whole darn movie and that's all they ever talk about."

It was still pouring, so Emily insisted that Beatrice spend the night. While Beatrice called her friend Libby to tell her she was stuck in town, Emily put fresh sheets on the pullout couch, clean towels in the bathroom, a new box of Kleenex and pitcher of water on the nightstand, happily obliging when Beatrice asked if she had anything a little bit stronger.

Emily said goodnight and went to write up her notes from the release ceremony. And that's when she realized she'd left Cathy's *Love Book,* and the letter to Charles, at Alice's.

A year after Emily and Charles had separated, Valentine's Day weekend, Zach and Emily had gone skiing with two other families. When they returned from the slopes after the first day, Charles was in the parking lot. He'd driven six hours just to give her a Valentine's Day present: a black pearl necklace she'd always wanted. Instead of feeling grateful for the gesture, she'd gotten angry, and told him he couldn't stay. She said she couldn't accept the gift and couldn't explain it to him, or anyone, including herself. She still felt like a horrible, unforgivable person, not worthy of anyone's trust, least of all his. She remembered how defeated he had looked when he waved to Zach from the car. How could she have been so unfeeling?

She went into Zach's room, something she often did when he was with Charles. Yoda was on Zach's bed dressed in a Knicks jersey and cap, more thug than Jedi master. Emily pressed his hand. "Will I ever find love?" Yoda's blue eyes blinked. His ears wiggled. *"Simple question, simple answer. No."* She asked again. *"Hmm, squeezed too hard, you have."* The third time, the master refused to speak. She put Yoda back on the bed and turned out the light. Yoda's eyes suddenly lit up like green marbles in the darkness. *"Feel the force all around you. Then clear the answer will become."*

CHAPTER FOURTEEN
TOUT DE SWEET

WHEN FREDDY TOLD BEATRICE TO MEET HIM at the Oak Bar on Thursday and that she was in for a surprise, she wanted to be ready on all fronts, mentionable and otherwise. She hadn't given much thought to undergarments except in a utilitarian Land's End sort of way. Probably not since Albert died. Had it been ten years already?

The salesgirl at Agent Provocateur had looked at her like a curiosity when she walked in. Her feathers were already a little ruffled from the frigid welcome, but when the salesgirl suggested that she might find the lingerie department at Lord & Taylor more her style, Beatrice made it clear she had no intention of wearing panties from the fifty-shades-of-beige granny section. She wasn't going to let this buxom brunette sexpot in a lab coat intimidate her.

The salesgirl arched her eyebrow, and then smiled. Beatrice knew she'd win her over eventually. Game on.

"I have just the thing," the young woman said, opening the mirrored drawers behind the long glass counter one by one until she found exactly what she was looking for, and draped a few barely there wisps of silk over her arm.

In the dressing room, though, Beatrice lost all her nerve. She sat on a tufted boudoir chair and counted the minutes until she could make her sortie without losing face. *It didn't feel right*, she'd say. Then the curtain parted and a glass of wine appeared, conveyed by an arm tattooed with two interlocking Venus symbols. Next, a pair of patent-leather slingbacks and body glitter.

Tipsy but fortified, Beatrice emerged, wearing a short white silk robe, her legs shimmering like a bronze figurine. Twenty-five years of Jane Fonda had a silver lining.

The salesgirl adjusted the hook-and-eye closures. "You're one hot mama."

Beatrice thanked her. And it was true. She was still attractive, no matter what the odometer said. She didn't feel half bad either. The Love Lava was flowing!

At the counter, the salesgirl slipped a three-pack of neon condoms gratis into the shopping bag and recommended Beatrice try the Drone, a pair of remote-control vibrating thong panties.

"Your man can pilot you from across the room at a cocktail party," she said.

"No thanks," Beatrice replied. "I like to be the pilot in command."

"Take it anyway," the salesgirl whispered. "You'll thank me."

Sitting at the bar in the Oak Room on a high green stool all "tarted up" waiting for Freddy (already twenty minutes late), Beatrice felt as conspicuous as a red cape in a bullring. What must the other patrons be thinking? A woman alone at a bar at four in the afternoon? She felt like some sort of specialty AARP prostitute waiting for her geriatric john.

The place looked different since the last time Beatrice had been there before the renovation. Impossibly newer. Her memories of mayhem in the dark corner booths were wiped clean with the recent renovation. The coffered wood ceiling gleamed. Never in a million years would she have guessed that the famous murals of Central Park in winter had been intended to be so vibrant, but then it was amazing what a person could get used to.

Decades of smoke-laced varnish had been stripped, revealing the painting's true colors: touches of pale blue moonlight on the Pulitzer fountain; the red lipstick of hopeful young women strolling the southern end of the park. She remembered feeling that way herself in the early days, racing across Grand Army Plaza to meet Albert on the rare weekends they spent together.

Freddy entered the Oak Bar, trailing clods of dirt from his white-knobbed shoes. Obviously he'd been golfing, or maybe mowing the lawn. He looked "faux" dapper in his checked pants and yellow pullover. The green key blazer with gold buttons, however, Beatrice found a little smug. He kissed her and rested his hand on her lower back.

"Dewar's on the rocks," he said to the bartender.

Beatrice winced. She almost made a comment, but let it go. Freddy should be Freddy. Albert had always complained that she was trying to improve him. Still, Dewar's? And maybe he shouldn't drink *too* much. Didn't want her cowboy to have to pop one of those little blue pills.

"I hyperventilated on Metro-North," he said. "The conductor was about to call the paramedics. I told him I was just lovesick."

"Stop it, Freddy. You're acting like a schoolgirl. Now, what's this about a surprise?"

"You'll know soon enough. Malcolm arranged everything."

"Malcolm? Why did you even tell him?"

"What? Put the room on *my* credit card? Muriel would have a cow."

Somehow the man in the safari suit she'd run into on the Peter Pan bus, as sweet as taffy, did not quite seem the paradigm of discretion. Well, no sense worrying now.

Freddy downed his scotch and threw some bills on the bar.

"What's the rush?" Beatrice said. "I could stay here forever. I always think if I sit here long enough, a girl I used to know might show up."

"You incurable romantic, Beatrice."

"Hardly. I just feel at home in a place that's been around the universe a few times and had its share of scandals."

"We'll come back for a nightcap," he said. "I can't wait another minute."

The bellhop escorted them upstairs, regaling them with the history of the hotel, rattling off movie titles filmed on the premises, the famous celebrity guests. "You've heard the story of Cary Grant and the three English muffins?" he asked.

"Who hasn't?" Freddy answered.

"It's rare to meet such an aficionado as yourself," the bellhop said. "I usually do the teen tours and all they want to hear about is *Gossip Girl* or if the bathroom fixtures in the Edwardian Suite really are plated with 24 karat gold."

"I thought they were 14," Freddy said.

"No, 24, sir."

"I'm pretty sure they're 14," Freddy said. "I have a photographic memory."

At the fifth floor, the elevator opened. A little girl and her mother stepped on. The girl was sulking.

"I'm sorry, dear," the mother said.

"You promised," the girl whined.

Freddy gave an exaggerated sigh.

"We'll do it for your birthday next year," the woman said. "I promise."

The girl cheered up. "Can I bring my guinea pig?"

"Yes, sweetie."

Freddy shook his head. "Little girl, they don't allow pets at the Plaza."

"Actually they do," the bellhop said. "As long as they're in cages, under twenty-five pounds, and kept on a very short leash."

Beatrice looked at Freddy. It was tempting to make a joke at his expense. Again, she bit her tongue.

In front of room 1832, Freddy handed the bellhop five singles and ordered a bottle of champagne.

"The key, sir," the bellhop said. "Enjoy your stay."

Without turning on the lights, Freddy rushed her inside, pressed her against the wall in the small entry foyer, and kissed her. Now that's progress. A far cry from the altar boy she knew at Dartmouth. She heard his belt unbuckling and the jangle of pocket change as he slipped off his trousers.

"Don't you want to wait for the champagne?" Beatrice asked.

"Damn it," Freddy said. "I thought I had a rubber in my jacket pocket." He fumbled with the light switch.

The room brightened. The suite was a pink jewelry box. Above the bed, a neon sign flickered before settling into a cool pink light after the mercury vaporized. The Eloise Suite! Malcolm hadn't arranged this; Freddy had. She felt the same tingles of anticipation she had all those years ago when the two of them had collapsed into a sea of pink in his younger sister's Eloise-themed bedroom.

She wrapped her arms around his neck, but Freddy pulled away, reaching for his cell phone. "I need to call Malcolm."

"Please thank him for the pink surprise," she said. But from Freddy's tone, it was clear he was neither pleased nor amused. In fact, he was annoyed, angry even.

He stepped into the entry hall wearing only his green blazer and boxers and closed the French doors. "What on earth were you thinking, Malcolm? Romantic? Are you out of your mind? You always were a jealous little . . ."

After he finished dressing down Malcolm, he called the concierge and asked if they could change rooms. Nope. The hotel was totally booked up. He slumped at the foot of the pink bed. So Freddy didn't remember the first time he'd made love to her, but apparently Malcolm knew the story.

"Let's cut our losses," he said. "I'll call you a car."

"The room's paid for," she said, sitting next to him.

"How silly. You're right," Freddy softened. "You came all this way."

"And gladly, I might add."

"I'm very glad you did too." He stood up. "There's absolutely no reason not to take advantage of being in New York." He put on his overcoat. "If I hustle I can just make the 9:45."

"You're leaving because you don't have protection? I brought rubbers. What color would you like?"

Freddy didn't seem to find the assortment of neon condoms in her hand at all amusing.

"Really, Beatrice. Look at this ridiculous room."

"I can't believe you're letting something so silly, or anything, ruin the night."

"Malcolm ruined the night."

"You're a big baby, Freddy. When did you turn into a stick in the mud?"

Freddy looked as if she were speaking another language. He was straddling the doorway, one foot in, the other out.

"Just go, Freddy," she said, and he was off.

Moments later there was a knock on the door. A smiling waiter in a white jacket wheeled in a cart, a silver ice bucket, a bottle of champagne, and two flutes.

Beatrice handed him a twenty to pop the cork, then collapsed into a floral armchair. She made an attempt to turn on the flat-screen using the gold-plated remote, but could only get it to dim the crystal chandelier and adjust the thermostat. She rummaged in her bag for her Stephanie Plum novel, laughing when she came across the Drone, but the only book in her bag was that silly *Love Book,* a seeming force of nature which had once again insinuated itself uninvited into her tote bag. She tossed it across the zebra carpeting and searched for some other distraction, but the only thing to read in the entire place were Eloise books.

How nauseating! Then, in the stack of books, another title caught her eye: *Eloise's Guide to Life, or How to Eat, Dress, Travel, Behave, and Stay Six Forever!*

Beatrice read the first page: *Getting bored is not allowed.*

The little kid certainly seemed to have it all together.

She drew a bath and undressed. It was only after taking off the bra from Agent Provocateur that she realized she hadn't removed the legendary Lessons of Seduction tag. Underneath a black-and-white photograph of a woman wearing the skimpiest of white lace thongs: *Leçon n°114. L'emmener jouer dans le grand bain.*

Take him to play in the deep end.

If she wasn't going to listen to *The Love Book*, she certainly wasn't going to take advice from a bra, although it was admittedly a good marketing campaign.

After soaking in the marble tub, the body glitter rising to the surface like an oil slick, Beatrice wrapped herself in a pink chenille robe hanging next to a matching pint-sized one. Curious, she put on her reading glasses and read the instructions on the back of the box of the vibrating panties. *Batteries not included.* Of course. But a 24 karat gold–plated remote control had to be good for something.

Before falling asleep between crisp white sheets, she said to herself: *I am Beatrice. I am sixty-nine years old. I'm an Oklahoma City girl. But tonight I'm staying at the Plaza.*

C HAPTER FIFTEEN
À LA CARTE

CATHY PULLED INTO THE PARKING LOT at Ruby Tuesday, purposefully choosing a spot with no cars on either side. Her bumper had already "fallen off" twice when she'd tried to back up while stuck behind a garbage truck. She couldn't believe she'd agreed to go on a blind date, especially with one of her father's lodge brothers, and probably wouldn't have if not for the fact that the other day when she opened *The Love Book* to do her daily meditation, a white feather magically appeared as if out of the ether and landed on the exact line she was reading: *Create a flight plan and learn to fly. Your dreams have no limits.* It was a sign. Of what, however, had still to be determined. So, when her father said he wanted her to meet his lodge buddy, Bob Plume, who lived near Teterboro Airport, she knew it was the universe guiding her yet again.

Cathy had always been especially attuned to coincidences and happenstance; fortuitous accidents or forced delays masquerading as obstacles; chance meetings and glimmers of synchronicity; but especially signs of divine intervention, like a white feather miraculously appearing out of thin air with dating advice. Miraculous, even though she had been finding feathers all over the house since she'd patched her grandmother's feather blanket with a strip of medical tape, too lazy to get a needle and thread.

She entered and waited at the bar. It was happy hour. She

scanned the crowd; dubious at best. What a relief not to be there for a punitive mission. She ordered a cranberry juice spritzer from the bartender, pleased for once to be waiting for someone besides the maître d' to help her with her coat and pull out her chair. She'd worn a demure outfit, a printed empire waist dress and her grandmother's pearls. It was always best to err on the conservative side. Her more funky outfits, like the floral pedal pushers that everyone had loved in Normandy, could wait until she and Mr. Plume knew each other a little better.

She closed her eyes and did a "sensualization" to get herself in the right Love Vibration. It had been a trying day at school. One of her students had freaked out during the eighth grade proficiency assessment exam and she'd spent two hours trying to calm him down so he could complete it. Standardized tests were a necessary evil in the public school system; federal funding for special needs programs was contingent upon it, but she resented it all the same. Like all the other teachers, Cathy "taught to the test" and as a result, her students always ranked among the highest in the district, but that didn't mean students who performed less well weren't gifted. She knew she could be a little Hallmarky sometimes, but her students weren't the ones with disabilities, they were the "able" ones, more open and connected to who they really were than "mainstream" students. She didn't believe that a student's self-worth should be measured by how well they could fill in ovals on a piece of paper.

Only a week ago, because of an outdated GPS, she'd happened upon a community for people with special needs, based on Rudolf Steiner's philosophy, an entirely different model of teaching that fostered independence and self-reliance. Seeing firsthand how much more was possible made Cathy wonder if she could do better.

She'd set out from New Jersey around noon for the second attempt at the first official Soul Mate Soirée, a tin of Wintergreen Altoids in her emergency backpack. She never went anywhere without mints! What she hadn't counted on was that somehow the GPS lady was set to French, and even after three months of Rosetta Stone level I and two weeks in Normandy, she still didn't know her *droit* from her *gauche* nor have any idea how to switch it back to English. She'd focused on the pink line guiding her route and said a quick prayer to Saint Anthony of Padua for a safe journey.

Everything had seemed under control and she was making good time until the GPS sent her toward the Whitestone instead of the George Washington Bridge. She continued despite her better judgment, assuming that the Magellan lady must have devised an alternate route because of traffic or some other unforeseen real-time obstacle. Satellite technology was very sophisticated. According to the French lady, she'd be at Alice's by *seize heures et demi*, which she also attributed to some sort of time zone glitch. Then when she saw the sign for New England she panicked and took the nearest exit, but the GPS seemed to be taking her still further off the beaten path, down winding unpaved roads. She kept reminding herself that it was the journey, not the destination, and managed to remain calm until she drove into a ditch and was hemmed in by a herd of cows. Not even satellites could have predicted a bovine obstruction.

Vous êtes arrivé à votre destination.

The middle of nowhere was *not* her destination! She saw a sign for the Steiner community and went to ask for help. At least she'd left Mrs. Beasley with enough food to last the winter. There was no telling when or if she'd get where she was going now.

The bartender at Ruby Tuesday brought her drink and a bowl of mixed nuts. He was cute, though not as cute as the bartender at Pat's last week. She thanked him, but was careful not to flirt. She certainly didn't want to give him the wrong impression, even though it hadn't been Richie who'd gotten his signals crossed.

Her cell phone vibrated. It was Beatrice texting from the Oak Room bar: *Freddy's late. I'm already on my third Malbec.*

Cathy texted back: *All obstacles are for the best.*

Ruby Tuesday was filling up. At the other end of the bar, three overly made-up single women were sipping sodas and trying not to look desperate. Cathy wished she had a few extra copies of *The Love Book* on her. They could use a little help from the universe. She was about to advise Beatrice to go easy on the wine when Lawrence Weiner walked in. She quickly turned her chair, hoping he would pass by without seeing her, but he made a beeline right to her as though he had built-in sonar. Knowing Lawrence, he probably did.

"Hey there, neighbor," he said.

"Lawrence," she replied flatly.

"If there was an empty seat, I'd keep you company." At that very moment, the guy next to her stood up. Lawrence smiled. "Looks like my lucky day."

Cathy put her bag on the seat as a deterrent. "I'm meeting someone. He'll be here any minute."

Lawrence was still hovering nearby, cheering with the other patrons at the bar to whatever sports event was on. Cathy checked the time. A few minutes turned into fifteen, then forty-five—still no sign of her Mr. Plume.

Another text from Beatrice: *Freddy stormed out! All men are babies!*

Truthfully, Cathy was glad that Beatrice's tryst with Freddy at the Plaza had not gone as planned. She still wanted Beatrice to meet her father.

She was about to text back when a tall blonde wearing a Jets jersey entered. A man who looked like Captain Kangaroo with muttonchops, who'd been standing next to Lawrence the whole time, introduced himself to the blonde.

"You must be Cathy," he said. "Your father told me all about you. And you were certainly worth the wait."

Lawrence put his arm around the blonde. "No, she's with me. I'm Lawrence, a friend of Cathy's. Nice to meet you."

"And where may I ask is Cathy?"

Cathy wished she could disappear. "This is me," she said from the barstool.

There was a brief look of disappointment, then he said, "Well. Let's find a table, shall we?"

The waiter brought them special Travelzoo menus because Captain Kangaroo had a discount coupon. All through dinner, while he droned on about his two grown daughters, his split-level in Teterboro, and his tax certiorari firm, his cheeks growing even more chipmunk-like as he inhaled several onion rolls, she kept stealing glances at Lawrence and the blonde. They were sitting on the same side of an adjacent booth. She wondered if they were siblings. They seemed familiar with each other, relaxed and laughing and sharing food from each other's plates. But then she kissed him. Nope, definitely *not* his sister. Not even Angelina Jolie and her brother kissed like that.

Beatrice texted with an update: *Just took a bath in a tub with a 24 karat gold faucet. If you think I'm doing that hand mirror exercise, you have another thing coming!*

Cathy knew exactly which exercise Beatrice was referring to. She had no intention of doing it either. Naturally, she'd also skipped the self-pleasuring exercise. She couldn't even say the word *vulva* above a whisper and the last thing she wanted to do was look at . . . IT with a magnifying mirror!

Her phone vibrated again. Captain Kangaroo was talking so much that he didn't seem to notice that she had her phone in her lap and had been texting Beatrice since the waiter had taken their orders.

Has he stopped talking yet?

Nope, he can eat and talk at the same time.

Incroyable!

He signaled for the waiter. "More rolls, please."

Cathy stifled a laugh with her napkin. She sent another text to Beatrice but from then on it was radio silence.

After dessert, the waiter brought the bill and two mints, which her date quickly pocketed. He tallied the check using a small calculator on the front flap of his wallet.

"Let's see. Your share comes to $22.95 plus tax. With tip, that'll be $27.50. It would have been less if you hadn't ordered the fries à la carte."

She looked through her purse. "I don't have any change."

"Don't worry, just round up."

She cringed as he wrapped the extra dinner rolls in a napkin. Then she got another text, but not from Beatrice. This one was from Lawrence: *Halloween party, my house Saturday night! I'm going as Charles Lindbergh. Would you be my Amelia Earhart?*

She snapped her phone shut. So much for signs and synchronicities. Sometimes a feather is just a feather.

CHAPTER SIXTEEN
HANGMAN

EMILY LAY ON DUNCAN'S UNMADE BED reading submissions just as she had every day for the past two weeks, while he worked at his rolltop desk. She was wearing jeans and a black bra. Invariably, the rest of her clothes would be off by lunchtime.

Even though every book on divorce recommended not introducing children to a new romantic partner too early, Emily was ready for Duncan and Zach to meet. It wasn't the length of time they'd been together; it was the depth of commitment, and the relationship felt on very sure footing.

After a "long" lunch, Duncan glanced up from his computer. "May I read something to you?"

Emily got out of bed and wrapped herself in a patterned blue sheet with bamboo flowers. She sat on Duncan's lap while he read her the op-ed he'd written for the *Times*.

"I've been neglecting you," he said, caressing her with one hand, while scrolling to the next paragraph with the other. "You've only come once today."

After leaving Duncan's, she stopped at the health food store for some Duncan-approved ingredients, then went straight to Alice's. She'd been meaning to go back for Cathy's book, but kept forgetting. Justin and Stevie were behind the counter. Apricot was dressed like Pagliacci, hat and all. *The Love Book* was next to a display of beautifully decorated cakes.

Emily flipped through the pages. "Did either of you find a letter?" Her fingers were already stained red.

Stevie was putting a tray of fresh scones into the display case. She looked up. "I didn't, did you, Justin?"

"No, but we'll be on the lookout."

If only she hadn't written the letter to Charles in the first place.

"Would you like a cup of tea?" Justin asked. "Silver Needle Jasmine, right?" Emily nodded. He filled a tea filter with loose tea leaves. "You know, that *Love Book* is voodoo!"

"What do you mean?" Emily asked.

"Freaky things have been happening."

Emily fumbled in her bag for a pen and notepad.

"The day you left it, I read the introduction and out of the blue my ex calls and wants to talk. Then three guys tried to pick me up at Whole Foods. The same exact thing happened to Stevie. Her boyfriend pleaded with her to take him back. I told another friend about the book, she orders it, and that *very* day she bumps into her first love! Men are coming out of the woodwork. I just happen to be a little pickier than some other people," he said, winking at Stevie.

Emily had been experiencing something similar, but she was still skeptical. Of course, there was Duncan; and the security guard at Zach's school who brought her homemade pastries; and the man behind her at Ansonia Station who chased her down with a bouquet of irises; and the deli guy who'd never even smiled at her before and was now suddenly offering her free coffee and Hungarian lessons. The Law of Attraction at work? Perhaps, but there was also that small niggly detail named Charles, whom she couldn't seem to shake. There didn't seem to be any rhyme or reason. It was more like flypaper than enchantment. But what remained even more of a mystery was the author of *The Love Book,* whose identity seemed cloaked in a secrecy matched only by the witness protection program. She hadn't received a single response to her daily Twitter queries.

"I never realized I was in shortage mentality," Justin said. "I used to tell myself all the good ones were taken, I'm too chubby, I'm not tall enough, I work in a teashop for minimum wage. What*ever*! But it's really true; love is like oxygen. There's a limitless supply. I'm going to see if it works with money!"

"How did you leave things with Daniel?" Emily asked.

"It's over, but we cleared the air. Who needs to hold onto anger? Like Buddha says: it's like drinking poison and expecting the other person to die."

When Emily returned home she found a registered letter from a Park Avenue white-shoe law firm demanding that Charles's name be removed as guarantor on the proprietary lease before the end of the fiscal year. Buddha was describing Charles in a nutshell!

She was preparing dinner when Zach came into the kitchen, which meant he was probably hungry.

"Who's Duncan?" he asked. "And what kind of name is Duncan anyway? Does he own a donut store?"

"No, silly," she said, ruffling his hair. Charles had taken him to his Italian barber again, and now he looked like a mini Charles with faux sideburns. He had even started using gel when he combed his hair in the morning. "He's a writer friend of Mommy's. You'll like him."

"No, I won't."

"Just give him a chance."

"When is he going to be here?"

"In about an hour."

"Are there any pizza bagels left?"

"No, I'll pick some up tomorrow." She gave him a plastic Winnie-the-Pooh bowl full of pistachios to tide him over.

"Mom, I'm not a baby."

"I know," she said. "It's just a bowl. How about a hug, ladybug?"

He poured the pistachios into an NFL cup, grabbed a turquoise Gatorade he'd talked her into buying after soccer practice the other day, and said, "Peace out, Mom."

He returned a few minutes later with a pillowcase full of Beanie Babies. "I don't want these anymore."

"But you love them," she said.

"Mom? Beanie Babies?"

Emily rescued Princess Diana and the "Road Hog" squirrel with the leather jacket. The rest she stashed in the linen closet where she kept crumbling rolls of Zach's paintings from nursery school. The only "toy" that remained on the loft was the talking Yoda. Oracles, apparently, were grandfathered in.

Duncan arrived just before seven. "A rose for Emily," he said, handing a flower to her as if presenting it to the queen.

Zach came out of his room wearing a Knicks jersey and mesh shorts, dribbling a mini Georgetown basketball.

"Nice to meet you, young man," Duncan said, shaking his hand. "Do you play hoops?"

"Yup," Zach answered.

"What grade are you in?"

"Fifth. Can I have another Gatorade, Mom?"

"You drank the last bottle, sweetie."

"You don't want to drink that stuff, anyway," Duncan said. "It's just sugar, salt, and food coloring. Real athletes train hard and don't put junk into their bodies."

"My father drinks it and he played basketball in college."

"Really, where?" Duncan asked.

"Georgetown."

Zach was staring Duncan down. Emily wanted to take him aside and shake him. Charles had gone to Georgetown, played the occasional pickup game on weekends, but he wasn't a Hoya.

Emily had planned dinner on the terrace, but the wind was coming off the river and the napkins blew away, fluttering off like white doves. Zach was virtually silent through the entire meal, playing with his iPod Touch under the table. Duncan barely ate a thing, scraping the breading off his chicken cutlet and not even tasting the spinach soufflé.

"I used whole wheat breadcrumbs," she said.

"Look at the label. It's still processed."

"How come you dye your hair?" Zach suddenly asked.

Duncan dropped his fork and stared at the child with a look Emily had never seen before and could not interpret. "Don't be ridiculous!" he said in a strained voice.

Zach asked to be excused and cleared his plate and Emily's, but not Duncan's. He returned a little while later with a pad of paper. Pictionary? Tic-tac-toe? Maybe the evening could be salvaged. He smiled as he ripped off a sheet of paper and taped it to the sliding glass door.

On it, he had written: *I HATE DUNCAN.*

Luckily, Duncan was facing the opposite direction. She ripped the paper off the glass, and then chased Zach down the hall. She was wearing thick white socks and slipped as she rounded the corner. Zach slammed the door to his bedroom and secured the eye latch, but one good shove and she was inside.

"You are very lucky Duncan didn't see that. If you don't behave, you're grounded. From everything."

"I'll just go stay with Daddy."

"Even if it were your choice," she said, "which it isn't, I'll tell Daddy you're grounded there too."

"He never listens to you. Daddy's right, you only date losers."

"You don't even know him."

"I don't want you to go out with him."

"I'm the mother, and you're the child. That means that you don't get to decide these things."

"If you marry him I'm moving out."

If one of her friends had told her this story over tea, she

would have found it amusing, but she had so much invested in the evening going well that she couldn't hold back her tears. Zach had seen more than his fair share of tears, assumed the role of comforter more times than she cared to remember.

"All right, Mom," he said. "I'll play a game with him."

Emily tried to hug him, but he squirmed out of her arms.

Sitting on the arm of the couch as Zach drew a series of dashes on graph paper, Emily's heart felt full. She wished she'd been more understanding. It must be hard on a son to see his mother with a man who isn't his father.

The hangman was nearly complete. "Looks like you beat me fair and square," Duncan said.

"You still have more guesses," Zach prompted.

"I've always played with only six body parts."

"We always do the eyes, nose, and mouth. Sometimes ears and hair."

"Are those regulation rules?" Duncan asked.

Zach shrugged. "That's how we play."

"Okay, how about an N?"

"Good guess," Zach said, filling in two N's.

Emily leaned over to see if she could decipher the phrase: *I HATE D __ N __ __ N.*

She stood up. "Say goodnight, Zach."

"Mom! I was winning."

"Time for bed."

"Goodnight, young man," Duncan said. "Maybe we can throw the rock sometime."

"Yeah," he responded, feigning excitement, then muttered, "Not." He not only had Charles's haircut, he was acting like him too.

Duncan was scanning Emily's glass-fronted mission bookshelves and didn't look up when she returned to the living room. She and Charles had found the bookshelves at a flea market in Lambertville when they first moved in together. They'd restored and refinished them, replacing a few broken panes of glass, and filled the shelves with their newly merged book collections. Duncan was holding a copy of *Tess of the d'Urbervilles*. She couldn't remember to whom the book had originally belonged, her or Charles.

She stood next to him, put her hand in his back pocket. She hoped he hadn't overheard too much of the confrontation with Zach.

"That's one fine young man," he said, placing the book back on the shelf. "And so well behaved," he added, to Emily's relief, without a hint of sarcasm.

"Thank you. He gets that from his father."

After Duncan left, Adele Weisenbaum rang her bell. The timing was rather suspicious. Prepared to be grilled about the quirky but handsome man who had just left her apartment, she was surprised when Adele just said a curt, "This was delivered to me by mistake." She handed Emily a red envelope, sealed with a ladybug sticker, and slammed her door.

The envelope contained just a single sheet of onionskin paper. Written in a lovely old-fashioned script with a fountain pen was one sentence: *We are glad that our* Love Book *is in the hands of a fellow seeker.*

It was the first lead Emily had gotten. If only she knew where it was taking her.

C HAPTER SEVENTEEN
HOMECOMING

AFTER THE INCIDENT IN THE ELOISE SUITE, Beatrice didn't ever want to see Freddy again. But he'd called, sent flowers, apologized backward, forward, and sideways, and if people convicted of misdemeanors or Class D felons could seal their records, the least she could do was allow Freddy to appeal his case.

They'd met at the Oyster Bar in Grand Central for a half-dozen Bluepoints and two dry martinis before their 11:45 train to White River Junction, and, after slipping a five into the bartender's hand, two more martinis in to-go cups. Once in Hanover, right before the fifty-foot-high wooden structure was set ablaze on the quad, heralding the official opening of homecoming, she got a text from Emily.

Are you pinned yet?

No. Do you have a book deal yet?

She smiled. How had these four unlikely women become so bonded?

The bonfire was made of old railroad ties steeped in creosote, making it burn like mad. A fire truck was on hand just in case. The flames were so intense it looked like a rocket had just taken off as the incoming freshmen did laps around the green. She'd only worn a light shawl. The air was crisp, so Freddy offered her his jacket. Slipping her arms into the sleeves of his herringbone coat with the wide shoulders and smell of cherry pipe tobacco made her feel young again, cared for, protected, like her whole life lay ahead of her, not just a weekend together until Freddy's wife returned from her trip to Portland to visit the grandchildren.

"Remember skating on Occom Pond?" he asked. She nodded. "How about Winter Carnival 1957? When Malcolm and I had that sudden-death match? I'd say the stakes were pretty high then too."

Beatrice knew exactly which match he was talking about. The past seemed so close she could almost touch it. It was Valentine's Day, sophomore year. Beatrice's birthday. Freddy had been lacing up his hockey skates. Malcolm sat down next to him on the wooden bench. He was wearing a pair of well-worn hockey gloves. Freddy continued lacing his skates without looking up, as though Malcolm weren't there.

"Why don't we settle this with a little one-on-one while the ice is free? May the best man win."

Freddy had hesitated then reconsidered, unable to resist the challenge. He finished lacing his skates, removed the skate guards, and wiped the blades with a soft chamois. "Okay, you're on," he'd said, zipping up his jacket. He grabbed a stick from his equipment bag, then glided out onto the ice with the assurance of someone who'd been skating nearly as long as he could walk.

"Wa-hoo-wa," Malcolm said, knocking Freddy's stick with his.

"Yeah, wa-hoo-wa," Freddy said, returning the arcane Dartmouth expression, his eyes so fierce and piercing they looked as if they could cut ice.

They had played to the death, or so it seemed, as if it were a championship game and the entire season was riding on the outcome, only it was just the two of them, two brothers, alone, facing off on the ice. Neither Freddy nor Malcolm had noticed when Beatrice left the pond that night nearly fifty years ago, teetering along the wooden walkway on her white calfskin skates.

She'd let boys be boys. From the porch, she had watched as the two of them fell into that familiar rhythm of teammates, brothers able to anticipate each other's actions, moving in tandem even though they were adversaries competing for the same goal. She'd watched so many of their practice sessions, some in the middle of the night, depending on when the ice was free.

After the match, Freddy had swept her off her feet and spun her around. "The best man won."

But that was all ancient history. The bonfire was dying down. Beatrice pulled Freddy's jacket tighter around her. "What do you mean the stakes were high?"

"Nothing, Beatrice, nothing," Freddy said. "That was a long time ago, another lifetime. By the by, just in case anyone asks, we just 'happened' to run into each other."

"I'm not a ninny, Freddy. I know the drill."

"My no-nonsense gal."

He'd booked a room at the Hanover Inn—a non-themed room, he promised—and had made reservations for dinner at Jesse's Steakhouse. They were both serious carnivores, another thing besides no-fuss, no-muss relationships they had in common. He was glad she'd enjoyed the Eloise Suite, but he hadn't spoken to Malcolm since. It was childish, as if they were in grade school and Malcolm had put the key to Freddy's roller skates on the train tracks. Boys will be boys. Thank goodness she hadn't married him.

At Jesse's Steakhouse, Freddy and Beatrice followed the hostess to a booth in the back of the dimly lit tavern, conveniently located near the salad bar. They ordered steak, baked potatoes, and iceberg lettuce with blue cheese dressing. Freddy chose the wine, a nice pinot noir from a local winery. Beatrice liked a man who was concerned about his carbon footprint. Albert never recycled; he used to throw cans or empty bottles of single-malt scotch in with the regular garbage, mixing paper and plastic willy-nilly. Every day she'd fish bottles out of the trash, eggshells sticking to her hands, and even with her daily reminders, he still persisted in flouting the recycling laws. The funny thing was that after he died, she sort of missed his annoying habits, like finding his orange boxers and Gold Toe socks under the bed.

The waitress brought their salads. Freddy asked for olives and breadsticks. They were famished and quickly getting tipsy—they hadn't eaten anything since the Oyster Bar.

Freddy lifted his glass. "To us, my dear."

"Yes, to us. And to living like an oyster," she said. From the blank expression on his face she knew the reference to Flaubert's letter to George Sand had gone over his silver head. "How about to no strings attached!"

He reached across the table, taking her hand. "Actually, I wanted to talk to you about that."

The waitress set down a basket of bread and a ramekin of olives. Freddy waited for her to leave before continuing.

"I kind of like the idea of string," he said. "I was even thinking I like the idea of eventually tying a knot in that string."

"Well, cut it out!" she responded, laughing at her pun.

"Cut it out? Why? I thought you'd be happy."

"You're married, for one thing," she said.

"Married in name only. Muriel and I haven't been—how shall I say?—*intimate*, for the last few years."

"But you *are* married and if you want to keep seeing me, I suggest you stay that way."

"I don't understand, Beatrice. You and I were engaged. Now that Mother isn't here to object, I thought that's what you wanted."

"I never said that. You have a life, children, obligations. I'm not looking to get encumbered."

"Beatrice, be sensible."

"I'm the only one being sensible."

Freddy snapped a breadstick in half. "I'm too old to be

sneaking around. How would it look? I'll make sure that Muriel is taken care of, if that's what you're worried about."

"I'm not worried about Muriel," she said. "I told you, no fuss, no muss."

"I assumed you were just being coy."

"I'm a straight shooter, Freddy. I thought you understood."

"Nothing I can do will change your mind?"

"Nope. I'm pretty set in my ways."

"I guess we have nothing more to discuss then."

"Guess not," she agreed.

Freddy shoved a large green olive into his mouth, as if putting a stopper in a bottle, and poured himself another glass of wine, but left her glass empty. Their steaks arrived. He tucked his napkin into his collar and began to eat in stony silence. She tried to make polite conversation, but he was still pouting and pretended not to hear, so she gave up. She asked him to pass the pepper. After the third time, he finally pushed the pepper grinder toward her. How did they get from that feeling of safety she'd had watching the bonfire to this? From lovely to lousy in sixty seconds flat. She wasn't even sure that what she was saying about not wanting to get married was really how she felt or if it was merely a knee-jerk reaction, her automatic response to any situation that made her uncomfortable. She liked Freddy; in fact she might even love him. What she didn't like was feeling cornered. It was fight or flight. But what on earth was she afraid of?

No nonsense. That's how she liked it, or said she did. She thought of her decade-long affair with Albert, each successive year a carbon copy of the last, the intensity of their passion fading ever so slightly with each reproduction. But it was reliable, convenient, stable. Until his wife threw him out, calling Beatrice on a Sunday morning to tell her *she could have him!* He showed up at her row house, a lost Paddington Bear with his suitcase embossed with his initials, one of a matching set bought for his honeymoon. Six months later he was diagnosed with an inoperable brain tumor. She loved him, but she didn't want to care for him; she couldn't. Telling him to leave was the hardest thing she'd ever done.

"Freddy," she said now, her voice tender and soft, "it's a beautiful night. We're together. You planned a lovely weekend. Let's try to enjoy ourselves."

He smiled faintly and was about to speak, when all the blood suddenly drained out of his face and he broke out in a sweat. "I'm feeling a little . . . Can't catch my breath."

"Here, drink something." She reached for his hand and squeezed it. "I think we let things get out of hand."

He slid out of the booth, bracing himself on the table. "I'm going to splash some water on my face." He'd only taken two steps when he collapsed, his head hitting the floor with a clunk like a bowling ball.

"Freddy!" she shouted.

Then there was a blur of people rushing about. Freddy's body started to convulse. The manager arrived with a young bearded man wearing a Dartmouth-Hitchcock Medical Center fleece. The doctor checked Freddy's pulse and vital signs.

"Your husband has had a heart attack. I'm going to begin CPR until the paramedics arrive."

Beatrice felt like an interloper as she rode in the back of the ambulance to the hospital, a privilege only afforded to next of kin.

Beatrice hadn't known whom else to call when Freddy was taken to the hospital, except Malcolm. He told her not to worry; he'd be there before she knew it. Hanover was only two hours from Boston, but for Beatrice that wasn't soon enough. As she sat in the egregiously cheerful waiting area in this perfect soap opera–esque hospital with rolling hills, manicured grounds, and Stepford nurses, she felt a pit in her stomach. Had she caused this? The doctors said he'd had an "event," but that there had been no damage to his heart. She tried to be optimistic, pretended she was Cathy, but it was easier said than done. The only silver lining she could find was that Freddy's heart attack hadn't happened in flagrante delicto. Considering his prominence, the world didn't need another Nelson Rockefeller scandal splashed across the *Wall Street Journal.*

And then she saw Malcolm walking down the corridor, his cheeks flushed, wearing a blue hooded toggle coat and chinos. From a distance he could have been mistaken for an undergrad on his way to class, which gave her an immediate feeling of relief.

"I came as soon as I could," he said. "His doctor's been warning him about his high cholesterol for years. The stubborn old goat."

"So, the foie gras at "21" might not have been the best idea?" she said.

He laughed. "That's Freddy. He thinks he's invincible."

Malcolm brought her tea in a Styrofoam cup then went to talk to the ER doctor. Beatrice stared off into space, watching the steam swirl as if from a genie's lamp. A memory slowly surfaced: She was in a navy sailor suit and wide-brimmed hat sitting on a fence tangled with blackberry vines. She'd been waiting with the other kids for her mother to pick her up from the bus stop. She stayed there, as she did every day, until they'd all gone before walking the half-mile home alone. Her mother wouldn't return for another six months. She'd found a job in New York working for the Associated Press, an opportunity of a lifetime, and left Beatrice with her Aunt Sue in Oklahoma City. Poor little girl, Beatrice thought. If she were that little girl again, she wouldn't even want to speak to the Beatrice who was sitting in this soap opera hospital, still waiting for someone who would never show up. And to think, when she was at Alice's she hadn't thought there was anyone she needed to make amends to.

Malcolm was back and standing in front of her. It seemed

like only minutes had passed, but her tea was cold. Where had she been?

"Superman needs angioplasty," he explained. "It's scheduled for the morning."

"Oh my heavens!"

"Don't worry, Beatrice. Dartmouth has one of the best cardiac teams in the country."

After visiting hours were over, Malcolm drove Beatrice to the Hanover Inn. He inquired about vacancies, but it was homecoming weekend and the hotel had been booked for months.

"Gee, what are you going to do?" Beatrice asked.

"Spend the night at the hospital, I guess."

"Freddy booked us a suite," she said. "You're welcome to the couch."

"I couldn't," he demurred.

"At least come up for a glass of scotch. We have a bottle of nineteen-year-old St. Magdalene."

"Maybe just for one drink. It would be a crime to let that go to waste," he said.

Upstairs, Beatrice poured them each a dram. Once the scotch had "bloomed" and not a moment sooner, they would drink to Freddy's swift recovery. Truthfully, she didn't know which she had been looking forward to with more anticipation: consummating her affair with Freddy or tasting this exquisite and noble malt.

Malcolm placed a drop of spring water in each of their glasses and then lifted his. "Come hither, dear one. I've been waiting all my life for you. You are a thing to behold."

He was speaking to the scotch, of course. She followed suit with three long inhales, allowing the fragrance to envelop her.

"I didn't know my brother was such a connoisseur. He's usually a Dewar's kind of guy."

"He isn't. I brought the scotch."

"Perfection," he said, after taking his first tiny sip, then put down his glass. He looked as if he wanted to say something to her.

"What's on your mind, Malcolm?"

"Beatrice, may I talk to you, friend to friend?"

"I guess, if you must."

He took a deep breath. "Well, no sense beating around the bush. I know this is none of my business, but I think you should know that my brother is never going to give you what you want."

Beatrice sat up. "And what exactly do you think I want?"

"For him to marry you."

Her inner Betty Friedan bubbled to the surface. "Why does everyone assume that because at one time I had a uterus, all I want to do is get married? I'd rather be the woman a man wishes he were with than the one he wants to get away from."

"Are those really the only two choices? I was devoted to my wife Winnie, never looked at another woman. Don't you want your own special someone to share things with? Explore the world? Inspire you? Make you laugh? Hold you when you cry? Be there when you need him?"

"What does that have to do with marriage?"

"What I'm saying is Freddy already has that person."

The former DA was suddenly rendered uncharacteristically speechless. She'd never thought of it that way. She and Albert had had so many adventures together it hadn't occurred to her that anything was lacking, but had he been there when her mother died, or when she discovered she had to have a hysterectomy and would never bear children? No, he was with his wife and kids, where he belonged. She always thought that was the way she wanted it. It was fun and easy, an escape. But an escape from what? For him it was from the woman who kept his home and raised his children, cried when their grandchildren were born. Who lay next to him each night, who loved him despite his philandering. Who let him go, then took him back when he was dying because Beatrice hadn't wanted to deal with it. Why would any man leave that?

"I don't judge, Beatrice, but I know my brother. Don't you think you deserve more?"

Malcolm wound up dozing off on the armchair, sleeping like a baby, while Beatrice tossed and turned in the bedroom. She'd had no answer to his question. It was true. When Freddy had offered more to her, she'd pushed it away. It wasn't because she didn't think she deserved more. It was because she didn't think she could give more.

Freddy's procedure didn't begin until well into the following afternoon. It was some sort of robot-assisted surgery done through an artery in the groin, a routine procedure, but it was taking longer than anticipated. Beatrice hadn't planned on going to the hospital. She hated hospitals and didn't want to be there when Freddy's wife arrived. But Malcolm said her flight from Oregon had been canceled because of bad weather in Chicago and wouldn't be arriving until tomorrow. The doctors put in three stents, noninvasively, but he'd be in the hospital for two or three days.

Once visiting hours were over, Malcolm drove Beatrice back to the Hanover Inn. He went to park the car and Beatrice secured two seats at the bar. She ordered cornmeal-dusted fried calamari and pork belly sliders. While she was waiting, she reread an email she'd gotten from Cathy. She was still trying to figure out what the devil she meant by it: *All sins are attempts to fill voids. —Simone Weil*

She was about to respond, but ordered a double scotch instead. Twenty minutes passed and still no Malcolm. What could be keeping him? She hoped Freddy hadn't taken a turn for the worse. She went to see if he was waiting for her in the lobby.

A woman with wavy red hair was at the concierge desk. "I'd like the key to Freddy McBride's room."

"I'm sorry, I can't do that," the concierge said.

"You can't give me the key to my husband's room?"

"Both keys are out, ma'am. And I'm afraid we're completely booked."

Malcolm entered, and was crossing the carpeted lobby. The moment he saw the woman at the desk, he rushed over. "Muriel!"

They embraced. "Oh Malcolm! I was so worried. How is he?"

"He's going to be fine, no need to worry."

"Malcolm, this woman says I can't get the key to Freddy's room."

"That's our room," he said.

"*Our?*"

He waved Beatrice over. "Come, Beatrice, don't be shy. Let me introduce you." She reluctantly obliged. She had never been a shrinking violet, but this seemed beyond awkward. Malcolm put his arm around her. "Muriel, this is my paramour, Beatrice. We came for homecoming."

Muriel smiled. She had a pretty smile. Under different circumstances, they probably would have been friends. She looked a little worn after the cross-country journey and was about fifteen pounds overweight, but her avoirdupois did not diminish her attractiveness, perhaps even enhanced it.

"Malcolm could use a woman in his life," she said. "I can vouch for the McBride brothers, except they're as stubborn as mules. The doctor's been telling Freddy to go on statin drugs for years and now look!" She hid her face in her hands. "Sorry, it's been a long day. I've been worried sick. I just need to lie down. But there're no rooms."

"We have a suite, Muriel," Malcolm said. "With a very comfortable pullout couch. Come, let me carry your bags."

Beatrice went back to the bar and downed her double scotch, fortification for another sleepless night in Hanover.

CHAPTER EIGHTEEN
FERTILE GROUND

EMILY AND DUNCAN WERE SPENDING the weekend at his agent's country house in New Hope. It was the first time since the divorce that the thought of an entire weekend without Zach didn't seem like a bottomless pit. She knew she was way ahead of herself but she tried to imagine where Duncan's rolltop desk would fit in her apartment, or hers in his. It wasn't logical. Charles was logical, methodical, systematic, and it had driven her crazy. He read manuals cover to cover. But logic wasn't always applicable in matters of love.

That morning, she'd just finished her daily blog when the phone rang. She had a moment of panic, thinking it was Duncan calling to cancel.

"Mrs. Andrews? This is Apthorp Pharmacy."

Her doctor had called in a prescription for birth control. The automated system probably hadn't recorded her payment information.

"Yes, just a minute," she said. "I'll go get my credit card."

"No need. I'm calling to say your infertility treatments have been approved by your health insurance."

"Infertility treatments? My doctor called in birth control."

"This is Clarissa Andrews, isn't it?"

"No, *Emily* Andrews."

"I'm sorry," the pharmacist said. "Your number is still listed under Mr. Andrews's account."

Clarissa Andrews? Since when had Clarissa started using Charles's name? Had they gotten married? Zach would have said something, wouldn't he? Suddenly Charles's snit about her not packing Zach's blazer a few weeks ago made sense.

She'd already hung up before she could ask if her own prescription was ready.

Duncan's agent lived in a stone house built before the Revolutionary War with small paned windows, shutters, and wide plank floors. The walls were painted authentic colonial colors in keeping with historical records—Meeting House blue, Yarmouth Oyster, Shaker red. And lots and lots of pewter. It reminded her of a trip she and Charles had taken to Colonial Williamsburg except for the stacks of manuscripts and books written by Estelle's clients, most of whom, as in Duncan's case, were like family to her. Emily's heart felt full as though a new world were opening up to her. For the first time, she felt she was standing beyond the velvet ropes.

Estelle and her husband Claude made Emily feel so welcome, kissing her on both cheeks and expressing their approbation to Duncan. They sat in the summer kitchen at a long pine table. Claude poured the wine. The meal was lavish, and definitely not period: *choucroute*, bouillabaisse, cheese puffs (*gougères*, Duncan corrected her), and a perfect *tarte Tatin* which Duncan consumed with uncharacteristic gusto, never once asking for the list of ingredients in the crust.

Then began Emily's very polite interrogation. Where did she do her doctoral work? Had she read Julian Barnes's novel? Oh, she hadn't? But wasn't she writing about Flaubert? When she answered that she didn't have a doctorate but that she'd seen both of Flaubert's "real" parrots in Rouen, they tried another tack. What was she reading? When she told them she was re-reading *Pride and Prejudice*, they looked at her as if she was a precocious little child allowed to sit with the grownups for the first time. Duncan's last girlfriend, a Swedish professor of semiotics who had just received a Guggenheim and was living with a baroness in Italy, was mentioned as often as the wine glasses were refilled. *Say, how is the beautiful Petra? Did her agent sell the foreign rights at Frankfurt? I heard she was planning on completing her novel at Wissenschaftskolleg in Berlin. Tell her she either has to come back for Christmas or divulge her secret recipe for* vörtbröd.

Ordinarily, it would have made Emily shrink into less-than-ness, barely holding onto her sense of self, especially when she found out that Petra had not only been Duncan's live-in girlfriend, she'd been his student. But his fingers tracing the inside of her wrist made it all disappear, the way little things, like a pink toothbrush on the vanity in his cluttered bathroom, or eyeliner in the medicine cabinet, could be easily edited out like a stray comma.

"Emily has a book," he said, taking her hand. "Mark my word, it will be a stunning debut."

Estelle smiled too sweetly as she passed a plate of *petits fours.* "Do you have representation?"

"No, I'll just be happy if anyone wants it," Emily said.

Duncan leaned forward, elbows on the table. "What Emily means is that it will be making the rounds soon."

While Estelle and her husband were in the kitchen making espressos, Duncan chided her. "Don't ever do that again."

"Do what?"

"Act like a beggar. You'll just be happy if anyone wants it? No true professional would say something like that."

"I was just being honest," she said.

"In this business you have to promote yourself. You have to make them beg for a chance to see your book, not the other way around."

"But I've only written one chapter."

He shook his head. "Sometimes you make me feel like I'm wasting my time. It's like pissing into a violin."

After dinner they sat in the living room, the oldest part of the house, a former tavern. Emily's cell phone began blaring: "*Pick up the phone, pick up the phone, pick up the phone.*" Zach had personalized her ringtone again without telling her. Estelle and Claude smiled politely while she fumbled in her bag, then excused herself and found a quiet spot to take the call.

"Zach, is something wrong?" she asked.

"Daddy wants you to pick me up at ten on Sunday. He has a meeting."

"I thought he was taking you to the game."

"He says he can't."

Emily looked over at Duncan, who was standing by the fireplace talking to Claude, his elbow on the mantel. She was disappointed that they'd have to cut their weekend short, Duncan would be too, but he would understand. It was her son. And there would be many more weekends like this together.

"Well, can you, Mom?"

"Yes, sweetie, tell Daddy it's fine."

"He says don't be late. Gotta go. We just ordered Chinese."

When she told Duncan she had to be back early, he didn't take it quite the way she'd thought he would.

"Why the sudden change of plans?"

"My ex-husband has a meeting."

"Oh, I see. And you're the good little ex-wife who's supposed to jump when he says jump?" He began pacing. "Who's in charge here? You or your ex-husband? I won't be held hostage to some corporate dweeb's whims."

Her first instinct was to defend Charles, but she knew it wouldn't go over too well. "I didn't think this would upset you," she said.

"You didn't think? Unbelievable! Don't you realize you're teaching people to disrespect you? If you don't stand up to bullies they'll walk all over you. And I don't want to be with a doormat."

Estelle and Claude were doing their best to pretend not to listen.

"What can I do to fix things?" she asked.

"Nothing. You made your choice. You have your priorities."

The next day they went to the farmers' market for fresh eggs and kayaked on the Delaware River, a perfect Saturday afternoon, but the mood was cool to say the least. Emily made a Dutch baby with caramelized apples, hoping it would be a palliative, but Duncan, who devoured Estelle's crêpes, wouldn't even take a bite.

In bed that night, however, he seemed in a much more conciliatory mood. "I think I know what can fix things," he said.

After an hour of acrobatics in the creaky canopy bed, she was more than ready for the final act, without which it would be akin to sitting through fifteen hours of Wagner's Ring Cycle without Brünnhilde's final immolation. It almost made her nostalgic for Charles's drive-through quickies. But Duncan was passionate and intuitive, the most generous lover she'd ever known. And a brilliant man. He blamed his inability to climax on the condom she'd insisted he use. Despite this, Emily was sure everything with Duncan would sort itself out, given enough time and patience, and she had both in abundance. They were connected on so many levels, she was certain they could overcome any obstacle.

Emily made arrangements for Zach to spend the day at a friend's house so she and Duncan didn't have to cut their weekend short after all, her way of repairing things. But Duncan spent the entire ride on his cell phone anyway, so she wondered why she'd even bothered.

She picked Zach up around five and they walked down a leaf-strewn Riverside Drive. At a red light, she tried to engage him in conversation but he only gave one-word replies. She didn't want to press him about Charles and Clarissa getting married, but it worried her that he kept so much inside. It had been the same with the divorce.

"Are you excited that basketball season is starting soon?" she asked.

"Mom," he said, as if she were the dumbest person in the world, "there's a lockout."

"I guess I haven't been keeping up with sports lately. So, what are you going to be for Halloween?"

"Halloween's for babies," he replied, then raced ahead on his silver scooter as soon as the light changed. He waited for her to catch up. "Can we go into the park? Jake taught me a cool trick."

It was getting dark, but he looked at her with that pleading expression she could never resist, the one that kept her reading him book after book when he was little despite it being way past his bedtime.

"Okay," she said.

"Cool. You're not going to believe it!"

The park was practically empty, just a few dog walkers and runners. Zach led the way down the cobblestoned path to the Soldiers' and Sailors' Monument.

"Stand over there. You'll have the best view," he said.

"Where's the hill?" she asked.

"No hill. I'm going to stair bash."

"Oh no you're not."

"I did it with Jake. I'm wearing a helmet."

It felt like yesterday when he'd toppled head first from the top of a slide. She'd cried more than he had as she'd rushed him to the doctor. Charles said she was overprotective. She was one of the few parents who still dropped off and picked up their kids. She knew she had to let him grow up sometime. Was sometime now?

"Please, Mom? I'll be careful."

She hesitated. "Okay, but promise you'll go slow."

Zach was perched at the top of the curved stone steps waiting for a slow-moving golden retriever and its corpulent owner to pass, when her heart began to race. She must be out of her mind to let him do this.

"Zach, stop."

"Why?"

"I don't want you to get hurt."

"You said I could."

"I changed my mind."

Zach threw his helmet to the ground, reminding her of the time Charles flung his briefcase into the street during an argument. She had a sudden flash of awareness: if she didn't do something, Zach might grow up to be a suit-wearing, briefcase-throwing man just like his father. But he wasn't Charles and she wouldn't let him pretend to be.

"That may work with your father," she said, "but not with me. Now pick up your helmet and let's go."

They walked the rest of the way home in silence.

Kalman was helping an elderly tenant out of a taxi as they approached the building. "Mr. Andrews is waiting for you," he said.

"Mr. Andrews?"

At the far end of the lobby Charles was sitting on a long wooden bench beside a large duffel bag.

"Dad?" Zach said. "Am I going to your house tonight?"

"No, Zachary, I was just walking by and thought I'd bring you a treat." He held out a small white bag.

"Watermelon gumballs! Awesome!"

Emily knew there was more to this impromptu visit than gumballs. "Zach, will you check the mailbox for me?" She waited until he'd scooted off then turned to Charles. "Is something wrong? Is it your mother?"

Charles wasn't one to show his emotions—he hadn't even

cried at his father's funeral—and this was the closest she'd ever seen him come to losing it.

"What is it?" she asked again.

"Clarissa threw me out."

Emily waited for the inevitable onslaught of blame. Somehow this, like everything, would be construed as her fault—she'd phoned one too many times, or Clarissa had found out about the mix-up with the pharmacy, or Charles had accidentally called her Emily (*that* scenario, she even found slightly amusing), but he just stood there silently, his arms heavy at his sides, staring at the floor.

Zach returned with a bundle of letters under his arm. "Speedy delivery! There's something for you, Dad." Emily had been hoping another red envelope would be among the letters, but just more bills. Zach scooted over to the elevator and pressed the button. "Mom, is it okay if Dad comes up? I want to show him my new Madden game."

Emily hadn't seen Charles unshaven since the summer after he graduated law school when they spent six months in Israel. After they returned to the States, he asked her to marry him. It was hard to see the old Charles—the adventurous, socially conscious, slightly dangerous one she knew when she was in grad school—in the man standing before her now.

"Can he, Mom?" Zach asked again.

Charles's eyes were ringed with shadows, his mouth tight. He'd had the same expression four years ago under the bare wisteria arbor when they told Zach they were separating. At the time she'd interpreted it as a lack of emotion, but now she wondered if it wasn't the opposite. He had too much emotion and was trying to contain it like a pressure cooker, the only way he knew how. If she couldn't extend herself for Charles, the father of her child, at least she could do it for Zach.

"Okay," she said. "And if he wants, he can even stay for dinner."

Like the flicker of a lightning bug, Charles's eyes brightened, unguarded, hopeful, relieved.

As they rode the elevator, Zach was talking a mile a minute. "Hey, Dad, can you help me with my math homework? And after dinner can we play catch?"

"Sure, Zach."

"And then watch the game?"

"I don't know, you have to ask your mom."

"Mom?"

"It's a school night, Zach. You know the rules."

Emily prepared herself for the *jawohl*, but instead Charles said, "Mommy's right. Don't you have a big game tomorrow?"

"With our archenemy. Can you come?"

Emily waited for Zach's crestfallen face. Charles hadn't made a single game this year or last, giving the usual excuses about work, an important meeting. She was always left to pick up the pieces. *He loves you, Zach. He'd be there if he could.*

But Charles surprised them both by putting his arm around his son and pulling him close. "I'll be there," he said as the elevator opened at their floor. "Tomorrow and every single game from now on."

Zach fell asleep before halftime. Charles carried him to bed then went to the front hall and put on his coat. Emily was in her pajamas and had pulled her hair up into a ponytail. She was wearing her glasses. She'd tried Duncan's cell at least a dozen times. Each time her call went to voice mail, her anxiety ratcheted up another notch. She felt like she was sinking with nothing to hold onto.

"Five thirty on Wednesday, right?" she asked, as if reading from a script.

He shrugged. "If I have a place for him to sleep."

Charles's first apartment after they separated had been a furnished studio with a Murphy bed, a small cot for Zach, an efficiency kitchen, and a huge spa-like marble bathroom. The first night Zach slept there, he'd cried and wanted to come home.

"Please talk to him, Emily," Charles had said when he called. "He asked me if we were orphans."

Nothing she said could stop Zach from crying.

"We're ruining his life," Charles had said when he brought Zach home twenty minutes later. She reminded him that he was the one who'd left, which was technically true, though she'd made it impossible for him to stay.

"Where are you going to go?" she asked him now. "Your brother's?"

"I don't want the whole family to know."

"A hotel?"

"I guess," he said, his shoulders slumping.

The same force that had initially prevented her from being kind in the lobby rose up again. It felt like the poles of two magnets repelling each other. Her default response would have been to bait him into a confrontation. She thought of that weekend in Vermont when she'd sent him away after he'd driven half the day to see her.

She got a blanket out of the linen closet. "The top bunk is made up. You can take Zach to school in the morning."

Charles looked as though she'd just thrown him a life preserver. One night. It was the least she could do. When she heard his electric toothbrush whirring, her body tensed just as it had when they were husband and wife.

C HAPTER NINETEEN
SNOW JOB

CATHY HAD BEEN LOOKING FORWARD to this weekend for months. *From Me to We: Manifesting Your Man!* The workshop of workshops where she would finally find the key. The only downside: it was at a yoga retreat in the Berkshires. A vegan yoga retreat. But the former Brownie believed in always being prepared and what this situation required was an electric teakettle and enough freeze-dried food for a mission to Mars: beef stroganoff with noodles, chicken à la king, scrambled eggs with bacon, Neapolitan ice cream, and low-fat Laughing Cow cheese. She'd lived off the stuff in college after discovering it not only survived, but improved, sans refrigeration. She wondered if NASA knew. She'd also bought a Garmin, because the salesperson told her she could download the voice of the navigator and David Hasselhoff was free! Next Monday Sean was giving a fire safety assembly at her school. Talk about a conspiring universe! She was long overdue for a personal day.

With David Hasselhoff at the helm, charting the course, she felt secure that she wouldn't get lost or wind up behind a herd of cows. And unlike that French GPS lady, he never snapped at her or made her feel inferior. Virtual or not, he was the only man in her life at the moment besides her father whom she could depend on.

That morning, she'd sent e-vites to Beatrice, Max, and Emily: *Soul Mate Soirée Skating Party! 11/11/11!*

It was an auspicious once-in-a-century event. A perfect day to get married. No bridegroom would ever forget his anniversary, not that she intended to wait another hundred years to walk down the aisle again.

Beatrice was the only one who'd responded so far. *I think SOS is more like it.*

Cathy was still puzzling over the statement from her home owner's insurance company. Her policy hadn't covered all the damage to the house from the fire, after all. Somehow, there was a $2,500 discrepancy. But when she called the contractor, he told her the balance had been paid in full. Was it the universe giving her a helping hand? When she inquired further he said a tall man, who he'd assumed was her husband, wearing a fireman's windbreaker, had dropped off a check. Lawrence Weiner! He'd try every which way from Tuesday to smooth her over and get into her pants, even resorting to surreptitiously paying her bills!

One thing Sean had been right about was that she'd been very lucky. Aside from extensive water and smoke damage, which had necessitated removing the wall-to-wall carpeting, the only structural repair that had to be done was to the roof rafters and the floor joists in the attic. But most of her personal possessions had been lost. Her soul mate altar, once a shrine to love, was a pile of embers. Gone were the fifty-three Buddhas she'd bought at the Antique Mall and the seventy-five different varieties of incense (although that certainly made for an interesting fire). The seven chakra candles that she religiously lit every morning and night had melted in the heat and looked like squashed dwarfs. Angel ornaments, fairies, and vintage valentines were reduced to ash, hovering like the "black butterflies" of Madame Bovary's wedding bouquet after she'd thrown it in the fire. The only objects that survived were a few seashells, associated with mermaid energy, a tile mandala she'd made at a Nichiren Daishonin workshop she'd thought was a cult, and a

VHS cassette of *The Lake House,* a movie that made her yearn
to be loved the way Keanu Reeves loved Sandra Bullock and
cry so hard Mrs. Beasley went into hiding for three days. The
video had melted like a chocolate bar left on the dashboard, but
somehow was still playable.

She'd spent days cleaning the soot and charred debris from
her soul mate altar. She'd polished the marble with baking soda
and powdered chalk until it gleamed like new. The slate had
been wiped clean. Luckily, Buddhas were a dime a dozen and
her soul mate altar would be cluttered up in no time. Among the
debris she found a silver dollar, which she took as a propitious
sign, a symbol of her desire that her soul mate be financially sol-
vent. She had put it in her purse as a kind of talisman, but then
ended up accidently throwing it into a tollbooth basket.

The first time she had walked through the house after the
fire she'd been shocked by the damage. She was disoriented, as
if she were on an ocean liner in rough seas with nothing to hold
onto. The ground was shifting beneath her. Her shoes echoed
off the hardwood floor, now stripped of carpeting.

Of course, when she'd looked out the window on that first
visit, whom did she see walking up the driveway but Lawrence,
wearing a terry sweatband and jogging shorts as though just
back from a run. Didn't he realize he'd never get anywhere with
her?

Before knocking, he looked up at the roof. Who did he think
he was? The fire marshal? He was still the same kid from fifth
grade who'd brought his father's miner's helmet for show-and-tell.

"Just came by to give you moral support," he said, peering
inside. "Looks pretty bad. Are you going to use an ozone generator for the smoke?"

"My insurance won't cover it."

"Sealers can be just as effective. But not oil-based; make
sure you use shellac. It's thin, so you can use a cheapo sprayer,
but I think you'd be wise to spend a little more and rent a com-

pressor. If you need an extra hand, I'm a gun for hire. A sprayer gun," he added, just in case the reason she hadn't laughed was because she didn't get the joke. "Gorgeous floors, by the way. I love old-growth eastern white pine. Who'd have guessed it was under that old shag carpeting?"

The sun was going down. Cathy was grateful for David Hasselhoff's soothing and confident voice guiding her, but she wished he was there in the flesh when she pulled into a sketchy-looking gas station. She hated self-service stations, another good thing about New Jersey. The clerk gave her a creepy look when she went inside to pay. She was definitely not going to ask for the key to the ladies' room. She reached for a tin of Altoids when she sensed a guy leering at her from the greeting card section. Who buys greeting cards at a gas station? He looked kind of familiar. Had she seen him on *America's Most Wanted*? He was wearing pleated blue Dockers (a questionable choice), but nothing says mental patient like a pair of brown slip-on crepe-soled shoes. He was still staring at her when she hurried out the door without her Altoids.

When she arrived at the yoga retreat, a blond guy at the front desk told her that the workshop had been canceled.

"Drat!" she said. "I've been looking forward to it for months. How come?"

"There's a freak snowstorm predicted and the presenter couldn't fly in. There's room in the Rumi workshop if you're interested."

"Thanks, but I have vertigo," she said. "Besides, it sounds a little out there."

He laughed. "I'm going to upgrade you to the wellness package. You get a complimentary massage. Dahval, our best Ayurvedic massage therapist, has time tomorrow morning. He's amazing. You'll feel like you died and went to heaven."

What was it about this area that kept putting up roadblocks

and making it impossible to leave? Two weeks ago it had been a herd of cows and now a freak October snowstorm. It must be a sign. She should be home in New Jersey, where she belonged, where cows were on packages of cheese, not roaming the streets, and even if there was a freak snowstorm, the snowplows would have it cleared by afternoon.

She reminded herself that all obstacles are for the best, but as she walked the Spartan halls—passing a roomful of hippies wearing saris and spinning as fast as dervishes—to her small white room with a single cot, a tiny sink in the corner, and no lock on the door, even she didn't believe it. The last thing she remembered before falling asleep was thinking the blinking red light of the smoke alarm was a firefly.

She awoke the next morning to the pleasant sound of a muted gong. She hadn't felt this rested in weeks. Starving, after two failed attempts at rehydrating eggs, she went to the dining room for a silent vegan breakfast. There was a talking dining room, but no one was in it so it defeated the purpose.

She had an hour before her complimentary massage, just enough time to take a dip in the Jacuzzi. Luckily, she'd brought her Miraclesuit. The salesperson at the Paramus Park Mall said that not only would it completely change her body, it would change her life. And so far, body-wise at least, it seemed to be living up to its promise, sucking, lifting, and reallocating what resources she had into a semblance of the desired hourglass shape. She noticed a *Clothing Optional* sign and was thankful, as she demurely shed her towel and climbed down the metal steps into the hot bubbling water, that it was single sex.

Two well-endowed naked women were lamenting the lack of quality men at the yoga retreat. Ordinarily she would have chimed in, but the sight of belly-flopping breasts on the water made her feel like keeping to herself.

"This is a bust," the blond one said.

"Yeah, tell me about it. I took a class at the Learning An-
nex on how to meet rich men. They recommended going to the
races, charity events, Christie's—but don't raise your paddle or
you'll go home with a Picasso. They told me to dye my hair red
and move to Fort Myers. That's where the highest concentration
of rich single men live."

"Did you meet any?"

The redhead leaned back on her elbows and laughed. "I
don't like rich men. I want an intelligent, faithful man. But I
already know where to find one of those: at the planetarium.
They're cosmic. But you have to burn all their clothes."

Cathy thought of Lawrence. Burning all of his sweater vests
and high-tech parachute pants might violate EPA standards.

A few minutes later she was escorted to a small room lit by
candles for her massage. A jar of Sole Mate callus cream was all
she needed to know for certain that a conspiring universe had
led her there. She undressed and slid under a soft white sheet,
lying facedown on the warm padded massage table.

The door opened. She felt a current of air move around her.
"*Namaste*. I'm Dahval."

"This is my first massage," she told him. "Not counting
those vibrating chairs at the Short Hills Mall."

"Close your eyes and relax. You're in good hands."

She flinched when Dahval touched her. At least she'd kept
her underwear and bra on, and Spanx underwear was heavy
duty. She tried Embracing the New Okay, an exercise in *The
Love Book*, to not judge her feelings, rather to accept the fact
that it was "okay" that things were not okay. It was "okay" that
she was nervous and that she felt like running out of the room.
It was "okay" that a stranger was unhooking her bra. It was
"okay" that his hands were touching places no man had ventured in years. And the reason it was "okay" (and this was by
far the most challenging aspect for her to reconcile, especially as
she lay half-naked on the massage table) was precisely because

it *wasn't* "okay." Embracing the New Okay had made so much more sense when she was reading it.

Dahval spread warm oil on her back. Soon all her inhibitions disappeared and this experience was not only "okay," it was incredible. Her body melted into the table. The last thing she remembered before she drifted off was how much she was looking forward to her freeze-dried Space Beef Stroganoff.

A little while later, her eyes fluttered open. Through the headrest, there as plain as day, she saw them—blue Dockers and brown, crepe-soled shoes. Mental-patient shoes.

Her body stiffened. No two ways about it, getting a massage from a mental patient was definitely not "okay." Operation New Okay was officially aborted until further notice.

For the first time since beginning this soul mate–seeking process, she felt truly frightened by her summoning abilities. She had been judgmental and suspicious at the gas station and the universe had responded in kind. Who was she to try to rearrange events like molecules in an atom to suit her own agenda? The laws of physics could tend to themselves. The universe didn't need a special ed teacher from Bayonne meddling in its affairs. There was an order to things beyond what she could see. But how in the world had she manifested an escaped mental patient in the first place? Where had she gone wrong? She imagined the local authorities finding her floating in a lake deep in the woods. *Cancel! Cancel!* She tried to act naturally. The last thing she wanted to do was provoke him into doing something drastic. She'd seen on an episode of *Oprah* that if a woman is attacked, she should never allow a "perp" to take her to a second location. *Cancel! Cancel!* She weighed her options. She could run out of the room screaming or remain silent in the hope that the mental patient would turn out to be a gentle giant like Lenny in *Of Mice and Men*. But didn't Lenny kill that baby rabbit? She prayed and tried not to react when the guy held the sheet and instructed her to turn over. She decided it was better to comply.

Prone or supine, what was the difference if she was going to be murdered? Logically, she knew it would be helpful to be able to give the police an accurate description of her assailant (if she lived to tell the story), but try as she might, she couldn't bring herself to open her eyes.

She smelled geraniums, then a whiff of alcohol, or was it chloroform? The mental patient placed his warm hands over her forehead. Was he getting ready to strangle her? Asphyxiate her? *Cancel! Cancel!* And then, just like that, he walked out of the room, closing the door gently behind him. She sat up, wrapped herself in the waffled sheet, and slid quietly to the floor. Before she'd taken three steps, she heard the squeak of crepe-soled shoes and froze. The door opened. In walked a young man with blond chin-length hair and blue eyes, offering her a glass of water with a sprig of mint. He smiled. Blue Dockers and mental-patient shoes had never looked so good.

Monday morning, back in New Jersey, Cathy led her class into the auditorium. The women in the Jacuzzi were right: the weekend had been a bust. She was still no closer to finding her soul mate. It took several minutes for her students to settle down. It had been her first night back in her own house and she'd completely forgotten to set her alarm. She still might have been sleeping if Lawrence hadn't called and woken her up.

"Why are you calling me so early?" she'd snapped.

"I wanted to catch you before you left for work," he said.

"But it's only—" Cathy looked at the clock. "Oh, fudge! I'm late!"

"You still haven't RSVP'd to the reunion."

"Why can't you take no for an answer?"

"I'll put you down as a maybe."

"That reminds me," she had said before hanging up. "How dare you pay my contractor!"

Her students kept asking what the assembly was about but

she had no idea. There were never assemblies on Tuesdays. But then she realized it wasn't Tuesday. It was Monday! How could she have forgotten to take her personal day?

The auditorium grew dark. Red strobe lights flashed and a siren began wailing. Sean and two firefighters—one in a blue uniform, the other in a firedog suit—walked onto the stage. She slumped down in her chair, hoping he wouldn't notice her. The kids cheered as the firedog pretended to spray them with a confetti hose.

"Firefighters always work in pairs," Sean said. "Can I get a teacher volunteer? I see one in the second row." He pointed to Cathy. "Who would like to see if Ms. Baczkowski can get dressed faster than Firefighter Bill?"

Her students began to cheer. She shook her head in protest, but the firedog ran down and escorted his reluctant volunteer onto the stage as circus music began to play.

The firedog jumped in his toy fire truck and started the countdown. "On your mark, get set . . . go!"

Sean fastened a mesh hood over her head and whispered, "Why'd you stand me up?"

"You know exactly why," she whispered back.

"I wouldn't be asking if I did."

Next, he helped her into a pair of insulated pants with suspenders, holding her arm as she stepped into a huge pair of steel-toed boots that came up to just below her knees. Firefighter Bill was way ahead of them, but pretended he couldn't find his goggles.

"Why didn't you return my calls?" Sean asked as he Velcroed her jacket and fastened the hook straps.

"This isn't the time or the place," she said.

The air tank on her back might as well have weighed a hundred pounds. She could never be a firefighter. She wouldn't be able to make it off the stage, let alone up a ladder. Next, he put a pressure mask over her head and a pair of thick fireproof goggles. She was already sweating. She felt claustrophobic, weighted down. The audience was cheering, the firedog was racing around, but everything was muted, as if she were underwater looking through a fishbowl, breathing through a tube, the way her father must feel when he's hooked up to his oxygen tank.

The firedog was blaring his siren. The auditorium was spinning. Cathy felt like she was about to keel over.

Ten, nine, eight, seven . . .

Sean put a huge helmet on her head. "I was really disappointed when you didn't show up," he said, his voice barely audible through the pressure mask.

Maybe it was the seeming lack of oxygen or the stress of being on stage, but suddenly she couldn't contain herself. There was no other way to describe it—she blew a gasket—going off on Sean the way she imagined her grenade extinguisher would have, if he hadn't sold it on eBay. "Baloney! You were only interested in my grenade!"

The firedog stopped racing around in his car. The auditorium grew silent.

"Uh oh," she said, suddenly realizing that her voice was echoing through the auditorium.

She pulled off the mask and lumbered off the stage. Sean was right behind her. She heard the students laughing. "The fireman wanted Ms. Baczkowski's grenade! It went off with a bang!"

"Wait up, Cathy," he called. He caught up to her at the end of the hall. "Just tell me why you fell off the face of the earth. Then I promise never to bother you again."

"You really don't know?"

He shook his head. He was at least half a foot taller than she was without her heels.

"The grenade? You told me you'd take care of it for me?"

"I did. I sold it."

"At least you admit it."

"I still don't get it." He rubbed the back of his neck. "You changed your mind about going out with me, that's fine, but when I didn't hear from you after I paid the contractor . . ."

"You're the one who paid the contractor?"

"You didn't know?"

"I had no idea. As much as I liked that grenade, I really did need the money. How can I ever thank you?"

"Let me take you out tonight. I've never seen a woman look so hot in turnout gear."

Cathy peered down, blushing.

"I'll take that as a yes. Pick you up at seven. I'll be the one in the red fire truck."

Driving home after work, the misgivings began to kick in. Instead of a sense of elation about her date with Sean, she felt dizzy, off-kilter. Was it vertigo or her inner compass telling her she was veering off course again? After a few speed-up slow-downs and a missed exit or two, she finally made up her mind, pulled off, and turned the volume down on David Hasselhoff. It was autopilot all the way to surprise her father.

She used the key under the mat. The lights were on in the kitchen and the sink was full of dishes. The pot of coffee on the stove looked like it had been made days ago. Her father wasn't in the den watching the news like he usually was at this time of day.

Like Ariadne's thread, she followed the cord of his oxygen tank through the house and finally into her mother's sewing room, rechristened the guest room, just off the pantry.

"Dad? It's me, Cathy," she called.

No reply.

From inside, she heard what sounded like . . . cries of pain?

"Dad, you all right?"

The first thing she noticed when she opened the door was

her father wearing the blue terry cloth robe she'd bought as a visual representation of her soul mate's imminent arrival. The second was that his home care nurse, a hefty woman in a pink uniform, was kneeling between his legs. Changing his oxygen tank? Down there?

"Dad?"

Startled, he pulled the robe around him. "For Pete's sake, Cathy! You scared the bejeezus out of me! Can't a man have some privacy in his own home?"

The zaftig nurse rose as unobtrusively as possible, maneuvered around the various medical devices, and slipped out.

Cathy's hand flew to her mouth. "Oh my God, Dad! In Mom's sewing room?"

CHAPTER TWENTY
BLIND TRUST

SOMEHOW GARRETT COAXED MAX into trying on dresses at Saks, dresses with sequins and beads, a red strapless gown that cost a small fortune, and then a knee-length, champagne silk halter dress that floated over her body and made a quiet whispering sound when she moved. "I like it when you dress like a girl," he said. The fabric was as cool as his hands on her hips as he pressed her against the mirror in the dressing room. She'd never played games like dolls or dress-up as a girl and had no idea they could be so much fun. When the saleswoman asked if they needed any assistance, Garrett told her that so far they were doing fine and secured the door with a chair. When they emerged, Max's handprints remained on the mirror like a bouquet of daisies.

Garrett was being honored for his work on global warming, a black-tie dinner at the Kennedy Center. He hadn't asked her to go—she always had back-to-back clients on Fridays and hostessed at Antoine's—but she'd arranged for a friend to cover her shift and planned to surprise him.

The next day Max returned to Saks for the dress. The two yards of lighter-than-air silk cost more than she made in a month. Luckily, the blond trust-fund baby, Pam's former client, had agreed to pay twice her usual rate. After leaving the glittery perfumed maze on the first floor of the department store, she went to St. Patrick's Cathedral to light a candle for Calvin, an antidote to the blatant commercialism. The sanctuary was filling up with afternoon worshippers. Max thought of the expression in Calvin's eyes the last time she saw him. She'd been so angry she'd pushed him away when he tried to hug her. The tiers of votives blended into a shimmering amber waterfall of flames. At the door, an old woman was asking for donations. Max dug into her pockets for some change, then impulsively emptied all the money she had on her into the woman's basket. She'd have given all the money in the world to redo that day.

She had an hour, more than enough time to do her one hundred flights, train her clients, and still make the eight o'clock Acela to DC. She'd never been late for a session and her clients knew the drill. If they weren't there on the dot, tough luck. She had three clients that afternoon: Gina, the bionic trophy wife; Gina's frat-boy son; and the trust-fund baby at three. She'd promised to push him until he puked. She and Pam still weren't speaking, but she wasn't about to turn down a paying client. Like Calvin always said, one man's loss is another man's gain.

She stepped out into the hall at the same time as the drug dealer. His ferret was on a pink leash with a matching leopard-print harness.

She smirked. "Pink?"

"Only color I could find," he said, pushing his sunglasses up onto his forehead. "This little bandito's been getting loose. Freaking out the tenants. The other day I found him on the tenth floor. You're still trying to run away too, I see."

"You have to train if you want to get anywhere in life," she said.

"How will you know when you get where you're going?"

"Easy," she said. "When I win."

"I'd challenge you to a race, but you'd have to give me a head start. No way I could do one hundred flights in sixteen minutes, forty-eight seconds."

"You're timing me?"

He laughed. "You're like clockwork. Have fun climbing to nowhere, Shorty. Me and the bandito are off to Jones Beach."

"Just remember to close the fire door," she said.

Simon laughed. "I keep telling you, mon, it—"

"Yeah, yeah. And these," Max said, holding out a bag of cigarette butts, "aren't from the fuckwads in the apartment above me."

"You have to *be* the love, Shorty. Like it says in that *Love Book*."

"I told you, no more quotes. I threw that book out for a reason."

After her one hundredth flight, all she wanted was fresh air. Sixteen minutes and forty-five seconds. Still room for improvement. She propped open the fire door, but the brick she used wasn't heavy enough and before she could react, it slammed shut. There was no knob on the outside and banging would do no good. Right now she actually would have been thrilled to have the drug dealer timing her. Something told her she was going to be late for her appointment with the bionic trophy wife. Always a first time for everything. It began to snow, huge lavender flakes as large as daisies falling from the sky. She put her arms under her T-shirt and sat below an overhang, watching the steam billowing out of the boiler chimney.

The summer before seventh grade, Max and her best friend Jessica had biked down to Walker's Point to see the blowing cave. Her parents, Didi and Carl, were entertaining on the wraparound porch, drinking daiquiris. They gave the girls money for pizza and ice cream and told them to be back before dark. It was high tide. Max held out her hand while Jessica inched her way out onto the slippery boulders. They found a good spot on the bluff overhanging the water and sat shoulder to shoulder, waiting for the first wave to burst through the opening of the cave. Finally, a wave crashed onto the rocks, spurting out and drenching them both. They screamed into the wind and hugged

each other, pretending to be lost at sea. Neither of them noticed
the car that had pulled over on the side of the road. A dark-
haired man got out and asked them where the blowing cave
was. Before Max could warn her, Jessica said, *Over here.* The
man ventured out onto the boulder, and sat down next to her.
He laughed raucously when the first wave hit and leaned into
Jessica. Max told Jessica it was time to go home. The man said
he was a producer looking for pretty girls to be in his movie.
Had they ever seen Endless Summer? Max pulled Jessica to the
road and told her to get on her bike. Her parents were waiting.
Jessica refused to go. She'd always wanted to be in a movie. She
said that Max was just jealous. Max raced home to get her father but he told her to stop making up stories. *If Jessica doesn't
come home immediately I'm calling her parents.* Max rode the
half-mile back to Walker's Point, her eyes stinging with the salty
spray. It was nearly midnight by the time she found her friend,
shivering, wrapped in a thin blue towel, her long hair tangled
with sand and seaweed. *Please . . . please don't tell my parents,*
Jessica wailed. Max never told anyone. *You've made a spectacle
of yourself again, Maxine,* her father said when she finally got
home. *Did you even think about the consequences? You're a
delinquent!* In the fall, they sent her to live with Calvin. They
thought he'd knock some sense into their wayward daughter. If
he couldn't, nobody could.

Max could barely feel her toes. It was dark and several inches
of snow had accumulated when the fire door finally opened. As
much as she would have liked Garrett to be her savior, at that
moment she didn't care if it was the creepy porter who always
stared at her ass when she passed him on the stairs.

    It was Hector. He helped her up and wrapped her in his
green parka, still warm from his body.

    "What took you so long?" she asked.

    "Listen, bitch, for all I knew you and the pilot were on your way to Peru." He pulled her close. "I've been running around the city all day looking for you."

After a warm shower, again wearing Hector's huge coat, along with sheepskin boots and nothing underneath, she stretched out on the futon couch.

"Where is your pilot, anyway?" Hector asked, handing her a mug of tea.

"In Washington. He's getting an award."

"Let me guess: he didn't ask you to go."

"None of your fucking business."

He smirked, nodding condescendingly. "Just like I thought. Jacques Cousteau's in a relationship."

"Just because you're a prick doesn't mean there aren't some decent guys out there."

"And you think you found one?"

"Maybe I have."

She slipped off Hector's coat. The bathroom mirror was still fogged up despite the exhaust fan. She wiped away a circle of condensation, applied lip gloss, and ran her fingers through her hair. Ignoring Hector's whistles when she emerged wearing the silk dress, she unzipped Calvin's army duffel and began packing.

"Where are you going?" he asked.

"DC."

"No fucking way," he said, grabbing the bag. "You have hypothermia."

"Give me that," she shot back, shoving him as hard as she could in the chest.

Hector held his hands up in defeat. "Okay, be a dumb bitch. See if I care. Just don't come crying to me when the guy dumps your sorry ass," he said, storming off.

She sent Garrett a text, *Arriving in DC at 11. Wearing the silk dress . . . nothing else,* then hoisted Calvin's bag onto her shoulder. She was locking the door when her phone pinged.

It's only colleagues and spouses. You'd be out of place.

She felt like she'd been punched in the gut. Calvin had taught her not to show the merest hint of vulnerability. One thing she'd never do was admit to Hector that he'd been right.

Fuck you too, she texted back, then dropped her bag and kicked her door.

The drug dealer came out of his apartment. "Everything okay, Shorty?"

"Does it look like everything's okay?"

He smiled, checking her out. "I'd say so."

"If you like girlie shit," she said.

"Girlie shit looks good on you."

She was about to unlock her door, then changed her mind. "Is it all right if I come in for a minute?"

"Be my guest," he said.

Simon's apartment smelled like incense, probably to mask the smell of weed. She'd expected a total mess, but the studio, a mirror image of hers, was tidy and minimalist. Nothing out of place. The ferret was sleeping on a sheepskin bed by the radiator. On the windowsill, on top of a stack of thick scientific texts on subjects ranging from neuroplasticity to quantum physics was *The Love Book.* Maybe he sold used textbooks to med students. Max peered through the blinds into Simon's garden. Underneath a bamboo arbor of hanging ferns were pots of exotic plants still blooming, despite the light dusting of snow: elephants ear, peacock orchids, birds-of-paradise. Three wrought-iron chairs around a stone fire pit. This was hardly the junk heap and cannabis tent she'd expected; he'd created a sanctuary. A drug dealer with a green thumb.

An unopened bottle of Cuervo sat next to the television. Two years ago that wouldn't have even gotten her through the night.

Suck it up, Max, Calvin had said. She'd just come home from the ore pit. Calvin was on the phone, his back to her. He was wearing a chambray shirt and overalls. His boots were caked with mud. *I suppose it'll be good for you to be with people your own age,* he said. He hung up and stood by the window staring out toward the pond as if he were looking for something, though his eyes had already begun to fail him. *I won't go,* she said. *They can't make me.* She ran out and locked herself in the shed. Calvin pounded on the door with his huge fists. *Open the door right now!* he shouted. *You told me I could stay with you forever. Suck it up, Max. That's life. Shit happens, people die. The only thing you can count on is that people will always disappoint you. Deal with it.* She came out and buried her face in Calvin's chambray shirt. *But not you, Calvin.* His chest expanded, then collapsed. *Yes, Max, even me.*

One month later, he shot himself.

Without a word, she unzipped the halter dress and let it fall to the floor in a pool of pearl-colored silk. Simon seemed momentarily caught off guard when she reached up and unclasped the straps of his overalls, but quickly regained his senses. His hands caressed her torso like a sculptor, finally resting on the curve of her hips. His body was smooth and perfect, muscular, ripped, and lean. Max put her hand under the waistband of his striped cotton boxers. She would have expected something flashier.

"Whoa, Shorty, what's the rush?" he said, pulling away. "How about a glass of *vino*? We barely said hello."

"Shut up, Simon," she replied, pushing him onto a chair and straddling him.

He held her still with one arm while he reached behind him into a desk drawer. "Let me put on a boot," he said, opening a condom with his teeth. Then, unable to resist any longer, he groaned, "Lord have mercy," and pulled her to him.

She closed her eyes, letting her body take over. In her mind she was racing up a never-ending flight of stairs. One step at a time. One more flight. One more landing. Just a little further. But she knew she could never go high enough.

With Simon's large arms around her, she felt small, safe. She

caught herself before she came. She wasn't doing this for pleasure. It was to level the playing field, get back at Garrett.

Suck it up, Max. That's life. Deal with it.

When she knew Simon was close, she held his hands above
his head, waiting until his body shuddered before getting off
him. He leaned back and took a deep breath. "Ah, the agony."
She pulled on his overalls, the straps barely covering her chest,
leaving the dress on the floor. No more girlie shit for her.

"Why the haste, Shorty? Your turn. Time to eat under sheet."

"No thanks, I'm good."

C HAPTER TWENTY-ONE
TEXAS SIZE

MONDAY MORNING EMILY MADE CRÊPES for Zach. The batter was a little gloppy, but nothing a good dousing of syrup couldn't remedy. She waited for the fancy French crêpe pan to heat up, a "present" from her ex-mother-in-law along with the two-volume set of *The Art of French Cooking*. The merest hint of snow on brownstone rooftops was the only evidence that remained of last weekend's freak October snowstorm. How quickly things could disappear without a trace.

She hadn't expected to see Duncan ever again after the disastrous weekend at his agent's house. He'd finally returned her seventeenth message and they'd had a three-hour scorched-earth conversation. He told her she was a hack writer, that she dressed "conventionally," and complained that she didn't even read the *New York Times* correctly. So, when her friend at the *Daily Beast* had asked her to go to DC last Saturday to interview the recipient of an award at the Kennedy Center for their online edition, she'd accepted without hesitation. Duncan wasn't going to be inviting her to any must-attend literary events in the foreseeable future. During the interview, the award recipient and Emily had more than a little flirtation. He was handsome and intelligent and it took her mind off Duncan. She'd gone back to his hotel for a drink and some more flirting, but once she made it clear that the evening wasn't going any further, he told her he had an early flight in the morning. And, big surprise, when she did some research, she'd discovered the guy was married.

She was still dutifully completing the exercises in *The Love Book*, but was having serious doubts that the results would be even remotely newsworthy. That week's chapter was "Space Clearing." It was supposed to make room for new love, but felt more like Emily-purging. Negative emotions were attached to every item in her closet like antitheft security tags. Guilt, to a misshapen sheer black dress with silk bows on the sleeves she'd worn without the slip for an illicit night with Nick when she should have been with Charles and Zach in the Catskills. Inadequacy, to the voluminous floral tunic she'd worn for Zach's bris when her mother told her she'd weighed less after giving birth than before. Self-doubt, to an embroidered top that Duncan said looked like something a granny would wear. Defeat, to a pair of jeans she'd had since high school that she tried on occasionally, hoping someday to be able to zip.

A few days later, after her third trip to Housing Works and returning to a now empty closet, Duncan called, and her banishment from his enchanted kingdom ended. The world was on its axis again.

"I shouldn't have called," he'd said, sighing. She could picture him pacing around his living room with his headset.

"Is something wrong?" she asked.

"I don't want to burden you with my troubles."

"You're not. You could never." And she'd meant it. Being allowed into Duncan's inner circle felt like a privilege, even if it sometimes entailed mundane tasks like picking up dry-cleaning, proofing galleys, or waiting for the cable guy.

"It's the book party," he said. "Why can't anything be easy?"

His next book was coming out in a few months. It had a Valentine's Day release date.

"What's the problem?" she asked.

"Tom's apartment isn't big enough. Plus, they just recovered the furniture and pickled the floors. They don't want another disaster like when Fran Lebowitz came in with a nail in her heel and pitted the hardwood floors."

"Isn't there anyone else who could host the party?"

"Lara offered, but it's really not ideal. The critic for the *New York Times* walking up five flights for some smoked fish?"

Hearing Lara's name sent an electric jolt through her body. "Couldn't you have it at your apartment?"

He laughed. "I guess Lara's will have to do."

"I suppose I could host it," Emily said impulsively.

"You mean it?"

She nodded, trying to convince herself. The only thing she was certain of was that she didn't want Lara to do it.

"I love throwing parties," she had said. "It'll be fun."

"Thanks for stepping up to the plate. One thing, though . . ."

"What's that?"

"No kids, this is business," he said before hanging up.

Emily understood, but would Zach?

Then she remembered that Charles was still sleeping in Zach's room. But February was a long way off.

Charles walked into the kitchen wearing new blue flannel pajamas with fold marks and slippers.

"Have you seen the real estate section?" he asked, shuffling through the pile of yesterday's paper.

"It's on the dining room table."

"I'll take Zach to school today."

"That would be great," she said, pouring the now milky batter into the pan.

It had been exactly two weeks since Charles showed up in her lobby. *One more day*, he'd say every morning, and she'd relent. It was a slippery slope, and getting more slippery by the day. Zach was different with Charles around—bubbly, smiling, eager to help. It was as if the sun had come out suddenly after a long dark winter.

Duncan called while she was doing the dishes. Charles was on her computer. He'd already adjusted her chair. When she sat at her desk she felt like Goldilocks in Papa Bear's chair.

"I'm calling to invite you to Liam's book party," he said. "It's at seven."

"Tonight?" she replied quietly. She didn't let on that Charles was there; it might send the wrong message, especially after the way Duncan had reacted to a late-night text from Christophe. *Midnight blowjob*? he'd asked. Emily had laughed it off. But still, what purpose would it have served to tell him, especially at this stage of their relationship when things could be so easily misinterpreted—like a basket of exotic fruit, or a harmless flirtation in Washington.

"Tonight at seven," he said. "There will be lots of people you should meet."

What was it about those words that she found so seductive? Zach didn't have school tomorrow (another Jewish holiday) and she'd promised they could go to Dallas BBQ for dinner, he was treating, and then to *Puss in Boots*. Networking and meeting agents and editors was part of her job. How many of Zach's games had Charles missed because of work? They could still have dinner, and Charles could take him to the movie. She knew if she didn't go, Duncan would invite someone else.

Zach zoomed into the kitchen, grabbed a plate of Nutella crêpes, and zoomed out.

"Hey, don't you want to sit down?" she called after him.

"No time. I don't want to be late for school."

Clearly he wouldn't mind if she went out tonight.

Zach wore his "dress-up" shirt, a black collared shirt with a zipper that he'd worn to each of his camp dances last summer, evidenced by the photographs on the camp website. At Dallas BBQ he asked the hostess to seat them in the upper tier by the railing. He liked to look out over the rest of the diners. He'd chosen Monday because Sundays were crowded with extended families dressed up after church or celebrating birthdays. It was five fifteen. Just in time for the Early Bird Special.

"What are you having, Mom?"

"Chicken, probably. How about you?"

"Chicken. It comes with soup and cornbread, and French fries, baked potato, or yellow rice. Which do you want?"

"A baked potato."

"I'm having fries. Daddy always gets rice."

Zach placed their orders. When the waiter asked if they'd like anything to drink, he said, "Just water. But can we have those little umbrellas?"

"What a special treat," Emily said. "We haven't gone out in a long time."

"Remember, it's on me."

"I'm so lucky to have such a wonderful son."

He pretended it was no big deal.

"You sure it's okay with you if Daddy takes you to the movies?"

"It's just a movie, Mom."

Soon their soups arrived. "Isn't this a good deal?" he asked. "Nine ninety-nine for two half chickens."

"You sure can't beat that."

He tasted his soup. "Pretty good. But I like the chicken soup at Gabriella's better."

"I think it's delicious," she said.

"Mom?"

"Yes, sweetie?"

"You know Sasha?"

"Of course, what about her?"

"I think I like her."

"You've always liked her."

"No, I mean *like* her."

Zach had known Sasha since preschool. He used to say he

liked her rhinestone headband. When they had playdates, neither of them would utter a word the entire time. Occasionally they'd nod or shake their heads in response to questions like, *Do you want to make rainbow cookies?* or, *How about we go to the Children's Museum to see the Dr. Seuss exhibit?*

One night when Emily was tucking him in, Zach asked her to tell him the story again about how Charles had proposed at the Whispering Wall in Grand Central, about how he'd blindfolded her and led her down the stairs, and the oyster dinner later with all of their friends.

"What did he whisper?" he'd asked.

"He said I was made in heaven for him and that he wanted to spend the rest of his life with me."

"And then what?"

"Then we went to the Oyster Bar."

"Did you find a pearl?"

"Yes. Four years later, when you were born."

Afterward, he was quiet. The glow-in-the-dark constellations on his loft were fading. He played with her pavé diamond wedding band, something he did when he was fighting sleep and about to nod off. Then he asked, "What if Sasha loses it?"

"Loses what?"

"Her headband."

"Don't worry," she told him, "she can always get another one."

"But it won't be the same one."

"Zach," she'd said, kissing him on the forehead and tucking him in, "headbands are replaceable. What you're feeling right now, you can never lose."

Emily was relieved he hadn't asked her to retell that story now. She knew what it felt like to lose something she thought she'd have forever.

Their dinners arrived and Zach asked for extra barbecue sauce. "Can I bring you anything else? Something to drink?" the waiter asked.

"No, we're good."

"Actually, I'll have a Diet Coke, please," Emily said.

"Regular or Texas size?"

"Regular."

Zach put his hands in his lap. He opened his wallet and counted his bills. His face fell. "You don't need a soda."

"Don't worry, Zach, I'll pay for it."

He threw his napkin on the table and pushed out his chair. "Why do you have to ruin everything?"

On the subway platform, she played with the little paper umbrella Zach had left on the table. Why couldn't she have been satisfied with water?

The book party was on the top floor of a brownstone in Brooklyn Heights and was so jammed it took Emily fifteen minutes to cross the room to get a glass of wine. And when she returned, Duncan barely acknowledged her. As they were leaving the party, an attractive redhead kissed Duncan's cheek and said, "Hey, sexy, your roots are showing." Duncan had laughed it off jovially, a little too jovially, then said, "Ah, you know how it is, Jasmine, summers in Biarritz, winters in the BVI. Still working on your little novel?"

Zach was already asleep by the time she got home. She would have gotten back earlier, but Duncan persuaded her to come up for one of his forty-five-minute "quickies." Charles was in the living room reading.

"Have fun?" he asked, looking up from the *Economist*. From anyone else it would have been an innocent question. From Charles it sounded like an attack.

"How was *Puss in Boots*?" she responded.

"We went to *The Rum Diary* instead."

"The Hunter S. Thompson movie? Charles, that's an R-rated movie. He's only ten."

"He loved it."

"But he wanted to see *Puss in Boots*. Just because you didn't want to see it doesn't mean you can take him to an inappropriate movie."

"He'd still be watching *Winnie-the-Pooh* if you had your way."

"Next time, can we discuss something like this?"

"Why, Emily? So you can veto me? At least I was with him."

"That's not fair."

"Whatever you did must have been very important to have disappointed your son."

"Zach didn't mind."

"If that's what you want to believe," he said.

"Look who's talking? You cancel on him all the time."

"For the record, Emily, we didn't actually see *The Rum Diary*. He's my son too. You're not the only one who wants to protect him."

At her desk, she readjusted the ergonomic chair to fit her body contours. The fat naked man from across the courtyard was staring at her. She pulled down the shade so hard it flapped right back up to the top. Tomorrow she'd pick up her birth control.

C
HAPTER TWENTY-TWO
AISLE SIX

CATHY FED MRS. BEASLEY then heated up a Lean Cuisine. It was only four thirty. Dinners were starting to get earlier and earlier and she feared that she was slipping into spinster syndrome. Season one of *Downton Abbey* was already in the DVD player. She looked out the window. A red Mini Cooper pulled into Lawrence's driveway and a blonde got out. Cathy's ex-fiancé Rob called again and left a message. This time he was crafty, using his mother's hip operation as an excuse, and she almost fell for it. But instead of taking the bait, she did something more proactive and called Sean. She wasn't sure if he was her soul mate or not, but did her last memory of sex have to be the sight of Rob's paunch and black dress socks? Maybe Beatrice was right: what was the harm in taking those dogs for a walk? Willing to risk listeriosis, she put the Lean Cuisine back in the freezer and drove to Rite Aid.

It had been awhile since she'd had sex, and just the thought of it felt like she was about to parachute into enemy territory. Luckily, she knew where she was going, which aisle the feminine products were in, so she didn't have to ask. And phew! Instead of the leering manager who always looked her up and down like a lollipop, a mousy woman in a red uniform was hunched at the register.

With the aisle to herself, Cathy began discreetly filling her basket with the essentials—sprays, douches, probiotics, deodorizing powder, and depilatories—with the purpose of making her more feminine by stripping her of all evidence of her natural physical state. We wouldn't want to offend Romeo's sensibilities with the taste of a real woman.

She pretended to be looking for antiperspirant when two twenty-somethings joined her in aisle six.

"Nah, Astroglide's too viscous," a tall brunette with an artfully messy chignon said as she scanned the shelves. "Tried this? It heats up."

"My gyno gave me a sample but it made me feel like I was microwaving a Hot Pocket in my hooha."

"How about these?" the brunette asked, holding up a box of horse-pill-sized gel capsules. "These will keep you wet and ready for up to four days." Cathy had seen the product on an episode of *The Dr. Oz Show,* and anything Dr. Oz recommended was the modern-day equivalent of what the *Good Housekeeping* Seal of Approval had been to her mother, with the exception of neti pots, which frankly seemed unsanitary.

The second woman waved it off. "I'm sticking with extra-virgin olive oil. Plus, if Justin is lucky he gets his daily dose of omega-3s."

After they finally walked away, Cathy debated buying the gel capsules. If she prorated it, she could almost rationalize the cost. She'd just have to make the effort to get her money's worth. *The Love Book* was twisting her arm through her pocketbook now.

When she brought her basket to the register, mouse woman was gone. The manager smirked as he slowly scanned each item, even calling for a price check on the Liquibeads.

When she pulled into her driveway, the red Mini Cooper was gone. Lawrence, wearing his stupid tasseled loafers, was on the roof adjusting his satellite dish and trying to disengage some wisteria that was smothering the antenna. Hopefully he'd disappear before Sean showed up in his big red truck to put out her latest conflagration.

Her newly purchased potions on the vanity, Cathy drew a bath and "lit" a flameless candle. Once submerged, she closed her eyes, but no matter how many affirmations she did, she was unable to erase from her mind the image of her father and his home care nurse in her mother's sewing room. The huge pink posterior, the bobbing head, and Mr. Soul Mate-to-be's blue robe!

The annoying whir of Lawrence's bushwhacker further distracted her from finding inner peace. Poor wisteria! Why can't men have any decency? Typical Lawrence; he'd sacrifice beauty for television reception.

Mrs. Beasley nudged the door open and, after dipping her paw into the water and shaking it off, pretended she could still fit on the narrow windowsill, and began making birdcalls.

"Mrs. Beasley, you haven't caught anything in your sixteen-plus years on this planet, what makes you think you will today?"

Something pinged against the screen. Too early for acorns. A neighborhood kid with a sling shot? Cyrano?

Then another ping and another. Beetles!

Mrs. Beasley batted the screen. Sadly, she had already been declawed when Cathy adopted her from Bideawee and couldn't even catch a dead potato bug.

The feminine cleanser had a pleasantly clean fragrance with hints of something unmistakably familiar to any young American girl. *Essence de Barbie Doll*, that irresistibly alluring and unattainable ideal of femininity. No wonder this stuff flew off the shelves!

All depilatorized, powdered, and sanitized, her pH balanced, her pheromones neutralized, she inserted the amber-colored Liquibead into what looked like a miniature rocket-propelled grenade and, with the target in sight, cocked the weapon and pulled the trigger. But somehow the gizmo malfunctioned and instead of the Liquibead going where it was supposed to, it shot out and ricocheted off the medicine cabinet.

She adjusted the prorated cost then reloaded. Channeling Dirty Harry, she squeezed off another shot. This time, the projectile hit Mrs. Beasley who, still engaged in a game of beetle badminton, barely flinched. She vowed to cut her losses if the next one also went AWOL, when Mrs. Beasley started gagging. A trickle of amber liquid dripped down the side of her mouth.

God was punishing her for even contemplating having sex!

"Mrs. Beasley!" she shouted, dropping the applicator and the third precious Liquibead, which rolled behind the radiator.

Trying to open the cat's mouth like the vet did was easier said than done. Mrs. Beasley hissed and squirmed away, backing up until the screen bowed from the weight of her hindquarters. A little more gagging and frantic scrambling and the screen fell completely off. Mrs. Beasley was now half in and half out the window, more out. Cathy froze. Should she let the cat find her own equilibrium or grab her by the tail, possibly frightening her, or worse, causing her to plunge from the second-floor window to certain death? She prayed for divine guidance from all sources, God, the universe, and St. Gertrude of Nivelles, the patron saint of cats, before making her decision. But Mrs. Beasley was gone!

As fast as a firefighter, Cathy pulled on her magenta *Love Stinks* skunk scrubs and climbed out onto the roof. The pitch was steep and the tar shingles were sticky. So much for her spa pedicure. Every so often a furry tail was visible snaking along the rain gutter.

Lawrence, still on his own roof, turned off his weed whacker. "Don't move," he called over, "I'll be right there."

A few minutes later, he appeared at the top of a ladder with a cat carrier. Mrs. Beasley cowered under the eaves, but with Lawrence's gentle prodding she was eventually coaxed into the box. Cathy put her foot on the first rung. "Mrs. Beasley! Are you okay?" she shouted. In the distance, an approaching siren could be heard.

Lawrence laughed. "Just like on *Leave It to Beaver*."

But he wasn't laughing when the fire truck stopped in front of her house and Sean jumped down from the cab. Cathy smoothed her hair and tucked her shirt into her skunk scrubs.

"Thanks again, Lawrence," she said. "You saved the day."

He turned to go. She hoped it was the weight of the ladder that was making his shoulders slump. Walking toward Sean, Cathy felt as if she had been struck by a giant tuning fork. Every cell in her body was vibrating, awake. Sean took the carrier from her hand and let her lead the way to the house. "Nothing sexier than a woman in scrubs," he said.

When he lifted her in his arms as if she didn't weigh a thing and carried her upstairs, quoting Shakespeare—*"Thou wouldst as soon go kindle fire with snow / As seek to quench the fire of love with words"*—she was glad she'd remembered to close the curtains. The sight of Lawrence with a power saw would have definitely ruined the mood. And this time, when she excused herself to give the Liquibead one last try, she hit the mark.

Ten minutes later, there was a crash that sounded like metal garbage cans being knocked over by raccoons, and then a call for help. She peeked through the blinds.

Lawrence! He was lying on his back on top of the garbage cans. What did the guy expect? Who in his right mind wears tasseled loafers to work on a roof?

C HAPTER TWENTY-THREE
NESTING INSTINCT

BEATRICE HAD FINALLY RETURNED to her Lark Street row house after a month helping Libby convalesce. Though loath to admit it, New Jersey had grown on her. That morning, she'd embarked on a decluttering project (how on earth had she amassed so much junk?) when, out of the blue, Malcolm called.

"I'm driving up to Albany for an ornithological emergency tomorrow," he said. "Any chance you can put me up for the night?"

"An emergency? What kind of emergency? Did Mr. Fox get in the chicken coop?"

It turned out Malcolm had organized a group of environmental conservationists and biologists to oversee the Dunn Memorial Bridge rehabilitation project and make sure the peregrine falcon's nest wasn't disturbed. He'd been there last spring to assist in putting leg bands on the falcon chicks, five in all. Beatrice was aware of the baby falcon webcam—she had a friend who'd sent her the link—and last year had even watched the live feed of Mama peregrine disemboweling a squirrel and feeding it to one of her baby fuzzballs, a touching if grisly maternal gesture.

She said sure even though she had never been keen on overnight guests. But Malcolm was Freddy's brother, so she couldn't very well say no. Besides, it was only one night.

"I'm a very good houseguest," he said. "You'll barely know I'm even there."

Somehow she doubted that Safari Man could ever fly under the radar.

Albert had been the last person to sleep in the guest room when he became too sick to walk up the stairs. French doors opened onto a small courtyard with white wrought-iron chairs, a Paris street lamp, and a steel obelisk for climbing plants—Beatrice's little Parisian sanctuary—but Albert had often felt too chilled to go outside. Underneath some bed linens was the rubber sheet still in the packaging she'd bought when he became incontinent. Not long after, a few days before Thanksgiving, Albert's eldest son came to pick him up. Albert had kissed her and thanked her for the love and said he'd see her after the holidays. But both of them knew that would be the last time before he died.

Never in a million years did Beatrice think she'd ever be saying this, but now that she was home, she actually missed having someone around. She and Freddy had been speaking every day since he'd been released from the hospital. But talking on the telephone was different from having someone to gripe about things with, to annoy, and to blame when things went wrong. A stolen moment here and there didn't quite fill the gap. If Libby hadn't fallen off a horse, Beatrice might never have known she even *had* a gap.

She'd put on some pounds taking care of Libby, the same fifteen pounds she'd lost and regained since college, and would probably continue to. There was something about the goal being within sight, but just out of reach, the striving and yearning to realize some fantasy image of herself, that was more seductive than attaining it. Once she achieved her goal, then what? She'd just put the pounds right back on and continue the cycle. She was tired of yo-yoing.

She dusted the banister on her way upstairs. Her landlord had recently painted the halls and stairwells and white dust had settled on every surface as if last weekend's snowstorm had blown in through the leaded glass windows. But there were happy sights, like the bluebells and a few fuchsia tea roses, still blooming in the garden despite it being almost the first week of November.

Beatrice's clutter purge continued for the rest of the afternoon. She moved her bed away from the wall where it had been crammed in underneath the eaves. Albert used to swear every time he hit his head getting out of bed in the morning. Maybe she'd read it in *The Love Book* or in a magazine at the physical therapist's office waiting for Libby, but apparently it was better feng shui to be able to walk around both sides of the bed and also significantly reduced the likelihood of concussion.

She emptied an antique milk crate to improvise a nightstand for Freddy, who was coming up next weekend when his wife was in Oregon visiting the grandchildren again. She took down an oil painting above the bed of a girl sitting by the shore and hung instead a colorful bark painting of two birds she'd bought at a market in Mexico. But there would be no pink crystal swans and husband-and-wife tortoises, however much Cathy tried to persuade her that pairs were good for relationship harmony. This wasn't Noah's Ark, for goodness sake.

She was carrying down another bag of castoffs to take to Goodwill the next morning when Malcolm pulled up in a maroon station wagon. Such a solid, dependable family car, the kind that tells a story of a marriage, like fingerprints: a wife who drove her three boys to baseball practice every afternoon; delivered platters of Christmas cookies for Boy Scout jamborees; and cut coupons for her weekly shopping trips. So dependable and *so* boring!

He was wearing his birder outfit: green windbreaker, tan walking shorts with green knee socks, and his safari hat. An overgrown Boy Scout, carrying two bags from King Kullen. His legs were very pale and slightly pasty looking. Shorts were definitely not his best look. She'd never liked pale skin. Freddy was always tan. She'd assumed it was a result of playing so much golf, but seeing how pale his brother was, she wondered whether his healthy glow had been cosmetically enhanced.

"What do you have there, Malcolm?" she asked from the top of the stoop. She was not a cook and didn't plan on learning today.

He started up the limestone steps. "I thought you might like some cranberries from the bog behind my house on the Cape."

Cranberry sauce was the one thing she actually knew how to prepare and was her standard Thanksgiving offering. She might not be able to cook, but she could definitely stir.

"Come on in. Sorry for the mess."

"You have a lovely place," he said. "Charming, just like you."

"Pshaw! Enough of that. Your room is right back here."

Malcolm put his overnight bag on an old steamer trunk she used as a coffee table and looked out the French doors. "Asters and goldenrod still blooming, I see."

"The weather's been so mild."

"Ever see hummingbirds in your garden?"

"Can't say that I have."

"I'm sure there've been a few nosing around. They're easy to miss. You really have to pay attention."

She didn't know why, but she was suddenly feeling uncomfortable. They'd shared that suite at the Hanover Inn for two nights and there hadn't been an awkward moment. Why now?

"There are fresh towels in the powder room. There's only one bath and it's upstairs. I guess I should get back to my clutter-removal duty. If you need anything, give a holler."

"Any interest in *tagging* along?" He chuckled. "Birder humor. But seriously, we could use all the hands we can get."

Beatrice thought about the thirty years of clutter still waiting to be sorted and organized. The weather was crisp and sunny and though she was not, and planned never to be, ornithologically inclined, she could use the air. "Well, gee. That might be fun!" she said. "I don't want to be *cooped* up all day."

"A birder in the making!" Malcolm beamed.

"Don't count your chickens!"

"Toucan play at this game!"

"I call fowl!"

On the ride over to the Dunn Memorial Bridge in his boat of a car, Malcolm filled Beatrice in on the latest details of Freddy's recuperation. She tried to act as if it was news to her and that she hadn't just spoken to him that morning. In the stark sun coming through the moon roof Malcolm's skin looked even pastier than it had before, and the holes in his safari hat cast a web of shadowy dots on this face as if he were in very low-definition. He seemed to wear that silly safari hat everywhere, even inside. It reminded her of Monsieur Homais in *Madame Bovary* asking permission to keep his fez on for fear of "contracting a coryza," a nasal congestion and bird disease which, considering where they were going, made her chuckle.

In the pocket of the passenger-side door was a pair of mini binoculars. Beatrice lifted them to her eyes and looked out into the distance, but all she saw was her own nose.

"Those were Winnie's," Malcolm said. "You're welcome to borrow them."

"I prefer my own two eyes to see things, thanks."

"Put them around your neck in case you change your mind. You'll probably need to adjust the diopter. It should be on the right-hand side somewhere."

"Listen, I'm not turning into one of you, so you might as well stop trying."

She realized she might have been a tad brusque, so when Malcolm launched into an ornithological lecture, she listened politely, contributing a well-timed "You don't say" or "Fascinating!"

"It's really a terrible shame, but in the 1960s, because of

the use of the pesticide DDE, peregrine falcons nearly stopped being a nesting species, but thankfully, because of work by the DEP, the species has been gradually repopulating as more captive birds have been reintroduced."

DDE. DEP. Beatrice felt like she had just picked some lousy tiles from a Scrabble pouch.

"It might also interest you to know that instead of nesting on cliffs, falcons adapted and became urban birds, building nests on window ledges and under bridges, up and down the Hudson River in places like New York City and Albany. But this requires monitoring by environmentalists to make certain that their nesting boxes are protected from urban disturbances like construction or bridge renovations."

"Fascinating!" Beatrice fiddled with the strap of the binoculars, winding it around her index finger like a tourniquet.

"And I don't know if you're aware of this," Malcolm continued, "but peregrine falcons bred in captivity, more often than not, choose wild mates."

This was the one fact that she really did find remotely interesting. She supposed she could be considered the wild one in the relationship, definitely by Freddy's mother's antiquated standards. She hadn't been good enough for his mother's born-and-bred-in-captivity Highland Park society son.

Once at the site, Malcolm's whole demeanor changed. His eyes sparkled as he greeted and coordinated the two groups in attendance for the bridge climb—all volunteers from the Audubon Society and the Peregrine Fund. At the last minute, Beatrice had put Winnie's binoculars around her neck. There might be something she wanted to get a closer look at. She zipped up a dark green Audubon windbreaker and joined the group inspecting the nesting boxes and perching bars (basically lookout spots from which the falcons waited for unsuspecting prey). Another group was making sure that the aging webcam was in working order. Malcolm's passion and devotion to the cause was infectious, and the other volunteers, though decidedly odd, were very pleasant characters, definitely birds of a feather. Before she knew it, she'd offered her legal services on a committee next spring, realizing only later when her cell phone rang and she saw that it was Freddy that she might not even be in Albany during next year's nesting season. She let the call go to voice mail. She'd get back to him later when she had some privacy.

After the inspection was completed, Malcolm suggested that the group visit a birdhouse in Washington Park, in the historic district, which happened to be just two blocks from Beatrice's apartment. The rest of the conservationist group wanted to go to the Albany waterfront with the hope of spotting some snowy egrets and green-winged teals and, with any luck, a brown pelican. Malcolm bid the others, "Adieu! Until spring migration!" and he and Beatrice were off in his Subaru, which was without a doubt one of the sportier cars of the birder set.

The structure was more a high-rise condominium than birdhouse. Over thirty feet high, it was a hodgepodge of rustic and whimsical houses intricately carved, some like gingerbread houses, others miniature Swiss chalets, arranged helter-skelter one on top of the other. Beatrice lifted the binoculars to her eyes. In magnification, the birdhouse looked like an Alpine village. She could almost imagine herself entering one of the tiny cottages with a front porch and calling it home. And she knew exactly which one Cathy would choose: a Victorian confection right next door.

Beatrice was half-listening as Malcolm told her about the artist William B. Schade, and how he had carved the birdhouse out of a single piece of cedar. It reminded Beatrice of Jenga, the game she used to play reluctantly with her sister's children at holidays. She was always pulling the wrong block out, often on purpose, causing the rest to come crashing down. In many ways, her own life often felt like a game of Jenga with a touch of *The Sorcerer's Apprentice*. When one block was removed, another popped up in its place. Here in the park with Malcolm, though, everything seemed simple. The birdhouse was a magical construction, a tiny world unto itself. And to think she had lived within walking distance for thirty years and had never seen or heard of it! What other treasures could be hiding right under her nose?

Back at Beatrice's, Malcolm made a fire in the wood-burning stove and Beatrice poured two glasses of Caol Ila, knowing he would appreciate it. She had friends from the DA who could down a bottle of single malt like soda pop. For these dilettantes, and for Freddy, she deigned to keep a bottle of Dewar's in the liquor cabinet.

Freddy! She'd completely forgotten to call him back. She told Malcolm she had to take care of something upstairs and went to call him.

"Has my brother bored you to tears yet?" Freddy asked.

Beatrice put her feet up on the ottoman. "We're having a pleasant enough time." She was actually having a splendid time, but with Malcolm and Freddy's rivalry, there was no point rubbing it in. She thought of that silly commitment quiz in *The Love Book* and it occurred to her that she'd been keeping herself on a short leash, but calling it freedom, and she had to be the one to cut it.

"Listen, Freddy, there's something I need to tell you."

"Should I be sitting down?"

"I've had a change of heart," she said, not intending the pun. "I know I said a lot of things, but the truth is, I do want to marry you."

"Darling, you've made me the happiest man in the world."

They both agreed that Muriel didn't deserve to be hurt and that if they approached this "dis-union" in the kindest, most honest and heartfelt way, everyone would wind up reaping the benefits. There was no rush. Everything in good time, but by

February 14, Beatrice's seventieth birthday, his health permit-
ting, they planned to be officially engaged and married the following September.

"The world is our oyster," Freddy said before they hung up.

Beatrice let the smarmy line go. She had to cut the man
some slack. He was still recuperating from a heart attack. Hopefully, he'd be back to normal by February 14.

After dinner, roast rosemary chicken with fresh cranberry
sauce, which Malcolm prepared while still wearing his birding
outfit, and another glass or two of scotch, Beatrice began to
feel all warm and fuzzy about her future life with Freddy; her
brother-in-law-to-be Malcolm; and this odd new sisterhood she
was cobbling together with the women in the soul mate group.
Yes, she was tipsy, but even if she didn't see them very often, she
felt a kinship with each of them, and their nearly daily emails
had forged a bond between them that matched or even exceeded
ones that spanned decades. They were more open with each
other than with anyone else in their lives, at least that's how
Beatrice felt. They were helpers, fellow travelers, dare she say
cocreators?

Around eleven, the phone rang. It was Cathy. Maybe it was
the scotch, or this right-out-of–Norman Rockwell domesticity,
but Beatrice suddenly wanted to share her good fortune with
someone and whom better than Cathy? She wouldn't believe it. It
was even more improbable than Beatrice moving to New Jersey.

She handed Malcolm the receiver. "Would you mind hanging this up? I'm going to take this on the extension upstairs."
Malcolm nodded, barely looking up from his iPad.

Sitting in her striped armchair under the eaves, looking out
over the garden, she debriefed Cathy. Before she knew it they
were talking wedding gowns, bridesmaids, and registering for
wedding gifts.

"Whoa, Nellie," Beatrice said. "I'm getting married, not
having a lobotomy."

Malcolm poked his head in the doorway.

"Hold on, Cathy." Beatrice covered the receiver with her hand. "Did you need something, Malcolm?"

"Just about to take a shower and then turn in."

"Fine, Malcolm. I'm on the phone."

He closed the door behind him. Beatrice heard running water.

Whether it was impulse or inspiration, Beatrice found herself inviting Cathy to Rob Roy's birthday bash. Libby still wasn't in any condition to make the seven-hour trip to Montana. It was too late to cancel without losing her deposit, and, as chintzy as the Rocking Horse Ranch in Whitefish, Montana, probably was, she couldn't pay for a double-room occupancy herself. Cathy was thrilled at the invitation. She'd always wanted to go to a rodeo.

A floorboard creaked and then she heard Malcolm's elephantine footfalls on the stairs. She told Cathy she'd call her tomorrow with the details. She'd already hung up before she realized that she'd forgotten to ask Cathy why she'd called.

Malcolm was in the kitchen wearing a robe over a pair of navy pajamas with white piping, warming up a glass of milk, the first time she'd seem him *sans chapeau*, revealing a less-than-hirsute pate, another thing that distinguished him from his brother with his thick shock of silver hair.

"Helps me sleep," he said, pouring the milk into a mug. "Join me?"

"No thanks. Nothing ever works for me. I've been an insomniac for years."

"Winnie and I always shared a glass of warm milk before turning in. I find if I add a few cloves I have even sweeter dreams."

With Albert, it was another glass of scotch and in the morning she could never remember her dreams. Maybe that's why the years seemed to blend together.

"I'll send you a dream pillow," Malcolm said.

"A what?"

"It's a sachet of hops, chamomile, valerian, skullcap, and lavender. I make them myself from herbs in my garden. You'll sleep like a baby."

"I'm not into all that hocus pocus."

"Don't knock it till you've tried it. Sleep is vital to a person's well-being." He stirred the milk with a wooden spoon she wasn't even aware she had. "You know, Freddy and Muriel will be celebrating their forty-fifth wedding anniversary next June."

"God, that sounds awful." She'd said the line so many times it was automatic now.

"He's never going to leave her."

"Listen, Malcolm, it was swell spending the day with you and your bird-watching friends, but from now on you should keep your opinions to yourself."

"I've seen it happen before with other women."

"Well, I'm not *other* women," Beatrice said, pouring herself one last drink before retiring.

The next morning, after a pot of strong coffee, Malcolm on his way back to Boston in his Subaru, Beatrice found a copy of Peterson's *Field Guide to Birds* in the guest room that Malcolm must have left behind. What a bother! Now she'd have to waste an hour standing in line at the post office. She flipped through it and saw that he'd inscribed the inside cover.

> *To Beatrice,*
>   *You never know what you might find right in your*
> *own backyard.*
> *—Malcolm*

CHAPTER TWENTY-FOUR
TRICK OR CHEAT

HALLOWEEN HAD NEVER HELD MUCH APPEAL for Emily. It wasn't just that she had been terrified of vampires ever since seeing *Dracula* at summer camp (the George Bush masks actually freaked her out most of all), it was the uncontrollable urge to devour the entire bowl of leftover candy, in hierarchical order, until only strawberry Charleston Chews remained, her self-esteem diminishing in direct proportion to the amount of candy consumed.

Little by little, since Duncan came into her life, her kitchen had been purged of anything nonorganic, processed, or sugar-laced. Even ketchup. The only remotely decadent items remaining in her pantry were bars of 72 percent ethically harvested, rain forest dark chocolate, basically crayons, which would never satisfy her the way her old standby, a one-pound bag of M&Ms, could.

Zach had been invited to his first-ever coed sleepover at Dylan's Candy Bar. He'd been vacillating between going dressed as a hippie or baseball player, finally deciding on Elvis, and had been practicing his hip gyrations in the mirror for days. Emily had seen enough Little Mermaids, Zombies, Harry Potters, and Angry Birds to last a lifetime, and since Zach wouldn't be home, she didn't put her name on the building's trick-or-treat list. But Charles had. He'd bought mini candy bars, carved a pumpkin, decorated the vestibule with spiderwebs, and resuscitated his

Green Lantern costume. She was already anticipating the quiz-zical look from Adele Weisenbaum, trying to guess the identity of the guy in the green mask, skintight jumpsuit with "rippling" abs, light-up logo, and shiny boots.

After an early breakfast meeting at Bouchon Bakery with her friend David, the editor, Emily went to the Columbus Circle gym to take an exercise class. The third sticky bun had done her in.

This was not the super-mommy-on-the-go crowd she was used to at the Upper West Side club. This was where the beauti-ful people worked out—models, newscasters, talk show hosts, fashion designers, moguls, and celebrities—in eco-friendly fibers and pseudo low-key vibe. Some didn't even mix with the hoi polloi, gaining entry into an even more exclusive area with pri-vate cabañas and fancy French towels, not by flashing a mem-bership card but with a retinal scan.

It still surprised her how uninhibited women could be in the eucalyptus-scented locker room, putting on makeup, blow-drying their hair, and chatting about mundane things, com-pletely naked. She found an empty locker, turned her back, and pulled on her loose black yoga pants, racer-back tank, and one of Zach's hoodies. She didn't hate her body, but she didn't love it. She could look decent naked provided there was good light-ing, she had a little color, a push-up bra, heels, wasn't retaining water, and made no sudden movements. She was already regret-ting venturing out of her comfort zone. And the full-length mir-ror confirmed her worst fears. She looked as frumpy as she felt.

The long wooden bench was already nearly occupied by a row of women who looked good in ponytails and no makeup, an unofficial queue. Finally, the door to the studio opened and a wave of perspiring women poured out and the next class filed in. Drips of sweat dotted the floor. She found a spot near the center, not too close to the front. She liked to have someone to follow as the instructor walked around realigning the women into perfect chakra-balanced poses.

The stereo system began blasting, louder than usual for an
intenSati class. The instructor entered, tucked her short blond
hair into a black bandanna, and adjusted her mic. When she
turned around, Emily realized it was Max. She waved, but Max
seemed not to recognize her. Class began, not with guided meditation and sharing, but with instructions called out like a drill
sergeant. Emily tried not to cause anyone bodily harm as she
alternated between roundhouse kicks and uppercuts, but she
could barely tell her left from her right.

"This is intenSati, isn't it?" she whispered to an older, very
fit woman in front of her.

"No, KarateStrike."

She was about to grab her things and slip out, but Max
caught her eye and smiled. With that simple acknowledgment,
she found enough courage to ride it out. What was the worst
that could happen?

The last person Max ever expected to show up in her class was
Emily. There were always a few lost souls unfamiliar with her
reputation, but never on a Friday. Fridays at 9 a.m. were for
diehards. Occasionally, a newbie managed to make it through
the class, but it was rare. Most never came back. Several left in
tears. Her classes were no joke and that was the reason they always filled up. There was a waiting list for her spin class. Women
loved the competition; she gave them something to aspire to,
but it was the men, cutthroat condescending business bastards,
reduced to groveling toads, who were most desperate for her
approval. Max derived pleasure in making them believe they
could keep up, maybe even seduce her, then leaving them in
the dust. It was a mental game. She could bring any man to his
knees. Until Garrett. No one had hurt her like that since Calvin
told her she couldn't live with him anymore.

Pam was in the front row. She had a towel on one side of
her and a water bottle on the other, marking her territory. They

hadn't spoken since Max fired her as a client at the Maritime Hotel. After the warm-up, Max called out the moves for the first combination. She was expecting Emily not to last five minutes, but while she wasn't performing the combos with grace or intention, she was keeping up. As the moves became more complicated, though, Emily seemed to lose her focus. Pam didn't try to hide her annoyance, and if it hadn't been obvious enough, she made it clear with a roundhouse kick that nearly knocked Emily off her feet.

Pam tapped Emily on the shoulder and pointed behind her. Looking chagrined, Emily navigated her way to the back of the room. The only available spot was behind a pillar.

Max wasn't going to allow Pam to run the show. "Did you all take spaz pills this morning? Drop and give me twenty. And no girlie push-ups. On your toes." She did ten plyometric push-ups with claps to show them she meant business.

While the class was grunting and trying to keep up with her count, Max pulled Emily front row center, shoving Pam's towel aside. Emily looked as though she had been thrust into an orchestra seat without a ticket.

"Take off your sweatshirt," Max said. "It's show time!"

Emily unzipped her hoodie. She was about to tie it around her waist when Max grabbed it from her. Just as she suspected: Emily's upper body was lean and defined. She had the posture of a dancer. Why was she the one hiding when Pam, with her jelly rolls, was wearing short shorts with zippers on the side?

Pam was clearly disgruntled at having been supplanted, but Max wouldn't even look at her. She turned up the volume and stood facing Emily.

"Do what I do, like you're staring in a mirror," she said. "And then imagine I'm someone you want to kick the shit out of."

Tentative at first, Emily shadowed Max's movements, a fraction of a second off, like bad lip-synching. Once she got the hang of one combination, Max switched it up so she couldn't go on automatic. Just as she had the night in the hedge maze in Normandy, she let Emily take the lead, surprising Max with her ability to anticipate her next move before even she did, though Emily didn't seem the least bit aware of it. As she and Emily sparred, Max felt a sense of ease. For some reason she didn't feel competitive with Emily like she did with the others. There was no need to keep her guard up because there was nothing to prove.

After class, Emily sat on the bench outside the studio, drenched in sweat, drinking a bottle of water, a towel around her neck.

"See you at spin class tomorrow?" Max asked.

"If I can walk," Emily said. "Are you going to the Soul Mate Soirée next week? 11/11/11 is a once-in-a-century event."

Max smiled. "I'll probably live to regret it, but I said I would."

Pam caught up with Max and begged her to train her again. Max ignored her, enjoying watching her squirm.

"Look at me. I can't go to Vail looking like the Michelin Man."

Max wouldn't have said yes, but she'd lost her job at Philomel after telling one of Antoine's partners he could suck her dick.

"Okay, if you promise not to be such a bitch."

"I promise," Pam said, crossing her heart. "Are you busy tonight?"

"Why?"

"I have two extra tickets to the Devil's Debauchery Ball. Bring your oceanographer. Did you see that article about him winning that award at the Kennedy Center in the *Daily Beast*?"

"He's history," Max said.

"You should still come. Invite Hector."

As if that was an incentive.

Max glanced over at the bench where Emily had been sitting, but she'd disappeared into the locker room.

Emily dropped Zach off at Dylan's Candy Bar for the Halloween sleepover. Sasha was wearing a long blond wig like Daryl Hannah in *Splash*. She grabbed him by the hand and the two of them ran off without saying goodbye to take advantage of the all-you-can-eat candy frenzy. It was rush hour, and taxis were scarce. Even the double-articulated buses were crammed full. Emily began walking, annoyed at having to fend off overly solicitous pedicab drivers. She entered the park at Grand Army Plaza, hoping the crowds of tourists and the nauseating smell of hot dogs and candied nuts would recede. But the drive was still open to traffic and she was caught in a riptide of horn-blaring livery cabs. She waited for a white horse pulling a carriage with red fringe to pass before crossing over to the footpath. A few lone skaters were gliding across the ice at the Wollman Rink. The sound system was playing a tinny version of a Beatles song so stripped of character it was unrecognizable.

The melody was still playing in her head as she headed underneath the canopy of elms on Literary Walk and through the Wisteria Pergola. The day she and Charles told Zach they were separating, the latticework roof was a purple sun-dappled arbor. Today it was choked with gnarled, leafless vines, much more fitting for that sad occasion, as neither she nor Charles had been able to find the right words.

On the other side of Terrace Drive, she leaned against the limestone balustrade and looked out over Bethesda Fountain. The Angel of the Waters was presiding over a dry fountain basin. Emily dreaded telling Max about her encounter with Garrett in DC, but had the situation been reversed, she'd want to know. Then, as if the universe had been listening to her, she received one of Cathy's inspirational emails, a quote by Tom Stoppard, and she was off the hook: *Every exit is an entry somewhere else.*

The clouds parted in the distance and the lyrics of the Beatles song suddenly came to her: *I'll follow the sun.*

If Garrett was history, why stir the pot?

An odd feeling came over her when she walked through the front door, as though she were visiting an ailing maiden aunt with a tin of butter cookies.

The Green Lantern was glowering. What had she done now? The doorbell rang. Charles picked up the basket of candy and opened the door. In unison, Spider-Man, a pirate, a ballerina, and a six-foot-tall blue M&M yelled, "Trick or treat!"

"Look, Dad," Spider-Man said, pointing at Charles as he grabbed a huge handful of candy, "it's the Green Giant!"

"Actually, I'm the Green Lantern," Charles corrected him. "And leave a few for the other kids."

"But you're holding a green corn," Spider-Man said.

"That's my Gatling gun."

"Looks like corn to me."

Charles's temples were pulsing. "It's not corn. Want me to try it out on you?"

"I'll spray you with my Spinning Web Blaster," the boy said, holding up a red and blue can of Silly String.

Emily took the basket from Charles. "Juliette, is that you?"

The little ballerina nodded, then looked at the floor. She was holding a small plastic pumpkin. She reached in and took one Smartie.

"You can have another one," Emily said. The ballerina shook her head then hid behind her father. "Okay, kids, say trick or treat."

"Happy Halloween, Green Giant!" Spider-Man taunted, then ducked into the elevator.

Once the door had closed, Emily asked, "What's wrong with you? Why'd you have to be so mean to Adam Klein?"

"I don't give a shit about Adam Klein, although someone

should teach the kid some manners. I think I have the right to know if the mother of my child is into BDSM. The courts might rule to change custody."

"What are you talking about?"

He pointed to a large white box tied with black ribbon on the front hall table, which had obviously been opened. Kalman told her she had a package, but she'd been hoping it was another red envelope.

"This is addressed to me," she said.

Underneath several sheets of orange and black tissue paper was a latex bodysuit, dog chain with studs, hooker shoes, and cat-o'-nine-tails. She read the card: *I'd like to make an appointment for a private screening . . .*

It was from her chiropractor. She'd been going to the guy for years with nary an untoward comment or inappropriate glance, until last week, when he told her she "stirred" his soul. She knew better than to think *The Love Book* had cast some kind of weird spell on her, but still. Even more disconcerting was that a chiropractor would encourage a woman to wear six-inch heels.

Maybe it was the sight of Charles in that silly Green Lantern outfit, or the sugar buzz from eating two Twix bars, or the high from the kickboxing class, but she felt playful, not angry. "It's my Halloween costume," she said, holding up the corset. "Like it?"

He shook his head. "You've lost it this time."

She picked up the cat-o'-nine-tails and slapped it against her palm. Charles tried not to smile. As soon as her back was turned, he shot her with his Gatling gun. Their eyes met and for a split second a different Charles was in front of her, the one who used to light up and spin her around when he picked her up for dates.

He was staring at her. The jack-o'-lantern he'd carved was flickering on the table. "How'd we let things get so screwed up?" he asked.

Emily didn't know what to say. There wasn't an answer. The bell rang, and his whole demeanor changed, his face becoming impassive, opaque, as though he'd put his "Charles" mask back on. Emily opened the door. It was Clarissa, wearing her white fur vest, and Duncan, with a bit of spiderweb in his hair. Strangely, Emily felt guiltier about the huge basket of candy she was holding than the cat-o'-nine-tails still dangling from her hand.

"I'm an idiot to have believed you," Clarissa hissed.

"It's not what you think," Charles said.

"Oh really?" She looked at Emily. "You told me she was staying with her loser boyfriend."

"I take offense to that remark," Duncan said. "Do you know who I am?"

Even in the middle of this scene, Charles and Duncan paused to shake hands.

"Charles Andrews. Zach's father."

"Duncan Lebow."

"This is bullshit!" Clarissa said. "You shouldn't have married me if you weren't over Emily."

"I *am* over Emily."

"If you're not downstairs in five minutes, we're done."

Charles stared at the descending red numbers. Emily had never seen him so cowed. When the elevator came back up, he pushed past three squealing goblins to get inside. His green cape got stuck in the closing door. A less graceful exit was hard to imagine.

At Duncan's insistence, and with a bit of ingenious contortion, Emily changed into the S & M costume. When she emerged, Duncan was sitting at her desk, flipping through her manuscript. "Mind if I take a gander?" he asked.

She nodded, trying to interpret the micro expressions flitting across his brow. "It's got legs," he said, after reading a page. "If you'd like some input, I'd be glad to give it a read."

"I wouldn't want to impose." The truth was, it felt too soon, in the same way that she'd kept Zach out of direct sunlight until he was six months old.

"Don't mention it," he said.

Red pen in hand, her ergonomic chair adjusted once again, he began scribbling furiously, crossing out lines, writing entire paragraphs in the margins.

"What do you think?" she asked, trying to sound nonchalant.

"I'm ten pages in and there's no story." Across an entire page he'd scrawled, *So what?!*

"This is the first piece of fiction I've written since college," she said.

"Look, if you want me to make nice, then you have the wrong guy. If I say that your writing makes me want to vomit, I'm just being honest."

"But you're not saying that, are you?"

"Are you a pro or are you an amateur? Because the way you're acting makes me think I'm wasting my time."

Emily crossed her arms, feeling exposed in the tight latex outfit.

"And the little French bon mots you throw in to give it authentic texture . . . *Quel cauchemar?* That's not French! It's another example of monolingual, xenophobic, ethnocentric people thinking that it suffices to translate idiomatic French literally."

Obviously annoyed, Duncan put down his pen. He looked up, his scowl turning into a smile. "Now, *finally*, something I like."

Around midnight, Emily heard the front door open and slam shut. She hoped Duncan hadn't awakened, but not only was he awake, he was half-dressed and searching for his jeans, which had been flung somewhere in the heat of the moment, along with Emily's S & M costume.

"Emily?" Charles called from the entryway.

"Whose apartment is this?" Duncan asked.

"Mine," she said.

"Then I suggest you change the locks."

Emily didn't respond. She hadn't changed the locks for reasons that wouldn't make sense to anyone and right now, not even her. She decided it was also probably best not to tell him that he'd mistakenly put on her jeans instead of his. He left without another word. When he cooled off, he'd realize he'd overreacted. He might even find humor in the situation. She'd never dated a man who could fit into—let alone looked better than her in—her jeans.

Charles was in the kitchen eating the last of the granola bars she'd been saving for Zach's lunch.

"What happened?" she asked. "The Green Giant couldn't talk Cruella into taking him back?"

"You really picked a winner this time," he said. "That guy's every bit the jerk that Zach's been telling me he is."

"And Clarissa's a prize?"

"Compared to Mr. Hyde she's an angel. But you can turn any man into a monster."

"I'm really glad you said that," she said, turning to leave. "Because I was actually feeling sorry for you."

Max waited outside Capitale for Hector to arrive. She wouldn't have accepted Pam's invitation to the Devil's Debauchery Ball except that Hector said he was getting tired of seeing Max dragging her mopey ass around since Garrett had shown his true colors.

"Meow!" Hector said, trying to kiss her.

She turned away. "Two ninety-nine down the drain," she said.

They'd agreed to go as "Cat and Dog," like Frank Sinatra and Mia Farrow at Truman Capote's Black and White dance. It was easy and cheap. All they needed were two half-masks from the party store. Max was dressed all in white with a white cat mask. But Hector had made an executive decision. Instead of a tux and black dog mask, he was dressed as He-Man from *Masters of the Universe*. He said he'd rather defend the realm of Eternia than dress up like a singer his grandma used to swoon over. But the real reason was that Hector didn't feel like himself unless his muscles were showing, and showing they were. He looked good, but it still pissed her off. Now she was only half a costume. A Cat without her Dog, just like Hector was a He-Man without his She-Ra.

The Venetian Ballroom was packed with all manner of angels and demons engaging in "debauchery" on the dance floor. The cavernous space was bathed in red light. The sixty-five-foot coved ceiling glistened like the honeycomb in Calvin's beehive. Pam was in another of the many opulent ballrooms, surrounded by her usual coterie of "close" friends; i.e., anyone she'd known longer than a month and had something worthwhile to bring to the table, unlike Max and Hector, whose sole utility was to make Pam look good. She'd opted for a pornographic Little Red Riding Hood. Her "date" was dressed as Don Draper (the lazy man's costume), lamenting that they hadn't gone to Webster Hall after the Halloween parade in the Village.

"They're having flying vampires and a virgin sacrifice," he said.

"This is the place to be. Heidi Klum can't be wrong," Pam replied, pointing to a tall woman in an elaborate Cleopatra costume.

"That's not Heidi Klum."

"Don't take my word for it; read *Junebug* tomorrow."

Don Draper nearly choked on his black martini. "If that's Heidi Klum, I'm Seal."

Their table was ready. They followed a woman in a skintight alien costume up a flight of marble stairs to a catwalk overlooking the ballroom, through a small bar, and into a room with lilac banquettes, padded white leather panels, and an enormous half-moon window with wrought-iron bars, a vestige, like the underground vault, of the days when the building had been a bank.

They ordered transfusions. Max didn't say anything when the waitress mistakenly placed one in front of her. She wrapped her fingers around the stem and twirled it like a flower, but didn't lift it off the table. On the wall above them was a water-damaged mirror painted with the words: *But past who can recall, or done undo?*

"What kind of gibberish is that?" Don Draper asked when he saw her looking at it.

Calvin had read *Paradise Lost* to her every evening after dinner. Before kissing her goodnight, he'd tell her, *Remember what they say: well-behaved women seldom make history.*

Something brushed against her shoulder. She turned, though she didn't need to. She knew it was Garrett standing behind her. He was wearing a tuxedo jacket and jeans, holding a peacock feather.

"You have to talk to me sometime," he said, eyeing the fuchsia-colored drink in front of her.

"Fuck off, Garrett."

"Five minutes," he said. "That's all I need."

Max picked up her glass as if about to throw it on him. "Don't say I didn't give you fair warning."

"So that's it?"

Hector stood up. "You heard her, dude. Take a hike."

Garrett looked at Hector as if trying to assess the nature of their relationship. "Okay," he said, "I understand. I'll respect your wishes."

He leaned toward her as if about to kiss her. His breath brushed her ear. "Book Nine. The Argument."

After he was gone, several people at the table began whispering and pointing to Mr. and Mrs. Beetlejuice making out on the dance floor. Max stared up at the water-damaged mirror until Milton's words swam in front of her eyes. She pushed her chair away from the table. Hector stood up to prevent her from leaving, but she put her hand on his shoulder.

"I might not be back," she said.

"I thought you were different," he said. "Not just another stupid girl."

CHAPTER TWENTY-FIVE
POT LUCK

SEAN TURNED OUT TO NOT ONLY BE GORGEOUS, but also everything in a man a father would want for his daughter. And the universe seemed to agree.

Before going to bed last night, Cathy sent one of her inspirational messages to her Flaubertian sisters, a quote by Neale Donald Walsch she'd once read on a tea bag: *You cannot let go of anything if you cannot notice that you are holding it.* Then, as she did every night, she placed *The Love Book* under her pillow for good vibrations. But in the morning, when she went to do her soul mate exercise for the day, it was gone. She searched high and low, in every cabinet and drawer, even the refrigerator (she'd once found the television remote in the butter dish), but the book had vanished without a trace.

Maybe it was the universe's way of telling her she could stop looking. She'd found her soul mate. She and Sean had clicked on so many levels, she was sure they would in bed too, once the time was right. It wasn't just that he thought she was sexy in her skunk scrubs, although that certainly didn't hurt. It was the sense of comfort she felt when she was around him. He was like family, not in a creepy-cousin kind of way; she could trust him. But most importantly she'd learned that her soul mate wish list wasn't carved in stone, commandment style—it was a guide, a blueprint, a scaffold in support of a relationship, sort of the way a modular closet could be reconfigured to suit anyone's needs. So what if he had a beer or two or six in the evenings and sometimes in the morning? It was part of the fraternity or brotherhood, or whatever it was called between firefighters, a way to bond and relax, not an emotional crutch as it had been for her mother.

The other night Sean dropped by after work. Luckily, she was wearing a cute outfit and had an entire tray of stuffed shells in the freezer. Even though Cathy was 100 percent Polish with documentation all the way back to the Kosciuszko Uprising of 1794, he said it tasted exactly the way his Italian grandmother on his mother's side used to make it. He asked if she had any wine, but the only liquor she had in the house was a bottle of Cointreau, a tablespoon of which she'd used to make the chocolate cloud cake for her cousin's bridal shower. And though he'd drained the bottle, he didn't seem the least bit impaired, probably a drop in the bucket for a six-foot-two, 180-pound hunk like Sean. And hunky he was. Eau de Barbie was child's play compared to his intoxicating firefighting pheromones. He was Ken on steroids. And though they did some serious heavy petting and kissing, Sean said he wanted to make their first time special.

Tonight was the pot luck dinner at the firehouse. Sean was making his famous Texas chili. The theme was "Hot Stuff" so Cathy made brownies with a dash of cayenne and wore the red leather dress she'd bought at the mall last year but had never summoned the courage to wear. It had been a little on the tight side, but it was on sale, and now after just a week of dating Sean, it zipped up with no wiggling or coat hanger necessary. She didn't realize until she was halfway to the firehouse that the full-length zipper worked both ways. This was definitely not a church dress. The whistle of approval from Sean silenced any residual doubts she was still harboring.

She sat next to her father at a long table in the firehouse kitchen while two firefighters retold the story of Sean carrying her out of her burning house. Pots were simmering on a six-burner stove. Two apple pies were baking in the oven. Sean brought over three bowls of chili.

"So, Mr. Baczkowski, does it meet with your approval?" he asked.

"Mighty good. Has a nice kick to it. Kind of sneaks up on you. Careful, son, when we Baczkowskis like something, we never want to let it go. You know that show *Hoarders?* That's us. Still got all my old forty-fives and my children. So watch out."

"My father's only kidding," Cathy said.

"Cathy's right," her father said. "For the right price, I might part with my princess."

"Doesn't scare me one bit," Sean responded. "In fact, I kinda like the idea."

"This one's a keeper, Cathy."

"Care for a game of billiards, Mr. Baczkowski?"

"Please, call me Jack. Get ready to be whooped, Mr. Fire Chief."

While Sean and her father played pool, Cathy talked with a few of the other wives and girlfriends. Not that she was keeping track, but Sean was already on his seventh beer and they'd only played two games. It was the tiebreaker. Sean racked the balls and her father called stripes then took the break shot.

Cathy's heart felt full. She hadn't seen her father so happy in a long time. Maybe not since her mother died. All her worry over the "incident" in her mother's sewing room now seemed inconsequential. The father she knew and loved was back.

As the night wore on, the party migrated outside. It was a beautiful night. The moon was full and there were fireflies, or so Cathy thought, until someone told her they were embers from the fire pit. Sean had one hand on her thigh, a beer in the other.

"I don't want to break things up," her father said, "but I think it's time to call it a night."

Sean wiped his hands on his jeans and stood up. "How would you like a ride home in the truck, Jack?"

"I'd love it, but then Cathy would have to drive home alone."

She was relieved that her father had so graciously turned down Sean's offer. Any other night, as long as no alcohol was involved, it would have been a very welcome gesture.

"I'll make sure she gets home," Sean said.

Her father zipped up his jacket. "Well, in that case, where do I buy my ticket?"

"I don't mind driving you, Dad," Cathy said.

"How often do you get a chance to ride in the cabin with the fire chief?" He kissed her on the forehead then walked toward the fire truck. "See you tomorrow at church."

"Dad, wait."

"Excuse me, Sean. My daughter's just a little overprotective. You know, ever since her mother died, God rest her soul." He walked over to where she was standing and put his hands on her shoulders. "Princess, everything's fine. You want to begrudge your father some fun?"

"Why don't I come along?" she said, as if her presence, like a St. Christopher Medal, would somehow protect him, the way she used to think if she waited by the window from the time her mother left the house until her car pulled into the driveway, she would be safe.

Sean stood at attention, one hand on his heart. "I promise to stop at every red light and never go above the speed limit. I'd just like some time alone with your dad."

She knew she was probably worrying for nothing, but in her mind she saw flashing lights and a lifetime of regretting this moment. *Cancel! Cancel!* It was only two exits on the turnpike and Sean didn't *seem* drunk. Her father pulled his arm away when she tried to help him into the fire truck. He looked smaller, less sturdy in his slightly rumpled Master Mason windbreaker with the square-and-compass crest. Sean turned on the flashing lights. Her father waved from the cabin. He was wearing a fire helmet. Cathy stood near the edge of the pavement on a strip of grass near the flagpole. They started to drive away.

"Dad! Stop!" she shouted.

Sean jumped out of the cab. He was smiling as he walked toward her. "Is there a problem, Kit Cat?"

"Yes," she said, "it's just that I don't think you're in any condition to drive after all those . . ."

Sean still had a smile on his face, but his posture had completely changed. His hands were clasped behind his back and his legs spread slightly, army style. "All those what?"

"You know what I'm talking about."

"No, I really don't."

"Sean, you've been drinking beer all night."

"Cathy, I'm a firefighter."

"And that's my father you're driving home."

"Do you really think I would do something so irresponsible? Is that who you think I am?"

Her father came over to try to make things right. "Kitten, there's no need to make such a fuss." But Sean was already walking toward the firehouse.

"Dad, he was drinking."

"Malarky! Sean wasn't doing any such thing."

"I saw it with my own eyes," she said. "You tried to deny Mom's drinking for all those years too."

Her father took a deep breath then shook his head. "Don't speak about your mother like that. Listen, Cathy, this isn't just about Sean having a couple of beers. I guess this is my fault. I let it go on too long. But after your mother died . . . and now, well, I'm just worried if you don't stop trying to control things you're going to find yourself alone. Because nobody wants to be with a dictator. And I don't want that for you."

"I'm sorry, I was just trying to protect you," she said after a long pause. She looked down. The two-way zipper on her dress was buckling like a misaligned train track.

A lump was forming in Cathy's throat. Her father had never spoken to her this way before. She felt like she didn't know him at all. Maybe he had been showing up all this time as the father she wanted him to be, just as she had been playing the role of the daughter she thought she was supposed to be.

C HAPTER TWENTY-SIX
TRUE NORTH

EMILY WAS IN THE VESTIBULE at the Belnord, about to ring Duncan's doorbell for the third time, when the door swung open. A small girl wearing a blue pinafore looked at her expectantly. Her golden hair was swept off her face with a white ribbon.

"Astrid, *ma chérie*, who is it?" Duncan called from the other room.

"I don't know, Papa." The girl waited for Emily to introduce herself. "I think it's one of your *fillettes*," she said with a shrug, then retreated to the couch where she was playing with a Madame Alexander Anastasia doll dressed in a gray-belted coat and matching toque.

Duncan had never mentioned Astrid's existence. Naturally, Emily was curious to know who this little girl's mother was, but she also wanted to know what the deal was with all these "fillettes." Willing herself to remain poised and calm, she smiled when Duncan appeared, his shirt buttoned up wrong.

"I see you've already met my darling Astrid."

"Yes, she's adorable. I didn't know you had children."

"As far as I know, she's the only one."

"How old is she?"

"She'll be six in March."

"I would have thought she was older."

He laughed. "Typical American. In Europe parents believe

in exposing children to real life, not mollycoddling them."

Emily's throat felt tight. "When did she arrive?"

"She and Petra flew in yesterday."

Thoughts were swirling in her head. She looked around the apartment for signs of the Guggenheim grant–receiving, *vörtbröd*-making Petra. Finding none, she relaxed slightly.

"Petra is in Princeton at a symposium," he explained. "In case you were wondering."

"I wasn't—"

"You're transparent. I can read you like a book."

She wasn't going to let her insecurities get the better of her. She'd been doing that too often recently. "I'm really glad you called."

She and Duncan hadn't seen each other since last week, on Halloween.

"Well, as you can see I have a slight encumbrance," he said. "You know how that is."

"Your daughter is hardly an encumbrance," she replied, ignoring his tone.

"It's a legal term of art. Don't be so literal." Duncan re-buttoned his shirt and then bent down to kiss Astrid on the forehead. "Papa will be home soon. Be a good girl for Emily."

"You're going out?" Emily asked.

"I shouldn't be too late."

"Weren't we having dinner?"

"Oh, yes. I'm glad you reminded me. I told Astrid she could order whatever she likes. It's on me. I left twenty dollars on the mantle."

There was no question in Emily's mind that she and Duncan had a date tonight. And here he was expecting that she'd baby-sit for a kid she didn't know about instead, and worse, without even asking her. She was about to voice her concerns when he leaned in close and whispered, "I have plans for you when I get back," and all of her indignation flew out the window.

* * *

Astrid fell asleep in Duncan's bed watching *Chitty Chitty Bang Bang*. Duncan should have been home an hour ago. Emily tried his cell, but from somewhere under the piles of papers on his desk came the "Flight of the Valkyries" ringtone. Tonight none of the books on the shelves beckoned. The only thing she noticed was dust, everywhere, copious amounts of it, on the mantelpiece, along the baseboards, picture frames—the same dust that had looked almost charmingly insouciant the first time she was here. Now it just looked grungy. Crumbs, dirty plates, and junk mail covered the dining room table.

Emily saw a stack of yellow Kodak envelopes with a rubber band around them. She told herself she wasn't snooping, she was just passing the time, as she opened envelope after envelope. There were dozens of photographs of beautiful and exotic women, some topless, with Duncan on adventures in places just as beautiful and exotic.

She heard soft footsteps from the hallway. One of the photographs slipped to the floor. Astrid, wearing one of her father's T-shirts, which on her was as long as a dress, sat down and looked at it.

"Here, let me put that back," Emily said.

Astrid rubbed her eyes. "You don't look like one of Papa's fillettes."

Emily glanced at her reflection in the darkened window.

As this little girl stared at her with her clear blue eyes, Emily felt a terrible emptiness. She didn't want to be one of many. With Charles she'd never doubted that she was the most important person in the world to him. She thought about her twenty-ninth birthday. Her parents had made reservations at their favorite Italian restaurant. The four of them shared a tiramisu with long silver spoons, no champagne, because Emily was eight months pregnant. Charles had made a toast. *Here's to the most beautiful pregnant woman in the world*. Reflexively, Emily hid her hands in her lap as though she was a child about to be reprimanded, and looked at her mother. The lines between her brows had deepened as if drawn with charcoal. Her father took his wife's hand. *No one is as beautiful as you, my dear.* Charles had been overjoyed to find out they were having a boy. Emily was too, though she never told anyone the real reason was that she didn't know if she could be a good mother to a girl, another thing she had in common with Emma Bovary.

Astrid tugged at Emily's arm. "Can we watch *Chitty Chitty Bang Bang* again?" She was holding the DVD.

"Sure," Emily said, but she was barely listening.

An hour later, the buzzer rang, bringing Emily back to reality. The movie was already half over and Astrid was curled up beside her on the couch, sucking her thumb. For the first time that evening Emily noticed how dirty the little girl's fingers were and she felt a pang of guilt. She paid the delivery guy and set the containers of food and paper plates on the coffee table.

"Come, Astrid," she said, gently removing the girl's thumb from her mouth. "Let's go wash up for dinner."

Astrid stood on a stool so she could reach the sink. Her hands felt so tiny in Emily's as she washed them with warm soapy water. After drying them with a dark blue towel, Emily searched in the medicine cabinet for a brush. The sliding mirror was covered with fingerprints and splattered with toothpaste. The only brush was a dusty Mason Pearson. As tangled as Astrid's hair was, she couldn't allow it to touch the girl's golden hair.

"I want to be Truly Scrumptious when I grow up," Astrid said as they settled back on the couch after eating, to resume watching the movie.

"Why?" Emily asked.

"Because then I would be beautiful and everyone would want to pick me first," she replied matter-of-factly.

"Pick you first for what?"

Astrid looked up at Emily, her eyes wide. "Don't you want to be picked first?"

Emily considered the depth and meaning of the girl's words. She thought about Charles and Nick and the strange triangle she was in now.

"Why are you sad?" Astrid asked.

"I'm not sad. Maybe a little. Sometimes."

The girl leaned her head on Emily and closed her eyes. "I pick you," she said.

Emily softly stroked Astrid's cheek. "And I pick you."

Around midnight the front door opened. Without even taking off his coat Duncan retreated to the bedroom to make a phone call. Astrid, still awake, picked up her doll and followed him. Emily could only hear Duncan's muffled voice. After waiting for twenty minutes, she considered leaving, but his words had been so seductive. *I have plans for you when I get back.* Hearing no sounds coming from the other room, she tapped gently on the bedroom door, then peeked in. Duncan was fast asleep next to a sleeping Astrid.

He opened his eyes, blinking in the light. "Emily, I forgot you were still here." His voice was gravely. "Call you tomorrow. Thanks for pitching in."

C
CHAPTER TWENTY-SEVEN
ON *THIN ICE*

IT WAS 11/11/11, the auspicious once-in-a-century date that Cathy had chosen for the Soul Mate Soirée. Beatrice couldn't remember if this was Cathy's second or third attempt to marshal all the members of the Soul Mate Soirée—a skating party—but it looked like it was going to come off without a hitch, until Max called and canceled at the last minute, off to some exotic place, maybe Peru, with her oceanographer boyfriend. The bus ride from Albany had been more trying than usual. Beatrice had sat next to a teenager listening to some sort of rap music on his iPod. Even with his headphones, she could hear every word: *Girl drop it to the floor, I love the way yo booty go . . .* By the time she arrived at Port Authority, she had a colossal headache but could freestyle with the best of them.

Emily and Cathy were skating on the rink in Bryant Park. To Beatrice, Bryant Park was still a vast but seedy patch of grass behind the library that attracted drug dealers and homeless people, a former potter's field. She and Libby had attended a rally to end the Vietnam War on the green and listened to Judy Collins with 40,000 other protesters. Who would have guessed that in a few decades, with the help of generous donors, it would be turned into a French-inspired tourist trap. Sure, it had been cleaned up, glammed up, and sanitized like Times Square, and walking through it at two in the morning no longer posed a threat, but something was lost in the process of trying to whitewash the past. It always was.

Beatrice had brought her skates and her rabbit-lined skating jacket, and had been looking forward to practicing her three-turns and backward crossovers, but after lacing up her skates, when push came to shove and it was time to venture out onto the ice, she couldn't do it. She held onto the guardrail, teetering on her white figure skates, and watched Cathy as she awkwardly made her way around the perimeter of the ring. Beatrice only left to give Freddy a call once the girl had found her balance and didn't look like she was about to face-plant.

When Cathy told her they were meeting at Lily O'Brien's, Beatrice had been thrilled. Finally, a place with pub food and a liquor license! What she found instead was a glorified and overpriced candy store. And the snooty waitress had the nerve to offer her a senior discount! She wasn't out to pasture yet. In fact just last week, at a Code Pink rally, one of the members had asked her if she'd be willing to offer her legal services for the Albany affiliate of Women Against War. She'd helped organize the Grannies for Peace Valentine's Day "Reverse the Surge" demonstration, for which she had been remunerated with a hot pink tote bag. A year ago she would have jumped at the opportunity, but since reconnecting with Freddy, her life had taken a different turn. How could she possibly commit to anything when she didn't know if she would be in Italy or Istanbul come February?

She sipped her scalding hot chocolate, a fancy-schmancy concoction called a Lily Vanili. Emily and Cathy were still at the counter trying to decide what to order. She removed the pink satin beauty queen sash Cathy had presented to her emblazoned with the words: *Bride-to-be!* She was still pretty steamed by Freddy's reaction when she called and told him about Rob Roy's seventieth birthday bash in Montana next week. *You're not going, are you?* he asked in that hushed, judgmental tone of his. *You bet your boots I am,* she'd answered. *Give me one reason why I shouldn't. I won't dignify that with a response.*

You know very well why not. Freddy, it's been fifty years, for heaven's sake. I had lots of beaux. Get over it.

She regretted neither her tone nor her answer and still didn't, but maybe telling him to "cram it, jam it," one of the rap lyrics she'd picked up on the bus ride from Albany, had been a bit much. After all, he was recuperating from a heart attack.

Cathy handed out pieces of poster board divided into what looked like wedges of a pie, along with magazines, scissors, and glue sticks. Several other patrons looked on with curiosity at this giant art project. Cathy explained the meaning of each of the eight sectors of the treasure map. Something about trigrams each corresponding to one aspect of life: career, spirituality, family and friends, wealth, fame, love, creativity, travel, and an empty yellow circle in the center representing balance and peace.

Beatrice was flipping through an issue of *The New Yorker* when she came upon an amusing Victoria Roberts cartoon of a miniature husband in a fishbowl on a desert island. The caption summed up perfectly her feelings about marriage after the call with Freddy: *He's the cutest thing, and when you get tired of him you just flush him down the toilet.* She grabbed a pair of scissors and glued the cartoon right in the center of the poster board. Cathy, who'd appointed herself Max's manifestor ad litem, was putting the finishing touches on Max's treasure map, positioning an image of a woman at the top of Mt. Everest "just so" before applying adhesive, the ultimate commitment. She glanced up to see how her other students were progressing, took one look at Emily's treasure map, and gasped. "You don't have a single image of partnership or a loving happy union!"

"Sure she does." Beatrice pointed. "Right there. See? Nothing says marital bliss like Vera Wang."

"The woman's alone, staring at the waves as if her betrothed was away at sea. That's not union, that's longing."

"Same difference," Beatrice said. "It's implied."

"You don't want to play around with the law of attraction," Cathy warned. "I should know. It's quantum physics. Vibrationally speaking, this woman says *alone forever*."

"Vibrationally?" Beatrice laughed. "I don't know how cutting out and gluing a picture of Brad and Angelina onto a piece of poster board will tell the universe anything about you except that you subscribe to *Us* magazine."

"Brad is very family-oriented. And if I were you I'd take off that cartoon."

Treasure maps complete, Cathy pulled out a can of pink glitter spray from her Mary Poppins bag. She gave the can a shake. "Now for the magic!" She was about to press the nozzle when the waitress told her that glitter was not allowed in the establishment. Cathy explained that it was nonaerosol, nonflammable, and nontoxic, but it was clear that this waitress was not going to budge, even where the law of attraction was concerned. Emily understood. In preschool, whenever Zach brought home an art project with glitter, she'd find sparkles all over the house for months afterward, once even right on Charles's nose during couples' therapy, which amused her and which she didn't feel the need to mention. Cathy obediently put away the spray can, but as soon as the waitress was out of sight, each treasure map got a quick dusting.

For Emily, the effect of a little bit of sparkle was startling. What had previously been a nondescript 22-by-28-inch piece of poster board with a hodgepodge of generic images from *Martha Stewart Living, Modern Bride,* and *Redbook* suddenly seemed to shimmer with possibilities. Her treasure map was a glittery enchanted path through the Candy Cane Forest and over Gum Drop Mountain leading to her perfect life. She'd caved to Cathy's pressure and glued on a photograph of a bride and groom hailing a yellow taxicab. She wished she had a reset button. If she had the chance she'd do so many things differently. Surprisingly, none of the images seemed out of reach, none of

them except the *New York Times* best-seller list she'd cut out
then crumpled up and stuffed in her pocket—too much of a
stretch, even in fantasy. Her coat pocket began to vibrate, a karmic warning sign. She hoped it was Duncan calling to apologize
for the babysitting incident the other night, but it was Clarissa.
All the ebullience she'd felt about the future drained out of her.
Candy Land quickly turned into a game of Chutes and Ladders,
sucking her into a dark abyss. She ignored the call and the two
after that.

"Cruella?" Beatrice asked.

Emily nodded.

"You need to stick up for yourself. Don't take any guff from
that gold digger. Bitches ain't shit but hoes and tricks."

Emily laughed. "I'd never have pegged you to be a Dr. Dre
fan."

"You have to stay current," Beatrice said.

After settling the bill, Cathy handed out laminated instruc-
tion manuals. "Remember, at exactly eleven minutes and eleven
seconds after eleven, make a wish—soul mate related, of course."

"And what, pray tell, are *you* going to wish for, Cathy?"
Beatrice asked, wrapping a purple plaid scarf around her neck.

Oblivious to the sarcasm, Cathy answered, "To be engaged
to my soul mate by Valentine's Day."

"That's less than three months from now. Be realistic."

"The universe doesn't differentiate between a button and a
castle," Cathy said.

"Huh?"

"I knew it!"

"Knew what?" Beatrice asked.

"You didn't read the chapter. Now that you're engaged, the
worst thing you can do is get complacent."

They left Lily O'Brien's and walked across Bryant Park.
The skating rink had just been freshly Zambonied. The ice glistened, untouched, no trace of the countless crisscrossing paths.

The three women looked at each other. Without a word, they laced up their skates, even Beatrice, linked arms, and glided out onto the ice. At precisely eleven minutes and eleven seconds after eleven, they stood in the center of the rink and made their wishes.

CHAPTER TWENTY-EIGHT
LOVE PULSE

THEY'D BEEN AIRBORNE less than twenty minutes and already Beatrice was second-guessing herself. Maybe inviting Cathy to go with her to Rob Roy's seventieth birthday bash had been a mistake. But the ticket was nonrefundable and she wasn't about to give Freddy the satisfaction of not going. Cathy was doing one of her kooky love quizzes, deliberating before filling in each answer as if she were taking an exam. Sure, it was harmless enough, until Cathy suggested for the third time that Beatrice take her own Self-Love Pulse.

"Ask me again and I'm changing seats," she said, getting up to go to the lavatory.

A bunch of rowdy NRA-card-carrying types were hooting and making raunchy comments to the flight attendant. Beatrice had never liked being ogled, and she'd turned many a head in her day, but she didn't like *not* being ogled even more. She returned to her seat and reclined her chair. She needed a drink like nobody's business. Finally, the flight attendant arrived with the drink cart. She handed Cathy a ginger ale and a cocktail napkin then asked Beatrice what she'd like.

"A bloody mary, no ice, with a twist."

"I'm sorry, I can't do that," the flight attendant said.

"I have cash."

"We're not permitted to serve alcohol in economy. Only in first class."

"They can get sloshed if they're filthy rich but not back here?"

"We're trying to protect our passengers from Economy Class Syndrome."

"What on earth is that?"

Cathy glanced up from her quiz. "It's deep-vein thrombosis. Dr. Oz says that dehydration may be a risk factor."

"Your Dr. Oz is an idiot! Then why do they allow liquor in first class?"

"Leg room," Cathy said. "It can even be worse in a window seat."

"That's a lot of hooey," Beatrice said.

"It's still our policy, ma'am."

"What if I show you my compression stockings?" she asked, even though she'd never worn the ghastly contraptions and never planned to. "I'll do calf exercises every half hour."

The flight attendant smiled patronizingly. "May I get you something else?"

Beatrice exhaled, mostly for effect. "I'll just have a can of Mr & Mrs T and try to use my imagination."

In first class a bridal party of giggling tipsy blondes had been popping bottles of pink champagne and passing around canapés since they'd reached cruising altitude. Next time Beatrice would plan ahead and sneak on one of those tiny minibar-sized bottles of booze. Freddy always traveled first class. Nothing but the best. If he were here she'd be drinking Veuve Cliquot and staying in a suite at a four-star hotel, not the Rocking Horse hole-in-the-wall Ranch. Beatrice checked herself. She'd made a promise to her mother after her father abandoned them to never be beholden to any man. And that wasn't about to change.

An hour later, the plane hit a pocket of turbulence. The Fasten Seat Belt sign blinked on. Cathy gasped and clutched Beatrice's arm. "This is my worst nightmare!"

"What is?" Beatrice asked.

"Falling out of the sky from thirty thousand feet." The plane hit another rough patch. Her grip tightened around Beatrice's arm. "My father tried to convince me not to go. I knew I should have gone back for my St. Christopher Medal."

"Calm down," Beatrice said. "It's just a little turbulence. Nothing to worry about."

"But what if the generator blows out again? It's not like they can juice it up from all the way up here."

Right before takeoff, as they had begun taxiing from the gate during the in-flight safety demonstration, the monitors, lights, and air-conditioning suddenly went off. The captain had assured them it wasn't a safety issue and that they'd start it up again and would be off the ground shortly, which they were, and then it was smooth sailing. But it had rattled Cathy enough for her to pop the other half of some kind of tranquilizer she'd taken before boarding, which luckily kicked in quickly.

Beatrice was starting to lose circulation in her arm. "The generator's working fine," she said. "The lights are on, see?"

"Right now they are."

"And they're going to stay on. Look, no one else is panicking, not even that little kid there."

"Are you sure we're not going to crash?"

"Of course not. Why don't you take another of those whatchamacallit pills and try to sleep. When you wake up we'll be there."

"I'm going to speak to the pilot."

Cathy unfastened her seat belt. She was fleet of foot despite three-and-a-half-inch heels and was about to cross the great divide. Beatrice wasn't terribly worried. With a little luck she'd meet the love of her life in business class, Beatrice would get her bloody mary, and all this silly love-conjuring business would finally be over.

The Self-Love Pulse Quiz was lying open on Cathy's seat. *True or false: Pursuing my life's purpose takes precedence even if it means disappointing someone I love.* Cathy had circled *True*, then crossed it out and circled *False*. *Not true for me right now.* Poor dear. She picked up Cathy's pink pen: *Follow your heart, but take your brain with you.* One of her mother's favorite mottos.

They hit another pocket of turbulence, causing even Beatrice's heart to skip a beat. A moment later she heard a series of loud pops. Those bridesmaids could certainly put the bubbly away! What followed next was a cacophony of muffled shrieks. Beatrice tried to get a glimpse of what the commotion was, but all she could see was a huge white cloud in the aisle. Gripping the seatbacks, she set forth until she reached the first class cabin. And there it was: a despondent Cathy was on the floor, engulfed in tulle, as a hysterical bride and her attendants frantically tried to stuff the bride's voluminous wedding gown, now puffed up like a mushroom cloud, back into its once vacuum-sealed garment bag. It didn't take long for the prosecutor to assess the situation. The open overhead bin and the puncture holes in the garment bag the precise diameter of Cathy's spiked heels told the whole story. Beatrice was reminded of another one of her mother's favorite sayings: *Always put your best foot forward, but don't step on other people's toes.* Didn't the poor girl's mother ever tell her to wear sensible shoes on an airplane?

Beatrice was waiting for Cathy on a huge tan Naugahyde sofa in the lobby of the Rocking Horse Ranch, a glorified Motel 6 with antlers. They'd been in Whitefish less than two hours and already the girl had spoken to her father five times. Beatrice's cell phone rang. It was Freddy.

"I'm not pleased, Beatrice. Not pleased at all. You didn't even give my feelings the slightest consideration."

"Hello to you too," she said. "I didn't know I had to ask for your goddamn permission."

"Really, Beatrice. That sort of language is not very becoming."

"You know what you are, Freddy? A stuffed shirt!"

"Think about how this looks. No wife of mine—"

"Save that kind of talk for Muriel."

"I can see that I'm not getting anywhere with you. I'll call you later when you come to your senses."

"Don't bother. I have."

Beatrice snapped her phone shut. Let him stew in his own jealousy a bit. She was peeved, but not so peeved that she didn't burst out laughing when she leaned back and found herself staring into the nostrils of a giant stuffed elk above the huge stone fireplace. Everything in this place was enormous. The scale had one benefit: it made her feel positively petite. To pass the time, she flipped through a book about native game and after five minutes knew more than she cared to about elks, genus *Cervus elaphus*. She learned that an average bull weighs over five hundred pounds (the antlers alone could weigh forty!) and that male elk prefer to live alone or with other male elk until mating season, when they roll around in the mud, sharpen their antlers on trees to intimidate other bulls, then lure unsuspecting females into their harem. If (heaven forbid!) a female elk were to wander out of the harem for greener pastures or fly to White-fish, Montana, the bull will merely grunt. But if another bull happened to be having a birthday party, the bull will turn into a possessive beast, going to any length to reclaim what is his. The only man she could think of at that moment who didn't fit that stereotype was Malcolm, who, at least from what she could tell, was far less testosterone-driven than his older brother. Albert had certainly had his moments of bullheadedness. If only she hadn't been just as bullheaded herself, maybe they could have enjoyed the last six months of his life together.

Cathy arrived and they rode the old-time trolley up the mountain to the lodge. The only other person on the bus was a geezer wearing a bedazzled white fringe jacket, Wrangler jeans, a belt with a huge buckle, and turquoise cowboy boots. He looked like he was on his way to a rodeo. When he tipped his ten-gallon hat, Beatrice smiled. After being totally ignored on the plane, it felt good to be acknowledged, even by an octogenarian Rhinestone Cowboy in Whitefish.

Rob Roy was still the handsome engineer who'd gone off to join the Peace Corps after college. On prominent display were photographs of him with his doting wife Ursula and their five boys posing in exotic settings, riding elephants, socializing with the locals, even surrounded by pygmies.

He gave her a huge bear hug. "You missed your chance, Red," he said. "All this could have been yours."

"This lodge?" she asked. "In Whitefish? Gee, thanks."

Beatrice hadn't been aware until then that the Rhinestone Cowboy had been standing right beside her the whole time. Damn *Love Book*!

After cocktails, dinner was served in the dining area, a circular room with a panorama of the mountaintop. They put Cathy at the "kids table" and Beatrice with the swinging-seventies set. She was seated next to a dapper gentleman named Harvey and across from a white-haired conservationist with a goatee who had published a book of haiku. On her other side was the conservationist's wife, a chatty woman from South Carolina. Beatrice tried in vain to tune out her high-pitched screeching bird of a voice. The men at the table were fit and flirtatious preening peacocks, wearing brightly colored cashmere sweaters under tweed jackets, the women duller than drab hens. Beatrice stifled a laugh. Maybe Malcolm was right: she might just be a birder in the making.

The waiter brought out cold Waldorf salads doused in a thick creamy dressing. As the dinner wore on and the wine glasses were filled, emptied, and filled again, the men became even more flirtatious, the women red-faced and giddy. When Beatrice stood to go to the ladies' room, her chair was swiftly pulled out as though she had a personal butler at the waiting. It was the cowboy!

"At your service, ma'am."

The rest of the evening, Ed chased her around like a prize steer. He was dumb as a post but very good looking, and she found the attention, even from an old coot like Ed, undeniably appealing. After dinner, when the men retired to a wood-paneled smoking room, Beatrice followed. As a former prosecutor she was accustomed to being the only female in a room. It reminded her of those early heady days when she'd had to earn her chops in the male-dominated world of the DA's office, following the path blazed by Charlotte Smallwood-Cook, the first woman district attorney in New York.

She'd only had one scotch, but she was tipsy enough to burst into song. She touched Ed's knee. "*I can see by your outfit that you are a cowboy.*"

Ed glanced down at his slightly worn fringed jacket. "I saved my best duds for tomorrow night."

She hit him playfully on the arm. "I think you look just fine." Never mind that he didn't get the reference to that old Western song, he was damn cute and getting cuter by the minute. "Where are you from, Ed?" she asked, leaning on the arm of his chair.

"Wild Horse Canyon. Lived there since I graduated from Worcester Poly Tech. I'm a civil engineer, just like Robby."

"I've always wondered if the rumor about cowboys is true . . ."

"Say?"

"You know, that cowboys are supposed to be the best in the West!"

He laughed. "You're one spicy gal, Beatrice. Mind if I call you Trixie?"

"Suits me. I've also heard that engineers do it to specification," she said, winking.

She felt a tap on her shoulder. Cathy motioned for Beatrice to follow her. What could have flustered the girl now? She hoped it wasn't something with her father.

"Don't be gone long, Trixie," Ed crooned like a sick cow.

"Be back in two shakes!" she replied.

As soon as they were out of earshot, Cathy said, "Beatrice, you're flirting!"

Beatrice smiled. "I'm not flirting; I just want Ed to know how cute I think he is."

"But you're betrothed! Doesn't that mean anything to you?"

"Haven't you ever heard the expression, *Flirting is a woman's trade, one must keep in practice*? That's a line from *Jane Eyre*. You should read it."

"Dr. Phil wouldn't approve," Cathy said.

"Like I give a hoot. Dr. Phil, Dr. Oz, they're both quacks."

"What about Freddy?"

"What about him? He's in Westchester with his wife and I'm in Whitefish. Don't worry, I'm not about to run off with an old cowboy to Wild Horse Canyon. I'm just having some fun."

Cathy glanced at Beatrice's glass of scotch. "I think you've had enough."

"Loosen up, babe. It'll do you good. Now if you'll excuse me, my cowpoke awaits."

It wasn't until the end of the evening that she realized Cathy had taken the trolley back to the Rocking Horse Ranch. She wasn't Cathy's babysitter. Or her mother, although it felt that way sometimes. Right now she had more important things on her mind, like the nightcap she was planning to have in the Jacuzzi with the Rhinestone Cowboy.

Snowflakes were falling like fairy dust. Beatrice sipped her champagne, mesmerized by the curls of steam coming off the warm bubbling water, trailing up into the night sky. Ed refilled her glass. She felt like she was back in college, hoping she wouldn't get caught skinny-dipping in the Notch.

Ed sidled up closer. "I've never met a woman like you. You make me want to be a better man."

Albert had said that too. If only he'd meant it. Beatrice had learned long ago to take people as they were. They weren't about to change and neither was she.

"You're just drunk."

"I'm not. I swear. It's like I was struck by lightning." He leaned over and before she could turn her face away, his lips were on hers, and they were soft lips, not chapped, home-on-the-range cowboy lips.

"Beatrice!" It was Cathy, zipped up like an Eskimo in her puffy sky-blue parka, her hands on her hips.

Ed slid down lower in the water, hiding his face under the brim of his hat.

"Hey, babe," Beatrice said, "what's shaking?"

"I thought we were friends," Cathy said.

Beatrice grabbed a towel and carefully made her way out of the Jacuzzi. "What are you talking about? Of course we're friends."

"A real friend wouldn't make me an accomplice."

"Listen, kid, I was a DA for twenty-five years and sitting in a Jacuzzi with a pruney old cowboy is not an actionable offense, even in Whitefish."

"Maybe it would be a good idea if I change my flight and leave first thing in the morning. I don't want to waste another personal day."

"Suit yourself," Beatrice said. "But if I were you, I'd spend less time meddling in other people's lives and more on yourself. You have a lot of growing up to do."

"At least I wouldn't be cheating on my fiancé."

"But you don't have one, do you?" Beatrice said.

"I will."

"Not with that attitude you won't."

Ed pushed back his hat and, dripping wet, slowly made his way out of the water. His boxers looked like they were about to fall off his skinny hips. Maybe that was why cowboys wore chaps.

Beatrice put on her robe. "I'm going to see about changing rooms for the night."

"Don't bother," Cathy said. "I already tried."

"Great. And thanks to you, my only other option is hobbling away. And let's consider this my resignation from your ridiculous Love Club."

"Fine."

"Fine."

As they walked to their room in stony silence, Beatrice had a sense of déjà vu. She'd painted herself into a corner again, just the way she'd done with Albert.

C HAPTER TWENTY-NINE
LOST AND FOUND

EMILY SAT IN A TAXI, waiting for Zach to finish soccer practice. It was Friday, early dismissal. The driver was growing impatient. "He'll be out in a minute," she told him, not even aware that it had already been fifteen minutes. She was replaying a telephone conversation she'd had with Duncan last week. *I've decided to forgive you*, he'd said. *Forgive me?* She'd forgotten what they were currently fighting about. *Yes, I forgive you. I'm a very forgiving man. No need to apologize. I can't fault you for your shortcomings.* Duncan was the keynote speaker at a symposium in Chicago. Emily had been looking forward to the trip for weeks. No distractions, no Astrid, no Charles, just the two of them. She assumed he was calling to cancel. *I understand if you'd rather I not go*, she'd said. *No, I'm a man of my word. And it's already booked. But this is going to be a make-it-or-break-it weekend.*

Finally, a little after one, a flood of sweaty boys in soccer uniforms burst out of the school. Zach slid into the back of the cab. His face was flushed and he had an icepack on his wrist.

"What happened?" Emily asked.

"Jeremy kicked me with his cleat."

"What did the coach say?"

"He told me I should get it X-rayed."

Emily checked the time. She was picking Duncan up to head to the airport in an hour. "Should I take you to Dr. Kahn?"

"I'll just wrap it with an Ace bandage when I get home."

Zach still had his doctor's kit from when he was in nursery school. One or another of his stuffed animals was always in the ICU, wrapped head to toe in an Ace bandage.

"You're going to the Rangers game tonight. I'm dropping you at Daddy's office. Maybe you shouldn't go."

"It's fine, Mom. It doesn't even hurt anymore."

"Are you sure?"

"Totally. I can get more ice at the Garden."

Her phone rang. It was a friend from journalism school who worked at the Library of Congress. Emily had asked her to help track down the author of *The Love Book*.

Zach was playing with his talking *Lost in Space* keychain attached to his backpack. "Danger, Will Robinson! Danger!"

She shushed him. "Zach, quiet, I'm on the phone."

"Hey, Mom, Ben invited me to his birthday party. It's a scavenger hunt. Can I go?"

She put her hand over the phone. "Go to what?"

"Ben's birthday party. We're going to drive around in stretch Hummers!"

"We'll talk about it later. Mommy's working."

"Sorry, Mom. One more thing: Sasha and I broke up."

"One sec, Zach," she said, continuing to jot notes in her date book. It looked like she might finally have a lead. By the time the cab arrived at Charles's office building, it turned out to be another dead end.

Duncan was on the phone when Emily picked him up in the taxi, and still was when they passed the World's Fair Unisphere in Flushing Meadows on their way to LaGuardia Airport. When she'd told Charles she was going away for the weekend, she was surprised that he was so accommodating. *I'm not the enemy, Emily.*

It was rush hour and traffic on the Van Wyck was heavy.

Duncan had gotten off the phone and was checking email. Emily moved closer to him. "My *Observer* article is online," she said.

"Really proud of you, Emily. We're going to have to celebrate . . . Ah! Finally! I'm booked on *Leonard Lopate*. I meant to ask you, has anyone else RSVP'd to the book party?"

"The reporter from the *Times* can't make it."

"What about Liam?"

"He hasn't responded."

"Have you called his publicist?"

"Not yet," she said. "I'll do it Monday when we get back."

"I'm a little on edge, that's all. Let me know when you're ready. I'd be happy to ask my agent's assistant if she'll take a look at your book. She'll do anything for me."

At the airport, Duncan said he only had a hundred-dollar bill and would she mind paying the fare. Then he asked for a receipt, which he folded and slipped into his wallet. Just as they were about to take off, Emily got a text from Charles: *We're at the orthopedist. Zach's wrist is broken.*

The first thing Duncan did when they arrived at the Drake Hotel was call down to complain about the glare from the glass-topped desk. When Emily suggested he close the curtains, he said, "And work in a dungeon?"

After he berated the manager for twenty minutes, they were upgraded to a suite and offered a complimentary dinner. Duncan ordered Caesar salads, no croutons, extra anchovies, even though she'd told him she hated anchovies, and grilled salmon.

She changed into a new outfit she'd bought especially for the weekend. A tunic over gray skinny jeans (tighter than she remembered) tucked into boots. In the mirror she was finally able to get a glimpse of the Emily that Duncan had been trying to coax out of her with his tough love and, at times, difficult personality.

She felt some cramping. Now? She'd been waiting weeks for her period to come so she could start her birth control. Did it have to be on a weekend when she and Duncan were trying to repair things, get things back on track?

Duncan was rummaging through his suitcase. "Damn it! I forgot my lumbar pillow. I can't work without it. I'll get lumbago."

"I'm sure there's a Brookstone in the mall."

"I just ordered room service."

"I can go," she said. "I'm not really hungry anyway."

"I'd go myself but I need to make some calls." His gaze lingered in the deep V of her top. "Is that a new outfit?"

She nodded.

"You really should shop downtown. If you *sapé*-ed yourself in a more *aguichante* manner, you might get *baisé*-ed a little more often."

"*Baisé*-ed?"

"I thought you spoke French," he said. "I've never been with a woman who wasn't at least bilingual."

She didn't need Google Translate to know he wasn't being complimentary. She had two choices: she could get defensive or be appreciative for the guidance. She chose the latter. It didn't occur to her until later that there might be another choice.

In the lobby, she stood next to a poster for the symposium with a blown-up photograph of Duncan, and called Zach's cell phone again. For some reason she felt uncomfortable talking to him in Duncan's presence. This time he answered.

"How's your wrist, sweetie?"

"Fine. It doesn't hurt at all. I got an orange cast. I can't wait to show it to everyone when I go to Ben's."

"Ben's?"

"I told you about it. Hold on, Mom, Daddy wants to talk to you."

"Bad news, Emily," Charles said. "I have to go to Detroit tomorrow. On business."

"You said you'd take care of Zach while I was away."

"You think I want to go to Detroit?"

"Where's Zach going to stay?" she asked.

"Clarissa said he could stay with her."

"Clarissa?" She was about to tell Charles off, but he'd put Zach back on.

"Gotta go, Mom. The elevator's here."

"Okay, see you Sunday. I love you."

"Right back at you."

Zach was fine. Then why did she feel sick to her stomach? All these weeks waiting for her period to come. Could she possibly be pregnant?

Duncan was wearing noise-canceling headphones when she returned and slipped into the bathroom. Her hands trembled as she unwrapped the pregnancy test and waited for the results. Zach was ten; he'd be in high school in a few years and then off to college before she knew it. Three minutes later she went to tell Duncan the news. Would he be happy? Where was Yoda when she needed him?

She waited until he looked up. "Duncan? Can I talk to you?"

"Hold on, I'm in the middle of answering an email. Can it wait?"

"Not really."

He took off his headphones. "Well? What is it?"

She took a deep breath. "I'm pregnant."

He leaned back in his chair. "Hmm. That's a piece of news. Who's the father?"

"What do you mean?" she asked.

"Who's the father? I always use a condom."

"Not *every* time," she said.

"Still, it hardly seems likely."

"I'm not sleeping with anyone else, Duncan. You know that."

"Your ex-husband is living with you, you get mysterious midnight calls . . ."

"Duncan, you can't be serious."

"Oh, I am. Quite. Other women have tried to entrap me. Star-fuckers, every one of them."

Emily threw the lumbar pillow at him. She missed, unfortunately, but the remainder of his uneaten Caesar salad was now in his lap.

Several hours, a pair of shoes, and a deep-dish pizza later, Emily returned to the hotel to get her things. Duncan wrapped his arms around her when she walked in the door.

"Emily, I'm an ass," he said. "Forgive me?"

She pushed him away and started packing. She had a friend in Wicker Park who said she could stay with her.

"Please, Emily. I'm thrilled by the news. Come, sit. Let's talk about all the wonderful things we're going to do. Snowsuits! The zoo! Bedtime stories!"

She stopped at the word *snowsuit*. He helped her off with her coat and led her to the bed.

"You're so beautiful. You're going to be the sexiest pregnant woman I've ever been with."

She let the comment go; she didn't want to be her mother. She and Duncan were together. He was on board. There was no competition.

"I've been under a lot of stress," he said, unbuttoning her blouse.

Then his cell phone rang. He looked at the number, raised his hand as if to say it was important. "I'm with someone, Lara. Yes, I know. I'll see you in a bit. Twenty minutes, probably. At the bar." He ended the call. "Now, where were we?"

Emily sat up, folding her arms across her chest. "Lara's here?"

"There are hundreds of people here. Why shouldn't she be here? She's interested in the subject."

"Did you invite her?"

"To have a drink?" he asked. "Since when is there anything wrong with my research assistant and I having a drink?"

"I mean to the symposium," Emily clarified.

"I refuse to have this conversation. You're making me regret giving you a second chance."

Emily began to feel panicky, shaky. Her tongue was dry. She was having trouble swallowing. "I'm really thirsty."

Duncan brought her a glass of ice water from the room service tray. "You're probably dehydrated from the flight," he said soothingly. He sat with her on the edge of the bed while she drank it down. "Better?"

She nodded. "I'm really sorry, Duncan. I don't know what got into me. It must be the hormones."

"Emily, *ma petite*."

She looked down. "Not for long."

He laughed. "You'll still be *ma petite*, even when you're a fat cow at nine months."

She started to cry. Duncan pulled her close. "How can I reassure you? Do you want to talk about snowsuits again? How about we go dancing?"

She put her head on his shoulder. "Please, just forget I said anything."

"Done. I'm glad you decided to be rational. We both let things get out of hand." He kissed the top of her head. "For all I know I invited her when you and I were on a break."

"When were we on a break?" she asked.

"Emily, don't start. I meant it when I said this is a make-it-or-break-it weekend."

"In other words, I'm on probation?" she asked.

"Your word, not mine," Duncan said.

"What word would you use for a cheat?"

Duncan got up and began pacing. "You have no right to act like a jealous girlfriend. You're the one who can't be trusted!"

The static electricity from the pile carpeting was making his hair stand up on end. She'd never noticed the tufts of hair sprouting from his ears. She barely recognized the man ranting and raving in this palatial hotel suite. This wasn't the charismatic man who'd charmed her at the literary salon.

She was waiting for a lull in the invective so she could reason with him, trying to ignore the fact that he had just called her a cunt-head whore, when she realized the only rational explanation for why she was still listening to him was that she must be a glutton for punishment. But she didn't need Duncan for that. She'd been punishing herself for years. For ending her marriage, for wanting attention from another man, any man, even her own father when she was a young girl and her mother resented anyone taking attention away from her, especially her own daughter. Maybe it had to do with the child she was carrying, or something else, but she felt protective, the way she did with Zach. If she was going to be anyone's mother, love another human being, she had a responsibility to protect herself, even from her own self-destructiveness.

"Look, Emily, I appreciate everything you've done for me, especially offering to host the book party. But this is abusive."

One of Cathy's inspirational emails sprang to mind: *You cannot let go of anything if you cannot notice that you are holding it.* All at once she realized that the axis she had been clinging to like a buoy in the ocean was nothing more than a wet noodle.

"A lack of self-esteem doesn't entitle you to behave any way you please, even if you actually are pregnant."

"You're absolutely right. I have no self-esteem. Because if I did, I wouldn't be here listening to your bullshit."

The moment the plane touched ground at LaGuardia the next day, Emily thanked God and the entire universe that she'd landed safely, and vowed to always put Zach first. No one would ever come between them again. Her phone vibrated. She had five messages, all from Clarissa.

"Zach went to Ben's scavenger hunt party. He and Sasha are lost in Grand Central."

A wave of nausea flooded her body. She pushed her way off the plane. Passengers looked at her as if she was crazy. She needed air. She could barely see the numbers as she dialed Clarissa's cell.

Clarissa met her at Grand Central. The police had been alerted and were searching the station. Ben's mother looked like she'd been up for days.

"Any word?" Emily asked.

Ben's mother shook her head. "I should never have let him talk me into this. I knew they were too young."

Clarissa looked like she was about to spit fire. Emily had been on the receiving end of Clarissa's venom too many times to count and braced herself.

"You got that right," Clarissa said. "They're ten! A person would have to be a freaking moron to let kids go off by themselves in this city."

Emily turned to her. "Stay out of this, Clarissa, he's not your son."

Clarissa looked stunned. Emily might have sat for a moment with the feeling of power she derived from finally standing up to Clarissa, if she hadn't been so worried about Zach. She looked up at the large four-faced opal clock, trying to fight off tears. The seconds ticked like a metronome. Everything around her seemed to be in slow motion. Her knees started to give out. "Zach, where are you?" she asked, but all she heard back was static. She was a terrible mother. She shouldn't have gone away this weekend. Why hadn't she listened to Zach in the taxi? She'd made so many mistakes. She'd do things differently with this child, but what about now? Zach was lost.

And then, as if the dial on a radio had been tuned, the signal was suddenly clear and she knew where Zach and Sasha were. She led the way downstairs to the Oyster Bar. There they were, standing under the vaulted tiled ceiling at opposite corners of the Whispering Wall, just as she and Charles had fourteen years ago.

Sasha's mother ran to her daughter and lifted her into her arms. Emily stood under the arch and whispered, "Zach, get your butt over here."

Zach's voice echoed back: "Mom?"

She ran to him and hugged him tight. "You had us all worried. You can't run off like that without telling someone where you're going."

Tears were brimming in his eyes. "The limos left without us. I did what you told me to do if I ever get lost. Go to a landmark and wait. Did I do the right thing?"

"Yes, Zach, sweetie," she said, wiping away his tears. "You did exactly the right thing."

"You weren't really worried about me, were you, Mom?"

"No, honey," she said, ruffling his hair. "I know you can take care of yourself."

Clarissa was standing near the entrance of the Oyster Bar, her teal-blue coat wrapped tightly around her. Without makeup and her usual three-inch heels, she looked almost childlike, not much taller than Sasha. Emily thought about the mix-up with the pharmacy about Clarissa's fertility treatments. She remembered the fear of never being able to conceive after a succession of miscarriages, before she got pregnant with Zach.

"I think someone else was worried about you, though," she said.

"Clarissa?" he said quietly.

She nodded.

Zach hesitated the way he had the first day of kindergarten, as if waiting for a sign from her that they would both be fine. It had taken every ounce of restraint for Emily not to run into the classroom and snatch him back. As she watched Zach walk toward Clarissa, she still had the urge to shout, *Come back!* but she didn't want him to bear the burden of her fears. Now she was carrying another child, the child of a man she didn't care to ever see again. How could she protect this unborn baby from those feelings?

Zach gave Clarissa a high five. At first Clarissa looked as if she wasn't sure how to react, then just as quickly she let her Balenciaga bag fall to the ground and opened her arms wide. Emily's heart felt like it was going to burst open in a million directions like a million dandelions scattered in the wind, off to a million destinations.

Her phone rang. "Yes, Charles, everything's fine now. We're all together."

So this was what it felt like to let go without fear.

CHAPTER THIRTY
GRACEFUL EXITS

THE WEEK AFTER GETTING BACK from Montana, things went from bad to worse. First Cathy's basement flooded; then Mrs. Beasley had to have emergency dental surgery; her car battery died; 20 percent of the teachers in her school district were being furloughed; and she and Beatrice still weren't speaking. The lemon squares she'd sent with a Hummel card had gone unanswered. And to top it off, her stylist convinced her to get Zooey Deschanel bangs. As she was driving home from the salon, her cell phone rang. She wouldn't have answered it at all, but it was her father.

"Hey, Dad, everything okay?"

"Everything's fine, Princess."

"Oh good," she said, relieved.

"I'm just calling about Thanksgiving."

"Oh! I'm making a double recipe of spaghetti casserole. That way we can have leftovers. It's always better the next day, don't you think?"

"Listen, kitten," he said, "I'm not going to be at Thanksgiving this year."

"What? What are you talking about?"

"I'm going to the Dominican Republic with Mary," he said.

"Who's Mary?" Cathy asked.

"You met her the other day."

"Your home care nurse?" she asked, nearly running a red light.

"Yes, Mary. She has family down there. Two daughters and five grandchildren. I'm sure Teresa and Mike will have room for you."

Thanksgiving was their tradition. *Promise me you'll always be my princess*, her father had said after her mother died. Cathy was sixteen. The promise she'd made to him had been carved in stone. She'd never let anything or anyone come between them.

"Kitten, I found someone I care about. I want to enjoy every precious day I have on this earth and I want that for you too. You're going to love Mary, once you get to know her."

"I'm sure all her male patients do," she said.

"Just give her a chance."

Cathy grunted. She wasn't planning on getting to know Mary. She'd already seen enough of her. She felt like she was about to detonate, the way she had at the fire safety assembly, except she couldn't blame it on the turnout gear.

"Princess, come on. Life goes on."

"I'm aware," she said. But her life didn't feel like it was going anywhere. Maybe Veronica was right: she had no life. "Go, have a great time." She didn't mean it, and she hoped he could tell.

For the first time she could remember, she hung up without telling her father she loved him. She felt abandoned. She'd never imagined that one of the ties she'd ever have to renegotiate would be to her own father.

Her car seemed to be vibrating and driving at a snail's pace. Considering the kind of week she'd been having, it didn't surprise her. And just her luck, Lawrence was pulling into his driveway at the exact moment she was. All she wanted was to get inside, try to fix her hair, and hide under the covers with Mrs. Beasley.

"Hey, Cathy," he said.

"Lawrence."

"Nice haircut."

Cathy suddenly burst into tears. "It's awful! I look like a labradoodle!"

Lawrence seemed mystified. "Did I put my foot in my mouth again?"

"No, this has nothing to do with you," she sobbed. "This time," she added.

"I've been told I'm a pretty good listener. You want to come in? It might make you feel better to talk. I can make tea."

She didn't know why, but she found herself saying, "Okay."

Lawrence's kitchen looked like it had been decorated by a senior citizen addicted to the Home Shopping Network. Cow-themed knickknacks were everywhere. He filled two Holstein mugs with water and put them in the microwave. He fumbled with a tea bag, spilling tea leaves all over the red countertop and floor.

"I have another tea bag somewhere," he said, rummaging through a drawer. "Wait a minute. I can do even better than that. Voilà! Swiss Miss!"

Always on the lookout for inspirational messages, Cathy read the quote on the discarded tea bag, but this one left much to be desired: *You can go amazing places when you quit stepping on the brakes.* It belonged on a brochure for a car dealership.

Lawrence set the mugs on the Formica table. He gave her a plastic spoon still wrapped in cellophane. She took a sip of the tasteless tepid drink, crunching on the rock-hard marshmallows.

"Too hot?" he asked.

"It's fine."

He took a sip. "Maybe next time I should read the instructions." He pretended to push an imaginary button. "The cone of silence has been deployed."

"You'd never understand," she said.

"Try me."

What did she have to lose? She didn't give a hoot what he thought anyway. Once she began talking, though, she couldn't stop. She told him everything—about alienating Beatrice, her father canceling Thanksgiving, even Mrs. Beasley's dental surgery. For a jerk, he was a surprisingly good listener, and when he wasn't talking, he actually wasn't that bad looking. But what was with the sweater vests?

There was so much more weighing on her, though she wasn't about to tell him about her "almost" fling with Sean. She needed to talk to someone "higher up" about that. And soon.

"And I'm going to have forty kids next fall," she said.

"Forty kids? Holy moly!"

"*Students*, Lawrence."

"I know. I heard about the furlough," he said.

"And as you know, my house burned down."

"Anything else?" he asked.

"Don't you think walking in on your father getting a *blow job*," she mouthed the words, "would be enough for a lifetime?"

"Yeah, that's intense."

She began to tear up. "It was awful. And I don't get it. None of this is on my vision board!"

Lawrence looked pensive. "I had no idea fellatio was covered by Medicare."

Cathy scowled. "I can't believe you just said that."

"Sorry. That was a failed attempt at humor. I thought it would make you laugh."

"It didn't."

"I guess you're going to leave now," he said.

"I should."

"Anything I can do to make you feel . . ."

Cathy was about to chastise him when the ludicrousness of the conversation they were having in this crazy cow-themed kitchen suddenly hit her and she began laughing uncontrollably. Lawrence appeared stunned at first, but then he started laughing too.

"What are we laughing at?" he asked a few minutes later.

"Your Medicare joke. It *was* kind of funny."

She took a deep breath. She felt lighter even though nothing had changed, at least not in her life. Then they sat in silence. The sun was streaming through the frilly eyelet curtains making a kaleidoscope of daisy patterns on the table.

"Hey, Lawrence?" Cathy began.

"Yeah?"

"Remember that night at Pat's Tavern?"

He nodded.

"I'm sorry I said you had love handles. It was just your sweater."

"That's okay," he said. "I'm sorry I said I liked your boots."

She smiled.

"If by any chance you and Mrs. Beasley find yourselves alone on Thanksgiving, you're always welcome here. I usually have about thirty people, give or take a few munchkins and various other creatures."

There were only four green vinyl chairs at the cramped fifties-style table. She couldn't believe she was actually considering spending Thanksgiving with Lawrence Weiner. But she had no-where else to go and if she was having car troubles, it was an easy commute.

"Mrs. Beasley has plans," she said, "but I'm free."

On the way back to her house, she burst out laughing again and didn't stop until she'd walked inside, taken off her coat, fed Mrs. Beasley, and changed into her *Love Stinks* scrubs, this time not ironically. The mental image of Lawrence Weiner, the man who couldn't boil water, trying to juggle thirty Hungry Man frozen turkey dinners, was so ludicrous it made her forget everything that had happened during this disaster of a week.

There was a message from Sean on her answering machine: "*Hey there, stranger. Got a call from your dad. He says your spaghetti casserole is not to be missed. If you need a date for Turkey Day . . .*"

* * *

It wasn't until Beatrice had been back from Montana for a week that she realized how much she missed Cathy. But she wasn't about to call. The girl had crossed a line. And for Beatrice, once that line was crossed, there was no going back. She wouldn't let Little Miss Prissy or anyone, even Freddy, cramp her style. She had her pride. She also had the Rhinestone Cowboy's email address. But now, she kind of missed the little brat. Cathy was *her* little brat. And who was going to be her bridesmaid now?

Last Saturday in Montana, after another tipsy dip in the hot tub, Ed had told Beatrice she belonged in Montana. He said she had a little cowgirl in her. For Beatrice, even three short days in Whitefish, where every free moment had been programmed with rodeos, huckleberry cooking sessions, and county fairs, was beyond stultifying, though it was kind of nice to be the only female elk in the harem.

The next day, everyone had piled into white Outbacks and driven to Glacier National Park for the Cowboy Cookout Ride. As far as Beatrice was concerned, the only redeeming aspect of this three-hour ride through no-man's-land had been the Triple-A Alberta steak dinner waiting for her under the "shady pines." The rest was just a matter of not falling off.

She had still been feeling a little wobbly, having had a touch too much to drink the night before and the night before that, but when she saw Cathy in her floral stirrup pants and white high-top sneakers on a Shetland pony, she nearly fell off her horse. Luckily, she and Ed were riding double and he made darn sure with those cowboy thighs that she stayed right in the saddle.

"I thought you'd left," Beatrice had said icily.

"I couldn't change my flight," Cathy replied. "I thought you hated horses."

"Easy there, ladies," Ed said.

It quickly became evident that Cathy was allergic to horses—highly allergic—and had neglected to bring her EpiPen. The girl had lugged her "emergency" backpack all over Normandy, but to Montana the only survival item she'd thought to bring was a magnetic Bear Bell, as though a little tinkle could fend off an angry bear. Beatrice waited for the medic to arrive and wound up missing the cookout, the whole raison d'être of being on horseback to begin with. Ed saved her a s'more, but that didn't even begin to make up for it. And Cathy's feeble, "I'm sorry," had only made her feel even more put upon. Besides, it was clear that the apology was for making her miss the steak dinner, not for judging her for a little harmless flirting with the cowboy.

On the flight home, Cathy had gripped the armrests in anticipation of an imaginary unforeseen calamity about to befall her and her fellow passengers. She was in the middle seat, and Beatrice, chancing a case of Economy Class Syndrome, was by the window. During a particularly rough pocket of turbulence, Cathy's knuckles had turned white. Beatrice pretended to be asleep. Every once in a while she'd steal a glance out of the corner of her eye just to make sure Cathy hadn't lost consciousness.

One sleepless night in Albany, after tossing and turning more than usual, Beatrice decided to drop Ed a line. She still couldn't believe the geezer even had a computer. But lo and behold, before she'd logged out she received a response. He said he was tickled to hear from her. He even called her his *darlin' lass*. She liked the sound of it. She liked a lot of things about Ed. Malcolm was right, it was nice to be someone's one and only. She and Ed corresponded all night. It was harmless fun. A distraction while she was waiting for Freddy to settle his affairs with Muriel, though who knew how long that would take. He hadn't even broached the subject with Beatrice in quite some time. When she asked him if he was having second thoughts, he said he just needed time. Another two weeks, he kept telling her, and then another. He'd better not send her a basket of apricots. Ed was halfway across the country, what harm could it do? But

when she received an email the next afternoon from the Rhinestone Cowboy's "other" *darlin' lass*, she knew that not only was
this not fun anymore, it had never been harmless.

Thanksgiving morning, Beatrice rose early to prepare her signature cranberry sauce with the cranberries from Malcolm's bog.
Like every Thanksgiving for the last twenty years, she was going to her friend Bob's. Even when Albert was alive, they never
spent holidays together.

It was only eleven when she finished her morning routine,
but it was a holiday, so she poured herself a scotch. She rinsed
the cranberries in a colander with ice-cold water. She knew the
recipe by heart and barely needed to measure. One cup white
sugar to two cups water. No, wait; it was two cups sugar to
one cup water. Or was it equal parts? It rattled her that she
couldn't remember the proportions for a recipe she had made
dozens of times. Maybe drinking before noon was not such a
good idea, after all. As she was transferring the cranberries from
the colander to the saucepan, half of them spilled onto the floor.
Her knees cracked as she bent down to clean them up. She was
rubbing the pain away when she noticed something small and
white, the size of a head of garlic, tied to the handle of the low-
est cabinet.

It was Malcolm's sleep pillow, a silk bag embroidered with
a few lines by Emily Dickinson:

> *"Hope" is the thing with feathers—*
> *That perches in the soul—*
> *And sings the tune without the words—*
> *and never stops—at all—*

She inhaled the scent of lavender and chamomile. Beyond
the French doors in the courtyard, something was fluttering
around her asters, still in bloom even this late in November. At

first, from its bluish-greenish iridescent wings, Beatrice thought it was a dragonfly. But as she watched the wraith-like creature hovering above the goldenrod, she knew it was much too large to be an insect. Malcolm had asked if she'd ever seen a hummingbird in her garden. By the time she'd located Peterson's *Field Guide to Birds* to check, it was gone. But funny thing: she suddenly remembered the exact proportions for the cranberry sauce.

She picked up the phone on the kitchen wall and called Cathy. "Just reaching out to wish my favorite maid of honor a happy Thanksgiving."

After watching the Macy's parade, Cathy set out to the firehouse for Thanksgiving dinner, her spaghetti casserole in an insulated cooler on the backseat.

For the first time in their relationship, David Hasselhoff led her astray. After driving in circles for an hour, she found herself once again at the convenience store where Sean's brother worked. As hard as she tried, she couldn't find any significance in her being there. The store was closed for the holiday; she couldn't even go in for a box of malted milk balls to send to Beatrice.

She pulled into the parking lot to try to reprogram David. It was drizzling lightly so she put on the wipers. As her GPS tried to locate her position, she watched as droplets of rain formed tiny constellations on the windscreen before being wiped away to reveal a lamppost with two signs with white arrows pointing in opposite directions. One said *Parking*, the other *Change Machine*. She took it as a sign that she needed to take a leap of faith, though it was a stretch even for her.

She tried to back out of the spot, but her car wouldn't move. It was a rainy Thanksgiving Day and it could take hours if she waited for a mechanic.

When Sean arrived in the fire truck, he said she just had to take her emergency brake off. *You can go amazing places when you quit stepping on the brake.* Stupid tea bag!

Everything about Thanksgiving at the firehouse was perfect. Sean was the man of her dreams. She felt like she'd known him forever. Then why was she so miserable? When Sean dropped her off at home later that evening, there was a basket containing an entire turkey dinner and a mini giblet pie for Mrs. Beasley. *Thought you and Mrs. Beasley might be hungry. Hope everything is all right.*

How could she have forgotten to tell Lawrence she wasn't coming? She already had a long list of things she needed to ask forgiveness for, even longer than her Toxic Ties list. She started up his walkway, but turned around. It was late and she didn't want to interrupt a family gathering. Besides, she wasn't sure she'd even be welcome now.

The door swung open. A portly gray-haired man in a sweater vest called out, "Ahoy, there! We've been waiting for you."

"You have?"

"Yes, you're the guest of honor. Lawrence," he said, "it's Mrs. Beasley!"

Lawrence was in the kitchen washing a roasting pan. He had on a frilly yellow bib apron over a dark gray sweater and pretty normal-looking jeans.

"Hey, Cathy," he said. "I didn't think you were going to make it."

"I'm so sorry. I should have called. Something came up."

"No worries. You came for the best part. How are you at whipping cream?"

She smiled. "I've been known to whip up a froth."

"I bet you have," he said, smiling.

The kitchen was warm and inviting and smelled like home. She thought of her father in the Dominican Republic and for the first time she felt happy for him.

While she whipped the cream in a glass bowl, Lawrence

prepared his "famous" banana bourbon layer cake. Slices of bananas were caramelizing in melted butter; cow-shaped oven mitts on his hands, he carefully poured in a cup of bourbon then set the bubbling syrup alight, shaking the pan until the flames died down and the alcohol had burned off.

"*Ecco!*" he exclaimed, arranging the caramelized bananas on top of the cake.

"I didn't know you liked to bake," Cathy said.

"I have a few tricks up my sleeve."

For once his sweater actually did have sleeves!

"You know the reunion is Saturday night," he said. "I think I can scalp you a ticket if you change your mind."

Change. There it was again.

"Who knows, maybe you'll meet your soul mate there," he said.

"That's so cliché, don't you think?"

"Yeah, I guess." He wiped his hands on a dishtowel. "But I can't help it."

"Okay, you win. But I reserve the right to change my mind again." She smelled smoke and tried to locate the source. "Um, Lawrence . . ."

"What?"

She pointed to the drawer next to the stove.

"Not another flaming potholder!" he said.

She laughed as Lawrence tossed the potholder into the sink. "Don't you just hate it when that happens?"

At home, she put on a Lanz of Salzburg flannel nightgown and looked out her bedroom window at Lawrence's house. Smoke was coming out of the chimney, lights were blazing. Before going to sleep, she sent an email to her Flaubertian sisters, a Chinese proverb she had all but forgotten: *My house having burned to the ground, I can now see the moon.*

C HAPTER THIRTY-ONE
FINAL FLIGHT

INITIALLY, CATHY HAD TAKEN MAX'S OFFER to host the next Soul Mate Soirée as a good omen, as encouraging as a flower sprouting from a crack in a sidewalk in a sketchy neighborhood, a harbinger of love having taken root in inhospitable terrain. But al fresco, on the roof of her building? The first week of December? During flu season?

But that was tomorrow. She still had a whole day of now to get through.

Today's assignment in *The Love Book* was Cultivating Silence. No television, no phone calls, no music, and obviously no talking for an entire day, not even to Mrs. Beasley, who seemed quite content to be left alone. Cathy didn't see how not talking would help speed up her soul mate's arrival, but she'd already made an executive decision to forgo the "Make a Vulva Puppet" project and she only allowed herself one skip per week. For Cathy, silence was the equivalent of wearing no makeup. Her only remedy was to escape into romance. So, like a doctor writing a prescription for a patient, she decided a Harlequin romance administered *quaque hora* would get her through the day, with the added off-label benefit of helping her tweak her soul mate intentions in time for the new year. She found comfort in romance novels. They always ended up the way they were supposed to. After suffering trials and tribulations, heartbreak and obstacles, true love triumphed. Luckily, her Harlequins were

stored in a corner of her father's basement and hadn't gone up
in smoke with her Nancy Drews. She'd sneaked them out one
morning when her father was at his lodge meeting. While she
had come to terms with her father's Thanksgiving assignation in
the Dominican Republic, he was no longer speaking to her for
basically calling Mary a sex worker.

Two dozen Harlequins were fanned out across her living
room. Fabio on horseback. Fabio on a cliff. Fabio the Viking
lover. How to choose! Somehow mixed in among them was a
lone self-help book: *The Middle Passage: From Misery to Meaning in Midlife*. She was always so vigilant about keeping romance and psychology in separate boxes. It was her mother's
book—her name was written in pencil on the front cover and
she'd marked her place with a yellowed postcard from Normandy. As far as Cathy knew, neither of her parents had ever
left the country.

She put the book aside; Beatrice might get some benefit
from it. To her surprise, though, once she was in her comfy
wicker chair in the sunroom, the Harlequin she'd chosen did
not entice her. Instead, she was drawn to the book her mother
had never gotten around to finishing, marked with an unsent
postcard from a place she'd never visited. Cathy opened it to the
spot where her mother had left off and read a few lines: *Many
of us treat life as if it were a novel. We pass from page to page
passively, assuming the author will tell us on the last page what
it was all about.*

The next day, as Cathy was driving into the city for the Soul
Mate Soirée, this time with Alan Rickman guiding her journey (she and David Hasselhoff had parted ways—amicably, of
course), she realized she'd not only enjoyed the silence, but she
didn't need to know what happened on the last page.

Oysters, quail eggs, caviar, blinis. Max never would have

thought she'd ever be hosting a Soul Mate Soirée on her own rooftop oasis. But then so much had changed since Normandy.

One of her clients was an architect and had a friend in the Department of Buildings, so there was no delay or red tape. The decking was completed in a week. He'd even helped her install heat lamps and white pine benches. Twinkle lights were strung from the railing. The elevator only went up to the thirtieth floor, so Max placed mini votive candles leading up the next five flights. She had never given a dinner party. Store-bought guacamole and chips didn't count. Her mother Didi had thrown lavish dinners, a thrice-weekly affair. Calvin would have roared with laughter at the sight of Max, his favorite "grandson," making bishop's hats out of linen napkins.

She'd left just enough time to do her one hundred flights. She checked to make sure Simon wasn't lingering in the hall before leaving her apartment; it had been tricky avoiding him these past two weeks. She put an extra twenty pounds in her backpack. If she had any chance of winning the Empire State Building race, she'd have to be able to carry twice that much and it would have to feel as if her backpack was filled with helium, not bricks.

The first year she did the Run-Up, the initial rush of climbers had the force of a crashing wave. She'd tried to push through the mass of scrambling, jostling bodies, but she'd felt like she was being carried by a riptide.

Her backpack was heavy, but not that much heavier than usual to explain the resistance she felt today as she climbed. As always, the shadows began to catch up with her. With each passing landing the stairwell seemed to grow darker, and with the darkness, the doubts crept up behind her. What if she didn't win? What if she would never be good enough? Usually she could push through these feelings, but today, the harder she pushed the stronger the resistance became, as though bungee cords were attached to her ankles. She closed her eyes, trying to ignore the pain in her quads, but her muscles were in spasm. She heard a loud crash on the landing above her, then out of nowhere a furry white creature darted between her legs. By the time she realized it was the drug dealer's ferret, it had disappeared. Then, before she could react, someone grabbed her from behind. She struggled to get free but the tip of a blade pressing into her skin drained all her strength.

Emily stood in front of Max's building, removed her pink cashmere gloves, and rang the buzzer for the third time. She'd called Max's cell, but gotten no answer. Just when she was about to give up, a tall, handsome man with dreadlocks opened the door.

"If you're looking for Shorty, she's on the stairs," he said.

"I'm sorry, who?" Emily asked.

"Max. She's doing the stairs. She told me she was having a rooftop party. I'm Simon, her next-door neighbor."

Emily held out her hand. "I'm Emily."

"Pleasure to meet you. Any friend of Max is a friend of mine. I happen to be heading up there right now, to find my bandito ferret. You can come with me, unless you'd rather walk."

She laughed. "I'm not bionic like Max, and this bag is pretty heavy." She switched hands so the circulation would return to her left arm.

Everyone was bringing a dish for the soirée. Emily's contribution was the dry ingredients for Soul Mate Cookies, which she'd layered into decorative Mason jars. She'd been amazed when she found the recipe online, yet all manner of soul mates and sweets were readily available with a click of a button. She'd felt empowered measuring brown sugar and pink M&Ms without Duncan to tell her that sugar, in any form, was poison, though now that she was pregnant, she had become even stricter about her own eating than he was. But sugar, she discovered, wasn't light.

"Here, let me get that for you." Simon put out his hand and took the bag, then pressed the elevator button.

On the thirtieth floor, Simon went off in search of his ferret and Emily climbed the last five flights alone. She stopped on every landing to catch her breath. Most of the votive candles had been blown out by a draft. She expected to hear sounds of the party with each passing floor—music, laughter—but there were none, just the squeak of her shoes on the tacky steps. The stairwell narrowed, growing slightly brighter the higher she climbed, illuminated by a weak sun filtering through a dirty pyramid-shaped skylight.

On the top floor were two dented metal fire doors, both rigged with alarms. Afraid to set one off, she peered down the staircase, hoping to see Simon so he could tell her which door led to the roof, but there was no sign of him. She jiggled one of the doorknobs, which wouldn't even turn. The other seemed stuck at first, but eventually creaked open into what looked like a boiler room. Steam hissed from a configuration of pipes on the ceiling in the cavernous, barely lit space. The only light was a dirty low-wattage bulb with a glow-in-the-dark traffic pull chain. Oddly shaped nooks, recessed into the wall, radiated in various directions. The floor began to vibrate beneath her as some sort of motor or HVAC turned on, the sound louder than the garbage trucks that rumbled beneath her window and kept her awake at five in the morning.

She took a few steps inside, peering around the bend, hoping to locate the door to the roof. Something was moving in a corner. She stopped, just able to make out the shape of a large hunched man in a secluded alcove on the far side of the room. He was wearing blue coveralls and crouching down, working on something. She waited for him to finish before asking the way to the roof, but as her eyes began to adjust to the darkness, she saw that the object the man was bending over was actually a woman, lying facedown on a stained futon, her hands tied behind her back. Emily registered details: a torn white tank top, running shorts, blue backpack. She momentarily froze as panic pulsed through her body, then she began to walk backward slowly toward the door, careful not to bump into anything. A few more steps, she kept telling herself; she was almost back on the landing. Her hands trembled as she located her cell phone, warm in her palm. Two more steps. Breathe.

She'd made it to the door when the man grabbed the woman by the back of her hair—short blond hair—and turned her over. The woman struggled, kicking and screaming. "Get off me, you fucking son-of-a-bitch asshole!"

The instant Emily realized it was Max, something instinctual kicked in and she screamed louder than she thought she was capable, "STOP!"

The man turned, his shaggy hair covering his eyes. When he spotted Emily, he rose mountainous and began moving toward her. Without hesitation and from a place within her so deeply primal that she didn't have a name for it, she summoned all her resources and, using the sack of Mason jars like a medieval flail, swung it from the shoulder strap and brought it crashing down on the assailant's head.

There were footsteps and then a rush of activity. Time sped by like one of those flipbooks she used to read to Zach. Simon barreled up the stairs and straddled the attacker, pinning his arms behind him. Emily kneeled down to comfort Max who was just barely conscious, blood smeared across her face. Cathy and Beatrice arrived a few moments later, out of breath. Once Cathy realized what was transpiring, she accidentally spilled her spaghetti casserole down the stairs. Beatrice, in prosecutor mode, called 911, then snapped photos with her cell phone, which she promptly sent to a friend at the DA's office to cross-check with a police database.

Before long the paramedics and police arrived and arrested the man. After taking Max's vital signs, the EMTs lifted her onto a stretcher and, careful not to slip on spaghetti casserole, brought her to the hospital.

Simon escorted the three shaken women downstairs. In the vestibule, they saw another man in handcuffs—the real drug dealer—the chain-smoking pothead who lived on the second floor. Max's assailant was one of his clients and had gained entry through the unlocked service entrance. It turned out that Simon was, if not an actual brain surgeon, as close as it gets. He was a professor of neuroscience on sabbatical from the University of the West Indies in Kingston, Jamaica. He had recently decided to stay in New York, accepting an offer from Rutgers University.

Beatrice, Emily, and Cathy were in the waiting area at New York–Presbyterian, each on a different color fake Eames molded plastic Eiffel chair. They still hadn't gotten any information about Max's condition. Beatrice reassured Cathy for the third time that their friend was not going to die. Emotions were running high and Emily feared that if Cathy asked Beatrice even one more time, Cathy would be in the ER too.

Emily turned just as a man wearing a leather bomber jacket stepped off the elevator.

"I'm here to see Maxine Forsythe," he said to the nurse at the intake desk. He removed his jacket and sat down across from the three women. Emily hid behind a magazine.

Beatrice leaned close. "Who's the Robert Downey Jr. look-alike?" Emily's nonresponsiveness only seemed to fuel her suspicions.

From behind a copy of *People* magazine, Beatrice added, "Oh, please let my instincts be wrong and don't let that be Max's Garrett."

He was staring at Emily. Once he'd finally placed her, he greeted her warmly. "Thank you for the flattering piece you wrote about me. I hope I can live up to it."

"I don't think you'll have a problem," Emily replied.

"I'm here visiting a friend," he said. "You?"

"So are we," Beatrice interjected, assuming the role of spokesperson, watching his reactions like a hawk. "We're here to see our friend Max."

Garrett looked slightly stunned, but recovered quickly. "I rushed over as soon as I heard what happened. She's been through so much. I don't want to cause her any more stress, you know what I mean?"

"Perfectly," Beatrice said.

"Please tell her I was here."

After he hurried away, Beatrice explained the situation to Cathy, who hadn't put the pieces together. "Poor Max," she said.

Emily remained silent. Her arms were wrapped around her like a straightjacket.

"I wonder what she did to attract all this," Cathy said.

Beatrice peered over her glasses. "Did I hear you correctly? Are you blaming Max for some sicko in a stairwell who gets his jollies by attacking women?"

"I'm not blaming her; I said she might have attracted it."

"Listen, kiddo," Beatrice said, "let's get one thing straight. I humored you by going along with your woowoo soul mate sorcery nonsense, but this goes beyond. You can't blame the victim for being attacked."

"It's energy," Cathy said. "I'm not saying it's anyone's fault. You wouldn't be with a married man if you were really available. Like attracts like. Max has to clean up her vibration or this might happen again."

Beatrice was fuming. "I can't believe what I'm hearing! *Clean up her vibration?* I spent twenty-five years as a prosecuting attorney. I've seen children, some as young as five years old, testify in court that they were molested by their father. Are you saying they attracted that? How about the pregnant mother who was caught in the crossfire of a gang-related shooting? Did she attract that? Did her unborn child?"

"*Ho'oponopono*," Cathy said to herself.

"What are you muttering?"

"It's an ancient Hawaiian forgiveness prayer. It means to put things right."

"Honopohooey!" Beatrice said. "I'm surrounded by dingbats."

"Please don't yell at me, Beatrice," Cathy said.

"It's the only way I can get your attention. Wake up," She snapped her fingers in front of Cathy's face. "You're living in la-la land. I hate to break it to you, but this is the real world and you can't control everything that happens by vibrating peace and love. Did that help your mother when she was diagnosed with cancer? Did it help her stop drinking?"

Cathy put her head down; she had tears in her eyes. "I told you that in confidence," she said quietly.

Beatrice sighed loudly and moved to a blue chair on the other side of Emily. "Help me out here. She won't listen to reason."

Emily tried to mediate: "Beatrice is right, sometimes bad things just happen."

"Finally, someone said something reasonable." Beatrice had barely finished her sentence before Emily broke down and began sobbing.

"I'm pregnant," she said.

"Pregnant?" Cathy whispered.

"Yes."

"Well, that's a fine mess," Beatrice said. "I suppose the father is the guy you just broke up with?"

Emily nodded.

"Are you going to have it?" Beatrice asked.

"I don't know."

"How far along are you?"

"Eleven weeks."

"Time's a-wasting," Beatrice said, leaning back as though the case was now closed.

Cathy sat next to Emily and held her hand. "Can't you try to be a little more supportive, Beatrice?"

"He's married," Emily said quietly.

"Who is?" Beatrice asked. "The baby daddy?"

"No, Max's boyfriend."

"Are you sure?"

"Unfortunately, yes."

"Oh my god," Cathy said, "how are you going to tell her?"

Beatrice scoffed. "Tell her? Why? So she can clean up her vibration? The only thing she needs to clean is his clock."

"She has to tell Max," Cathy said. "It's the right thing to do."

"Tell me what?" Max asked, walking toward them on crutches, her head wrapped in a bandage.

When they left the hospital, none of the women were speaking to each other and it seemed unlikely that they ever would again. This was the first time all four women had been together since Normandy and it looked like it would also be their last. They once again seemed to be four strangers lost together in a maze.

On the New Jersey Turnpike, Cathy suddenly felt too dizzy to drive and pulled onto the shoulder. Alan Rickman was silent. She doubted David Hasselhoff would have been any more helpful. She needed to clean this up on her own. Her hands were trembling as she dialed her father's number.

"Dad, it's me. I'm sorry. Please forgive me . . ."

CHAPTER THIRTY-TWO
GOODNIGHT MOON

THE FOLLOWING WEEK, both of Emily's 11/11/11 wishes came true: an editor at *O, The Oprah Magazine* who'd been following her blog wanted her to do a Valentine's Day article, and Charles and Clarissa reconciled. Emily knew her wishes hadn't been technically "soul mate" related, as Cathy had instructed, but they were as close as she could get. She should have been thrilled by the news, over the moon, but instead she felt empty. She was finally getting some traction on her career as a journalist and she would soon have her life back. She had been imagining this moment for months. But all she could think of was that she was pregnant and alone, and had no one with whom to share the news. As incomprehensible as it seemed even to her, the person she most wanted to tell was Duncan.

She was only wearing a camisole and jeans and hadn't even brushed her hair. She threw on her down coat and grabbed her purse. She knew she couldn't take a moment to look at herself in the mirror, the equivalent of stepping on a scale before an ice-cream-sandwich binge.

It was an intensely bright, cold day. The wind stung her cheeks as she walked up Broadway. But she felt invigorated, more purposeful and awake than she had in weeks.

Duncan answered the door, wearing a pair of faded jeans and a T-shirt. He looked surprised and relieved when he saw her.

"I came to return this," she said, handing him the red raining-cats-and-dogs *New Yorker* umbrella.

"Come here, you," he responded, pulling her close. "And you," he added, kissing her abdomen.

Even as she was melting in his arms, a place she'd said she'd never allow herself to return to, Emily registered every change since she'd last been there. The new comforter on the bed. A bird's nest with three blue eggs on the mantle. A steamer trunk by the window.

"Maybe I shouldn't have come," she said.

"Yes, you should."

He led her to the bed, kissed her, then unclasped her bra. But Emily's eyes were focused on a long blond hair glinting from the folds in the sheets. She had the urge to inspect it, wrap it around her index finger, examine its texture, the subtle variations in gold and yellow. Instead, she swept it to the floor. She was not going to act out of fear. *False evidence appearing real,* she repeated in her head, until she believed it.

They didn't make love. There wasn't enough time; he had an appointment. *Later. Tonight. I have plans for you.*

They kissed at the door and Emily floated down the stairs. Duncan watched her the way he had that first day they met at Barnes & Noble. "I'm putting the champagne on ice," he called after her. "So proud of you."

In the courtyard, she looked up at Duncan's window. She was hoping he'd be looking down. When she turned, she saw Lara walking out of the shadows of the cobbled archway. She was holding the hands of two little girls. One was Astrid. Suddenly, Emily felt queasy.

Lara walked right up to her and smiled. "I can't believe you're still here," she said.

"That makes two of us," Emily answered.

The sun was too bright, magnified as if through a telescope. She put up her hood to shield herself from the wind and sun and eyes of passersby and walked home in a complete fog, past the familiar shops on Broadway, without the slightest awareness. The streets were a blur, like time-lapse photography. If there were any thoughts, she couldn't identify a single one of them. Then, as if she'd blinked, she was standing in the lobby of her building.

"How are you, Mrs. Andrews?" the doorman asked in greeting.

Kalman was on vacation in Montenegro visiting his family. His replacement was Tulus, a small man who looked like he was wearing his father's oversized suit. He was sorting the mail in a metal pushcart. She took the stack of catalogs and periodicals he handed her, only realizing in the elevator that he'd mistakenly given her Mrs. Weisenbaum's *Women's Wear Daily*. Upstairs, two other issues, wrapped in plastic, were waiting on the vestibule table. Adele was probably visiting her daughter in Larchmont and Tulus didn't know to hold her mail. She'd have taken them inside, though it was hard to tell what might set Adele off.

In her tiny alcove office, still wearing her coat, Emily adjusted her chair and turned on her computer. Strangely, Mrs. Weisenbaum's television was blaring through the wall. She dashed off and posted her blog entry for the day. She and Charles were picking Zach up early and taking him to a Columbia-Georgetown basketball game. They had decided both of them should be there when Zach heard the news that Charles was moving back in with Clarissa.

When she stepped out of her apartment, paramedics were carrying Mrs. Weisenbaum on a stretcher. Adele's daughter had panicked after not being able to get in touch with her mother by telephone, and discovered her lying on the floor. Apparently, her back had gone out and she'd been like that for days. Emily was unable to take a full breath. She felt like there was a lead weight on her chest. If only she'd notified someone when she'd had the chance, sparing Adele her nearly three-day ordeal.

Emily held the door as the paramedics maneuvered the stretcher into the elevator, in the process accidentally knocking Mrs. Weisenbaum's mail off the vestibule table. When she kneeled down to collect it, she discovered a red envelope between two issues of *WWD*. She waited with Adele's daughter until her mother was safely in the ambulance before opening the envelope. Inside was a single sheet of onionskin paper with the cryptic words: *When you find what you're looking for, you will find us . . .*

Emily was running late so she met Zach and Charles at the basketball game. When she arrived, she spotted Zach sitting next to Charles, wearing his Hoyas sweatshirt. She stood for a moment watching them in the stands. They looked at ease, laughing and sharing a container of popcorn. It was rare that she saw the two of them together like this, from a distance, when they weren't aware of her presence, and she almost didn't want to intrude.

Zach waved. She climbed the shaky metal bleachers and sat down on the other side of Zach. He offered her some popcorn. "Have you ever been to a game?" he asked.

"One or two," she answered.

"I'll tell you what's going on if you don't understand."

"Okay," Emily said. Charles was studying the roster, but from the slight twitch of his eyebrow, she knew it had registered.

The first year she and Charles were dating they went to nearly every one of the Knicks' home games. They sat in the seven-dollar nosebleed section before the Garden was renovated and the blue seats were turned into skyboxes affordable only for Wall Street types. She even had her own Knicks jersey, just like Zach. Those were the days before partner dinners and firm outings, when Charles thought she was the perfect girlfriend and liked her best in a T-shirt and jeans.

"Let's go, Hoyas!" Zach yelled. "Air ball! What? He fouled him! Did you see that, Mom?"

"He was definitely fouled," she said, resting her arm around his shoulder. He didn't pull away or make a face. Even Charles smiled at her once or twice.

After the game they went to the Carnegie Deli. Both Charles and Emily had hesitated when Zach suggested it. It was where they'd had their first date. But then maybe it was exactly the right place to talk about new beginnings. Zach chose a booth near the window. He asked if he could have a Shirley Temple. Emily said sure. Zach could have a Shirley Temple with three cherries, anything he wanted, as far as she was concerned.

"When did we last come here?" Zach asked.

"I think it was with Uncle Jack after we saw *The Scarlet Pimpernel*," Charles said.

"And before that?"

"With Grandma."

"And before that?"

"I don't think you'd remember that," Charles answered.

Emily knew what he was thinking: that was the day she told Charles she was pregnant with Zach and she had a craving for kreplach soup. She thought about the child she was carrying now, the child she had decided to have and raise on her own. Max's attack had put everything in perspective. The baby would be born in June. She'd turn the office into a nursery. The only thing she hadn't figured out yet was how to tell Zach.

The waiter took out his pad and pen. "Okay, bossman, what'll it be?"

"Two pastrami sandwiches, French fries, extra coleslaw, one half-sour and two sour pickles," Zach said, proud to be doing the ordering.

"You got it."

After the waiter left, Zach asked, "You like the sour ones, right, Mom? And you like half-sour, Dad, right?"

"I'm amazed you remember that," Charles said.

The boy smiled. "Kenneth said I have a really good memory. I just need to study harder."

"Sounds like good advice."

"I guess." Zach took a sip of his drink.

Charles wiped his hands on his jeans. "Zach, your mom and I have something to tell you. Remember I told you Clarissa and I were having problems?"

Zach nodded. "Yeah."

"Well, we talked and worked things out and I'm going to be moving back in with her."

Zach was fiddling with the *Lost in Space* keychain on his backpack. "Warning, warning. That does not compute."

"When?" he asked.

"Tonight."

Zach was quiet. He looked down and began shredding his napkin. "Sasha and I broke up."

"I'm sorry," Charles said. "We know how much you liked her."

"But we got back together."

"Oh, that's good."

"Yeah, we still have unfinished business," Zach explained.

A few weeks ago, one of Emily's copies of *The Love Book* had vanished. Now she was pretty sure she knew where it had gone.

"Unfinished business? What do you mean?" Charles asked.

"You know, like you and Mom."

Charles ruffled Zach's hair. "Let's talk about something else, okay, kiddo?"

"Why did you and Mom get divorced?"

"Zach, we've talked about this." Charles gave Emily a help-me look. "Your mother and I love each other, but we don't want to be married anymore."

"What about all the unfinished business?" Zach asked.

Emily reached out and touched her son's hand. "What unfinished business?"

"Forget it," Zach said.

"Tell us, sweetie, we want to hear."

Zach's chin quivered. Emily could see one of the star-shaped scars on the side of his cheek from when he'd had chicken pox.

"Me," he said. "I'm not finished yet."

Emily went to tuck Zach into bed. Charles said he had some work to take care of, but Emily knew it was because he was afraid he might lose it in front of the boy.

Zach was hugging Yoda. They were both dressed like Hoyas. Emily sat on the edge of the bed. "Do you want me to stay until you fall asleep? I can read to you if you want."

"You think I'm a baby."

"Sorry. I forget sometimes. It's like I blinked and suddenly you were ten years old. I know I've made lots of mistakes, but from now on I'm going to be a better mom."

"Mom, please don't get all mushy."

"I'm proud of you, that's all."

"For what?" he asked.

"You know."

"Yeah. I'm proud of me too."

She gave Zach a kiss and turned out the light. "Sleep tight. Don't let the bedbugs bite."

"Mom, you promised."

"Sorry. Goodnight, Zachary Andrews."

"Goodnight, Emily."

"Zachary!" she said, trying to sound stern.

"I mean, goodnight, Mom." She was about to close the door when she heard him say, "Goodnight, bears sitting on chairs."

She pressed her forehead against the door, tried to swallow. *Goodnight Moon* had been his favorite book. They used to recite it together every night.

"Goodnight comb," she answered.

"Goodnight brush."

"Goodnight bowl full of mush," she said, glad for the darkness.

"And goodnight to the little old lady whispering 'hush.'"

"Love you, Zach," she said.

"Love you too, Mom."

Charles was standing in the front hall with his suitcase. His face was drawn, the circles under his eyes darker. "Poor kid," he said. "We ruined his life five years ago and now I'm ruining it again."

"No, Charles. You're wrong. Don't you see? He just helped us all move on."

Emily waited until she heard the front door close before she allowed herself to really cry. Afterward, she felt as if she'd been punched in the stomach and wrung out like a rag. The fat naked man was standing in the window across the courtyard. The very sight of him made her wince. She felt a stabbing pain in her side. She splashed cold water on her face. She'd never had such a strong physical reaction to emotional pain before. Then she felt a warm gush between her legs. She sank to the floor and hugged her knees to her chest as if she could make it stop.

She heard footsteps. Zach couldn't see her like this. She braced herself on the side of the tub and tried to stand, but the cramps were excruciating and all she could do was curl up on the tiled floor.

No, please God, no.

And then someone was kneeling beside her, wiping her forehead with a cool wet cloth.

Charles?

"You're going to be fine. The ambulance is on its way."

C HAPTER THIRTY-THREE
ADIEU, BERTHE

CATHY'S SISTER CLAIRE MADE THE CALLS. Cathy was too bereft. There was a viewing at the funeral parlor Tuesday morning before the graveside service, then refreshments at the house. It had been totally unexpected, Claire said. Thankfully, there hadn't been any suffering, but death was never easy. Emily hoped Max and Beatrice would show up. Even if none of them were speaking to each other, Cathy needed friends around her.

Before driving out to New Jersey, Emily stopped at William Greenberg Desserts for two pounds of assorted butter cookies. This was a sad occasion and she hoped two pounds would suffice.

The saleswoman in a starched chef's apron assembled the cardboard box, lined it with a precut sheet of wax paper, then placed it on the scale. After asking if Emily had any preferences, she began filling the first layer from trays of cookies behind the glass display case. "No biscotti," Emily instructed. "Heavy on the linzer and chocolate chip." Even though she wasn't keen on the almond cookies, they were always a hit with some distant elderly relation.

Small children with grandparents and nannies with carriages entered the tiny Madison Avenue store, standing in the long line for a sticky bun or mini pink-and-white cookie. Emily thought about each of the Greenberg cakes she'd ordered for Zach's birthdays and now, after losing the baby two weeks ago, about the ones she never would.

The box was filled with layer upon layer of cookies. The woman pulled a length of red ribbon and began wrapping the box, winding it around her finger before tying it into a bow. Emily had never been to a Christian funeral before and was dreading the open casket.

"I'm going to a funeral," Emily said. "Are cookies appropriate?"

"Cookies are always appropriate," the woman said. "But I'll give you a white ribbon instead."

The men directing cars in the parking lot of the funeral home looked like mafioso types with deepset eyes and slicked-back hair, though more likely they were off-duty policemen looking to supplement their pensions. A guy wearing a white bow tie and windbreaker, eating a bagel, directed Emily to park at the far end of the lot. She signed in and hung up her coat.

Cathy and her family were greeting mourners in the front of the chapel, next to an arrangement of flowers. Cathy was wearing a floral dress and navy cardigan. Her hair had been straightened into a neat bob. She smiled and kissed people, clasping their hands as they offered soothing words. She seemed to be holding it together. Emily avoided looking at the open casket at the front of the chapel. She did glance around a bit and determined that neither Max nor Beatrice were there.

"Yes, it's for the best," Emily heard a short woman behind her say. "She's at peace now."

Emily almost said something, but refrained. They were probably casual acquaintances and she didn't want to embarrass them. The line moved forward. It was almost Emily's turn to pay her condolences when Max arrived on crutches.

"Thank you for coming," Cathy said to Emily. "It means a lot to me that you're here."

She felt comforted by Cathy's warm embrace. She smelled like lilacs. "How are you holding up?"

"It happened so fast," Cathy said. "I don't think it's really hit me yet. But there was no suffering, which is a blessing."

Standing next to Cathy was a short man with a white carnation in his lapel. A woman in a pale blue suit entered the chapel and sat down at the white piano. As soon as she began to play, the man with the carnation started sobbing uncontrollably. Cathy put her arm around him, trying unsuccessfully to console him.

At a loss for words, Emily glanced at the funeral program: Faithful Companion Funeral Home. Inside was a collage of family photographs: Cathy with a kitten in a basket; Cathy pushing a cat in a stroller; an older man, probably Cathy's father, holding a cat wearing an Easter bonnet.

"Emily, this is my father," Cathy said. "Dad, this is Emily, one of the women I met on my bike trip."

"Your father?" asked Emily.

"I'm sorry," he said, wiping his eyes and blowing his nose into a white handkerchief. "Please call me Jack."

"I can't tell you how glad I am to meet you." Emily felt like throwing her arms around him. "I'm so sorry for your loss."

He nodded solemnly. "Thank you, that's much appreciated. At least it gives us comfort that Mrs. Beasley is with Dr. Doolittle, may he rest in peace."

Emily finally got up the courage to look at the casket. Inside the wooden box the size of a bassinet, curled up on a pink knit blanket, was Mrs. Beasley with a catnip mouse.

Cathy smiled. "My sister left out one tiny little detail. My great-aunt almost fainted when she saw my dad. In case you were wondering, Dr. Doolittle was a Persian blue."

After the service, Emily and the other mourners filed out to the parking lot. The funeral procession hadn't gotten three blocks when it began to pour. The sky in the distance only looked darker and more ominous. The box of Greenberg cookies sat beside her. In the past, it would have been opened and all the linzer cookies would have been gone. But today it remained untouched. She no longer had the desire to eat in secret. They would be even more delicious shared, and there were enough to go around.

The immediate family sat on folding chairs under an awning set up around the graveside in Pet Lawn Memorial Park. Surrounding Mrs. Beasley's eternal resting place was her beloved Dr. Doolittle, along with Sparky and China Lei, Cathy's hamsters, who had both died under mysterious circumstances, and Cloud, her blue parakeet.

Emily stood on the periphery, barely able to hear the eulogy. The heels of her suede boots sank in the wet grass. Max was on the other side, shivering in a thin running jacket.

In the distance, marching determinedly up the hill, came Beatrice, her auburn hair tucked under a jaunty purple newsboy cap. Instead of her usual open-toe sandals, she had on a pair of patent-leather rain boots. From her purse, she removed a tiny umbrella the size of a peony. It seemed fitting for a woman who put herself first. Miraculously, when unfurled, it was as large as a beach umbrella.

Beatrice beckoned to the other women. Calling a silent truce, they all put aside their resentments, for now, and took shelter together under the umbrella.

Cathy started to cry. "I didn't think you'd come."

Beatrice put her arm around Cathy. "I couldn't very well leave you all to get washed away in the rain again, could I?"

The minister recited the Prayer of Saint Francis:

O Divine Master,
Grant that I may not so much seek
To be consoled, as to console;
To be understood, as to understand;
To be loved, as to love.

After the Lord's Prayer, the casket was lowered into the ground.

"Goodbye, Mrs. Beasley," Cathy said through her tears. "I'll miss you."

As they walked to the line of cars, the rain began to let up and the sun came out, but the four women still stood together under one umbrella.

CHAPTER THIRTY-FOUR
BE MINE

NONE OF THE WOMEN SHOWED UP for the final Soul Mate Soirée the day before New Year's Eve. Cathy had used her frequent flyer miles to head to the Dominican Republic to ring in the New Year with her father and Mary. Just as her father had predicted, it didn't take long before she and Mary were bosom buddies. Beatrice was packing up her Lark Street row house and Max and Emily still hadn't reconciled. While hurt that Garrett had concealed his marital status, what Max found unable to forgive was Emily's deception.

Emily's plans for New Year's Eve consisted of cocooning herself in goose down and watching old movies. These plans were derailed when her friend David, the editor, called and invited her to a party. She said she wasn't up for it, but he was adamant. He even resorted to telling her about a superstition that whatever a person did on New Year's Eve was a harbinger for the rest of the year, and did she really want to spend the year alone? Being alone didn't sound so bad, but she grudgingly agreed. She began to feel more in the spirit as soon as she slipped into a black halter dress with iridescent paillettes and a pair of impractically high silver sandals she hadn't had any occasion to wear the whole time she was dating Duncan. She would have towered over him.

The party was at the home of a friend of a friend, in a town house across from the Hayden Planetarium. Furs and Burberry overcoats crowded together on the metal coat rack set up in the marble vestibule, and afterward, plastic champagne glasses tumbled down the carpeted stairs like loose change.

David went on the grand tour of the five-story rococo house with the hostess, a petite blonde who produced Off-Broadway plays, while Emily mingled with the bejeweled women and clean-shaven men in the elegant parlor. Just five months ago she would have been star struck by her surroundings. But the literary milieu she thought Duncan would give her access to now seemed like a gilded cage. More than a few people had met her with Duncan and felt the need to bombard her with questions, pressing her for juicy morsels about his forthcoming novel and whether it was true that Scorsese was planning to turn it into a series for HBO. Then, as if serving gossip on a silver tray, they'd offer their own unsolicited tidbits in return, things she'd have preferred not know. Like that he and Petra were back together, after he'd tired of his assistant Lara, who couldn't refrain from acting like an assistant.

Finally, Emily escaped to the balcony; her only companions two little girls throwing confetti onto passersby below. She leaned against the wrought-iron railing, gazing at the celestial blue glow from the dome of the planetarium, which somehow contained infinite universes. It had been almost a month since the miscarriage, and still every time she thought about Charles showing up, a lump formed in her throat. She knew that every year she'd calculate how old her son or daughter would have been, just as she still did with each of her other three miscarriages.

The little girls went back inside; they'd run out of confetti. The planetarium was cloaked in an opaque pink haze. She was tired and shivering on the balcony, bare-shouldered, having not wanted to wade through the throngs to get her coat. When the French doors opened behind her, sounds from the party floated out: laughter, music, glasses clinking in celebration. Couples kissed, arms entwined, as the sky exploded with color. After the fireworks, the party soon began to thin out, the guests migrating to the next social event on their calendars, or rushing home to impatient babysitters.

David joined her outside holding a glass of champagne. "I hope this is a better year for you. Not all men are like that Duncan guy, you know."

She nudged him as she reached for the last glass of champagne from a server. "I'm swearing off men," she said.

He put his jacket over her shoulders. "It's a well-known fact that if you want good luck all year, the first person to enter your home after midnight New Year's Eve should be tall, dark, and handsome, preferably bearing gifts. I can pick up some Hostess Cupcakes at the deli."

"That's one thing I know for certain," she replied. "No man over four-foot-eight and no sweets will be crossing my threshold for a while."

With the approach of Valentine's Day, Emily began to feel wistful about her Soul Mate Sisters. Maybe it was because the article about *The Love Book* had just come out (the author's identity still a mystery), or that she'd given the caterer a nonrefundable down payment for Duncan's book party. She had formal invitations printed with RSVP cards, though she had no idea if any of the Soul Mate Sisters would even want to be in the same room. Mistakenly, she'd ordered one extra as though she were an invitee, not the hostess.

Every day she hoped another red envelope would arrive, providing her with the answers she was looking for, but it never did.

Zach and Emily spent days looking for just the right Valentine's Day present for Sasha. They walked up and down Broadway, but nothing was quite right. Hello Kitty paraphernalia and clothes were too boring. Finally, on Valentine's Day itself, in the window of a tiny notions shop a block from Zach's school, he spotted the perfect gift. A rhinestone tiara. They went in and inquired about the price. He checked how much cash he had in his wallet, and then asked the salesperson to ring it up. His serious demeanor and deliberateness reminded her so much of Charles, until his face lit up and he impulsively told the salesperson he'd take two more. That was all Zach, through and through.

"Are you sure?" Emily asked. "Remember what we talked about? You can't lose what you're feeling?"

"Just in case," he said. "She might want to share one."

"That's sweet." She pulled him close.

When they walked out of the store, Kenneth was at the corner, revving his motorcycle.

"Hey, Kenneth!" Zach called. "Mmm . . . bacon!"

"Mmm . . . pie!" Kenneth responded, giving Zach a big grin and saluting Emily before speeding off.

"Kenneth's really cool," Zach said. "Did you know he can quote every single episode from *The Simpsons*?"

Emily laughed. "Who wouldn't like a guy who could do that? Do you want to invite him to Alice's sometime?"

Zach gave her a look.

"Dallas BBQ? Early Bird Special?" she asked.

He smiled. "I'll even let you get the Texas size this time!"

They stopped at Alice's for scones and peppermint tea. They sat at Zach's favorite table, glass-topped with an *Alice in Wonderland* tableau inside. Emily was so busy looking at the charming miniature scene, she didn't notice at first that the lovely older couple she'd seen outside Barnes & Noble were seated right next to them, exotically dressed as always. The woman had on a multicolored hat with earflaps and a harlequin jacket, the man a red-velvet blazer and striped blue trousers.

"Excuse me," Emily said. "I hope I'm not disturbing you, but I've seen you around the neighborhood and just want to tell you that you inspire me."

The man chuckled. "You'd like to be like us when you're

in your golden years?" He had an accent she couldn't place.

"I want to be like you *now*," she said. "I've never seen two such vibrant, connected, and joyful people before."

"Thank you for saying that," the woman chimed in. She too had a European accent and the most beautiful porcelain skin. "We just live every day to the fullest. Life is a gift."

"I know this might seem odd," Emily said impulsively, "but I'm having a small Valentine's Day party tonight. My son will be there and a few of my closest friends. We live right down the block." She reached into her purse. "I even have an extra invitation. Don't feel obligated," she added.

"Brock and Lavinia," the man said, shaking Emily's and then Zach's hand. "And we'd be delighted. Wouldn't we, dearest?"

"Yes, sounds perfectly lovely."

"Do you live in New York?" Emily asked.

"No, we're just here for a bit," Lavinia said. She touched Brock's hand and smiled, closing her eyes for a moment as if savoring a delicious piece of chocolate.

"Where are you from?" Emily asked.

"We met fifty years ago. In London," Brock answered. "We were both foreign correspondents. And we've been following our story ever since, wherever it leads."

"I envy your sense of adventure," Emily said, thinking about the invisible boundaries of her life, which she knew were not just geographic. Charles had always wanted to explore the world, live in exotic places, but Emily had resisted the idea. And when she did travel, her greatest worry was that she'd never get home again.

"Home is where Lavinia is," Brock said. "Even during the winter we were snowbound in Kashmir with nothing but the most meager provisions and our love to keep us alive."

"Don't forget our Olivetti," Lavinia said, her eyes sparkling.

Brock nodded and kissed his wife's hand. "Yes, and we still use it to chronicle our never-ending love story."

After paying the bill, Emily felt inspired to leave her dog-eared copy of *The Love Book* on the antique sewing table. She inscribed it with a quote by Saint Thérèse de Lisieux before sending it on its way: *It is there for each and every one of us.*

Emily and Zach walked home down Amsterdam Avenue, the familiar stores now long gone like timestamps of his childhood: Vinnie's Pizza, where he had his first slice; the penny candy store, where he loved to scoop Swedish fish into a white bag; Pug Brothers, for a small buttered popcorn and to play with the owner's dogs. They passed the barbershop where he'd gotten his first haircut. Something—perhaps the twirling red-and-white barbershop pole, a glint of sunlight, or a little whisper from the angel of just desserts—made her turn and look in the window. The sight of Duncan sitting in the first chair with silver foils in his hair was, without question, the "highlight" of her Valentine's Day.

Kalman gave Zach a high five as he held the door. "Mrs. Andrews, sorry . . . I mean Ms. Jordan, there's an Express Mail letter for you."

Inside was her new Social Security card. She celebrated with a glass of pink champagne and felt like a schoolgirl as she practiced writing her name over and over. Now hearing *Emily Andrews* felt strange, as if she'd found an outfit she hadn't worn since college that still fit but was strangely out of date.

At three o'clock on February 14, Beatrice waited at Pier 12 in Red Hook where the *Queen Mary 2* was berthed. The water was choppy. She and Freddy were booked to set sail next month for an eight-day transatlantic cruise. Tonight, he'd made reservations for her birthday at the only four-star hotel in Brooklyn. They'd take a stroll along the pier and have dinner at Morton's. He'd promised to order fish. She couldn't bring herself to tell him the other night on the phone that she'd rather be with her Flaubertian sisters.

In another life, Beatrice would have arrived at the dock like an heiress, enrobed in ermine, her twenty-seven-piece set of matching luggage conveyed onboard by porters, and, after the *Bon voyages*, she and Freddy would embark on the adventure of their lives. But this wasn't the society pages or a Deborah Kerr movie. It was real life. *Her* life, and there was no script.

In the distance, like Humphrey Bogart emerging from the fog, she saw Freddy walking down the cobbled street. She peered out over the water. The river was a sheet of obsidian.

The letter she'd written to Freddy was crumpling like a carnation in her sweaty hand. *Love Book*, I know I pooh-poohed you, but please don't let me down now.

She felt a hand on her shoulder. It was the moment of truth. Here goes nothing. She turned to see . . . Malcolm in a safari hat.

"Malcolm? What are you doing here? Where's Freddy?"

"Beatrice," he said, taking her hand. "Beatrice, dear . . . how can I say this?"

She pulled away. "Don't waste your breath, Malcolm, I know what you're going to say."

"You do?"

"Yes. Freddy sent you to let me down easy. Muriel needs him and he needs her. He thinks the world of me. I'm the only one he's ever loved. He's an old dog who has trouble with new tricks . . . blah, blah, blah. Does that sum it up? The coward couldn't tell me in person? Like a real man? When push comes to shove, he sends his little brother to do the dirty work."

"Don't blame Freddy," he said. "He's never been good at dealing with feelings. Old school. He was afraid you'd be devastated."

"Tell your brother whatever you think he wants to hear— that I fell to pieces, that I'll be pining away for the rest of my life, anything that will make that old dog feel better."

"Freddy doesn't know what he's doing," Malcolm said. "I never would have given up all those years ago if I thought he would hurt you, but the best man won."

"What do you mean?" Beatrice asked.

Malcolm sighed. "If I'd had any idea he'd chicken out on you a second time—"

"It was your mother who put the kibosh on our engagement, not Freddy."

"Mother? Why would she do such a thing? She was awfully fond of you."

Beatrice finally understood what Freddy had meant at homecoming when he said the stakes had been high. Malcolm had been the goalie on the Big Green hockey team. The one protecting the net from a rush or onslaught by the opposing team. It seemed so fitting. He'd always been there. Even now, when she didn't need him, he was there to shield her. After the match, when Freddy raced up the stairs, scooped her up in his arms, and said, *The best man won*, it hadn't been about her at all, but about beating Malcolm, and still was.

A seagull was pecking at a piece of bread some kid had thrown in the river. She thought of that releasing exercise Cathy had wanted them to do. Casting Off the Castoffs? Dumping the Chumps? If she'd had a loaf of bread now, she certainly had plenty of things she'd like to unload.

"I'm not a trophy, Malcolm," she said. "And I don't need Freddy or anyone else, for that matter, to protect me."

"I know that, Beatrice. We were young and dumb. Trust me, he'll regret this for the rest of his life. But he lacks courage and always did. Come, I'll drive you home. Where's your luggage?"

"Baggage free," she said. "One thing you should know about me, Malcolm, since I think you and I are eventually going to be good friends, is that I ain't no hollaback girl. I came to tell him the same thing. I just had the decency to do it in person."

Cars honked above on the Brooklyn-Queens Expressway.

She was shivering. Her eyes stung. Maybe she wasn't so tough, after all. Malcolm wrapped his scarf around her neck and offered her his soft leather gloves.

"Thank you," she said.

"It's what you do for the people you love."

A quote by Eckhart Tolle surfaced like stars on a dark night: *And within that stillness there is a subtle but intense joy, there is love, there is peace.* She hadn't realized how much the stillness scared her and that she had been trying to mask it with busyness, background noise, and a lot of scotch, which only deferred the pain.

"Enough of this smarmy stuff," she said. "How would you like to go to a Valentine's Day party?"

"How could I forget? Happy birthday, Beatrice. You get younger every day."

"You know what, Malcolm? That's a big pile of baloney. But I hope there's more where that came from."

She tore the letter to Freddy into little pieces and threw it in the water. Now she was ready to set sail.

Zach and Sasha were in the kitchen dipping strawberries in chocolate. Sasha had on her new rhinestone tiara and Zach was wearing a Knicks cap she'd given him. The kitchen looked like it had been hit by a chocolate tsunami. On the front hall table were three pink manuscript boxes and Cathy's copy of *The Love Book*, which Emily still hadn't returned.

The doorbell rang. Beatrice and a tall man in a safari hat were standing there in the hall.

"You must be the lucky guy," Emily said. "It's nice to finally meet you, Freddy."

"I'm definitely lucky," the man replied, putting his arm around Beatrice. "But the name's Malcolm and the pleasure is all mine. Now, if our beautiful hostess will point me in the right direction, I would be delighted to do the honors."

"The pink champagne is in the fridge," Emily said. "My son's the one covered in chocolate."

He turned to Beatrice. "Club soda with a splash of cranberry and a twist?"

She nodded.

"Ladies, I shall return anon."

"I like him," Emily whispered. "He's a keeper."

"I have a feeling he's more of a never-leaver," Beatrice said.

"What's with the binoculars?" Emily asked.

"Oh, these?" Beatrice laughed. "With Malcolm you have to be prepared. We had a couple of hours to kill so he took me on a guided parrot safari in Brooklyn."

Emily hugged her. "I'm so glad we're all together again."

"All of us?" Beatrice asked.

"No, Cathy didn't RSVP."

Beatrice's smile faded. "Sorry, I don't mean to be a Debbie Downer. Are we the first ones here?"

"Max and Simon are in the den."

"Simon?"

"I'll fill you in later."

The morning of the Run-Up, Emily had waited with Simon outside the Empire State Building. She'd brought a thermos of tea. Her hood was covered with wet snowflakes. The tower runners, wearing shorts and long-sleeve shirts, were congregating in the marble lobby. There was a cacophony of echoing voices, then a thunder of footsteps.

"Did you tell her I'd be here?" she'd asked Simon.

"You think I'm batshit?" he said, smiling.

A few minutes later, Max had limped out of the building. When she saw Emily and Simon standing together she began to cry. Emily didn't know if it was because Max was in pain or relieved to see them. She held out the thermos. Max took a sip and smiled through her tears.

"I couldn't even make it past the twentieth floor."

"Don't worry, Shorty," Simon said, opening his jacket and pulling her close. "There's always next year."

"As long as my cheering section is here, I don't care if I come in last."

Zach and Sasha were wearing long white aprons, passing around hors d'oeuvres on trays like at a fancy cocktail party. Sasha's mother and father were chatting with Kenneth and David in the living room, and Max and Simon were in the den playing Guitar Hero. Max was wearing a Columbia sweatshirt; she had enrolled for the fall term. The next time Emily peeked in, Malcolm was fast-fingering the whammy bar like a pro. Zach called winners and sat on the couch between Simon and Max. He whispered something into Yoda's ear and squeezed his hand, smiling at the answer.

After dessert and coffee had been served and cleared, the doorbell rang. From the kitchen, Emily heard cries of delight. Her flute refilled, she joined what appeared to be a love fest in the foyer. Cathy was arm-in-arm with a guy in a sweater vest.

Beaming, Cathy shared the news that she and Lawrence were moving to Canada at the end of the school year. She'd applied for a one-year sabbatical and had been accepted to take a training course in Anthroposophic Social Therapy at the Ita Wegman Association, a community for people with special needs in British Columbia. Lawrence's mother had already begun knitting them each a pair of long johns for the cold Canadian winter, and was on "standby" for any future little Weiners delivered via stork.

Lavinia and Brock arrived in full bloom like an early spring. "We brought you a little something," Lavinia said, handing Emily a foil-wrapped bottle tied with red ribbon.

"You didn't have to," she said.

"Of course not, we never *have* to do anything. It's our pleasure."

It wasn't long before Brock and Malcolm were planning an alpine ski expedition; Lavinia and Beatrice were singing Irving Berlin songs at the piano; and Sasha was showing Max the proper way to wear a tiara. What sort of magic was *The Love Book* performing now?

There was a clinking sound. Zach had filled a flute with conversation hearts. Sasha was next to him, trying to balance the manuscript boxes in her arms.

The boxes were distributed, one each to Max, Cathy, and Beatrice. Zach explained, "When I say go, open them up. One, two, three, ready, set, open!"

All at once a shower of petals fluttered to the floor, transforming the parquet into a pink magic carpet.

Beatrice read the dedication on the title page aloud: "To Beatrice, Cathy, and Max. Three true soul mates." She smiled. "Right back at you, babe!"

"There's still time for some final tweaks," Emily said, winking at her. "It's a work in progress."

Soon, Lavinia and Brock stood to leave. "Regretfully, we must be off. Thank you for a splendid time," Brock said, kissing Emily's hand. "Luvie," he called to his wife, who was now exchanging contact information with her new best friend, Beatrice.

"Coming, Brocky. *Amour, tout autour!* Kisses all around!"

The last champagne bottle drained, Emily unwrapped the present from Brock and Lavinia. It was a heart-shaped carafe of Pomme Prisonnière. Calvados with a whole apple inside.

After everyone left, with promises to get together soon, Emily put her arm around Zach's shoulder and reached into his glass for a candy heart. *Be Mine.* She'd found exactly what she was looking for and it had been there all along.

10/2014